CLAIRE WORSLEY

The Secrets They Keep

First edition

This book was professionally typeset on Reedsy.
Find out more at reedsy.com

To my three sons,
Finlay, Caelan and Ehren,
I would have sucked at mothering a daughter.

Refuse to inherit dysfunction. Learn new ways of living instead of repeating what you live through…
- Thema Davis

Acknowledgement

I wrote the first draft of this book in the silence between parenting, teaching, and other responsibilities that swallow our time - in large chunks. So, I thank you, my readers, who use some of your precious time now to read this story.

Thanks to Kirsty. H, Kirsty LC and Pip for pep talks, gin, cake, and laughs. To Noel for being patient and making lots of coffee...

And to Nick Waites, who helped me understand how martial arts can help you develop greater emotional stability.

Thanks also to my family and friends, especially those who read and gave precious feedback on earlier drafts of this book- Nazia, Sian, Debbie, Cerys, Jan, and Finlay. To Jon Blake for always taking an interest and offering his wisdom and years of experience.

Finally, a big thanks to Laura Joyce, my editor for her calm and intuitive nature, and guidance, especially when self-doubt wanted to drown me.

If I've left anyone out - I thank you too.

1

Angela

Angela had read somewhere that abuse comes in many forms. And although she couldn't remember quite where she'd read that line, she recalled her physical response to those chilling words and relived it now. It was as though an invisible force punched between her eyes, clouding their usual sharpness and causing silent tears to salt her sallow cheeks.

A sense of dread crept over her like day becoming night as she sat on her new living room floor.

She glanced down to discover her arms folded across her stomach in a protective gesture warding off that invisible yet familiar threat. Angela wiped a runaway tear as her eyes wandered towards an old self-help leaflet that had slipped out of one of her books earlier. The words "Let us help you help yourself" forced her lips into a sardonic smile before she scrunched the leaflet into a tight ball and threw it into a rubbish bag nearby.

There were so few people who understood that she'd known—and suffered—the truth of those painful words. And that's how it would have to stay, she realised, as she unfurled her arms and pulled herself up from the dusty floor, using the stacked cardboard boxes in front of her for leverage. She looked down at those boxes now, seeing what she'd scribbled on them just a few days ago with a black marker in a trembling hand. Her possessions and memories thrown inside. In disarray.

Better to view a box from the outside, she consoled herself.

Angela massaged her lower back to ease the rising discomfort that threatened to consume her. How would she start this new chapter of her life at thirty-three with two children? She already felt older than her years; stained like the grimy magnolia walls around her.

A gloom lingered in the empty room like the remnants of bleak news. She lit another Bensons, the flame of the ignited match fuelling her guilt; she'd spent her last pound note on a pack of ten. A terrible choice. And one that played dark games with her, telling her she would never find a job to support the children—no one would want to employ someone like the useless woman she'd become.

She inhaled and filled her lungs with nicotine. With closed eyes, she listened to her pulse swoosh through her temples and reminded herself that she had survived the worst.

Abuse comes in many forms. The words that haunted her, perhaps read in a magazine or a newspaper article, or even some helpline, stuck onto a glass panel of a soiled telephone box surrounded by women's business cards offering sex for a price. Anyway, the phrase should have no relevance to her new life. And although her new set of circumstances had come in like an unexpected storm, early in 1982, she'd forecast them much earlier. In fact, for as long as she had experienced the need to escape her withering reality.

And now? Now wasn't the time to fathom if she'd been brave or reckless to flee their broken nest. She exhaled a haze of grey smoke, knowing one thing—she had done it for them, for her children.

Reaching into an opened box, she picked out the small, framed picture of her children. They both smiled up at her, Joel with his cheeky gaping smile and Catherine with a smile half-hidden by a hand—because of a gap between her two front teeth, which she hated. Angela ran her finger along the cracked glass that split the scene, then placed the frame back into the box, folded the flaps down, ready to take it upstairs later.

A moving shadow outside caught her attention. She stilled to listen. She wondered if her troubled mind was causing her to imagine things. Suddenly aware of the dimness of the room, she leaned towards the window and pulled back one of the dusty threadbare curtains left by the previous owners.

Thanks. Much obliged. She thought.

The old plastic rails, taut and resistant, finally relented. A dull March light broke through, exposing air choked with dust particles and a windowsill stained with cup rings and dark red splotches like spilled blood. She opened the window out onto the unkempt garden and sloping narrow street beyond. A single bare tree stood alone in a muddied lawn, with no fence for security.

And then she saw that the blue Range Rover parked on her driveway yesterday had gone. Her nerves tingled. Who had moved it and when?

She could see Catherine stood on the pavement, looking down the street towards the park. Had she seen someone?

As she flicked ash out of the open window, her teeth bit into the fleshy corner of her mouth. Had the stress she'd endured for so long changed her? Changed the essence of who she once was? Angela thought so. Danger now lurked everywhere.

Without warning, a male's voice behind her interrupted her scattered thoughts. Angela swung round quickly. The movement made her dizzy. Disorientated. She gripped the windowsill to steady herself.

Her vision blotted with dots of blue as she tried to focus on him stood there, a stranger in her house.

'You okay? Didn't mean to startle you. Your daughter said to go on in!'

He stood in the doorway with arms suspended above him as he held the door jamb. The corners of his lips curled upwards as if he had every right to be there.

Angela folded her arms across the rise and fall of her chest. A nervous heat rose up her neck and face like a tidal wave of shame and fear that flushed her skin. *Who is he? And why is he in my house?* The sound of her own altered breathing filled the space between them as an arsenal of familiar defences took hold of her.

She turned, her back tense, and pushed the cigarette butt into the already filled glass ashtray with force. She wasn't prepared for this. Faint music trailed in from the radio in the kitchen. "Joan of Arc", one of her favourites. The familiar lyrics reminded her to be strong. *At least it's not him!*

She swore under her breath and turned to face the man again. He continued to stand there, unmoving, as the light caught dashes of green in his hazel eyes. One of his hands dropped from the door jamb and brushed an ashy blonde curl from his face. The action bothered her. She sensed her own vulnerabilities in the moment and disliked him for it.

'Scuse me ... What the hellu you doing in my bloody house?'

Her tone killed his smile. He shifted his weight from one foot to another. Looked down at himself for a second. His hesitation and lack of response made her stomach tighten. Her eyes darted around the room.

What was he going to do? What will I do if...

Then he scrunched his face up. A grimace.

'I just... I thought.' He stopped. Stared at her again, then sighed. 'It was my car on your driveway and…'

Before he could finish, she snapped back like an animal under threat. 'Well. You have no bloody business parking there.'

He continued to stare at her as his hand rubbed across the top of his other arm drawing her attention to a strange oriental-looking tattoo. Her eyes shifted down to his trainers. The laces were loose and undone and snaked across the wooden flooring each time he shuffled his weight from one foot to another. Yet, his eyes continued to watch her in a manner she couldn't fathom, as if she was some curious creature he'd never witnessed before.

Her delicate hands began to tremble, so she pushed them deeper into her armpits to try to further conceal her nervousness. She needed him to leave now. To get out of her house. He seemed reluctant to go. Hadn't he already caused her enough anxiety parking up on her driveway the day she'd needed to move into her new home in a hurry?

Then, as if he'd finally registered her hostile mood wouldn't give way for anything better, he turned to leave, dragging those laces with him. Then he stopped. Glanced over his shoulder as if forgetting something.

'I'm staying next door if you need help with anything. Anything at all. It's the least I can do. Really.'

Angela watched from the window as he strode briskly along the pathway towards her daughter who stood with a few children on the pavement. They exchanged a few words. He glanced back towards the house, nodded, then disappeared round the hedge out of sight. She sighed with relief. Like a habit, her nervousness around men would be hard to kick into touch.

A couple of hours later, Angela had managed to put aside her restless thoughts about the intrusion of the strange neighbour. With a bucket of cloths, disinfectant, brushes and sprays, she'd set to work with Catherine's help. They wiped down scuffed and dusty skirting boards and stained walls until her knuckles ached. With mops, they cleaned the parquet flooring, damaged like an old used jigsaw with missing pieces. And managed to empty some boxes of their contents and move the rest upstairs. Angela looked around, satisfied with their efforts.

It was gone twelve when they took a break and Angela sauntered into the kitchen, eyeing the nauseous mustard and black gloss décor which was chipped, and exposing the woodwork in places. A poky space, cramped with any more than two people stood in there at one time.

She took two glasses from a small shelf above the worktop that doubled as a breakfast bar and filled them with ice cubes from the ice tray. In one glass, she poured a large shot of vodka from the bottle she'd placed under the sink the day before. She topped it with orange juiced and poured a coke into the other glass for Catherine.

She carried the drinks into the lounge, gave Catherine the glass of coke then sank into the sofa next to her. Catherine frowned toward her mum's glass.

'Bit early for that, isn't it, Mother?'

Angela tutted. 'It's bloody needed after the morning I've had.'

'What do you mean? Is it the guy from next door?'

'Well, yes. That aside from other things.'

'He did feel bad about it, Mum. I don't think he realised we were moving in.'

Angela rolled her eyes. 'Oh. I see. You've already spoken then, love?'

Catherine pulled back a little and scrunched her nose. 'Really. Don't be like that. He seemed pretty cool to me. His name's Gethin.'

'Bloody hell, Cath. I thought he was weird. He stood in the doorway, by there like, and just kept staring at me. He didn't even try to apologise for the hassle he's caused us.'

'Did you give him a chance?'

Angela sipped her vodka. 'That's not fair. He could have if he'd wanted to.'

They both sat in silence as they sipped their drinks. Catherine folded her legs under her as Angela dipped her fingers into the glass and plucked out an ice cube. She popped it into her mouth and enjoyed the cold tingling sensation as she crunched down into the ice with her teeth. The smaller pieces melted away on her tongue. Disappeared. So did her thoughts with each gulp of liquid that passed her lips and flooded her body. Like a wave of calm, the vodka helped to purify all that negativity that wanted to invade her head.

Catherine huffed in the quietness dividing them.

'Anyway, I think I'm going to like him. Seems a pretty normal kinda guy to me. Nowhere near weird.'

Angela swayed her head back and forth. 'Christ sake's, Cath. How can you say that? You don't even know him.'

She shrugged. 'Call it a hunch, Mother. Not everyone is...' Her words fell away. 'Come on, Mum. Things are going to be different here, you'll see?'

'Are they now?' Angela reached over and tickled her daughter's side in an attempt to break the growing tension between them.

It was happening often these days. Catherine squirmed away from her mother's hand with her glass held in the air to avoid any spillage. Her sleeve slipped down towards her elbow. On her smooth olive skin, Angela saw several thin marks, like paper cuts. Some raised and red. Angry looking.

'Hey. What are those marks?'

Catherine shot up from the sofa. Grabbed at her sleeve to cover her arm.

'Nothing. It's from surfing.'

'Really. They don't look like nothing, Cath?'

'Do you always have to go looking for things to have a problem with, Mother? For God's sake.'

7

Angela took a long, intense look at her daughter. She knew she would have to tread carefully. Her hand gripped the vodka glass as if it might slip through her fingers any minute. She heard her controlled tone as she spoke, frosting the air between them.

'You do not talk to me like that, young lady. I'm still your mum.'

Catherine scowled. Her face darkened with emotions that Angela had yet to understand.

'Yes. A mum who drinks fucking vodka for lunch.'

Angela's eyebrows shot northwards, a frown like hair line cracks before an eruption cast a visible confusion on Angela's face. Catherine had never sworn at her before. And for once, Angela had no clever retort to her daughter's caustic words. Even if she'd thought of one, she'd never have said it because she'd made a promise. A promise to herself for her children. In their new home, there would be no screaming or shouting of abusive words. At least not from their mother.

She remained on the sofa and watched in silence as her daughter, with a stone-cold expression, stomped up the stairs. The bedroom door slammed shut as Angela lifted her glass to her lips. Where had her daughter's once soft and kind nature disappeared? Angela shook her head. She knew she was kidding herself. Catherine was older now, fifteen. She knew things. Had witnessed things.

Angela was under no illusion what the marks on Catherine's upper wrist were and why they were there. Like all of them in the family, her daughter carried troubles. Memories that weren't easily forgotten. She'd even read about it somewhere. How some youngsters cut themselves to relieve pain or loss. She understood. Hadn't she done the same? She still had the scars between her toes and her buttocks—hidden from sight from herself and others. There were many forms of abuse and many ways to conceal them, too.

As she held her glass of vodka in both hands, she watched the liquid catch and refract the light from the room. Fragments of ice knocked and pulled away from each other in the tight space. Seconds later, Angela watched as the glass hit the wall opposite like a mini explosion and splintered into a thousand pieces. Vodka and orange stained all her earlier efforts. She cursed herself for not doing more to protect her children. Then she stood and began picking up all the broken pieces scattered across the floor of their new home.

With a damp cloth she wiped away the sticky juice from surfaces with a vigour motivated by the heaviness in her chest. Has she not scratched and scrambled her way out of that other existence? She sighed as she scanned the room again. She'd brought so little with her from that other life. An old gingham sofa taken from the children's old playroom in the other house, a nest of coffee tables, a television, and an old dining table with mismatching chairs. And, of course, the framed blue silk kimono given to her by her father. But she hadn't cared about that then or now. She had what mattered most … her children and a future worth living. Yet, those darker thoughts crept at the edges in shadow. Was she kidding herself? Did she really have the strength to make the Street their new home? A safe place for them. Somewhere they could start again.

For the second time, someone startled away Angela from her frayed loose thoughts, this time by the telephone. She panicked—a knee-jerk response. Then she remembered. She'd been told they were reconnecting the phone lines and would be testing the line for her. She picked the bright red telephone up from the windowsill and answered it.

'Mum, wait!' Catherine stood on the stairs. Her voice laced with concern.

'They're probably just checking the line, Cath. Chill.'

'No. Let me answer… Please.'

'Hello. Battersea Dogs' Home?' Angela turned and grinned towards

Catherine. Something was wrong, though. She recognised that look.

'How. How did you get this number?'

His cold, contemptuous snigger felt like a belt tightening around her chest, making it difficult to breathe. She looked out at the cherry tree in the garden. Surely, she should see buds of life by now. Early March. The raw, bare branches waited still. She breathed in again, inflated her chest against the tightness.

'Colin, you can't do this anymore.'

She waited for the vitriolic response that would come. It had always been that way. He had always tried to control her boundaries, dictate the rules, and make the decisions. As the verbal attack ensued, the warmth of alcohol in her veins rounded the edges of his sharp, scornful voice. She trembled less. Maybe her body now understood the physical distance between them.

Catherine looked down at her from the stairway.

She mouthed. 'I know ... It was me. Sorry!'

Angela shook her head at her daughter and gestured to Catherine to return upstairs. Her jaw tightened.

It was obvious he would have manipulated Catherine into giving him their number. He had a way about him. Yet, something didn't feel right. Surely, Catherine knew the risks of him knowing where they might be. Would she have taken that risk?

Then she did something, so out of her own realm of behaviour that she almost seemed separated from herself. She placed the phone back on the receiver. Just like that. Light as a feather until the sound of the click danced towards her ears. She'd silenced the voice that assaulted her. For now.

She lowered herself into a dining room chair and straight away wondered what might come of such an action. Would he attempt to ring back? Let her know she'd overstepped the mark? She sat staring out the window so lost in a maze of twisted thoughts she missed Joel come in and Catherine move light on her feet down the stairs behind her and into the kitchen.

The phone rang again. She swallowed. Snapped her tongue against the roof of her dry mouth. She knew it would be him. From the corner of her vision flickered Catherine. She swiped the phone before Angela could respond.

'Hi Dad... Yes, thank you. Mum has popped out. No. I can't. Don't say that. It's not true. I don't know when.' Silence. 'Joel's calling me. Have to go now. Yes. Okay. Bye.'

Catherine placed the phone back down on its cradle and without another word disappeared into the kitchen and returned with two hot drinks.

Had she really just done that at fifteen? Cut her father dead in his tracks. What had he said to her? Angela looked at Joel who sat in the chair opposite her playing his new game, *Vermin,* on his Nintendo. His eyes fixated on the small screen of his hand-controlled gaming device. She sighed.

Angela wasn't in the habit of attaching more importance to her own ways over others. But Catherine's interference had bothered her, made her feel even more inadequate. Did Catherine's actions mean she lacked confidence in her own mother's ability to protect them?

'Thank you,' she said, as Catherine put a mug of coffee on the table in front of her.

'I've made Joel some lunch, too.'

'No, not for that. The phone call. But you know I wasn't expecting you to do that, right?'

Catherine shrugged her shoulders.

'I had to do something.'

'Not really.'

Catherine folded her petite frame into the dining chair next to her mum, wrapped her arms around her knees, and rested her chin on top of her knee. At that moment, Angela saw how truly beautiful her daughter was.

'I don't want to see him, Mum.' She glanced towards her brother. 'And I don't think Joel should either.'

Joel nodded. 'Yeh, it's more fun with you anyway, Mum.'

'Is it?'

'Yeh, Dur.'

She watched as his fingers moved quicker with the ever-increasing bleeps of his console as he spoke. He must have lost the game, as he stopped and looked up. 'And I have a cool park to go to and lots of friends with BMX's. I guess Dad can see us another time, I don't mind …' With that, he smiled, jumped off the dining chair and disappeared upstairs to his bedroom.

'Catherine. I understand. There are things you and Joel should never…' She wondered why her words felt so hollow. 'You won't understand yet…'

Catherine lifted her head from her knee. 'But Mum, I do …'

Angela glanced upstairs towards Joel's room and raised her hand asking her daughter to stop.

'Please. Catherine, you really do not.'

'Mum, I'm not blind. I could see how impossible it was for you.'

When would Catherine be old enough to understand it all? The desperate and ridiculous need she'd felt for so long to keep her family together, to try and make it better despite the damage that had been caused.

Twenty minutes later, as her children settled at the table to eat Angela couldn't shake the feeling that Colin wouldn't rest. She knew the hidden truths that lay behind his perfect presentation, and the narcissistic pride that kept them all in its grip. Fleeing his tight grasp might not be enough to keep them safe. Her actions would be perceived as a ruse by him, a threat even, given what she knew.

There was no knowing what he would do.

2

Gethin

'And don't forget, ring your parents, Geth. They miss you.'

Gethin nodded and stuck his thumb up with a wry grin. 'Got it.'

He watched as the car slowed to take a left at the top of the street. Dina's slim arm continued to wave out of the car window, her husband's eyes fixed on the road ahead, as they disappeared and away from the estate.

Gethin stood barefoot for a few moments on a gravel spattered pavement in front of Dina's driveway, his hands pushed deep into his jean pockets, his shoulders hunched around his neck like a lost child.

He should consider himself fortunate. She'd let him have *their* house for two whole weeks at least, depending on her husband's new contractual work. Since their days studying journalism together in London, Dina understood Gethin—and the privacy his work required.

As his eyes wandered along the terraced houses opposite, he smiled. Gethin saw Dina, much like a sister. They even argued and teased each other, as siblings often do, to the dismay of her husband. But

Gethin could always rely on her. And he did.

Children's laughter drifted up from the park at the end of the street. He saw them scramble up coloured climbing frames like warriors, jump off moving swings whilst several other children, like cannon balls, shot around the enclosed area.

An old, rotund woman stood outside her house on the terrace end, hands on her wide hips, her hair swung up in a bun, as she watched the children and smiled. Occasionally, she would call something out towards the children, then smile again whilst shaking her head.

He glanced down at Belflo, who sat a yard or so away from him. The cat stared back at Gethin, as if searching out his intent. Then, Belflo miaowed with an air of dissatisfaction directed towards Gethin.

'The feeling's mutual. You'll need to stay out of my way, you overweight eunuch.'

Belflo's whiskers twitched before he pulled himself onto all four paws, waddled across Dina's front garden, and pushed his way through the hedge into next-door. Gethin squinted and peered through the hedge after him. He saw flashes of a familiar blue between the dark green foliage. *Damn.* He'd forgotten his battered old Range Rover parked on the driveway next door.

'No one's been living in that house for months now.' Dina's husband had said a couple of days before. He'd taken Gethin's keys and parked up on the driveway of the empty house.

Then why had he also spotted several bags of rubbish that filled the dustbins at the end of the Driveway at No 10?

He heard footsteps, then the voice of a young girl; a chuckle and a bike being pedalled away down the street, gathering speed towards the park.

'Be back for lunch, Joel. Okay?' Her voice called down the street.

Christ. There are people living next door.

Gethin turned on his heels into Dina's house to find his trainers and car keys. The sudden movement made him light-headed. Too much whiskey the night before? He rubbed across his forehead and hoped it wasn't a sign his headaches had returned to. He couldn't help but wonder if Dina's husband had known, parked his car there on purpose. Perhaps he sensed Gethin wasn't so keen on him.

He grabbed his keys from the pocket of his jacket and made haste back outside. As he rounded the narrow concrete path, he almost collided with the young girl he'd heard earlier. She wore black loose dungarees which were rolled to the ankles and a striped long-sleeved t-shirt. Tucked into the large pocket on her chest, with its head poked out sniffing the air, was what Gethin could only assume was a small rat. Gethin blinked.

She looked away from the creature and at Gethin, startled by his sudden appearance.

'Sorry. Didn't mean to frighten you.' He jutted his chin out toward his car. 'I'll move my car now.'

The young girl tilted her head.

'Ahh, it's your car.' She glanced at the keys in his hand. 'I'll warn you. My mum's not happy about it. At all.'

He nodded slowly. 'They… I thought the house.' He stopped. And looked down at the young girl who stood barefoot in front of him.

'I'm Gethin.' He stretched out his hand. 'I'll be your new neighbour for a while. Who's this little fellah?'

She studied him with a small frown as she brushed wisps of wavy chocolate brown hair away from her face. She wiped her hand down the side of her dungarees and reached out to shake him. Her eyes rested on the tattoo at the top of his right arm.

'Catherine. And this is my female rat, Daisy Duke.'

With one small shake she let go, moved around him, and dumped the bag she'd held in her other hand on top of the already filled dustbin.

'Well. Hello both. I'll move my car then apologise to your mum.

16

How does that sound?'

With a small chuckle, Catherine nodded. 'Okay. Good luck with that one. She's inside cleaning. Go straight in.'

She didn't hear him knock or call out hello. He walked straight in, as suggested by her daughter. Then lingered there in the doorway and watched her stood near the windowsill. Mesmerised.

Music drifted in from behind him. She appeared lost to the world. Sunlight lit her platinum blonde hair white-gold and framed her still figure like an energy field. He felt like an intruder. Knew he should say something. Then she turned round.

At first, she looked terrified. Then, like slick oil which bled and darkened the deep blue of the ocean, her appearance changed. Her ice-cold stare hardened the space between them. Her arms crossed over her chest as the cigarette between her delicate fingers continued to release grey, swirling smoke. She turned and stubbed it out in the ashtray behind her, then turned with suspicious eyes back towards him. He wanted to move. His legs felt like lead weight.

This time, she spoke. The words whistled like an icy wind through her tightened jaw. He heard a familiar accent in her voice. Cardiffian, which he knew so well.

For a few moments, he seemed to lose all control over his vocal cords. He couldn't find his words as he became acutely aware of his own body taking up space in the doorway. He dropped his arms from the door jamb and plunged them into his jeans' pockets. He muttered some words. Then he turned and left.

Within a few minutes, he found himself back at Dina's. Shaken-up. Beads of moistures shimmied down his pulsating forehead. He rubbed at his temples. Wondered why his grey matter had refused to engage, to let him down in such a manner?

Had I apologised? Given my name even?

His hangover furthered his growing discomfort. He held his

stomach. It churned below his hand. Then he raced upstairs and threw up.

Twenty minutes later, he sat on the edge of Dina's black leather sofa with a glass of water and two paracetamol. The incident with the neighbour had unsettled him. And, of course, there was an obvious explanation. Her Cardiffian accent had reminded him of the stranger's voice. A woman who had called him late one night back at his flat in Highgate.

He folded over and picked his tobacco tin from the coffee table wondering if it was all becoming too much. He knew he was smoking a lot. Right now, he didn't much care; being back in Wales wasn't ideal for him.

He opened the tin, took out a slip of crisp white paper, and placed it onto his small rolling mat. With slender fingers, he gently sprinkled loose tobacco across its creased white surface. Slowly, he rolled the straw mat back and forth. Back and forth to form a perfect rollie.

Like a strange side show, thoughts of the last few weeks reeled across his mind's eye. He lit up and took a long, drawn-out tug on the cigarette as he remembered the words of the fearful woman with the Cardiff accent that had crackled down the line.

'There are things you don't understand. The dead girl found at Dulwich Park. She spent most of her childhood in that godforsaken place Radcliffe and there's something else you...'

Gethin flicked the gathering ash into an ashtray as he recalled the muffled sound of a male's voice in the background of the call. Fragments of an argument. Then the line had gone dead. The call must have lasted only around a minute. But it had left a shadow that stretched and pulled him like an invisible umbilical cord back home to Wales. A place that held memories he would much rather forget; many of them he already had.

The woman's voice had crackled with fear and urgency for sure.

And he'd detected something else too. Beneath the accent referred to as "Cardiff English" often heard on the outskirts of Cardiff City and so close to Angela's, his sharp ears had detected something else, an undercurrent of a foreign accent.

After doing a little research at the National Library in North London, he discovered a children's home called Radcliffe on the north-western tip of the Vale of Glamorgan. Gethin had grown up on the southerly side of the Vale in Penarth, a coastal town. Radcliffe had closed towards the end of 1978, nearly four years ago. Whilst still in London, he made several phone calls. No one could or perhaps *would* explain why it had closed. A few people he contacted appeared eager to end the call when he questioned them about the home. Unwittingly, they gave him a motive to pursue the matter further.

As he inhaled another lungful of nicotine, the same unanswered questions circled around his head like a carousel. Who was the woman on the phone? Had she been a friend to Penny, the young girl found dead under the thick and heavy foliage of rhododendron and azalea bushes in the American gardens of Dulwich Park? Or perhaps related? And who was the man who had interrupted the call?

Gethin wondered if the woman knew that he had an interest in the case. Was that the reason she'd sought him out? There were other investigative journalists more experienced than he was. He sucked the last bit of nicotine from the rollie in his hand and crushed the dying orange stub into the ashtray.

He also reminded himself how anonymous and unexpected sources could often be unreliable; at worst, they could purposely mislead an investigation. He picked up his glass of water and took a gulp. Yet there had been something sincere in her voice. He needed to find out who she was and how she knew Penny. Right now, he had no idea how he would do this. He glanced at his pouch of tobacco, wondering if he should roll another one when the sound of the phone jolted him.

Christ, what's wrong with me?

His eyes darted towards the phone on a shelf near the television. He sat there for a few seconds, not wanting to pick up, then leapt across the lounge, forgetting the glass in his hand.

'Hello. Geth?'

'Fuck.' Water spilled down his jeans and onto the thick shagpile carpet.

'It's Mark. You okay mate?'

'Yeh, fine. You?' Gethin wiped down his wet trouser leg, remembering that he had given this number to Mark, just in case. In case of what, he wasn't sure.

Mark's tone dropped. Almost to a whisper.

'They've only gone and bloody transferred me out of Scotland Yard. Some station filled with cranky old timers on the outskirts of London. Got no juice left in em.' His voice dipped further and Gethin imagined him scanning around as he spoke into the receiver. 'Someone didn't like me asking questions about *that one*, you know.'

The comment didn't surprise Gethin, although he was concerned for his friend. He sounded unusually fractious.

'Whoever's doing this is covering all areas mate. Boxes of evidence have gone… including that ring.' Long silences punctuated his words. 'You need to be careful Geth. Something ain't right here, buddy.'

'Any idea who it might be?'

'Nope. Not a clue cloner. And right now, it's too risky to be asking any more questions.'

Gethin nodded. 'Jeez Mark. I know how much you loved being in the thick of it down there in Whitehall. I didn't mean for…'

'Naahh. Don't sweat it, geezer. You're a friend, right? If I hear anything, I'll let you know—when the waters calm a bit. There are eyes watching me right now.'

'Okay. Understood.'

'Anyway. How's Dina and the wifey doing?'

Gethin couldn't help but smile at Mark's contempt for Dina's husband, and his assertion that it wasn't him wearing the trousers in that marriage. One meeting had been enough, a visit to London, a few drinks in a bar, a memorable evening for all the wrong reasons. 'He's alright. In small doses.'

'Never could see what she sees in him.'

'She's happy.'

'I suppose. Right gotta go and push some paper round a loada bongos. Stay safe friend.'

Gethin place the receiver back on its cradle, feeling blindsided by his friend's news. The ring was the only piece of evidence that identified the body. On the inside of the ring had been the words: *To Penny H love Mum.. X*

He glanced at the large clock that hung on the lounge wall, its face partially obscured by the light that poured into the room. The large black hands pointing to midday.

He still hadn't called his parents. A familiar guilt prickled. He consoled himself, knowing they might already be at bridge club. He'd ring later—let them know he was back in Wales. Not that he didn't want to speak to them, it was that his work commitments took up so much of his head space these days, he told himself.

Instead, he shot upstairs and changed into a pair of jogger pants and his favourite Zeppelin t-shirt. For forty minutes, Gethin worked through several Aikido positions, then sat in his familiar seiza position. Even when away from his Highgate flat, it was a routine Gethin enjoyed. It helped him to focus and prepare his mind.

When he'd finished, Gethin stood, put his hands together, and bowed graciously towards a small photo of Morihei Ueshiba he'd brought with him.

Then he strode across to the wooden cubby framing the television.

The shelves were full of albums, and reel-to-reels, and the cubby also housed the telephone, and a large stereo system. He ran his fingers along Dina's LP collection and plucked out a Rolling Stones album. Sliding the vinyl out of its sleeve with care, he held it by its circular edges and placed it onto the turntable. Lifting the stylus, he placed it onto the black spinning disc. Subtle crackling preceded the opening notes of "Sympathy for the Devil".

He closed his eyes. Despite the aversion he felt, he'd returned to Wales and for good reason. To find answers, too many of the dark questions that surrounded file 10.81. Strangely, an investigation he'd almost abandoned had now brought him back to the green lands he'd turned his back on.

3

Angela

There it was again, that all too familiar noise.

Thud…

Thud…

Thud.

Angela lay in bed, staring at the ceiling as her fingers clenched and unclenched the cool sheet under her. She waited, hoping the banging would subside and stop. Colin had always insisted on taking control of these matters, telling her to stay in bed. Now that old life worked against her in the unfolding moment. As if tied in one place, her body failed to act. She started to count the thuds. On the third she sat up, on the fourth she shifted her body to the edge of the bed, and on the fifth she planted her feet on the carpet next to her bed. She breathed out in the darkness of unfamiliar shadows.

They had nicknamed him "headbanger", and it had seemed amusing to start with. Now, Angela struggled to comprehend the oddity of her son's action, burying it beneath the sediment of other traumas and worries. She had thought it a phase, something that would stop once they were out of the other house and away from Colin.

She grabbed her old satin dressing gown from the floor and wrapped it around her shivering body. In the darkness she slinked across the room, trying to move her body around the unfamiliar dimensions of her new room. Her fingers grasped at the door handle and opened it.

Thud … Thud … Thud.

'Shit!' Angela's hands flew to her chest as she stepped back from the door as it opened suddenly. 'Catherine, what the hell you doing? I nearly peed myself.'

'Sorry, Mum didn't mean to frighten you like. Joel is banging his head again.'

'Yes, I can hear it, go back to bed. I'll sort it.'

Catherine gave her mother a peculiar look. 'Okay. But Mum… I think Joel might be trying to self-soothe. Someone in school was saying their little sister used to do it.'

Angela frowned. 'Maybe. Get yourself back to bed.' Angela wondered if the marks she'd witnessed on her daughter's skin earlier that day were doing the same thing for her.

She leaned in and kissed her daughter on the cheek. She could smell the oil paints. 'Cath, you shouldn't stay up so late painting.'

Catherine shrugged and shut her bedroom door.

As faint light from the streetlamp filtered through the smoky glass of the bathroom window through the open door, Angela tiptoed across the bare floorboards of the landing. They creaked below her feet, the sound a haunted chorus to bone hitting an unyielding wall.

She pushed her son's bedroom door open shocked to hear how much louder the pounding of his forehead sounded. Her own heart pounded in and out. Her limbs seemed to lose their strength as her eyes focused on his small body rocking back and forth alone in the darkness. Angela cursed herself for being a chickenshit. She was his mother and had to deal with this now.

In one swift movement she was across his small room, avoiding somehow the toys and books that littered his floor. She bent down over him, placed her left hand in-between his shoulder blades and reached her other hand to his forehead to restrict and cushion the impact. It worked. With his movement restricted, he calmed. She sat on the edge of the bed and watched him for a while, his sweet face calm as he drifted back into sleep.

She had watched him play earlier from the dining-room window. He seemed to love the street and his newfound friends. It was the most fun he'd had for as long as she could remember. It was a moment she wouldn't forget—seeing him so free and happy. He'd galloped indoors dirty and grimy, his chest heaving with exuberance, his dark eyes shining like a thoroughbred's. No worry whipped into his features. It had never been allowed before—dirt. As if dirt itself was something to be in fear of.

She stood and bent to grasp the bed frame from underneath with both hands, and in a moment of fierce effort, she pulled the bed away from the wall. Why hadn't Colin let her do that before when she'd suggested it? Why had she stuck to this position in a new house? Joel's sheet and *Incredible Hulk* blanket slipped away, disappeared onto the floor between the bed and the wall. She reached over the bed, grasped them, and pulled them back over her son's milky limbs.

She nestled in behind her son and tucked her arm under his neck and across his chest. With her other hand, she stroked his thick glossy hair and listened to his silk-smooth breathing. It was a wonderful feeling. She didn't want to let him go.

As Joel slept, she lay there marvelling at his attempt at hanging posters of his favourite characters: Luke Skywalker, *E.T.*, and *Raiders of the Lost Ark*. He had stood on a chair and stuck them to the wall himself. Long shiny strips of tape splayed across the wall in copious amounts. Each poster at a different angle. The walls of his room looked like a kid's scrap book. The sense of accomplishment had radiated from him as he'd descended the stairs to tell her what he had done. Anyway, she couldn't afford to decorate it at the moment, so it didn't matter. For now, it looked like a proper boy's room. An untidy space.

Angela moved her left arm up under the coolness of Joel's pillow. It ached from his sleeping weight. Her fingers touched something. Grasping the corner, she slipped it from under his pillow. About the size and weight of a photograph, she lifted it high above her head. A small amount of light fell upon it, and her world caved in a little. It was a photo of all of them during one of the family's rare and happier moments. Colin's hands rested on Joel's small shoulders. His smile as wide as the Darth Vader cap he wore. How photos deceive, she thought. The journey of a single parent was beginning to feel like walking across a floor covered in Lego pieces with a blindfold. Angela heard her breathing stutter inwards as the hollow pain in her stomach made her squeeze his small frame tighter towards her. She reminded herself many times things would improve, not just for herself, but for all of them. Careful not to wake him, she slipped the photo back under his pillow and shut her eyes to sleep.

Something had woken her. Small rivulets of sweat tracked lines between her breasts. Threads of Joel's hair stuck to her hot cheeks. She squinted towards his *Transformers* clock. The fluorescent hands read 1.30 A.M. She sighed. Crawling back to her own bed seemed pointless now.

Seconds later, she watched as the lights of a car turning into the quiet street sliced through the darkness of the bedroom and lit parts of the wall. She frowned. Puzzled by who it could be. Then she bolted upright. Listening.

What if it's him? The tightness in her chest told her she already feared it was.

Had he returned in the dead of night to drag them back to his lair? It wasn't an unimaginable reality; he had done similar things in the past. Her breathing consumed the silent room as she sat like a mannequin except for the thumping beat in her chest. Every cell of her body had become hyper-alert to the subtle sounds of the car outside, as its movement slowed to a stop. The engine clicked off. The car was now parked outside her house.

It is him!

The nausea rising from the pit of her stomach lurched upwards, making her light-headed. She knew she needed to move. The car door opened. She was ready to fling herself across the bedroom, downstairs to the phone. She heard clicking heels on the pavement and the snapping of bags being open and shut.

Where were the familiar weight of his footfalls?

Like a wild fox on a city street, she continued to listen for danger. Female voices whispered through the darkness. Angela closed her eyes and concentrated hard, thinking she might be imagining the sounds. She peered up towards the window, then with slow movements edged from the bed and to the windowsill, her curiosity replacing her initial fears.

A trio of woman stood below the orange glow of a streetlamp. Lit from above, their features appeared distorted and unnatural. Angela grimaced at the sight of them. They huddled in towards one another, speaking in hushed tones under the flickering light. It reminded her of a coven of witches. Even the branches of the cherry tree seemed to lean in towards them to hear their utterances. The orange night-light like a stark stage for their unfolding performance, set against a misty backdrop of thick unknowing.

She squinted as she tried in vain to detect what the ladies were giving their unwavering attention to. The tallest of the trio passed the small object around as though in some arcane rite. For a moment Angela found herself amused … "hot potatoes" came to mind. The thought itself arbitrary and unrelated to the moment. She felt herself tipping towards hysteria.

However, the strange scene compelled Angela: she was caught in the inescapable allure of the three soundless women. Only then did Angela consider she might know one of the women. The smaller one on the right could be Lisa, her new neighbour. She couldn't be sure, not sure at all.

Then her eyes drifted across the street where the row of darkened terrace houses lit with pinpricks of white in the vast black space above made her heart unsteady. So empty. So vast. Her little life seemed so insignificant in contrast. She peered down again towards the ladies and reared back in horror. One of them glared up towards the window. She ducked her head, not before witnessing all three heads turn towards her.

"Shit!" She caught her forehead on the edge of the windowsill as she dived out of sight. She rubbed in circular movements above her right eye, trying to alleviate some of the throbbing discomfort. Why did she want to giggle, laugh out into the space that held her? She slinked to the floor, wondering why the urge to smile … laugh? Then the word appeared like letter pieces from a game of Scrabble—freedom. She had experienced something new and unusual, a bit weird, but of her own doing. However, right or wrong her actions were this strange night, she had chosen them. In another world she would have appeased a controlling husband and lay like cardboard in bed unmoving, lost to a world of spoken instruction. She sat on the brown carpeted floor of her son's room for a while longer, feeling the edges of her lips curl and her heart inflate a little. Then, without hesitation, she stood upright and walked across the bedroom hearing the clicking of dispersing heels on the kerbside. She didn't turn to see, no need.

Opening her son's bedroom door, she glided across the landing and into her own room. She discarded her dressing gown, which fell to the floor and flung her knickers across the room ... just because she could.

Angela lay in her bedroom, staring up at the ceiling for the second time that night. This time, she lay above the sheets. Curtains opened a fraction. Her limbs lit in strips of light from outside. The bed clothes and cushions displaced. Angela wanted to savour each second of the feeling before it faded. She wouldn't sleep for a while, so she let her mind wander to the women outside. One of them had been her new neighbour, Lisa, she was sure of it.

The day before, or was it two days ago? Tired and agitated she'd asked Catherine to knock on their neighbour's door. She'd clocked Lisa peering from behind her neat net curtains a few minutes earlier. Now, as she lay in darkness on her bed, she scrunched up the soft skin around her eyes in shame as she remembered her own anger, her own rudeness. How she'd demanded an explanation for the Range Rover parked on her driveway, making it impossible to reverse the van that contained her life.

I must have looked a sight, Bensons ciggie hanging from my bloody lip and attitude dripping from every pore. Whilst Lisa stood there all neat and calm and smart in her blue twinset. Manicured nails and a manicured attitude to match.

And yet she appeared so different in the distorting light of the streetlamps tonight. Angela stretched her feet, her toes pointed towards the end of the bed. She turned them in small circular movements as she puzzled over the strange appearance of her neighbour. Then it came to her as clear as her daughter's bright green eyes. Her hair. Surely, a wig. Yes. Where was that Lady Di cut? Had Lisa been wearing a wig? Her hair, short and ash blonde yesterday, this dark night transformed into a cascading mane of shoulder length chestnut brown. Convinced she wasn't mistaken, she flipped herself onto her stomach and smiled as she lay across her bare arm. She felt curious. Something had switched on; she flipped her legs up from the knee joints and crossed her feet in the air, swinging them gently. What was their quiet and agreeable neighbour up to?

Angela fell asleep for the third time, her mind busied with images of haunting women made up like mannequins dealing packs of cards in slices of light and shadow.

4

Gethin

It was late evening when Gethin opened file 10.81.

He'd spent the early afternoon doing a few chores until he realised he hadn't seen Belflo since the morning. Gethin guessed the damned cat had disappeared in a show of total displeasure at his sudden arrival and residency on his home turf.

Gethin wandered up and down Dafydd Drive. His lips made a terse line of agitation. He didn't care much for "that fat cat" but he'd made a promise to Dina. To look after Belflo in return for staying at the house. He mooched about. Whispered the cat's name into dark corners, under hedges and parked cars. He felt the lingering winter bite in the air—reluctant to give way for the warmer spring months. Gethin shivered. He imagined the cat crouched down somewhere watching him. Full of smirky glee.

A curious neighbour from number 15, a few doors down on the other side of the street, wandered down his path. An opportunist.

'Bit chilly isn't it?' he said with a feigned quiver. 'What's going on?'

Bloody obvious, isn't it? 'Looking for Dina's cat.'

He nodded, a slow deliberate action as the sides of his lips pulled down. Hair as black as night stuck like glue to the sides of his pale, long face. His false smile and lack of honest interest were palpable as he stood there, hands clasped behind his back, rocking back on his heels.

God, I hate men who do that, thought Gethin.

He glanced across the road. 'Maybe one of those women over there has taken him in. Let any Tom, Dick, or Harry inside, they will.'

Gethin pulled his forehead down heavy over his eyes with a slow shake of his head. The man raised an eyebrow as he continued.

'This used to be a respectable street I hasten to add...'

He must have sensed Gethin's lack of interest in his proclamations because he changed his tone a little, glanced across the street, and sighed.

'Let's hope they see sense and find good men to take care of them.' He rolled back on the heels of his patent leather shoes again.

Men weren't always reliable in the business of caring, thought Gethin as he bent down and peered under another car. The man's feet shifted on the pavement. He made strange noises with his throat as if agitated by Gethin's lack of attention; obviously he felt his words merited more attention. Gethin stood and brushed a few pieces of tarmac gravel from his joggers. He noted the faint sneer given towards his Led Zeppelin t-shirt.

'Best get back in door then. Hope you find that cat. He's a bit overweight, wouldn't you say?'

Then, with a taut turrah, he turned and loped back down the path towards his front door. He stood there for a moment watching Gethin, waiting.

Gethin lifted his hand, said, 'See you then,' and forced a smile, hoping with all hope as the man shut his door that he wouldn't have the pleasure of the man's company any time soon.

The burgundy Rover on the man's driveway had several bumper stickers. One of them read, "Jehovah loves you". Gethin padded away, wondering what type of hellish street he was living on.

As the sun dipped behind the terraced houses and the streetlights blinked to life, Gethin gave up. He passed Angela's house and glimpsed toward the window where she'd stood earlier with a lost expression troubling her features. He thought he saw a glimpse of her moving up the stairs with her son.

As he called Belflo one last time and shut the front to the darkening, ink-blue skies, he reminded himself that cats were survivors. Maybe guilt gnawed at him a little. Either way. He had work to do.

Five minutes later, with a strong coffee in one hand, he stood at Dina's dining table. Paperwork spread fan-like across the surface of the oval shaped table. Darkness crept over curled edges of paper as natural light from outside completely diminished. He reached across to the wall and switched the overhead extendable lamp on. With a small metal bar, he pulled the large green glass shade downwards. He'd replaced the bulb earlier. It shone a light on the paperwork that had travelled from London with him.

For a moment, the room, or the action of pulling light towards his investigation, reminded him of his own eclectic lounge, his desk and coloured lampshades and cushions. He hadn't changed it for some years now. Hazel had liked colours. These splashes of colour reminded Gethin of her, he suddenly realized. He blinked. Shook his head. He needed to focus.

Breadcrumbs from his earlier sandwich littered the table. He brushed them away, then with that usual trepidation he lifted the familiar shaped brown envelope from the table. Inside were three photographs. He knew the risks involved in possessing them. However, it had become clear to Gethin, having witnessed these photos, that evil crept undetected in many minds. In order to unearth this evil, reality had to confront these spectacles of inhumanity directly. That was his job now.

Gethin took the photos and placed them alongside each other under the direct light. Different shots of Penny's exposed body mutilated and eaten away in places by city animals and insects. Her long, dark hair scattered around her head like a dark and swirling storm. Her patchy pale skin juxtaposed against the gloom and shadows, and the vegetation that might have concealed her lifeless, abused body a little longer than a few days had it not been for the smell of decay in the air. It had attracted the attention of a dog and his owner. A mild November meant decomposition had set in sooner.

Rarely did any image shock Gethin. However, these were different. The apparatus of her death made him confront reality itself. The head shot exposed the brutality he struggled to comprehend. Consumed in a darkness empty of any kind of benevolence.

Screwed into the sides of her skull were two small bolts attaching a mask-like contraption to her distorted features. The rough strips of metal worked horizontally and vertically across her features from the rough outer edges. A central metal plate had two small pin holes for eyes and below, a crude convex shape moulded into a nose. Cage-like and barbaric, the funnel metal shapes jutting out like microphonic ears at the sides of her head only added a sick cartoon mockery.

The final jolt of menace, which he'd read about in the report, was the rod inserted into her mouth. At the end of this, a small rotating wheel with metal spikes had torn her tongue into fleshy tassels. He remembered reading somewhere in his file that the torn flesh in her mouth had attracted blowflies which had laid eggs.

The post-mortem concluded she'd died from a heart attack brought on by her body being flooded with adrenaline. Sheer terror and pain had killed her.

He glanced up at his muted reflection in the tinted mirror opposite. Something flickered behind his right shoulder. Movement. He spun. And swore.

In the blackness outside, two bright marbles of colour stared inside. Accusation and disfavour bristled in his whiskers. A Blink. Then Belflo dropped away from the window.

Gethin heard the cat's hollow cries carry from the porch. He moved to the hallway and opened the front door. The corners of his lips upturned as the cat darted in with uncharacteristic speed. Aloof, with his tail pointed northwards, he leaped up the stairs out of sight again.

Gethin shut the door and returned to the table. At least the damn thing had returned and would be out of his way. He had much to dig into that required his full attention.

Hazel told him once she thought he suited deeply researched investigative work. He had a knack for getting others to talk she'd said. If he gave them his undivided attention with those large inquisitive eyes, they'd chirp right through to dawn, undeterred by the threat of a coming storm. There were things far worse than storms. He buried the memory of her voice. Hardened his focus towards his fact-finding.

Gethin picked up some statements and interviews paper-clipped together. Not one person who had attended the festivities at the park had reported seeing anything unusual. It was Halloween. Most people wore costumes and behaved a little out of character. Fancy dress often did this to people. Gethin shuddered. He hated artifice. And he hated Halloween.

He reached for his tin. Rolled a cigarette by hand, causing the paper to crease and crumple under his uneven pressure. He struck a match and lit it, sucked at the filter. He blew out circles of smoke and watched as they rose and faded. Like symbolic messages to the unseen. He was looking for trails.

He sat back into the spindle legged dining chair. Rollie hanging from his full lower lip. He knew the police investigation into her murder had been a shambles. Experienced officers replaced with what Mark had referred to as "sprogs".

'Mere apprentices who had no bloody idea what they were doing!'

Other members of the team he'd discovered were ex-military. They had no initiative, Mark had said. Happy to follow orders and not much else.

There were too many irregularities with the case. Evidence lost or not logged properly. Even simple lines of enquiry he'd discovered proved too difficult for the team put together for the investigation. He questioned how officers even experienced ones could make so many disastrous mistakes and errors in one case. Perhaps someone had orchestrated it this way? And why had the case been closed so quickly?

He'd investigated cases in the past where discrimination in the police force contributed to the failings of the investigation. He rummaged through layers of paper. Papers he really shouldn't have been privy to. He stopped to flick ash off his smoke. Plucked out the newspaper article he'd cut out of a tabloid around the time of the initial investigation.

The article claimed Penny had been a prostitute and drug user. He'd cross-referenced it with a copy of the post-mortem. They found no substances in her body except for red wine and traces of a meal of salmon, potatoes and asparagus found in her stomach.

However, the examiner highlighted old scars on her arms that indicated previous drug use and possible early damage to her liver.

Gethin sighed and rubbed his forehead. Was it possible that some failings simply came about due to a male orientated team who had no interest in finding the killer of who they believed to be a prostitute? A prostitute who had little history to her life, no traceable family or friends. She hadn't come up on a missing persons list. No one had found dental records to identify her.

Only then did it strike Gethin. There was a good possibility that he might be the only person in possession of certain evidence collected during the investigation. The only thing that had identified the woman was the small ring inscribed with her name. That ring had disappeared, along with other evidence. Gethin still had photos of it.

If someone intended burying the case and everything with it, Gethin's investigative work into who murdered Penny could put him in even greater danger.

He flicked ash that hung like crumbling cement into the marble ashtray as his foot tapped without a sound into the shagpile carpet. Then he remembered. The books from his Local Library in London were still in his car.

Barefoot, he scampered back out into the darkness, the cold on the soles of his feet making him shiver as he unlocked the car door and retrieved the books. The sound of the car door as it closed echoed in the silence. A dog nearby barked. He stopped and scanned along the street. The orange yellow light from long thin lamp posts split the terraces either side into light and dark. The hedges and garages that jutted out in intervals down the street created sharp angular shapes that jutted out like broken bone. He shivered again. His pace quickened as he returned down the path and indoors.

He settled on the sofa and opened one of the books. *A Concise History of Medieval England*. He flicked to the index. Ran his finger down a couple of pages until it stopped as if words had bounced away from the page and obstructed it. "Instruments of punishment and torture. Pg 106".

There they were. Several pictures of women with cage-like contraptions over their head: the scold's bridle. He thought he'd heard the word before. Below are other similar devices. *Shrew's fiddle*, *cucking stool, ducking stool.* Men used the bridle as an instrument of punishment, to torture and silence women who talked too much. Gethin's stomach flipped. Nausea. Bile scorched the back of his throat.

Despite his repulsion to the brutal devices that tightened his grip on the page, he continued to read how these bridles, also had a bit, sometimes with spikes, fixed into the mouth. To also silence the victim.

Was this why Penny had been caged? Degraded in death, or to death?

Gethin snapped the book shut and frowned. He reached into his pocket, took out his small pot of tiger balm and rubbed some in slow circular movements onto his temples to ease the growing headache.

Outside, rain now ticked in sweeping rhythms against the windowpane. The sound of it brought him back to his own flat again. Hazel had liked the sound of rain hitting cold glass. The way the world outside became blurred as she sat warm and comforted reading under the huge emerald lamp shade they'd bought at Camden market. Hazel had said once that the colour symbolized living together in balance and harmony.

Gethin stood and stretched then moved across to the sofa. He rolled his head back against the soft leather and closed his eyes. His mind dragged him back to thoughts of Radcliffe, that forsaken place. Then he slipped into a dark and troubled sleep.

5

Gethin

Gethin woke up on Dina's sofa, looked down at the woollen blanket that covered his bare chest, and groaned. His strange ritual had started sooner than he'd thought. He closed his eyes for a few moments and listened as the stylus crackled on the turning vinyl beneath it. He'd fallen asleep before turning everything off.

With a sinking sensation flooding his senses, he sat up and looked towards the pile of folded clothes in the middle of the lounge. On top of them, he could see the photograph of Hazel. He must have searched it out in his half-sleep, despite removing most of the pictures of her from sight after Dina had left. In his own flat, he no longer had photos of Hazel. He'd got rid of them. It had worked. Stopped his night walks in darkness. Dina still had photos of her, which was no surprise really, given that they'd all been good friends once.

Belflo sat and watched between the wooden slats of the staircase as Gethin lifted the photo and folded clothes from the carpet. The cat's whiskers bristled, and his tail looped and curled in spasms. Gethin threw a suspicious stare at him.

Did you see me do this? Search in the darkness for her and mock me?

Gethin plodded to the kitchen and slipped the photo in-between tea towels in the kitchen. He realised this was going to be tricky. He couldn't bin photos that belonged to Dina, but he didn't want his sleepwalking to become a burden. It made him more tired and moody.

He put his joggers back on and focused on his morning Aikido routine, bare-chested. It helped, especially the meditation afterwards. He didn't tell people he meditated. It seemed few people understood the merits of it. And he was done with trying to convince people otherwise. And of hearing the hidden mockery in their words.

After a quick shower, he bounced back downstairs, feeling rejuvenated and ready to continue with his research into Radcliffe Children's Home, and its connections, if any, with the murder of Penny. With renewed focus, and earlier distractions dissipated he reached into his beloved leather satchel for the article he'd copied from the British Library in Colindale a week earlier. He'd spent hours scrolling through old newspaper articles on microfilm reels for information about Radcliffe.

He placed the document on the walnut coffee table in front of him. The headline read:

"New girl's annexe for Radcliffe's children's home in Coed Derw."

Below the headline was a grainy photo that took up almost half of the page. It showed a large, Gothic-style building with steep pitched roofs and painted gables, even in the grainy image Gethin could see the ancient paintwork blistering away from the ornate woodwork. Attached to the left of the building was a modern annexe built with little consideration to the characteristics and style of the older building next to it.

A sizeable crowd of people, including children of different ages, stood in front of the new annexe. Taking centre position near the entrance to the annexe were several men. A ribbon hung across a set of doors waiting to be cut.

Gethin recognised one of them, the young Welsh Councillor Dylan Edwards. He'd become a member of the Labour Party about the time the idea of devolution became prominent on the Welsh Labour landscape. In his earlier and eager journalistic years, Gethin had written a few articles on the subject and spoken with Dylan.

Labour and its industrial heartbeat had monopolised many Welsh seats in parliament. It had been a fruitful time for someone like Dylan to join the Labour Party. He came from the right stock, his father being a miner and his mother a nurse.

Standing on Dylan's right smiling, with a pair of large scissors in his hands, ready to cut the ribbon, was the Vale Mayor. And to his left were two other men. One of them wore sunglasses and seemed to be looking over his left shoulder at something in the photo-shot.

Gethin dropped his eyes and scanned the article, picking out words and phrases that caught his attention.

An annexe built onto the older, existing building of the children's home … caring for our looked after children … A proud moment … Honourable George Davies Mayor … Superintendent Mr Wayne H. Thomas, Councillor Mr Edwards, and private financial contributors … delighted to … play and study rooms … new dorms and bathrooms for the girls … Celebrations followed with bouncy castles … small rides and some fun stalls… lovely cake stall… the wonderful Mrs S. Solomon … who has to date fostered over seven children from the home … including the delightful young Deborah pictured next to her.

In pen he highlighted several names, including Mrs Solomon, Dylan Edwards, the Superintendent, and the mayor. The brief, perfunctory descriptions of Mrs Solomon had piqued his interest. She seemed the perfect person to approach about Radcliffe Children's Home. Gethin would use every skill he'd acquired as an investigative journalist to glean what truth he could from those who might have known Penny, either by name or more personally.

Across from him on Dina's shelf he could see the large BT directory. He sifted through the delicate thin pages, searching out the section of sir names beginning with 'S'. His fingers ran down the small print as his eyes searched out Solomon, with a speed that came from experience of such things. There were five listed. That wouldn't be too difficult; he'd had worse.

The first number he dialled no one picked up. The second a younger woman who thought he was a cold caller, gave him a ticking off before ending the call abruptly. His third attempt proved to be more fruitful. Just.

Mrs Solomon picked up and said hello in a gentle, slow manner. Gethin warmed to her voice and softened his own tone to more match hers. Without delay, he introduced himself as an old friend of Deborah's.

With the old newspaper article in front of him, Gethin continued to regale all the good things he'd heard about her, including her baking for the children at Radcliffe. Her voice became a little higher pitched now as she seemed to exert her fragile mind in an effort to recall details from a past that had started disappearing into perpetual darkness.

For a while, he enjoyed listening to some of her stories, even if they were fragmented and silenced by absences of memory.

'Well, my dear. I'm afraid I find it difficult these days to remember the finer details. The grey matter doesn't want to fire up.' She chuckled to herself. 'But I do remember Deborah. She wasn't an easy one to forget. Sad really. Deborah was one of the sharper tools in the box. but couldn't seem to keep out of harm's way. Always breaking the rules and her curfews.'

There was a pause.

'Beautiful young lady. Half-Chinese and half-Portuguese, she is. But of course, you know this.'

Gethin nearly stumbled. 'Yes.'

She chortled. 'Deborah hated that mole though, always trying to cover it up. She was her own worst enemy, really.' The phone went quiet again.

'Didn't like rules, she didn't see … My husband, and I tried so hard with her, but eventually she returned to Radcliffe. She ran away again. Didn't return after that.' Mrs Solomon sighed. 'It wasn't long after that my husband passed away. They wouldn't let me foster being a single older woman. I carried on baking for the children for a while, which was nice.'

'I'm sorry to hear of your loss, Mrs Solomon.'

'Ohh, it was years ago now. The children at the home kept me going. Not now though. I wouldn't cope with all that excitement.' She went quiet.

Gethin detected a little sadness in her voice.

Mrs Solomon, I wonder if you remember another young girl by the name of Penny who attended Radcliffe? Her sir name might have begun with H.

'Mmm, Penny, no, I can't recall a Penny, but then my memory.' She blew out, exasperated with herself. 'There might have been a Penny! Oh dear, I'm not being much help. Perhaps Deborah could help you there?'

'Mrs Solomon, can you remember Deborah's surname? It's my turn to be forgetful now! It's been such a while and if she's married now, I guess it's changed?'

'Oh no dear, don't think she's the marrying type. Still Deborah Barmak.' She chuckled again. 'See, I remember some things.'

'Ah, yes, Barmak.' Gethin didn't enjoy playing these games with such a sweet old lady. But it was safer for now that she thought of him as an old friend of Deborah's.

'Well, you've been so kind helping me. Thankyou.'

Mrs Solomon didn't respond.

'Mrs Solomon. Are you okay?'

'My dear man.' Her voice broke away again with an uncertainty that Gethin had become accustomed too with people troubled by the words they wanted to speak.

'Deborah is, well. Um, sells her body, so sad. Doubt she's ever believed she's worth more. Poor lady.'

'I see. If I find her, I'll do my best to help her.'

'The Package ... no that's not it...' She spoke aloud, tracking her thoughts. 'The Pallet? Oh dear, it was some time ago now. Someone might have mentioned she was living there. I think it's a pub. I'm feeling a little tired now. Sorry, I guess it's not good news?'

'Please don't apologise. I've kept you on the phone too long.'

'Well, good luck. Lovely speaking to you, Richard.'

'Bye now.'

He placed the phone down. And wondered who Richard was? For a moment, he questioned the reliability of what she'd told him given her deteriorating memory. With a pen, he jotted down a name. *The Packet.* Her memory had served her well with that snippet of information. He knew the pub intimately. He'd frequented it himself down Cardiff docks as a youth.

Gethin

As the train rumbled into Bute Street Railway Station, Gethin viewed the whitewashed terraces stark against the steel grey skies. Had spring abandoned Wales? He smiled as he wondered if he might be luckier today. He'd taken the same trip yesterday. Left Dina's in the morning in his Range Rover, driven to Cardiff Central station, parked his car in one of the multi-story car parks and taken a train down towards the Docks. The journey took only five minutes from Central to Bute Street.

He came out of the station, pulled the collars of his vintage Gloverall duffle coat up around his neck. He crossed the road, then took a left towards the docks until he came to crossroads. Old buildings rose about him, some several storeys high, with large sills holding terracotta pots, others crumbling and decaying from years of erosion.

Tiger Bay had been an area his parents had deterred him from in his youth. To no avail. Many times, with friends, he'd ventured into jazz bars with Catholic girls wanting some thrills and dope. He'd spent several evenings in smoke-filled rooms listening to funk jazz as swift and heady dealings filled dark corners. Holding a pint of brown ale in one hand and a joint in the other, they had all thought they were all grown up and super cool. It had been a dangerous place for those who weren't local—despite this, Gethin had fond memories of the place. He'd always been treated well. His face must have fitted.

He crossed the junction, and several yards ahead the familiar wooden sign swung and creaked in the wind above the door to *The Packet* pub. The same feeling hit him as it had the day before. The pub had appeared different when viewed through the kaleidoscope of his curious teenage eyes. With a group of friends, he had ventured into, and explored *The Packet*. An experience worn like a badge of honour when regaling the story to their less curious peers.

Yesterday, he had also ventured into the pub, ordered a drink from a burly, brutish barman with a voice like coarse-ground pepper and found himself a quiet corner to sit. The seats were stained brown and torn in places, exposing stained, yellow filling. He'd lifted the strap of his satchel away from his chest and undone some of the toggles on his coat. Someone had left a newspaper on the round table across from him. He'd stretched over and picked it up to scan while he sat and waited. A haze of tobacco smoke had lingered just above his head, mixed with the smell of stale beer and sweat. He'd seen a few women with thick liner pencilled around soulless eyes, and lipstick bleeding into cracks around their mouths. They had glanced his way with a mixture of curiosity and hunger. Their attire had been more appropriate than his duffle coat for the stage that set their scene. The area had plenty of prostitutes. Many of them also hung about under the bridge further into town, where the old bled into the new.

Today, although still windy and grey, had a warmth that yesterday missed. It was his mood. He'd woken with no ritualistic pile of clothing set on the floor.

As he made his way to the public house for the second time, he still found himself in awe of how business types in suits mingled with what he thought of as a cultural soup of diversity. Things were changing fast, but the aromatic smells of West Indian food interspersed with sweet and spicy Chinese could tantalise the most conservative of taste buds. It reminded him of London, walks along Camden Market with Hazel. Her easy chatter as they perused the open food stalls. The sounds of Reggae mixed with swing jazz, and the Hindustani language. The latter of which he had heard during his several travels in India.

He still scorned the bad press the place received from other areas of the city. Now older in years and experience, he saw much of it as a matter of prejudice and ignorance. Bad press had convoluted all negativity towards the area. In his line of work, he had soon opened his eyes to the fact that corruption and vice existed everywhere, even in the most unexpected of places. With a little sadness, he considered the fact many in other areas of the city had avoided Tiger Bay and the docks because of such prejudices.

He stood for a moment outside the pub, watching his own reflection ripple in the old glass windows before going inside. Five minutes later, he returned with a pint of Brains in his hand. The spring sunshine clawed its way out on the horizon as he placed his beer on the small metal table outside and took his place on an old rickety chair.

He took his tin from his satchel and rolled a cigarette, cupping his hands to light it with his Zippo lighter. For a while he rolled it around in his hand feeling the coolness of the metal in his hands. Gethin took a moment to read the words scribed onto the side of the Zippo before depositing it back into the depths of his pocket.

He sat back and considered the brief interaction he'd had with the woman pulling pints behind the bar. Part of him had expected to see the barman from the day before, staring at him with those insipid distrustful eyes. With relief, and an air of contrived casualness, he'd made some light conversation with the woman then started asking other questions, watching her with interest as she responded. At first, she'd crinkled the soft tired skin around her eyes at Gethin, in an attempt to work him out. She pinched her lips at his inquiring questions. Then, as if having decided about him, she began to talk in raspy broken tones through lips clinging to a cigarette.

'She ain't lived here for a while now, daarling.' She continued pulling his pint as she spoke. 'Private one, that one.' The corners of her lips pulled up as she pushed the pint towards Gethin. She tried to suppress a sly laugh that snorted from her flared nostrils. 'Likes to fink she's a cut above ur station.' She turned, punching her brittle lacquered nails into keys on the till.

'That'll be 46p.' She held out her palm and sighed. He took a pound note from his wallet and placed it in her outreached palm.

'Thanks, daarling!' She turned back to the till for change. As she dropped it into his hand, she stopped, her dead watery eyes staring at him. She wanted to ask something; he sensed it. She didn't.

'She comes down yur for Brooks's sweet shop bout twice a week sometimes. It sells the best Turkish delight in Wales. Like I said, always thinking she was a cut above...'

Then she stopped talking and swiped a glance over Gethin's shoulder at a solitude figure sat cross legged in a dark corner of the pub. After that, she turned and started serving another punter.

Today, with a metal ashtray to fill with his ash and butt ends, he sat enjoying the sensation of observing life unfold in all its myriad of colour and spectacle before him. He sifted through an hour like this, jotting notes, nodding to passers-by, and taken in the spectacles of dock life as Spring air resilient in its duty, warmed the mood.

He stretched, pulling his shoulders back to relieve the tension in his lower back when someone flickered into view across the road, obscured in intervals by the relentless black cabs and buses. She walked head down, both hands pushed deep into her expensive looking trench coat. Despite the surrounding noises, he could hear the distinct click of her stiletto heels against the stone pavement. She must have noticed him too, her eyes for a second shifting across the street towards him, then back to the floor ... For a second, he wondered if she could have known he was going to be there.

He watched for a few seconds more as her glossy dark hair bounced around her beautiful face with each footstep taken. He squinted, trying to see more. Yes, there it was, below her left eye, the beauty spot Mrs Solomon had mentioned over the phone.

Christ! Is it really here? Could I be this lucky? Or did Mrs Solomon let her know somehow?

He grabbed his tobacco tin and stuffed it into the leather satchel which still hung across his shoulder. He moved across the road that cut across the thoroughfare whilst also keeping an eye on Deborah. And in a few quick, wide strides he walked alongside the unsuspecting young woman. He knew his behaviour might appear threatening to her. He went to say something. Too late. She stopped and stared at him. Her dark brown, almond-shaped eyes were a strange mix of smoke and steel.

'Fuck off!' She turned away from him and continued walking as if he wasn't there at all. Accustomed to this type of response in his line of work, Gethin continued to walk alongside her, calm and persistent in his manner.

He spoke in quiet tones, expelling snippets of what he already knew about her and his investigations. Her dark eyes flickered towards him every now and again. The only sign she was listening. They continued to move northwards, Gethin trailing her movements as she turned left onto James Street.

'Deborah, I just want to ask you some questions about Radcliffe. You used to live there, right?' No response. 'I spoke to Mrs Solomon a couple of days ago!' There was a noticeable twitch at the mention of Mrs Solomon. He continued. 'I think something happened there. That's why you ran away from there, isn't it?' She continued to ignore him—her heels clicked against the stone pavement more quickly, with more urgency.

'Please Deborah. I can help.'

She stopped and turned. Looked him straight in the eye. In that second, like momentary light through a camera lens, he saw the vulnerability she hid behind those dark steely eyes.

'Okay, not here. Follow me.'

Gethin followed Deborah as she turned right into Mount Stuart Square. It was quieter. With fewer people around, he sensed her tension ease, and her footsteps slowed a little.

Ahead of them, the most iconic buildings of Bute town rose above them in all its beauty: The Old Coal Exchange. She stopped for a

49

few seconds, raising her head to look around. Then she started again, scampering towards the old, grand entrance of the building, past the steps and along the east side.

She stopped in the shadow of an arched doorway. And turned to face him, her arms folded across the front of her. Her eyes flickered back and forth as she spoke, watching as strangers walked past.

'How fucking dare you follow me like this? Here. In broad daylight? Do you have any idea how dangerous this is?'

He shook his head. 'No, I don't. Maybe you can tell me?'

She shook her head at him in disgust.

'I know you went to Radcliffe, and I think something bad happened there?'

He knew he was taking chances making a statement like this.

She scowled at him, then dropped her gaze to her shoes as if mulling something over.

'We can meet and talk wherever you want. When you want?'

He wanted to gain her trust. He grasped the small business card in his pocket and passed it to her. On the back of the card, he'd written Dina's ex-directory number. A number she used for her own work. He knew using her number this way would make her angry. He'd deal with that another time.

'Please take this, it has a number on the back ... No one will talk about the place and now it's gone ... along with what happened there.'

She took the card from Gethin and flipped it over in her hands as she spoke. She breathed in. 'Why me?'

'Because I believe you know things about Radcliffe, and I sense you're one of the few people who has the courage to talk.'

She looked at him with those sharp dramatic eyes again, less convinced than him by his words, then she thrust the card into her mac pocket.

She shuffled a little, then looked past Gethin and down the street.

'Don't follow me like this again.'

'Got it.'

'Two o'clock tomorrow. Wait for me to call you. If you don't pick up, I won't ring again.'

He nodded. 'Okay.'

She pulled her mac tight around her tiny waist as the sound of laughter echoed into the square.

Mrs Solomon wasn't wrong about her beauty. It was hard to imagine this woman could be a prostitute.

She cast her dark beautiful eyes across the street once more before stepping out of the shadows and away in the opposite direction. Gethin watched her turn the corner out of the square. He stood there for a few minutes alone, wondering if she would ring him. Or would she just disappear out of sight?

6

Angela

Angela slowed to take the corner onto Dafydd Drive. The orange hues of spring dripped like nectar in the quiet car, across her sleeping son's face. Catherine sat in the passenger's seat next to her. A good time had tempered and coloured her features as she slept soaked in the afternoon sun.

For the last few days, they'd painted walls, repaired furnishings, and made the house more of a home. When the sun had slipped from behind the eternal clouds to offer spring, Catherine had insisted Angela should drive them all to Porthcawl to surf. The decision had proved to be a good one, despite Angela's reservations at first.

Now she beeped the horn gently. Smiled. Turned the car onto the driveway dispersing a colourful burst of excited children on bikes and go-carts. Her car wheels squealed and threw up loose pieces of tarmac, which drew more unwanted attention from the two women stood chatting on the kerbside.

Angela switched her engine off with a click and glanced over her shoulder. She'd met Lisa the day she'd moved in. And since then, saw her on several occasions leaving or returning home. On one occasion, she had, despite herself, exchanged numbers with her new neighbour. Catherine had encouraged her with a glance that said she should try harder to make friends.

When was that now?

She struggled to pull the details out. Her timeline felt foggy. Four, maybe five days ago.

The women's expressions appeared serious, thought Angela. Both women had their arms folded across their chest. Angela bit at the side of her lip and stared ahead at the peeled black paintwork of the garage door. The dull grey metal beneath exposed. Fuck. She couldn't stall leaving the car much longer.

Lisa's daughter Becky waved enthusiastically. Her dark blonde ringlets bounced as she nested on her bright pink bike. Ribbons at the end of each handlebar fluttered like Angela's nerves. She managed a perfunctory wave. Rigid smile.

Why can't I just casually get out of the car outside my house, on my drive? I'm being pathetic!

She took a deep breath, inflated her lungs, and breathed out, closing her eyes for a second. Things were different now. She unpeeled her fingers from the steering wheel and stretched them. It helped a little. She nudged Catherine gently from her golden ambience.

'Come on lazy bones, you've slept pretty much all the way home.'

Catherine stretched her arms, touching the roof of the small green Mini. She turned towards her mum.

'Hey, Mum, I saw something a bit strange at the…' Her words trailed off as she followed Angela's gaze towards the women stood on the pavement.

'What up? You okay, Mum?'

She nodded. 'Of course, why shouldn't I be?' Another lie. 'We need to move the surfboards from the roof.'

Angela opened the car door and avoided eye contact with the women. She helped Joel out and watched as he clip-clapped along the path in loose flip-flops, opened the door with the key she'd given him and disappeared into the house.

With Catherine, Angela moved the short turquoise board from the top of the car. She stood elevated on the car door frame with her back towards the woman. Catherine stood on the other side, using the small wall for leverage as she untied the thick straps slung across the board.

'Hi, Ang.'

Angela turned towards the ladies.

'Hi!' responded Angela. She heard the tension, the higher pitch of her voice.

The other one, tall and athletic, loomed over Lisa. Her jaw fixed tight, and her sharp auburn bob added to her hard appearance. *Unfriendly*, thought Angela.

'We've just come back from Porthcawl.' Angela scrunched her features, feeling embarrassed by her unnecessary explanation. She had no reason to explain herself.

'Lovely.'

An awkward silence fell on the moment. Angela returned her focus to removing the surfboard.

Lisa stepped forward. 'How silly of me! Angela. This is Veronica. Veronica … Angela.'

Angela turned to offer a courteous hello, only to be met with a sharp nod of acknowledgement from Veronica. That she appeared so immaculate, so confident, unnerved Angela more. She was everything Angela imagined herself not to be.

Her jaw tightened as she tried to control the ball of anger that spun in a fast fury deep in the pit of her stomach.

Why should a woman I don't know make me feel this way?

With her daughter, she lifted the board up and away from the car, feeling her pulse gather pace. She told herself to stay calm, not to react. Not to embarrass her daughter with an outburst of defensive, angry words.

She carelessly dropped the end of the board. Her cheeks flushed with a mixture of restrained frustration and embarrassment. She sensed the women watching.

Why don't they fuck off inside? Please.

She counted like she'd taught her daughter to in stressful situations. She forced a smile towards her daughter. 'It's okay. No damage.'

'Oh, Angela, before I forget. I posted an invite through your letterbox earlier. I'm having a party this weekend. It's short notice, I know.'

'That's nice.' Angela spoke without turning to face the women this time.

'Be a chance for you to meet a few others on the street.'

No bloody chance of that.

'Thank you for the invite.'

She hadn't had an invite to a party for years. The idea of being surrounded by unfamiliar people made her nerves twitch. Especially if Veronica was the kind of person who might be there. It wasn't her idea of fun, not at all.

Lisa turned and spoke to Veronica in inaudible, hushed tones. Angela saw the unfriendly Veronica shake her head with features that creased with dislike, maybe even mistrust.

'Anyway, Won't stop you with my chitter chatter. You must be shattered. Hope we see you Saturday ...'

With this, the ladies left the pavement and disappeared into Lisa's house. Angela breathed out, relieved that they had gone.

Although no stranger to neighbours who looked down on her,

something about Veronica felt oddly familiar.

Had she seen her somewhere before?

Only then did it strike her like a lightsabre in the dark.

The night in her son's bedroom.

One woman stood outside on the kerbside had turned, peered upwards with a scolding stare. She was sure that the woman was Veronica. Yet. Something was different. Out of place. Had she been wearing a wig too?

Was this the reason for the woman's iciness toward her?

Did I witness something I shouldn't have?

'Right, Mum, all done. We can move the boards into the outside toilet now?'

Catherine's voice tugged Angela away from her silent thoughts.

She watched as her daughter carried one board to the outside toilet space. The way the sun lit strands of her brown chestnut hair into bright copper. But she'd seen other things, too. On the beach. As her daughter's towel slipped away from her thighs as she peeled her wetsuit off. She knew her daughter had tried to hide them from her.

And whilst Catherine had left their side and surfed, Joel had confessed that it was he who had given their new phone number to their dad. Catherine had felt the need to protect her brother. But from whom? Angela recognised that her own anger, a result of her own emotional turmoil, had also affected her children.

Sadness tore at her insides. Here was she worrying about the strange behaviour of unfriendly neighbours when she should be trying to help and understand her own daughter's worrisome behaviour. Angela knew her mind was flipping from one bad scenario to another like something from a horror movie. And she desperately wanted to make it all better for her fragile family. She took another deep breath.

'Catherine, before you head off upstairs to paint, I'll stick the kettle on and make us a nice cuppa, alright?'

Catherine stopped and stared towards Angela, her eyes searching out her mother's intentions.

'That doesn't sound good, Mother. You only call me Catherine when you're mad or need—you know—*a talk* with me.'

Angela was stunned by how well her daughter had become attuned to the tone of her voice and her nature.

'I need to get Daisy Duke out of her cage and clean it.'

'Catherine, I saw them. The marks on your thighs.'

Catherine pulled a face and shrugged. Her eyes flooded with a deeper resentment.

'What you talking about? They're from the surfboard?'

'But Catherine I've…'

'Jeez, Mum, Do I look like I need your help? Anyway.' Catherine glanced at the watch on her wrist. 'Isn't it about now you pour yourself a drink?'

Angela was taken aback. The muscles in her shoulders tensed. Rarely, despite everything, did her daughter speak or respond to her in this way. She felt hurt and a strange sense of regret which pressed down on her chest.

'Catherine. Come inside now. I don't want to do this outside.' She hissed out the words through her teeth, pitching them low.

'Do what? As if anyone on this street bloody cares about us.'

Angela stopped and glanced down at the stony grey ground for a second, then she inhaled, sucking in the extra energy her body needed. She exhaled.

'And what do you think I care about, then?'

Angela waited for a response, but none came as her daughter walked around her and into the outhouse, the surfboard a screen that divided them.

'Pretending we are normal to others when we obviously are so not.'

As her legs threatened to buckle below her, Angela strode into the house- not quite wanting to absorb her daughter's words.

'Well. I need to wash your bedding, and Joel's, before dinner.'

'Tsk. Always hiding!'

She saw her daughter's head shake in her peripheral view. It took everything, every scrap of herself not to spout the familiar anger which moved like a riptide below her skin. In that moment she saw it. Felt it even. The same defensive behaviour she herself had used many times to hide her own mistrust of others.

It pained Angela that her own daughter might not trust her. Believe she could help, or be there if she fell. Like water seeping up from below, she wondered, had her daughter become so fiercely independent to hide the mistrust she felt towards others? Was the cutting a way to release some of her pent-up emotions? Angela believed it to be so and knew she had to do something.

She filled the kettle and stared down at the water as it overflowed, spilled, and splattered into the cold metal of the sink below.

A minute later, Cath stomped into the house.

'Catherine. I'm making a cuppa. Can't we at least try to…'

'Nah, I'm going to my room.'

'Fine.' Angela heard her own voice raw and unkind. She took a deep breath and breathed out: six slow ones. She clicked the kettle on and walked into the lounge.

'Please Catherine. Don't disappear upstairs like this. Not now.' The words caught in her throat, and she coughed to clear them.

Catherine stopped on the staircase and looked ahead as she spoke. 'There's nothing to talk about!'

'We both know that's not exactly the truth, Cath. For a start, you have a mother who is absolutely bonkers!'

Angela watched in hope as restrained tears tripped over themselves onto her daughter's burnt cherry cheeks.

In that moment, she could feel the pull of motherhood in a place that had become layers of sediment; hardened and compacted by harsher realities. She could feel it crumbling along with the emotions of her family. Hard rock had locked out any light until now. Angela watched as her daughter stood motionless for a few seconds, except for the small judders of her chest, then continued upstairs.

'Where you going, love?'

'To wipe the snot out of my cleavage!'

'Oh, fair enough.' Angela felt the corners of her lips blossom just a little. It felt like a small olive branch, and she would accept it knowing it might be all she had right now to show her daughter that she could be trusted. Trusted to veer her daughter away from a future that would cause her harm and unhappiness. She would have to find a way to do it.

Angela went into the kitchen to finish the tea. She also took a small shot glass from the cupboard above her head, filled it with vodka, and knocked it back in one. It helped take the edge off. There was only so much a mother could take in one day and still be there to support her broken family. It's not something she did often, just now and again to keep her sane. She knew Catherine always worried the drinking might become a bigger problem. Angela didn't think so.

The phone rang as she quickly swilled out the glass and place it back in the cupboard. She wondered who it might be? Her temples pulsated with a heated fear. Was it him again?

Her hand shook as she reached out for the phone.

'Hello?'

'Hello Angela, it's me. Lisa.'

Angela sighed with relief.

'Ummm. I wondered if Gethin had,'—Lisa hesitated—'apologised to you yet.' Another pause, 'For what happened. He's invited to the party too and well. I didn't want you to feel any more awkward than you need to.'

There was an uncomfortable silence. Angela sensed she was pushing for information. Perhaps that woman Veronica had put her up to it?

'He's very busy you know, an author I heard?'

'Yes, he's been round,' Angela said, dead pan in the hope her tone would say enough.

'Oh. Right. I see. That's good.'

Another silence.

'There was something else. Hope you don't think I'm being a nosey neighbour. I thought you might want to know. Some man knocked your door earlier. About two o'clockish, I'd popped back from the salon. Strange. When he saw me get out of the car, he left sharpish.'

Angela's hand tightened round the phone, turning the skin around her knuckles white. Her mouth went dry.

'A man. What man?' She heard the fear in her own words.

'Well. I don't know. Shortish brown hair, average height, I guess. Oh. He wore these cowboy boots. I remember them because they had a distinctive sound as he walked.'

Angela reached out and held the windowsill to steady herself.

'Angela, you still there, you okay?'

'Fine. Thanks for letting me know. Turrah.'

She didn't wait for a reply and set the phone down with a click.

He bloody knows where we live.

She tried to control the fear that lurched from every limb. She heard Catherine's footsteps on the stair way. Angela took a deep breath, turned, and smiled at her daughter.

Who was on the phone?'

'Lisa. She forgot to mention she's invited Gethin to the party. She thought I might want to know, given what happened. Apparently, he's an author. Can't see it myself.' She watched as her daughter opened her mouth to say something, then shut it again.

'You okay?'

Cath looked down before looking back up. 'I'm going out for a couple of hours.' In the crook of her neck nestled Daisy Duke, partly hidden by her long hair. Angela chose not to object. That rat gave her daughter more comfort than anyone else.

'Okay love. Back for dinner?'

Catherine nodded. A few seconds later, Angela heard the door close as her daughter left the house. She bit at the skin around her fingernails. She wouldn't rest until Catherine returned home.

7

Gethin

Gethin sat opposite Deborah in the café. A partition made up of small cubic shelves reached towards the ceiling, separating a small, shaded area from the rest of the bustling café. Plants and beach paraphernalia filled the shelves and gave them privacy as they sat opposite one another at the small round table.

Spring sunshine, in intervals, seeped through the large glass front of the café. He could just see the shoreline from where they sat. Dappled with colour by surfers and sunlight. Her suggestion to meet at a beach cafe had surprised him.

'I get the feeling it wasn't an easy decision for you, meeting me like this?'

Her eyes flashed up at him from below long dark lashes, away from the serviette she'd continued to fold and unfold. The only clue she was nervous. She turned her attention towards the window. Seagulls squawked and pecked at scraps; little morsels left on a table outside.

'I'm glad you did though,' he added, keen to keep her attention, wanting her to continue. Wondering if her sudden silence indicated she'd had a change of heart.

'As I was saying, I ran away from Radcliffe a few months before my fifteenth birthday, around May 1978. That would be... what nearly four years ago now, right?'

Gethin nodded.

'The place shut down by the end of that year.' She lifted the loose strap of her floral dress back up onto her shoulder.

Gethin continued to listen as she spoke of the dangers and struggles when living on the streets of Cardiff. How summer had passed into autumn, and the first chilly winds of winter rolled in without money. She'd begged and slept in shop doorways. Her life took on another devastating reality as the cold bit at her hungry body and starving mind.

He took his tin of tobacco from the inside of his pocket. There were several rolled cigarettes he'd made earlier. She shook her head when he offered her the tin. She didn't look like a smoker. Gethin considered lighting up himself. But closed the tin, deciding against it.

'I almost died. Thought it was just a bad cold inall, turned out it was pneumonia. If it hadn't been for Jean, I would probably be dead.' She huffed with sarcasm.

'Jean the fairy godmother.'

Gethin raised an eyebrow.

'She'd approached me a few times on the streets saying she wanted to help. I guess I must have looked a mess. I hadn't realised how unwell I'd become. You don't. All I could think at the time is that I wasn't going back there.'

'Radcliffe?'

She nodded.

'The weaker I became; the more attractive Jean's offer sounded. She made it so easy. Still remember those first few weeks. The safe house she put me in. It felt like heaven. Hot food, showers, and a warm bed. She even found me a doctor.'

As her words spilled into the space between them, Deborah reached for her denim jacket that hung on the back of her chair. She spread it across her lap.

'It was too late by the time I realized. My medication had included a concoction of unknown drugs. One month was all it took to be trapped and addicted.' She paused, her voice almost becoming a whisper. 'And a prostitute.' She lifted her cup and sipped the lukewarm coffee.

'Deborah. Who is this Jean?'

Deborah laughed. 'No one knows. We're not sure if Jean is even her real name.'

'We?' responded Gethin.

Deborah frowned, deep furrows of suspicion. She said nothing for a moment, then spoke.

'Yes, there's a few of us from Radcliffe that ended up under her poisonous wings.'

'Do you have names?'

The steely look returned as she shook her head. 'They are my friends. Why would I do that? I'm telling you this because someone has to stop this woman from ruining other young innocent girls' lives.'

Gethin flicked open his notepad. 'Do you mind? Helps me to remember everything,'

She shrugged. A lukewarm permission.

'Don't mention my name. Nothing must lead back to me. Do you get it?' She said this with such ferocity Gethin looked around at others sat in the café.

He lowered his voice. 'Of course. I give you my word.'

Do you think she's working with someone else?'

As he reached into his leather satchel for his pen, he caught a flash of aquamarine from outside the window—a surfboard.

Stood outside the window, to his disbelief, stood the neighbour's daughter Catherine peering in towards him. She smiled and waved. He looked away and didn't respond.

'Shit.'

Deborah frowned and followed his line of view. She coughed.

'Anything I should be worried about?'

'No.' He shook his head for effect. 'Don't know who she is.' He continued. 'So, this Jean. Do you think she's working with someone else? Someone who worked at Radcliffe?'

'I don't think so. It's hard to say. The strange thing is that she changes her appearance every so often, you know.'

'What do you mean?' asked Gethin.

'She wears wigs inall. You know. One day she's blonde, the next day a redhead.'

Gethin stopped scribbling and looked up at Deborah. 'Wigs?'

'Yeheh. And she's got a temper too. It simmers white hot under her skin. Not a shouting type of temper. You got me?'

'I think so.' Gethin continued to scribble down what she said.

Deborah drifted off in thought for a moment. 'Come to think of it I have heard her on the phone a few times. This voice she does, like she's trying to please or impress the person she's talking to.'

Gethin nodded. 'Maybe she's working *for* someone else, not *with*?'

Deborah shrugged. 'Maybe. One of the other girls says she thinks she might have something to do with a place called Makos. I think it might be a club.'

'Good, that's good Deborah.' He scribbled the word Makos, underscored it then tapped his pen on the pad. Gethin wanted to ask her about Penny. But, he'd waited. Listened to Deborah. Had let her do the talking.

'Deborah, what about the name Penny? Anyone at Radcliffe with that name?'

She scrunched her perfect little nose up and shook her head. 'No. I don't think so.'

'Okay. One more thing and that's it. I have something I'd like you to look at?'

She looked at her watch, her eyes flickered, as strangers moved around the café. 'It'll have to be quick. I've been too long already.'

Gethin took the newspaper article out of his satchel and placed it on the table in front of Deborah.

'Do you recognise anyone in this photo?'

She leaned over the table to take a closer look.

'Of course.' She pointed to Mr Thomas, the superintendent who managed Radcliffe and Mrs Solomon.

Gethin nodded. Is there anything you can tell me about Mr Thomas?

'Nope.' She sniffed.

'Have another look.' He tapped the paper with his finger. 'It might help you remember.'

She sighed and looked down at the photo again.

'I know her. She was always kind to me.'

Her finger tapped on the face of the young woman with wavy long hair who, unlike many others in the photo wasn't smiling.

'She was one of the carers. Foreign lady. Had a weird accent. Whenever she was on duty, she had these little sweets called sherbet pips. God, I loved those things.'

Gethin stopped writing and stared at Deborah in surprise. He leaned in to take a closer look at the woman she'd pointed to.

'And she always smelled nice. Funny what you remember. In the evenings she always came round the rooms checking in on us. Sometimes she would stay and sit on the edge of the bed reading us stories. She stayed with you longer if you asked.'

Gethin listened with interest. He thought back to the phone call he received back in London. Could it be here?

'Can you remember her name?'

'No. But everyone called her Nonnie, a nickname. She was different because she seemed to understand we were all lost in a world that had lost much of its meaning for us. She just had that way of making you feel everything was going to be okay. Some of those other staff. Like I said before. They had no right working with children.'

'Deborah, do you have any idea where Nonnie might be now?'

'No, I don't. I wanted to forget everything about the place.'

Gethin grimaced. 'Shame. Sounds like she really cared about you all?'

'Didn't stop her from leaving though ... did it? Afterwards, others left too.'

'Do you know why she left?'

'No. We were never told either. Although some younger kids told me they'd heard her arguing with other staff at Radcliffe. Something to do with the behaviour of some of the children. Then she left.'

Gethin sighed and nodded.

'The thing is I had a pretty face, so I kept being taken into foster care because of it. Like a trophy for desperate adults. Each time I returned from another failed placement with foster carers there were fewer familiar faces there. The older female staff who had been there for years were retiring inall.'

'Did they replace the staff that left?'

'Hell yeah, mostly men though. Like I said, they were tougher, waved their fists around a bit more. I guess they were employing more men to deal with the tougher kids.'

Gethin could see the ripples of emotions like a slow rising tide threatening something more potent. He knew he wanted to ask more questions about others in the photo. For now, he would have to wait. He didn't want to lose her trust. There was something in her mood.

Something had changed. He had the sense she knew more. He couldn't be sure.

'I really do need to go now.'

He put the pen down, folded the newspaper article and put it back into his satchel. Out of sight. He saw her relax a little.

Before putting her denim jacket on, she reached over and took his notebook and pen. He was about to object until he saw her scribble down a number.

'Here's a number to contact me on. Only ever between twelve and two o'clock weekdays.'

Gethin nodded as she slipped her track-marked arms into her jacket. She saw Gethin look.

'I don't do that anymore. I wouldn't be here sat talking with you if I did.'

'You also have my number. Use it if ever you need my help. Anything at all.'

She nodded and glanced over his head towards the door before rising from her chair. With a quick goodbye she left the café. She moved along the pathway, through the crowd and out of sight.

He lit a rollie and flicked ash from it into the ashtray—a blue ceramic dolphin with a concave belly. He pondered the realities of her life. She had flitted from one foster family to the next. She'd talked of some foster carers who blatantly pronounced the only reason they fostered was to build a nest egg for old age, having little or no real concern for her or other children they took into their care.

One foster carer she spoke of knew that Deborah was sneaking out of her window frequently at night and chose to ignore it, easier that way, less responsibility. Deborah had said she quite liked it to begin with until she realized they must care so little about her. Deborah returned to the care system not long after. She'd smashed the family's house to pieces; venting her hatred and resentment towards a world that offered little warmth, care, or love.

Gethin flicked through the pages of his notebook. Scanned what he'd written.

- Harsher punishments given out particularly by the growing male staff in the home. whipping with leather belts. Sometimes punching.
- Foreign member of staff left Radcliffe house under suspicious circumstances, 1977/8 very fond of the children/them of her. Went by the nickname Nonnie.
- Several young girls from home now prostitutes, who is Jean?
- Makos. A bar or club?

He sat back into his chair for a while and wondered if children caught in a cyclic habit of rejection, often reinforced any negative feelings they had about themselves. Perhaps this, like Deborah's life set them on a path of prostitution, crime, and drug abuse. It was no surprise to Gethin that so many youngsters that left the care system were failing in the wider community and falling into wrong hands.

He could feel the dull ache at his temples, something told him Deborah had chosen her words carefully. She knew more. He scrunched his eyes together tight and opened them again. He put his notepad, the newspaper article and tobacco tin safe in his satchel and left the café determined to find out more about the place called Makos.

8

Gethin

Gethin sat in Dina's back garden and curled his toes into the damp bristly grass. He enjoyed the sensation of early morning dew that cooled the soles of his feet. He'd completed a session of Aikido exercises in peace outdoors, a rare opportunity that had lifted his senses and placed him in a better mood.

Now, he could consider the resurgence of an old behaviour—with the calmness his body had forgone a couple of hours earlier. A behaviour that at one time had required medication and flipped him upside down into a welcome world of nod where nothing existed, not even himself.

He'd awoken again to a neat pile of folded clothes. Always with a photo of her searched out in his sleep and placed on top. He never remembered doing it.

Returning to Wales, a place where they'd shared so many glorious memories, had re-awakened the very behaviour that had threatened his sanity. He knew he should contact his therapist in London. The idea gnawed at him. Last time he'd had a session, he'd exploded out of the featureless therapy room. Sworn and shouted. As if, he was in some kind of drama: lights on. Cameras. Ready set. Go. The outburst had made him feel assertive. More in control. His therapist had cared to differ and labelled his symptoms. That had been the end of that uncomfortable relationship.

Gethin didn't like labels. *Dissociation*, the therapist had told him, scoring out each syllable with an exactitude that had backfired. Gethin had baulked at the label. He *was* stronger than all that bullshit. He'd thought that back then. Now he wasn't so sure. He had ignored the blank spaces of memory. Didn't we all have them? Gethin called them his safe spaces. The therapist hadn't agreed.

From up the street he heard the click of heels on stone, a car safety lock. He rose from the sun chair and moved a little closer to the slatted wooden fence. He peered through towards the brow of Lewis Drive. The glare of early morning shine obliterated his view. He could just make out the shape of a woman. He squinted to try and catch more detail.

A tall woman. Bobbed auburn hair. Athletic build. Her nose turned up a little. Her appearance polished and immaculate. Too perfect, thought Gethin as she stood near her white Mercedes. She peered down Lewis Drive. Did she sense him watching? He moved back a little feeling suddenly conscious of how he might appear—a peeping Tom.

She opened her handbag and took out a small brown bottle. He watched as she unscrewed the top and glanced about her before lifting the bottle to her mouth. Seconds later, with its top returned, she chucked the bottle back into her handbag, opened her car door and slid into it snake like. The car swung away from her drive, turned right, and sped off breaking the quietness with the purr of an engine.

Gethin hunched back to the sun chair. He closed his eyes, lifted his head upwards towards the passing sunlight. Blue and orange blotches floated across his eyelids, then disappeared. He thought about his meeting with Deborah yesterday. He'd ventured into the docks and Tiger Bay, even Porthcawl. Surely, he could do the city too. Did he have a choice? He tried to imagine Hazel encouraging him, telling him he must go to Makos. Find out if there was a link to Radcliffe and Penny H.

As the warm, spring air licked his skin, like the flick of a coin his thoughts spun to how such a morning would have been a spectacular view from the roof of his Highgate flat; he missed that subtle vibrating and shimmering city horizon on mornings just like this. He missed Hazel. And what they had shared.

He stood and stretched his arms above his head. He told himself he could do this. Hazel would be proud of him. That's all he needed to tell himself.

A sudden downpour thrashed the stone pavement as Gethin jogged straight into the Wimpy bar. The morning sunshine had dissipated into a rainstorm that wouldn't have looked out of place in a Noah's ark movie: relentless and foreboding. People gasped as they sat in the restaurant watching passers-by run for cover.

He shook his damp jacket off his shoulders and sat on the red plastic seating listening to the excited chatter and noises from the coffee machines filling the stifled air. Within a few minutes a young female waitress approached his table smiling holding a small white pad and pen. He looked at his watch, it was half eleven, a little early for lunch but he was hungry. He picked up the greasy menu and ordered some food and a coffee.

Ten minutes later he sat eating his guilty pleasure, a burger with relish and chips.

A dull ache descended again. He rubbed across his forehead wondering if the change in weather had caused it. He looked around the Wimpy bar, watching as condensation gathered into miniscule strands of water running down the inside of the windows distorting the world outside. The bodies and facial features of passers-by looking stretched and contorted into something inhuman.

He shifted in his chair and pulled his notepad out to reread his notes. Yet, his mind curled back in an almost perfect sphere to the morning he'd stood in Angela's doorway. He cursed Dina's neighbour, how she penetrated his thoughts without warning. Just like that, as he sat focusing on something else, something important, she would appear, no matter how hard he tried to expel her, she refused. It was irritating. It was messing with his logic.

She hates you Gethin. She won't ever forgive you Gethin.

Damn it, he flipped open the notepad and began reading his notes. He drew his attention towards the notes he's made earlier.

Maybe you should go next door and apologise properly?

'FUCK THIS!'

The gasps and shocked silent stares from other customers sat in the Wimpy bar clarified to Gethin that he hadn't imagined it. The words had jumped out of his mouth without warning. His shoulders felt tight as he cursed, to himself this time.

Tuts and whispers of disapproval filled the air until normal chitter-chatter resumed. Gethin pulled his white t-shirt away from his chest. It felt sticky against his skin. The heat gripped at his usual alert senses.

He breathed out and looked towards the young waitress who had served him earlier and waved for her attention. She approached him without a smile this time.

He paid up, tipped the young lady generously and hot-footed right out of there into the street where wet surfaces blinded you as the sun pushed its way through the gloom, only to disappear again. His Ray

Bans dropped away from his forehead onto his nose as he turned right, accelerating towards St Mary's Street hoping his next interaction would prove to be more successful.

He turned off Queen Street into St David's shopping centre, making his way towards the Hayes. From here he could cut through the large department store taking him directly onto St Mary's Street.

Once outside again, he walked down St Mary's Street, away from Cardiff Castle, which loomed behind him. He passed The Louis, a restaurant his grandfather had taken him to as a child. Some of the old ladies who waitressed there had entertained him in his youth, with their contrived rudeness. They were characters straight out of a Roald Dahl book. He crossed the road and scanned the large old doorways and facades of buildings several stories high still with the old lead window frames. At one time trams would have transported people up and down the street. He wondered if the street had been as noisy back then as it was now.

As he passed another portcullis, something made him stop and backtrack. A small brass plaque glistened on the wall, the words difficult to read. He moved closer, read it, and smiled.

He would have missed this small, mounted sign had he not known the place existed. It had the air of a place that attracted a certain type of clientele—the wealthy and affluent.

Makos Wine and Champagne Bar.

Gethin stood in front of the door with its large brass knob set in the middle. He pressed the small brass button below the brass plaque and waited. He glanced upwards and noticed the small camera in the corner of the doorway.

After a minute he pressed it again. He felt the satchel strap on his shoulder, the dampness of his trousers against his thighs. He shuffled a little, not too much.

A drip of water landed on Gethin's crown as he stood and waited.

He pushed the door in response to the familiar buzzing that signalled he could enter. The warm air inside hit his body as he stepped inside and lifted his sunglasses away from his eyes.

Two metres away from the door a steep staircase carpeted in orange and burgundy swirls rose in front of him. The walls were plain white with large portraits of members of the royal family. Nice touch, thought Gethin, wryly.

Gethin could hear and see little of the promised bar, Makos. His pace slowed at the foot of the staircase. A door opened, then closed, above him. A suited man, with a slightly stooped gait, appeared at the top of the stairs and stood there, his dark eyes fixed on Gethin. Gethin thought he saw the man sneer—or was it just a trick of the light? The man brought a hand twisted and warped by age to his mouth as he coughed and sniffed. Gethin noticed his untucked shirt with surprise. He stood back against the flocked wallpaper waiting for the man to descend and prepared himself for any altercation that might occur with the stranger. He had a feeling that something wasn't right.

As the man's foot hit the last step, he nodded curtly at Gethin. Gethin returned the curt gesture as he controlled his breathing and the pulsating rhythm at his temples. The trick was always to appear calm even when you weren't. He heard the door click shut behind him as he ascended the steep staircase.

At the top of the flight were several doors coming off a long narrow passageway. Ornate wall lights offered a subdued light to the claret wallpaper. As he walked down the wide passage the word *Irimi* flickered onto the screen of his mind. It meant entering. He had learnt this in Aikido. He felt his body adjust—ready.

Another smaller brass plaque on the wall, near carved wooden doors made him stop. He reached towards one of the door handles, then pulled his hand away. His attentions, focused in that moment on the blade thin gap between the doors. He breathed in and pulled his shoulders back. Then as if in slow motion he eased the door open as his ears heard the first murmurs of conversation.

As he stepped into the grand lounge, the murmurs fell away to silence. Faces turned towards him for a few seconds. He scanned with quick alert eyes sensing any formidable danger and continued to move across the lounge nodding with politeness to those who continued to stare. Others resumed their conversation in dulled tones. Privacy suffused the large space. The heady mixture of expensive perfume and aftershave hit his heightened senses as he approached the bar. It had a film of cold ice over it. Plush.

A few people sat at the bar. Not many. Two or three small groups sat in dark crimson velvet chairs around rosewood tables.

He ordered a whisky without ice from the young lady with a false smile behind the bar.

'Have you booked a table to eat, Sir?'

'No. Thank you.'

She nodded in return. 'I'll bring your drink to the table, Sir.'

He sat near the large windows overlooking St Mary's Street. Heavy velvet curtains pulled back framed the now silent world outside like a large and distant stage.

Gethin looked up as she approached the table with a whisky and put it down on a coaster. He's convinced he saw her scowl for a second.

'Thank you.'

He took a sip of the orange single malt, savouring the flavour. He could get more accustomed to being called "sir".

Struck by the sophisticated interior, his eyes wandered to the painted walls smooth as glass that glided upwards towards sculpted cornices and a ceiling fitted with elegant chandeliers. On the far right, gilded paintings hung on a wall surrounded by two other doors leading to smoking and private rooms. In front of the doors were two large billiard tables. He was waiting for a tap on the shoulder, he felt like the uninvited visitor, let in.

Unable to stay still, he strolled towards a wall that had caught his attention: a collage of black and white images put together. Frames of different sizes move around one another, showing a myriad of elegant women and handsome men, not all but most. He moved in closer scanning faces with his sharp eyes.

The hairs on his arms rose to salute his instinctive nature. He almost heard them bristle in quiet applause. He was looking right at her. Her hair looked lighter in the photo. It was hard to tell with a monochrome photo. She was smiling towards the camera, a relaxed and confident smile, as a gentleman's arm flopped around the top of her shoulders. His face vaguely familiar. Her body partially facing away from the camera, she'd turned her head for the shot.

In the background were others faces faded out. One of them played on the landscape of Gethin's memory—Dylan Edwards. Like a camera coming into focus other faces became vaguely familiar. To the left of her was the billiards table and behind an open door surrounded by gilded picture frames.

Penny when were you here and why?

Behind Gethin, a shadow in a black suit appeared after sidewinding past several tables. His presence gained little attention in the room, and Gethin could only catch him from the corner of his eye, not wanting to give himself away. The man's thrust his head forward, exposing a strong and muscular neck, his eyes dark and unmoving stared down at Gethin's whisky. His hand darted out, and he deposited something onto the table, next to the whisky glass. Seconds later, he was gone ... back into the shadows.

Gethin strode towards the bar.

'That's an impressive collection of photos over there!'

The bar-lady appeared uninterested in Gethin's presence. Her unsmiling face glanced towards him and nodded with an air of boredom.

'Bet you meet a lot of interesting faces here?'

She shrugged.

'Ever hear of a woman called Penny?'

'Nope.'

'That's interesting as there's a photo of her up there.' He nodded towards the wall.

She looked up towards the wall and shrugged again, her expression ugly. 'Those! Think they've been up there since the bar first opened. How would I know?' She didn't take her eyes off him as she spoke.

Gethin tried again. 'What about a woman called Jean, older, likes to wear wigs?'

This time Gethin caught the uncomfortable flicker of recognition. Her smile never reached her eyes. Without a word she picked up a cloth, turned her back and began to wipe across the back of the bar.

For a moment he stood, puzzled by her behaviour.

'Excuse me.'

She turned. Her demeanour less congenial than before.

She lifted her chin. 'Would you like to order another whiskey, Sir?' She glanced towards his table. His drink. 'Oh. I see you haven't finished your first.'

'I asked if you knew a woman called Jean?' As he spoke, he caught a glimpse of two figures stood in the shadows through a narrow doorway behind the bar. One of them disappeared, the other tall with bobbed hair stood there watching and listening.

He took a chance. 'Isn't that Jean?' He nodded towards the shadowed doorway.

The bar woman continued to ignore Gethin.

He persisted, knowing a bar like this wouldn't want to attract any obvious troubles. 'I have a few questions to ask Jean, about the girls?'

Only then did she look up startled at Gethin. 'Sir. I've told you...'

The lady in the shadows stepped out into the bar area smiling an acid sweetness. The younger lady disappeared.

'Hello, I heard you asking after me. Is everything to your liking, Sir? Or can I offer something else?'

'Hello, Jean.' He stretched his hand over the bar to exchange a formal greeting.

She reciprocated with an uninterested loose grip. Her lips pulled up in a false smile.

'Do you know of a woman who went by the name of Penny? Sir name possibly begins with H. She was found dead last November. In a park in London.'

Other guests must have heard his words and glanced towards the bar.

Jean's face scrunched up in disgust at Gethin's question. The smile still fixed to her arching lips, but her eyes had already flung a reactive punch.

'No, never heard of her. And could I ask Sir that you keep your voice down? This is a reputable bar with reputable clients.'

'Clients?' retorted Gethin. He had no response.

'I see, then perhaps you can tell me more about how you help to remove women off the streets. Then put them in far worse situations?'

Gethin could see the cool rage below her skin, the efforts made to control what she said next. Her eyes narrowed, her pupils like poisonous chasms of hate.

Keeping her tone low as not to draw the attention of others she leaned over the bar towards Gethin.

'What is wrong with people like you who find it so hard to believe that some of us want to do good in this world. Putting ourselves at risk each time we go out onto the streets trying to save the next vulnerable young lady from harm.' Her eyes flickered around the bar as she spoke.

Gethin unmoved by her sanctimonious story continued. 'There's a picture of Penny over there in your bar. He cocked his head towards the wall. She has her arm around a man's waist who looks way older than she is. The man smiling behind her is a local councillor. He's also been seen at a local children's home. The same home I suspect Penny attended as a young girl. Someone has clearly taken the photo in this bar?'

'This is a reputable bar with a high class of clientele coming through its doors each day and evening. I understand what you are implying, and it is preposterous and outlandish. I've never met this Penny you talk of.'

She was smug despite the lies that bled off her tongue like blood from a puncture wound. Gethin sensed Jean was used to having the upper hand—he also sensed she already believed herself to be untouchable.

'It's time you left Gethin. London is home, isn't it?'

He smiled. 'Home is wherever I can ferret out wrongdoing. It's a great hobby of mine and I assure you I do it well.'

'Hobbies can be dangerous when it puts you in places you don't belong.' She smiled again with burgundy lips pushed tight together before she turned and disappeared back into the shadows again.

Gethin walked back to his table to collect his jacket and bag knowing that he'd ruffled her feathers a little. Yet, her haughty arrogance bothered him.

On the table next to his unfinished drink, he could see something. A photograph. His shoulders tensed as he realised it was a polaroid of him and Deborah at the beach café. His heart sank. He looked up and scanned the bar. He swore to himself. Everything looked ordinary—as before. He'd not been able to get a good look at the person who'd placed it there.

There were still a few smaller groups of men and women enjoying a lunchtime drink, all executive and business types. He scrutinized each one looking for a gesture or behaviour that might give them away.

He knew the photo of Penny smiling down at him had mesmerised him for a moment. It had felt as if she was trying to communicate with him. Drawing him closer to the world she had inhabited. Now he knew darker forces were creeping on the peripherals of his own reality. Had he put Deborah in danger?

He placed the photo into his trouser pocket with urgency, picked his satchel and jacket from the back of the chair and hastened towards the doors to leave.

The hard white bones of his ribcage seemed to shudder with each quickened heartbeat. He understood the sensation of danger, it had a way of penetrating all your senses. Gethin wouldn't let the external signs of fear give him away.

His eyes darted back and forth at the doors as he moved along the silent crimson hallway. The sound of his heartbeat drummed in tune with his heavy footfalls as he descended the steep staircase. As he pushed the heavy door open, the sounds of the street, high pitched and jarring heightened his senses. He heard a clap as the door shut behind him. With his jacket still folded over his one arm he jerked left and picked up pace.

He raced across St Mary's Street heading towards St Morgans arcade. An ever-changing landscape had disfigured his memory of the city. Would the telephone box still be on the Hayes? He'd used it several times as a teenager.

As he turned left towards St David's centre, the red telephone box like a beacon against the grey of the building behind. A young lad stood inside making a call. Picking up speed Gethin approached the box and waited. His feet shuffled back and forth as he watched the lad drop another coin into the money slot. Gethin stared at him, willing him to end his call. He turned his back on Gethin sensing his agitation.

Gethin pulled his wallet from his jacket pocket and retrieved a few silver coins with trembling hands. As he shoved his wallet back into his satchel, the door of the telephone box opened. The lad looked at Gethin and scowled before walking away. In seconds Gethin darted into the small space which smelled of piss and stale tobacco.

He picked the dull grey receiver up with its coiled lead. Pulled his notepad out of his satchel and flicked the pages until he found the number Deborah had scribbled down. He slid a ten pence coin into the slot then dialled. Trance like he watched as the circular dial clicked back on itself each time he plucked at a number.

For years, he'd avoided public telephones. They made him think of the day he wasn't there to save her. She never did make it to India to be with him.

A click shook him back into the present. He remembered. *Only between twelve and two o'clock* resonated in his ears. He looked at his watch five to two. He thrust his free hand against one of the small glass panes of the booth and pushed against it.

'Hello. Deborah?'

No response. Someone was there, he heard the raspy breathing. Was it a male? If ever there be a time that the sex of a sound might be determined by its weight and whistle. Then now was it. Malevolent and threatening. Then the click and the infinite dead tone.

Gethin slammed the receiver down. His stomach churned. His head felt light and dizzy. The recognizable feeling of being too late for someone. He was in India, humid and sticky. Flies buzzing around his head as he tried in vain to reach someone, anyone by phone. He had screamed out, a sound that had felt so inhuman to him. The receiver in his hand he'd thrashed against the wall till it had cracked and split like bone. His knuckles raw. Blood everywhere.

He took several deep breaths and used his diaphragm to breathe. *What the fuck just happened to me?* He leaned against the glass panes of the booth ignoring the crowing queue outside.

Were they my memories or images created by an overanxious mind?

His Aikido instructor had taught him to take deep breaths in. He exhaled with a slow purring sound 'aaaaaaahhhhhhhhh' ignoring the strange looks and moans from outside.

After a minute he calmed a little. He heard a sharp rasp on glass and turned. An older man stood outside the telephone box. He gestured with a swaying thumb and annoyed expression.

Gethin pocketed his notepad, pushed against the door relieved to feel cooler air on his skin.

He turned to the man who'd knocked the glass pane.

'Fuck you.'

And he didn't care what others thought this time as he walked away. More than ever, he understood there were things he didn't understand anymore. That therapist was onto something after all. Gethin knew there were memories he'd forced into shadow, never wishing to see or feel them.

For now, he also understood he needed to put all this aside. He wanted to know if Deborah was safe. Someone must have followed her to the café. Or had someone followed him? It was possible?

Should he ring Mrs Solomon again despite the promise he made to himself to not ring the old lady again? It was a promise he wasn't sure he'd be able to keep now.

He felt the photo in his pocket. What would they do to her? And who were 'they?' A cold wind hit his cheeks as he turned off the Hayes towards the old red multi story carpark. He had a deep sense that other darker things were at play. He felt it in every ounce of his flesh.

9

Angela

Angela walked into the putrid, mustard, and black kitchen and peered through the smeared window into her back garden. A few daffodils had fought against the lingering cold. Their yellowness small beacon of brightness in an otherwise dull and troubled day.

Her mind was on the party that evening. A party she had fretted about going to the last few days. She imagined herself slipping from one space to another in stilettos that made her feet ache to avoid people who made her headache. Veronica, one of them, and Gethin, and that strange man across the road who stared at her as if she was the devil's work. The goddam street was freaking her out and all the time she had to pretend to her children.

She scrutinized the unfortunate low fencing that failed miserably to offer privacy from her neighbour Gethin. Those strange things he did in the garden; she didn't want to be privy to them at all. She guessed it was some martial arts. Anyhow, it freaked her out more. And she caught him spying on Veronica the day before at some ridiculous hour in the morning, as she'd woken early from a bad dream.

Why is he here?

She didn't trust him. His prying eyes always watching and searching for something.

Maybe he knows Colin?

She turned away from the window and scolded herself for such stupid, paranoid thoughts.

How could that be possible?

She reached up onto her toes for a glass from the wall cabinet. Being so petite had its disadvantages. She pushed the glazed door upwards with the tips of her fingers and reached in to retrieve a glass. She almost slipped on the cheap linoleum flooring and swore under her breath this time.

There was still some vodka left and orange juice in the fridge.

Why did I allow Cath to persuade me to go?

She wanted things to be different here, but now she had reservations. What if Lisa and her friends turned out to be like other so-called friends? She blew warm air out between her pursed lips in a slow rhythm- breathed in again, expanding her lungs to stay calm.

So, Veronica lived in a house as big as the one she'd lived in once. It didn't impress her. Set back a little on the bridge of Lewis Drive, the house overlooked Dafydd Drive. It didn't surprise Angela one bit that Veronica would live in a position of great vantage. It gave her a full view of the street and everything that went on in it.

Angela poured vodka into the tumbler, topped it with orange juice, and gulped it like she was trying to commit suicide. She frowned at the ugliness of the chipped black gloss of the woodwork, the old cooker with the grill set above the stove and the stone-built larder, the doors also painted with black gloss like dripping oil. So much to change. But where would the money come from? She hadn't worked for years. He hadn't liked it.

Her mind couldn't help but wander to those tumultuous years. She knew she'd developed a fear of social situations which lurked beneath her avoidance of people. She had so few friends barely worth mentioning. And these so-called friends. Most of them abandoned her, as if her friendship had been of no value to them. She had done the unthinkable. Finally rejected her husband's behaviour and grandiose lifestyle to be a single mother. *Unthinkable.* She wondered if she was living in the nineteen-eighties or the eighteen-hundreds?

She had become a risk factor. A contagion which could spread and infect their perfect little lives. It had been a painful realisation for Angela. She leaned against the kitchen side, crossed her legs, and looked down into her glass.

Fuck them. I didn't need them anyway.

She knew one thing for sure. She was happier now her life was no longer dictated by him at least...and sorry that she had listened to those who had encouraged the sweeping of unacceptable behaviour by partners quietly under the carpet like a dark, dirty secret.

Angela knew she'd always felt too ashamed to tell them the full extent of his behaviour—including the prostitutes. The stained shirts and pants. It still sickened her every time she thought about it. She quivered as she swallowed the cold liquid down.

And now he might already know where we live?

Was it even safe to go to Lisa's party? To leave her children? She shook her head at the thought of it. Then she understood her mind was skipping from one unpleasant situation to another again. Had she noticed this behaviour before?

She breathed in, exhaled, and walked into the lounge. Catherine sat on the rug with Joel playing a board game much to his delight, as Catherine usually disliked board games with a vengeance. It impressed Angela.

'You going to the party then, Mum? I think you should!'

'Oh, do you now?' responded Angela tartly.

'Yes. I do. Why not, Mum. Give you a chance to get to know your neighbours.'

Angela wondered if her daughter, like most teenagers, liked the idea of having the house to herself for a few hours.

'Neighbours aren't all that love.'

Catherine looked up from the board for the first time and frowned at her mum.

'What?'

Catherine shook her head. 'Nothing.'

'Yes, there is. I can tell.' Angela leaned against the doorway puzzled.

'It's nothing, really.'

'Go on.'

'Well. When we were at the beach, I saw the neighbour Gethin sat with a young woman at the cafe.'

'Was he now.' Angela tried to smile.

'I don't think he recognised me.' She paused for a moment. 'mum, I think he was pretending not to recognise me?'

Angela scrunched her face in puzzlement. 'Really. Why would he do that?'

Catherine shrugged. 'I don't know.'

'The girl looked all nervous when she saw me wave at him.'

'Forget it, honey. Nothing for us to be concerned about.'

Angela continued upstairs, knowing her daughter's words had caused her more discomfort than admitted. She bit at the corner of her lip as she wondered why this man seemed to appear at the most unexpected moments. Was it just a coincidence, or was he watching them? A cold panic descended. It splintered the normality she so desperately wanted to create for herself and her children.

Was she right about him?

Her chest and neck became hot and clammy. Catherine and Joel had been so excited by the prospect of their mother finding friends, going to a party. They desperately wanted to belong to something—a community. How could she let them down? She would have to put on a brave face and go to the party. All she had to do was stay for an hour or so, then leave. Job accomplished.

She flopped onto the edge of her bed. Her busy mind had already convinced her the invite was a gesture of sympathy. She was the sad, lonely female that everyone feared.

Near her bed, *Vogue* magazines were now stacked high with a single pewter lamp resting on top. A small art déco-inspired chair had several items of clothing hanging from it. On the wall behind hung her collection of small designer paper bags put in clip frames. Their handles used to hang them from small nails. It was an impressive look and economical way of making the wall a feature in a bedroom that lacked furniture and much detail. Angela had stacked her books up against another wall. At least until she could afford a bookshelf. Her books had saved her sanity many times.

She opened the fitted wooden wardrobe and run her fingers across several garments. Her hands resting on an old blue silk suit. Although a little faded, it was still in good condition. She pulled it out and viewed it with an experienced eye. The one trouser leg had frayed at the hemline.

Despite her weight loss, when she put it on, she thought it had potential. And the fraying. Well, that was easy. She would raise both hemlines. It wouldn't take her long.

Before she closed the wardrobe door, her eyes stole a glance towards the pink card patterns that hung the far end in darkness. Angela had a flair for fashion design. Colin had never discovered she'd kept them.

She had a natural talent for pattern cutting. He'd objected to this… their children wearing the clothes she'd designed and made. He often chucked them in the bin, claiming they were freaking disgusting, a mess. Over his dead body would his children wear them. She closed her wardrobe door. You bastard. *One day, she thought.*

Five minutes later, she carried her glass of vodka to the bathroom, set it upon the windowsill, put the plug in, turned both the hot and cold taps on, poured a generous amount of bubble bath and swished the water to create bubbles.

She undressed and stepped into the bathtub; her reflection flickered in the smoky, tiled mirrors opposite as she submerged herself into a delightful blanket of bubbles. It felt good. Some peace and privacy at last.

However, the rare ambience was short lived. Angela opened her eyes and stared blankly at the peach-coloured wall opposite. She heard a loud burst of knocking on the front door.

She froze.

It came again. The short, quick burst of knuckles on glass. Had she missed his footsteps along the path? Or had he walked across the garden to conceal his approach? The fear in her chest caused small wave like ripples on the surface of her bath water. She gripped the edge of the bath. All her senses heightened and ready.

She jumped upright, causing waves of water to cascade over the edge of the bath and onto the laminate floor below. She stretched across to the radiator and grabbed a towel. Stood and stepped out of the bath. Bubbles slid down her body. She wrapped the towel around her wet limbs. Small pools of water collected at her feet as she swung the bathroom door open.

'Um, Mum,' shouted Catherine from the bottom of the stairs … 'There's a lady called Gladys here to see you!'

By the time Angela made it to the top of the stairs, a strange rotund woman stood halfway up her stairway. She stopped when she saw Angela and smiled brightly.

'Ha-ha, you so funny stood there with bubbles stuck to your head. I called at wrong time, eh?'

Angela didn't respond. Just stood there stony faced.

'I'm Gladys, half-Welsh, and half-nuts, so they tell me, pahh. I come to welcome you to Dafydd Drive.'

'Pardon?' Angela stood with her hands now on her hips, staring down the stranger on the stairs. 'Who the hell are you?'

'I'm Gladys,' she responded cheerfully, ignoring Angela's agitated tone.

Angela couldn't speak for a second. This time, deep ravines strayed across her forehead, threatening something more intensely forceful. This was the second time in just over a week someone just appearing in her own home had caught her off guard. Was this normal? Was it a council estate thing?

Catherine stood behind Gladys, covering her mouth with her hand to restrain the threatening chuckles.

What was it with people around here just walking into my house when they fucking fancy?

'Sranje. I done it again, haven't I?' She shook her head and peered down at her orange floral apron.

'Please.' She placed one hand over her chest. 'Forgive me. Lived on street far too long.'

'At the bottom near the park I am.' She gestured with a tilt of her head. 'Your son, he is little prince, he is.' She held her chest again. 'So polite to me. He's fitted right in with the others. He has.' Her eyes widened and danced with a cheerful friendliness that reminded Angela of her own grandmother.

Angela noticed her son smiling and nodding at Gladys.

'Mum. Gladys is Russian. Isn't that cool?'

She softened a little towards this short rotund woman who pushed strands of silvery wispy hair back into the large clothes peg at the back of her head. Joel liked her. Then she remembered her neighbour

Lisa mentioning a woman called Gladys the day she'd moved in. How she looked out for children at the park.

'How bout I making a nice cup of cha for us? Start again?' She continued to stand on the stairway looking up. Her cheeks flushed purple, pink. And her eyes twinkled like diamonds.

'I'm drinking vodka,' responded Angela.

'Good.' Gladys grinned wildly. 'A welcome gift for you. Very good vodka.' With this, she turned on her heel, pulled a bottle of vodka from the bag on her hip and waved it in the air as she descended the stairs.

Angela nodded. Dumbfounded. She felt like one of those senseless nodding toy dogs on a car dashboard. No words would come as she watched Gladys descend her stairs and disappear towards the kitchen. Until she realised Gladys wouldn't know where anything was.

She shouted after her 'The glasses are in the second cupboard on the righ—'

'I'll show her, Mum.'

Catherine followed Gladys into the kitchen, a grin reaching to her eyes. At least her children were enjoying the moment.

Five minutes later, Angela sat at her dining room table in her daughter's dressing gown and her wet hair pulled up off her face, with a towel wrapped around her head. She pulled a small strand of hair loose and twisted it between her slender fingers.

Gladys sat opposite her; the vodka already poured from the bottle into two tumblers. The measures were even bigger than Angela allowed herself. Angela stared at the glasses. Why had this strange woman turned up and offered her vodka? Was this normal? Should she drink it? Was it safe to drink it? She folded her arms and smiled, tight-lipped and suspicious.

Somewhere, part of her knew she should ask Gladys to leave. These sorts of intrusions weren't commonplace to Angela and her small family. It made her feel paranoid. What if Gladys was fishing? Isn't that what streets like this were about? People knowing other people's business. She would need to be careful.

'What's this?' Angela flicked her eyes towards the bottle.

'Ahhh yes, my vodka. I drank neat,' she slid a glass across the table towards Angela.

Angela grimaced. Gladys tittered.

She lifted her glass and gestured to Angela to do the same.

'Za tvajo zdarovje!'

Gladys knocked back the glass of vodka, then smashed the empty glass down onto the table with a satisfied expression.

Angela's children flinched at the sound of the glass hitting the table. For a moment they stilled, as if expecting something else more dangerous. Then, realising everything was okay, they returned to their game.

Gladys looked on at Angela nodding her head and widening her eyes; a beckoning for Angela to do likewise.

'Shit. Here goes.' Angela took a gulp of her vodka. She held her breath ready for the uninvited toe-curling and unpleasant sensation of straight vodka soar down the back of her throat. It didn't happen. She looked over at Gladys, who continued watching her smiling and nodding.

'Good Vodka, eh! Vodka from the Russian empire itself.'

It was true Angela had never tasted vodka like it. And so far, she still felt very much alive. No dramatic clutching of her throat or deathly gurgling, just a softness she had never experienced before. She bit the inside of her mouth. She liked it very much.

'Very nice.' Angela emptied the last few drops from the glass into her open mouth. She snatched a look towards the unfamiliar green labelled bottle with something akin to lust.

Her tongue moved around inside her mouth to taste the lingering, subtle citrus flavours. She glanced at Gladys. The mood had changed. She looked down at the table and back at Gladys. Could this strange situation be unsafe for her?

For a moment, both women studied each other. As if trying to see what lay beneath the surface. Then as the vodka affected their senses and the mood Angela giggled. Out of nervousness or relief that she hadn't been poisoned after all. The moment of uncertainty made both women giggle. Which soon became raucous laughter—the type of which was shared by strangers who have witnessed something funny but mildly uncomfortable.

'Gladys why are you here?' spluttered Angela.

Gladys stopped laughing and poured another shot of vodka into both glasses. 'To persuade you to comes to Lisa's party.' She handed the glass to Angela this time.

'Why? You don't know me.'

'I do now. We drinks vodka together.' She chinked her glass with Angela. Swallowed the clear liquid back.

Angela noticed the old woman confused her tenses. Was it a vodka or Russian thing?

'And it's nice for you to meet new friends. I'm not supposed to say something.' She leaned in towards Angela and lowered her voice. 'Don't worry about Veronica. She just being Veronica.'

Angela downed the vodka, stood up, and collected the two glasses off the table. She restrained her mouth, knowing she was on a knife-edge—wanting to say what she thought of the rude woman. She didn't. News travelled fast on Dafydd Drive. Gladys must have sensed her reticence.

'Why don't you meet me outside lates so you not haves to walk in the party by yourself?'

Angela thought about it for a minute, then nodded. Vodka, considerate gestures, and a strange need to know exactly what was going down had slowly diluted her previous anxiety. And Gladys was right. She needed to venture out a little, take a few risks.

An hour later, Angela scrutinized her reflection in the bedroom mirror. Gladys's unexpected intrusion on her afternoon had meant less time to get ready. Once she'd left, Angela rushed upstairs and stitched the hemline of her silk trousers with the precision of a professional. A tipsy one.

It had been a long time since she'd made any genuine effort regarding her appearance. For many years, it had been easier that way; she'd soon convinced herself it was one less thing to fret about anyway. Less trouble.

Have I overdone it … too much maybe, she pondered? Moving closer to the full-length mirror, she dabbed the corner of her lips with a white tissue removing a small smear of red lipstick.

She took the silk jacket from its hanger and with her small clutch bag, carried them over her arm downstairs.

Catherine looked up.

'Wow, Mum, you look great!'

'Do you think?' She responded. 'Doesn't look too much, then?'

Catherine shook her head. 'Not at all,' she said, folding the board game away.

'You've missed a piece on the carpet there,' said Angela, pointing towards a small metal object.

'Oh yes … The top hat. Jeez, Mum, how did you see that from there? Joel always chooses this token when we play.' Catherine stretched across the rug to pick it up.

'Rich Uncle Penny-bags' top hat,' said Angela with a grin.

Catherine frowned at her mum, confused. 'Umm, you drunk, Mum?'

'Probably, after Gladys's vodka.'

Catherine offered up a rare, bemused look towards her mother.

'I used to play this when I was a young girl. Your nana told me it was a woman who first designed this game, not a man!'

Catherine pulled a face at her mum and shrugged her shoulders.

'I'll tell you about it. If you're interested?'

Catherine shrugged. 'Nahh! You're okay, Mum, thanks.'

Angela smiled and changed the subject. With a fixed, sober expression, she gave Catherine a list of instructions for the evening. Catherine took on the bored, blank expression teenagers often have when they feel they already know what you're telling them.

'Err Mum, you're only next door … really, do we have to do this again?'

'Yes, we do … you never know who might decide to come snooping or knocking on the door when I'm out.' responded Angela as she turned at the bottom of the staircase.

Catherine stopped what she was doing and viewed her mother with interest.

'Yes, the penny's dropped now has it. Any sign of him turning up and you ring the number I've left on the dining table. It's Lisa's home number.'

'Okay, Mum, just go and try and have some fun. We'll be fine.'

Angela moved towards her daughter and planted a kiss on her forehead.

'Gladys will be here now in a minute. Make sure you bolt the door behind me, and I'll use the key for the back door to let myself in later.'

'Yup … will do.'

Joel flings his arms around her from behind.

'Cwtch.' She twisted round in his embrace and wrapped her arms around his shoulders. He'd never spent an evening without her, at least, not one he'd remember. Her chin wobbled a little.

'Go, Mum. Before you change your mind.'

She let go of Joel and walked to the hallway.

'Turrah then.' Uncertainty speared her again.

'Catherine, I don't feel good leaving you both like this.' She lowered her voice so Joel wouldn't hear. 'What if he turns up?'

'Mum. I'm not going to answer the door to a soul. I have Lisa's number and your next door. Next door, Mum!'

She couldn't bring herself to tell Catherine that her father had threatened to take her brother away from them. That he'd said it would be his mission. *If we're splitting, then the same goes for the children,* he'd said with a nefarious grin. She knew he could do such a thing. Until this evening, she'd forced it from her mind.

10

Gethin

Gethin paced back and forth across the dining room, rubbing across the back of his neck. He stopped several times and glanced at the phone, then picked up the ritualistic pacing again.

He'd considered contacting the police. However, this might alert them to his investigations. They might start asking him questions. Mark's words punched at his chest. Someone at Scotland Yard is hiding the truth about Penny. Who she is and where she comes from. He feared more sinister retaliations if they discovered his investigations, his questioning about Radcliffe. He needed to be cautious. To stay safe.

The Polaroid had been a warning to him, too. A warning to stay away—another threat. If he spoke to the police, it could also make it much worse for Deborah. He sighed and dropped into a dining chair wondering how he could play this. He rubbed his temples, feeling the onset of another headache.

For the next forty minutes, Gethin turned to his Aikido. It helped him to re-focus, stay calm, and get his ki more in order. The investigation had become more complicated. It was beginning to feel like he'd opened Pandora's box.

His headache subsided. He stood and bowed in his ritualistic manner. Then he showered, dressed, and ate a quick dinner of pasta and arrabiata sauce topped with some grated parmesan and pepper.

He pushed his empty plate across the table and lit up. The first inhale of the evening was always one he savoured. He thought about the photo at Makos. Perhaps if he discovered more about Penny, it would help him find Deborah before something bad happened to her. He swallowed and tried to push the horrible thought away.

He needed to strategize. Think. He hadn't only seen Penny in the photographs at Makos, but also the face of Dylan Edwards. Although he'd been out of focus and in the background, Gethin had recognised him immediately. Dylan's face had also shown up in the newspaper article about Radcliffe's Children's Home. It could be coincidental, but something told Gethin it wasn't.

Gethin grabbed Dina's BT directory, flicked it open, and searched through the thin pages of numbers. He had half an hour, maybe more, before the City Hall offices closed. It didn't take him long. He dialled the number and after two rings, someone picked up.

'Hello. I would like to be put through to Mr Dylan Edwards's secretary, please.'

He heard a tut, then the gruff Welsh voice of an older man.

'Is this a joke, son?'

Gethin frowned. 'No joke.'

'Young man, that won't be possible. He died over two years ago.'

Gethin sank into the chair. It was a blow to his hopes of Mr Edwards shedding some light on Penny and her associations with Radcliffe.

'Please forgive me. I wasn't aware.'

He couldn't understand why he hadn't heard about this. Then he calculated backwards and realised it would have been when he was in India.

'That's okay, son. He was a remarkable man and a significant loss to us all. Very sad indeed.'

'Yes. I knew him. He had a lot of insight into what his Welsh constituents needed. May I ask?' Gethin hesitated. 'What happened?'

A low grumbling cough echoed down the line. 'He took his own life. People are sometimes fighting demons we have no knowledge of.' He coughed again.

Gethin could hear the crackling sound of grief collapse down the line. He knew he was pushing it.

'His family must have been in complete shock.'

'Yes, His wife found him in the garage. Car fumes killed him. There was little she could do to...'

'I didn't hear any...'

'We tried to keep it out of the papers for as... Damn. Who am I speaking to?'

'I'm an old colleague of Dylan's. I helped with a few of his charity campaigns back in the seventies as a young man.'

'Not the blasted press, then. Bloody heathens they are.'

'No. Just an old friend that's all.'

'For the sake and respect of the family, we tried to keep the details of his death quiet.'

'Mmm. Yes, of course. I understand.'

Silence.

'Well, thank you for your time. Just one more thing. I remember Dylan as a local councillor. He gave a lot of his time to supporting and improving the quality of life and education for children li...'

'Yes. Dylan was a respected man. Damnation. The man was the most committed to children's' welfare than any...'

'Yes. I know. Did he do any charity work for Radcliffe Children's

Home?'

Gethin heard the familiar click, then the flat hum of a deadline. Had the old man merely mistaken the call as ending or purposely cut the call short?

Gethin placed the receiver gently on to the cradle. Like before, he'd drawn a blank. No one wanted to talk about Radcliffe Children's Home. Was it fear? Fear of what might happen if they did? His chest sank deeper as he exhaled.

With fingers that strummed on the tabletop, Gethin understood he still had much to learn about investigative journalism. His newly found public responsibility—searching for the truth meant shovelling a load of shit and dealing with dangerous situations. He'd always been aware that unscrupulous characters lurked everywhere; and would go to great extremes to protect their sordid fiefdom rather than be exposed to who or what they were.

Why had a respectable man like Dylan committed suicide? Many people had admired the way he worked. He had been at the top of his game. What had impelled him to take his own life? What murky waters had Mr Edwards groped around in? Or had someone planned his murder to appear like suicide?

Sunlight scattered along a thin horizon, the remains of a day holding out until the world disappeared into darkness. In that space between day and night, the stillness often helped Gethin to view things differently. To see things through an adjusted lens.

His mind drifted to the photo of Penny again. Something he'd seen but not acknowledged fully—the strange markings on her left shoulder. Had it been a trick of lighting or possibly a tattoo? He couldn't be sure.

Gethin reached over, pulled file 10.81 towards him, and opened it. His memory told him the autopsy report had recorded no tattoos on her shoulder. He'd read it enough times to be sure of it. Perhaps she'd had it removed? He pulled all the photos from the envelope and plucked out one taken at close range.

When Mark had given him the photos, the lack of proper, detailed documentation of the crime scene surprised him. He knew the procedure usually involved overall, mid-range, and close ups of the crime scene. This then captured all the environmental elements and their relationship to the scene itself. It was a vital part of the investigative process.

Mark informed him later that these were the only photos available, most of them taken with incorrect exposure and at mid-range.

Back in London, he'd tried contacting the coroner. He'd sounded flustered and refused to speak to Gethin insisting the case was closed and no further communication with anyone was required.

Luckily, one photo he possessed come straight out of the pathologist autopsy suite. That was the one that showed him the most detail of her neck and shoulders.

With his magnifying glass, he swept across the photo as he scrutinised every inch of her left shoulder where the marking or tattoo should be. He pulled the magnifying glass away, then back in closer towards the image, hoping form, line, and shape might morph into something previously hidden.

He froze. There it was, faint and almost indiscernible amongst the purple-black discolorations and marked skin. He grabbed at a scrap of paper.

His sketch was crude. The black granite pencil giving some form to the shapes he pieced together. Once he'd finished, he lifted the sketch and observed it with interest. Each curved line came together forming a bird in flight.

He pondered how a pathologist might have missed it. Then Gethin asked himself what if he'd omitted the presence of a tattoo from the pathology report on purpose. Perhaps at the request of or forced by another?

Gethin moved from his chair and stretched his back until it clicked. He heard music and laughter drift through the open window. It must be people turning up for Lisa's party. His shoulders dropped; earlier, he would have enjoyed a couple of hours socialising, but now it was the furthest thing from his mind.

He rubbed across his chin with its late afternoon stubble. He'd picked at threads, hoping he would undo the seams that hid the facts of how and why Penny had lain dead in that park last October? But instead, other frayed threads appeared that added to the complexity of the investigation. He wondered if what he was about to unravel might be greater than he himself could manage. Did he have what it took to be a muckraker? Hazel would tell him "yes". So, would he travel to the eye of the needle, the place that had once gone by the name of Radcliffe? A place shrouded by trees, shadows and secrets.

11

Angela

Angela stood in her small porch waiting for Gladys. She looked at her watch, only three minutes until half past. She fiddled with the small chain strap of her handbag as she listened to the beating of music coming from Lisa's house.

Others turned up and spewed out of cars and taxis onto the pavement, excited party revellers without a care in the world. She stepped back into the shadows as she heard the cheers and laughter echo along the drive as Lisa welcomed each new party guest inside.

At half past, Gladys came up the street. Her cheery voice woven into other sounds on the street before Angela saw her on the kerbside. Glady's transformation from something akin to Mary Poppins to Ann Margret looking for another wild night surprised Angela. She suspected Gladys would have a stash of vodka on her somewhere, too. Her hair and make-up had a sixties feel to it and the black dress she wore flattered her curvy body. Around her neck and shoulders draped a beautiful blue and gold brocade scarf.

'Didn't keep you waiting, did I?' Gladys kissed Angela on the cheek. The gesture took Angela by surprise.

'No. Not at all.' Angela's fingers tightened around the bottle of wine she held. Her eyes dropped to the hemline of her trousers, checking again if they were the same length.

'Was helping the solynishko (little sun) into his pyjamas. He struggles a bit with the stiff joints, painful for him. Extra pill tonight.' Gladys guffawed. 'Knock him out for night now. Sleep on sofa bed tonight I will. My love snores like a giant.'

Angela nodded, not knowing what to say in response.

'Come on, let's go drink more vodka.'

Angela felt Gladys's arm wrap around hers, linking them together. She was being ushered into the unknown as they took the corner that led down the path to Lisa's front door. The sun had begun its descent before the streetlights blinked on, a lull, as Gladys knocked loudly.

A few minutes later Angela stood in Lisa's kitchen alone, whilst Gladys went to look for their host. The smell of alcohol, perfume and tobacco filled her nostrils as music blared from the stereo in the lounge.

The air thickened with cigarette smoke and the white noise of cluttered spoken words made her heart beat a little faster. Her legs weakened under her heavy weight.

She placed the bottle of wine on the kitchen side next to bottles of champagne. Surprised by the quality and quantity, she let her fingers stroke the labels with interest.

Angela stood with her back against the kitchen worktop as she peered out towards the hallway, unable to move, even to find a glass and pour herself a drink.

Why has Gladys left me alone like this? Have I been foolish?

She lifted the flap of her handbag and pulled out her cigarettes with a hand that trembled as she lit up. She cursed under her breath and wondered if she could make it to the door and disappear back home.

People continued to flood into the house. Some wandered into the kitchen with more bottles. For a while Angela stood there and pretended to show interest in the décor, the expensive Denby crockery on the oak shelving and the crystal light fitting that strangely suited. It chimed subtlety by the continued opening and shutting of the front door. Angela guessed she might be the only one who heard it.

On the count of ten, she breathed out and wandered into the lounge. She needed to move, to stop seeing disregard and dislike on strangers' faces.

Groups of people danced one side of the open plan space. Beyond them, in the corner, was a table with speakers and a moving orb that created blobs of colour that traced across surfaces and bodies like moving insects.

Below the table, a smoke machine threw out a white opaque smoke. Partially concealed figures moved in and out of focus.

For a while she stood at the bottom of the stairs that, like her own home, partitioned the two large rooms. Someone had put an ashtray on the open staircase. She killed her cigarette in it, then searched the room for Gladys whose laughter she could hear tumbling above the music.

Something in the corner of her eye caught her attention. Someone stood in the darkness at the top of the stairs, staring down at her. Angela felt goosebumps on her skin despite the heat in the room. Who was it? And as this thought lingered, Veronica appeared from out of the darkness, viewing Angela with distaste marking her features.

To avoid making further eye contact, she turned away as Veronica's heels hit the wood of the stairs, slow and menacing.

Angela dropped her attention to her handbag and pretended to look for something. She stiffened as she felt Veronica brush past her.

What the hell was that about?

Someone tapped Angela's shoulder. Startled, she swung round. Gladys stood there smiling.

'There's you are. Wondered where you'd got to.'

Angela responded with a tepid smile.

Gladys held two glasses in her hand. She passed one of them to Angela. 'I've put orange juice in yours this time. How you like it.'

'Thankyou.' Angela gulped the drink down in one go and proceeded to cough and splutter.

Gladys' eyes widened, visibly surprised by her action.

'Jeez, Gladys. You trying to kill me or what?'

'You alright. My lovely?' Gladys rubbed Angela's arm in a show of comfort.

'I understand, I do silly thing leaving you in kitchen this way.'

The feel of Gladys' hand on her bare skin made Angela stiffen. It wasn't something Angela felt comfortable with, and she edged away.

'I'm still getting used to your love of vodka, Gladys.' It wasn't the whole truth. Angela was regretting being there. She looked at her watch.

Over the sound of Blondie belting out "The Tide is High" Gladys leaned in towards Angela.

'You did a good thing getting out tonight. Have you seen Lisa yet?' Gladys scanned the room on tip toes. 'She'll be pleased you come. Come on. I sees her.'

Lisa greeted Angela with a warmth that made Angela relax a little. She handed her the birthday card she'd kept in her bag. As they chatted Angela discovered Lisa owned her own beauty salon in the nearby town. She'd suggested Angela pop in some time for a free treatment. Angela didn't want charity. She smiled and said nothing. *I can do this.*

Lisa asked if they'd seen Gethin yet. They shook their heads. Lisa told them he hadn't declined the invitation and thought there was still plenty of time.

The ball of tension in her stomach wouldn't leave her. As someone passed with a silver tray filled with champagne, Angela took one thankful to have something that might further dull her anxiety.

Lisa also took a glass and held it suspended in the air. 'It's Cristal, the best. Welcome to Dafydd Drive!'

'Thank you.' Angela held the glass by its stem and watched the tiny bubbles loosen and float to the top. She clinked glasses with Lisa, closed her eyes as the fluid run down her throat like quicksilver.

Each time the tray came round, she took another glass of champagne. She worried less about Colin, about Veronica, and as time ticked on, there was no show by Gethin.

At some point later in the evening, she'd squinted through the smoke and alcohol to see Veronica speaking to Sophie; she didn't look happy. They exchanged words without the eye-contact expected from good friends. Circles of coloured moving light shimmied across their bodies, giving them a crooked unsteady appearance. Veronica shook her head, then walked off, her face set like cooled molten lava.

Sophie picked another glass of champagne from the tray that was being brought around and knock it back in one go, returned it to the tray then picked up another. Then she walked towards a group of men stood near the window. All smiles and happiness. As if the moments before hadn't existed. Hadn't taken place. Angela understood the process.

Darkness glided in with a wild and bohemian mood. Overheated bodies, smiles galore, and some powdered noses were part of the scene. Copious bottles of champagne, too many to capture, with corks that popped like miniature firing cannons. The guests partied with few boundaries, something arbitrary and exclusive was truly being celebrated in the most ostentatious manner. It felt unparalleled to Angela. The exquisite drama that tingled and touched every part of her body. For the first time all evening, she was relaxing. Enjoy herself and smiling.

Ten minutes later Sophie jigged through groups of people towards Angela. Her skin glistened with the rising temperature. Angela could see the red wine now in her glass swish about perilously. Her hair, now tied away from her face, exposed how beautiful she really was. Smudged kohl pencil like storm clouds scattered around her black sparkling eyes as she bent towards Angela to say something.

She wore what looked to be a man's oversized large white shirt that skimmed her thighs. A wide brown belt hung loosely around her hips. Several colourful beaded necklaces hung from her slim neck. It was a look that drew attention. Particularly the attention of many males in the room.

'Oh bugger. Look. Done it again.' Red wine like spilled blood had soiled the one side of her oversized shirt. She rubbed at the stains with her fingertips, hiccupped, looked up and grinned towards Angela. 'To hell with it. Who cares?'

'Hi, I'm Sophie and I'm very drunk.'

Angela couldn't help but grin seeing the enormous effort Sophie was making to even stay upright.

'Hi. I'm Angela. I'm drunk too. Gladys's vodka.'

'Lethal stuff.' She beamed.

'Your Lisa's new neighbour, aren't you? Hic, how are you settling onto this crazy street...?'

'Good, thank you.' Angela wondered what type of crazy Sophie meant or was it just the alcohol talking.

'I heard that hot guy Gethin left that truck of his on your driveway the day you moved in. That must have been awkward?'

Angela nodded 'Yes, awkward for him.'

Sophie grinned and raised her glass in agreement.

'Lisa invited him to the party. But he tends to keep himself to himself. Doing some sort of research for a book, Gladys said. Shame. I think he's gorgeous.' She finished the wine in her glass with one large gulp, then grinned again. 'He can come and do some exploration on me anytime!'

'Research. What kind of research?' shouted Angela over the sound of a Supertramp track.

Sophie wasn't listening anymore, something else had caught her attention.

'Umm. Sorry ... what was that?'

Sophie peered towards the lounge window, obscured by the constant movement of people dancing or stood in shifting groups. Outside, shots of triangular orange light patterned the blackness on the street, not much else to see. Then, as her drunken eyes focused more, she stepped back in horror. She glimpsed a man peering in from outside the window.

His eyes shifted from side to side, as if searching for someone. Then he thrust his thick set hands onto the windowpane on either side of his head. His nostrils emitted little funnels of condensation on the windowpane. Angela gasped and looked around, seeing if anyone else had noticed him.

'Who is it?' gasped Angela.

Sophie was already edging towards the window, squinting through the throngs of revellers. Then, like a startled filly, she turned and fled, somehow clearing a large floor space full of drunk people. as "Rapture" By blondie blared from the stereo. She scrambled under the dining table, bringing a few glasses crashing to the floor. People turned their attentions towards Sophie to see what was happening. A few people cheered, not realising the danger.

Angela, with one hand on her fast-beating chest, returned her gaze to the window. He'd gone. She swallowed. Had anyone else seen him there? She squeezed her eyes shut then opened them. For a moment questioning if she'd seen anyone there at all? Were her anxieties creating all this? Making her more unhinged? But what had scared Sophie?

Angela moved on unsteady legs towards Sophie, who had folded her long frame into a neat parcel under the small dining table. A few people had gathered above her. Angela pushed through them. They thought it some kind of amusing spectacle, their senses and better judgement drowned in alcohol.

'You okay?'

Sophie shook her head.

Angela could read the emotion of fear like someone had etched it into Sophie's features. Maybe they had both seen him? Angela knew all too well how it felt to be seared with fear by the presence of a man. Angela shifted her body weight to kneel and heard a cry from behind. She'd stepped on someone's toe.

'Oh shit, sorry!' she exclaimed before looking up.

To her horror Veronica stood there, her arms folded across her chest and with eyes that burnt like hot rods into Angela's flesh. She scowled at Sophie, then turned and walked towards the hallway.

Sophie slumped further under the table, her demeanour flat and resigned, whilst Angela who had witnessed the small interaction between both women felt a heat that rose from her chest like a bubbling scolding geyser. Veronica behaved like a bully, and she'd had enough. She squeezed Sophie's hand, wondering why she cared so much.

'Stay here for a moment.'

She stood and strode with intent towards the hallway with a stream of objections running through her drunk mind. Her words slipped away as she watched Veronica open the door to the stranger from the window.

'Hello, can I help you?' If scared, Veronica hid it well. Stood in the doorway, almost filling the open-door space, stood a man of colossal size. His head leaned forward of his bulky neck and shoulders, and his jeans didn't conceal the mass of his full thighs. He was both striking and scary.

The stranger pushed his hands deep into his black bomber jacket. He smiled with a hint of menace towards Veronica.

'You know Sophie? I want to see her. She told me about the party.'

Veronica didn't even twitch. Her exterior measured and controlled as she spoke.

'There's no one here called Sophie—sorry. You must have the wrong house. And I don't think there's a Sophie on this street either.'

'Stop shitting me. She told me Dafydd Drive.' He narrowed his eyes as if sensing she was lying. Then he scanned the small crowd, stood behind Veronica, ignoring his cue to leave. He caught sight of Lisa. Angela frowned as she watched Lisa look away and slip behind the person stood in front of her. Something was wrong. Very wrong.

Others became fractious. Someone whispered to call the police. Angela wondered why Lisa wasn't dealing with this growing situation. It was her party, after all.

He guffawed upon hearing the police word and calmly lit a cigarette, as if still expecting to be invited in.

A male guest shouted, 'I think you need to leave, mate.'

The stranger in the doorway sucked his teeth in response.

Veronica turned towards the guest and glared. He shrunk back into silence before she returned her attention to the figure at the door.

'I really have to get back to my guests. Sorry I can't be of any more help. Bye'

Without waiting for his response, Veronica curtly shut the door. Through the mottled glass of the door, his silhouette lingered for a while, then it receded down the pathway, like a lost soul fading into the night.

Veronica stood near the closed door for a few seconds, deep furrows etched into her forehead. She looked furious. A curious emotion given the circumstances, thought Angela. There was more to what had just happened, and Veronica had done her damnedest to conceal whatever it was.

People flocked around her, asking if she was okay. Others made jokes, trying to relieve some of the residual tension. Lisa had already slipped away unnoticed.

Then a tingling chill lurched up Angela's spine. What if he went on knocking at neighbours' doors in search of Sophie? What if he went to her house? Would Catherine remember she shouldn't answer the door under any circumstances?

She pushed through the crowded hallway past Veronica and flung the door open to the shocked gasps from others. She fled down the path, hearing the calls of objections behind her as the cool air pinched at her heated skin.

The cold air seeped through the old silk of her trousers. Then she heard it, the screeching, metal on metal. Through the drunkenness, she tried to fathom what it was. She moved along the pavement towards the sound. Her heels barely making a sound on the concrete path. With eyes that quickly scanned the street like a frightened city fox, Angela saw no sign of the disturbing man who had intruded on the party. She glanced towards her own house. Everything seemed settled. Her head spun. She felt dizzy.

Another screeching sound that seemed closer than before froze her to the spot. Her throat tightened and restricted her breathing as her head turned slowly towards the sound. She moved nearer to the hedge that divided their houses.

She gasped.

Christ, it was Gethin. *What was he doing?*

She watched him in the darkness as his arms swung up, pushing the garage door back as far as it would go. It groaned and creaked with defiance, like damaged cartilage on joints. Then he stooped to pick something from the floor. As he came back into focus, she could see he was carrying what looked to be a pile of books or albums. Hard to say with eyes plundered by anxiety and alcohol.

She heard a click and light flooded the inside of the garage and along the driveway. He disappeared inside for a few minutes, then returned empty handed. Instead of closing the garage door as expected, Angela watches as he stood there looking around as if he sensed someone was watching him. It made her shudder; his behaviour seemed inflated with a strangeness she couldn't make sense of.

She stepped in closer to the hedge. Hidden by darkness and distorted silhouettes. She could hear her own heart thumping. Trying to beat itself out of harm's way.

She heard another click. Darkness smothered again. The garage door cranked shut, the sound of a car door being opened then shut. She thought she heard his car engine- being turned on. *What was he doing?* What seemed like seconds later the engine clicked off again as he left his car and with light footsteps scamper down the path and shut the front door.

For a short while, she remained rooted, unable to move. She looked up at her own home. It watched her with eyes unblinking, asking her to come inside where it was safe. Yet, something ruminated inside her, something different to what she'd felt before. A need-to-know thing. She turned back towards Lisa's house and told herself she couldn't leave without saying goodbye.

Angela wandered through Lisa's lounge, looking for Gladys and the others. Guests were leaving; it was already past twelve. Yet, the strange events of the evening had catapulted some guests into an atmosphere far less comfortable, forcing them to leave sooner. Angela sensed Veronica's dishonesty. Had others too?

The atmosphere in the house was now laden with an invisible weight which subdued the previous excitement. Smaller groups of people sat together, hands clasped around bottlenecks and glass stems. Heads slung low in conversation.

Occasionally their eyes twitched upwards towards the diehards who swung their loose unshackled bodies precariously close to where they sat.

Ashtrays brimmed, empty bottles and glasses littered the floor and surfaces. All their fizz dispersed and misplaced—just mementos of a fairground evening. The stale smell of tobacco and worn-out fragrances encouraged by the melancholic sounds of Billie Holiday accompanied Angela as she continued to search out Gladys.

Has Gladys left without saying goodbye?

Angela felt a small punch to her stomach. Lisa was missing. So was Sophie. Veronica, she didn't much care about.

Pushing past a young almond sweet couple who sat on the open staircase, legs entwined, Angela made her way upstairs to go to the toilet before having one last look for them before leaving. In the darkness, she pushed on the brass handle to no avail. *In use, just my luck.* Angela sighed as her eyes adjusted to the dark.

She noticed a thin strip of light framing the door opposite the bathroom. Then she heard hushed brittle voices. Out of a strange curiosity, she moved closer to the door to listen. One voice sounded distinctly and disgustingly familiar—Veronica. She was doing most of the talking, and she didn't sound happy. Angela stilled, knowing she should move away, return downstairs. Her feet wouldn't let her.

'What the hell were you thinking, Sophie? It's that kind of stupidity that will finish it. For all of us?' hissed Veronica—so sharp it cut through the quiet like a blade.

Angela continued to stand motionless as Billie Holiday's "Ain't Nobody's Business" dripped up the stairs, bittersweet like a warning. They drew Angela into something unpalatable but seductive.

'You're becoming a real risk, Sophie. You drink too much, say too much. For God's sake, why can't you just pull yourself together!'

'Sophie, are you listening?'

'Oh, give it a rest Roni. I have a headache. Can someone find me a paracetamol pleeeeasse?'

'Why? Why would you do it Sophie?'

There was a lull, then Sophie spoke again. Angela had to stifle a giggle; she could only imagine the expression on Veronica's face right now.

'He didn't see me Ver-on-ic-a! So, what's the problem?'

'Are you insane? You told him where we live! He could have recognised any of us.'

'I don't feel good, ladies.'

This time Angela heard Lisa's hushed tones.

'Please Roni. Perhaps we can talk this through tomorrow. I don't think you'll get much sense from her. She drank a lot tonight to be honest.'

'He recognised you Lisa. I saw it and so did you. Why defend her?'

'Oh, I forgot Roni. Forgive me for having a good time.' Sophie slurred as she spoke, each word coated with a sarcasm and contempt for the woman who criticized her.

'Sophie, your behaviour could ruin it for all of us—not just yourself. If you can't give a shit what I think, at least be concerned for Lisa.'

'For Christ's sakes she's passed out. She's not even listening. I'm done here. Maybe you're right. We might get more sense from her tomorrow.'

'I think so. I'll let her sleep there for tonight. Her mum has Jason.'

'Right now, I couldn't care where she slept, I'm going home.'

Angela backed away from the door like a novice on stilts. The bathroom door suddenly opened behind her. Gladys stood there blinking as she tried to read the situation.

Then the bedroom door swung open. Veronica stood there her steely grey eyes firing bullets at both of them. Angela felt like a trapped insect between pinched fingers. Who would speak first?

Gladys coughed, then spoke in a cheerful tone. 'Thanks Angela, my pelvic floor, it waits for no one including you.' She chuckled and burped. 'Oh, scuse me.'

She glanced at Roni's stony face, then back towards Angela. 'I not keep you waiting too long, eh?'

With a jerky shake of her head as if her neck muscles had turned to metal, Angela passed Gladys into the bathroom and swiped the lock. She fell back on to the toilet seat and dropped her head into her hands.

Angela's stomach churned, a mixture of alcohol and anxiety as her mind flipped images of the evening's events like pages in a photo album. She turned quickly, lifted the lid of the white porcelain bowl, and vomited into it. Hanging there she wondered why things had turned out this way. She was beginning to question the idea that she was drawing these troubles to her in a strange sublime way. Had an elongated life of torment become so normal that she naturally veered towards it unconscious of her own intentions? It seemed that way. She wanted friends, not enemies. She wanted certainty, not suspicion.

Dragging herself up, from her knees, she swilled her mouth out with water and spat it out into the basin. The action was satisfying and darkly amusing. She wished it was Veronica's basin as she rinsed her hands, the basin, then flushed the chain: She wouldn't have rinsed at all had it been Veronicas. Drying her hands, she might have thought herself crazy had she not known how close to crazy she had been before.

Without stopping to say goodbye Angela crept from the house: probably the best given the situation. As she turned the key in her own front door, one idea shone with clarity. She would shut her door to it all. Some things just didn't work out for her. Having real friends seemed complicated, riddled with further problems and issues of which she had no room in her life for. Perhaps Colin had been right about one thing. She didn't need friends.

She slipped her heels off and dragged herself up the stairs. Without removing her make-up or clothes, she crawled into bed, pulling the quilt right up over her face. And yet despite herself, despite everything, she still couldn't help but wonder what made Veronica so bloody vicious.

12

Angela

It was just past ten-thirty as Angela manoeuvred her car round and round the bends of the multi-storey carpark. Since leaving the house, Angela had struggled to shake off the awkward conversation she'd had with Gladys earlier that morning.

Why did she do it? Why had Gladys played down the events at the party a couple of nights ago? Even hinting, when Angela subtlety reminded her of some of the details, that Russian vodka and nerves tarnished Angela's perception—memories of the evening.

Was she trying to tell me I have a drink problem? Or that my own anxieties were over dramatizing events?

As her car took the last turn, she glanced at Joel sat at the back of the car playing on his hand-held game console. He couldn't help it. Joel hadn't realised his mum had avoided any contact with the ladies since the party. He'd opened the front door to Gladys, led her into their house before Angela had time to object. Gladys had tried to be sympathetic, even make some excuses for Veronica's behaviour.

Angela had to think about herself and the children now. They were the most important thing in her new home. And their happiness mattered.

Whatever they were up to she wanted no part in it. She couldn't risk it, especially if Colin was snooping around. He threatened to have the social services take the children from her once. He'd threatened many things, and that forced the decision that she should be careful what she became involved in right now.

A breeze swept through her car window as she turned onto level three.

'Nearly there, now!'

'Cool!' responded Joel between the bleeping and smashing sounds from his hand-held console.

Angela nudged Catherine. She slept a lot these days. Her long chestnut hair fell across her beautiful, impish features. A faint smell of turps lingered on her daughter's skin and clothes. She wore dark shadows under her eyes which matched her choice of clothing.

Catherine now painted well into the night. Filled the upstairs of the house with the smell of pungent oil paints and turps most evenings. She'd given up asking Catherine to make sure she had a full eight hours sleep each night. She never listened.

Angela wondered if her daughter had picked up the women's magazine left open on the dining table the night of Lisa's party… She hoped so. An article about self-harm featured on the centre pages. It included a small bio about a young girl, counselled through her habit of self-abuse. It had helped her understand and alleviate the thoughts and feelings that caused her to take a razor blade to her skin. Perhaps, counselling could help Catherine, after all she'd witnessed and felt the constant emotional bleakness caused by a decayed and abusive relationship.

They left the multi-storey carpark and headed straight to Queen

Street, where you could fall from one shop and into another from Newport Road right up to the castle. Shops housed in old white brick buildings stood next to the new, with large glass facades. Each showcased a multitude of fashions.

It took an hour to buy additional uniform needed because of growth spurts, a new jacket for Joel, he'd ripped his at the park recently, and some new underwear for herself. All paid for after she managed to sell her wedding ring in free adds. The last shop they dragged their feet into was *Chelsea Girl*.

Catherine found a dress and Angela encouraged her to try it on. It was an expense she couldn't afford, but the sheer enjoyment of watching her daughter prance about in front of the mirror like a pixie with a sherbet dip was worth every penny she didn't have.

She sat and waited in the dressing room area as her daughter changed behind a curtain and whittled happily in the process about some girl in school called Suzie who wore her skirt so short, she really shouldn't bend over, not even a fraction.

'Can you imagine Mum? Having to consider every little move you make could spell real trouble.'

Angela knew only too well, although she guessed her daughter didn't mean it quite the same way.

'How much is the dress, Cath?'

'One second. On no. It's £3.50. Is it too much?'

'I said it's a treat, didn't I?'

Colin had insisted his children always wear the best. Benetton. Calvin Klein. That was what they'd been used to. Angela had soon come to realise how these things had also acted as veneers of respectability, concealing his true nature. Angela had never really had a say in the matter. She would have preferred the money used for extra tuition for her children who had on and off struggled to focus at school.

'Are you sure, Mum?'

'Absolutely.'

Angela turned to speak to Joel. She bit at her lip as she looked up at other customers perusing rails. No Joel. Angela stood, then tiptoed. Scanned the shop. She called his name quietly. Apologetically. Nothing. She called again. A little louder this time. Her legs weakened. Customers turned. To stare.

The clatter of curtain rings scratched across the rail and startled Angela.

'What's wrong, Mum?'

'I can't find Joel. He's gone.'

'What? Mum, I'm sure he's here somewhere. He…'

Angela weaved between customers and clothes rails as her daughter's words trailed behind. Panic tightened her features. Her mind flickered with dark images of Joel banging on the glass of a car window, fear etched in his features as the car disappeared into nowhere. She knew what Colin was capable of.

She squeezed her eyes tight then opened them again scanning every inch of the shop for a glimpse of his blue *Transformers* t-shirt. Or the sound of his small console. Her face tingled as her breathing became sharp and shallow. Specks of white light dotted her vision. She held onto a rail for a moment. Tasted the bitterness of bile. Where was he?

What if Colin had followed them? Grabbed Joel? I wouldn't put it passed him. Oh my god!

She heard a high-pitched screech from the second floor of the shop. Angela sped up the stairs two at a time. As her foot hit the top step, she saw him knelt on the floor looking up at the old lady. His eyes were like large telescopes, scanning everything above him in nervous anticipation. Angela swallowed the emotions that threatened as she raced over. Her mind brittle. Ready to snap. Her hand tugged at her polar neck as she struggled to catch her breath. She wanted to cry out.

She couldn't. She mustn't.

'Sorry, Miss Lady, I was only hiding under there so I could see the game on my screen more properly, see!'

Her son lifted his console to show the woman. He turned towards Angela.

'Muuum. I didn't mean to frighten her. I was sat under there'. He pointed to a rail filled with jackets and long blouses.

Angela glanced at the old woman trying to read her mood.

'Joel, have you said sorry to this poor lady?' She knew he had done.

'Yes Mum, I did. THREE times' He looked up at the old woman again then stretched out his arm with the console in it.

'See this is the game. You can have a go if you like? I can show you how to play it.'

'No thank you my dear.' She looked at Angela, then back at Joel. 'But you really shouldn't hide from your mum like that. I'm sure she would've been terribly worried.'

Angela nodded in agreement, relieved that the woman had taken the incident so well. She bent down to pick the woman's shopping off the floor and handed it back to her.

'Thank you dear. He's a little charmer, isn't he?'

'Thank you. Sorry he shocked you like that!'

'Am I grounded now, Mum?'

The old woman chuckled at this. Pinched his cheek with a hand touched by age. 'Stay close to your mum now.' Then with a nod to Angela, slipped away.

By the time they had paid for Catherine's dress and left the shop, Angela had recognised something. A subtle change. She'd managed the incident without a hundred nervous apologies or worse still, an angry outburst with no consideration of others. Could she trust the thought that she might cope better now?

Angela and Catherine strolled down Queen Street towards the

car park discussing in minute detail, the incident in the shop. Her daughter chuckled as Angela relayed what Joel had said to the old lady. It didn't take long before Angela started laughing, too. Even if somewhere in the recesses of her mind, she knew she concealed what her initial fears had been. Laughter as an after tonic worked. That, for now, she was grateful for. She looked up and noticed Joel had inched further away from her again.

'Joel, you're walking ahead again. WAIT.'

He'd refused to hold her hand and always wanted to be ahead. A few metres away from them he stopped. The lollipop she'd bought him earlier grasped tightly in his one hand. His attentions drawn to a side-street, he grinned.

'What's he looking at?'

'I'm not sure?' Angela's brows inched together as if being darned by an invisible thread and needle.

As they approached Joel, she heard women shouting.

'Mum, don't we know her … you know, Mum, the one who always looks pissed off?'

Angela nearly choked on hearing her son's words as she tried to take in the scene a few yards down the side street.

'Shit. Joel, don't say that word, it's a swear word.'

He pursed his lips at his mum. 'But you just said "shit", Mum, that's a swear word.'

'JOEL!' She stared down at him.

'But Dad …' his voice sank into a whisper, then silence as he witnessed his mother's stare.

Veronica stood in the street next to a strange woman. They were arguing. The other women's voice louder and angrier with each syllable spoken. Her body moved closer towards Veronica as she spewed a vitriol that made Angela feel uncomfortable.

'Mum, are they going to duff each other up or what?'

'Joel, really, that's no way to talk. Come on, this won't do standing here like this. Let's go.'

It was at that precise moment, as if in slow motion, The other woman pushed Veronica back into the long black wrought-iron fence behind her. A handbag hit the floor, its contents spilled onto the pavement. A few people passing by gasped.

Angela dropped the shopping in her hands to cover her son's eyes. He pushed her hands away.

Veronica's face twisted with pain. Angela gathered her shopping ready to leave. Maybe Veronica deserved it. Then she stopped. Glanced back towards Veronica. She knew how it felt to be on the end of blows to the body. No one deserves it. Angela could see that the other woman was about to strike Veronica again. Angela turned towards her daughter. Bit at her lip. She sighed.

Catherine peered at her mum; her face crumpled. She put her free hand on her mother's arm.

'Mum, don't even think about it. Let's go. Please.'

Angela glanced past her daughter at the café on the other side of the High Street.

'See that café over there? Go and get yourself and Joel a drink. Sit inside and wait for me. Don't move. For anyone.' She said this so sternly she knew Catherine understood what she meant.

'No … Please, Mum!'

'I must help, Cath.' She knew if she walked away, she would regret it, but she also knew there was a good possibility she might regret staying. She bit at the corner of her lip.

Catherine shook her head and snatched the shopping bags from her mum. 'You don't have to help her, Mum. Look at how she's treated you? What about…'

'Don't talk to anyone and keep hold of Joel's hand.'

Joel shrugged with disappointment. 'They'll probably pull each other's hair out and stuff like that. I saw Tracy do it too Sian in ...'

'Joel, not now.'

He nodded. Grimaced towards his sister's hand.

Angela watched them enter the café, then turned and headed towards the women. They had drawn the attention of a few shoppers who stood watching but doing nothing.

'You're being ridiculous. Get off me. I have no idea what you're talking about.'

With her head forced forward towards the ground, Veronica held onto the black railings behind her in a desperate attempt to keep herself upright.

'You're lying.'

'You're insane.'

'Hi. Why don't you let go of her hair? Look around. People are watching. Take it from me. You'll regret it later.' Angela's voice remained calm but firm.

The woman flung her head around. Her lips were a thin red line you dared to cross. Small pistons of condensation shot from her nostrils.

But her eyes. Angela knew that look—the crystal shine of unfettered fear and desperation.

With her fingers still laced through the hair at the back of Veronica's head, she thrust her attention towards the small crowds of people gathering along the street.

'You think you know what this is about? You've no idea. Piss off.'

'Yes. You're right. but I assure you, this will not help either. Especially if this is about a man.'

Angela registered the subtle flicker of vulnerability in the woman's eyes. Then, as quick as it appeared, her brows warred towards each other. Her grip tightened and forced Veronica's head even closer towards the stone pavement.

Veronica turned towards Angela. The embarrassment visible in her eyes.

'Please get this lunatic off me?'

Angela took a risk. She moved in closer and put her hand on the woman's shoulder gently. 'Come on. You're upset. I'm sure you can sort this out some other way?'

Angela heard herself say the words and didn't recognise herself.

'I've told her it's not me. I don't sleep with other women's husbands.'

Angela wished Veronica would keep quiet.

'Not my thing. I work with him: that's it, Anna.'

The woman looked past Veronica as she spoke, as if she no longer heard her words. Vacant. Lost. Her mind cast somewhere else. Angela recognised the expression and took advantage of it. With her one hand still on her shoulder, Angela used her free hand to untangle and remove the woman's fist from Veronica's hair.

Veronica stepped back like an animal fleeing a trap. Both women had smeared make-up and red blotched faces. They stood in silence as their chests heaved. Veronica tucked her silk shirt back into her trousers. The other woman rubbed at her red ringed eyes.

'Sick bitch. All you care about is yourself and making money from others.'

Angela winced and stepped back. Was it time to leave, she asked herself? Whatever Veronica had done or not done was of no interest to her.

'I saw them. Your little love notes...'

Veronica shook her head in slow measured movements as she rubbed the back of her neck.

'I trusted you.'

Veronica rolled her eyes. 'It's him you can't trust, darling.'

The other woman shot Veronica a glare so powerful, you could almost believe you had just had a whiff of gun smoke.

'And the notes on the company headed paper? Signed Sexy V? The late-night meetings.'

Veronica smirked.

'You are wrong.' Veronica pronounced each word in isolation, dragging the sentence out for greater effect.

There was a pause.

Veronica sighed as she reached down to pick up her handbag and its contents.

'Yes, I work with your husband. yes, occasionally we do late meetings. Attend boring social functions ... But sleep with him... NO. Absolutely not.'

Veronica was telling the truth. Angela heard the apathetic, almost bored tone in Veronica's voice. She recalled what her son had said earlier and tried to hide her amusement. Her son was pretty observant for a nine-year-old. It impressed her.

Veronica took an expensive looking pen and a small piece of paper from her handbag. Scribbled something down and handed it to the woman without a word.

The woman read what was on the paper.

'What is this?'

'That's the Hotel where your husband has a rendezvous every other Thursday. That's her name, Ella Victoria ... V for Victoria.'

'Is this another one of your little games?'

'No. not at all. Had you given me a chance, darling, I could have told you this before all this... this ridiculous fiasco.'

Angela pitied the woman now. Chasing your husband's mistresses down must feel like hell, the feeling of self-worthlessness excruciating. It seemed so unfair that those women, thrust onto an unknowing path of disrespect and abuse by others often fell into behaviours that only caused them further harm and pain.

'He'll be there this Thursday ... always finds some excuse to leave the office, 2 p.m.'

The woman placed the note into her small green leather handbag, pushed the flap down until it clicked into place.

'I'll pay for those.'

Veronica looked down at the broken heel of one of her court shoes. She smirked. 'These. They're Louboutin!'

The woman frowned not understanding.

'Never mind,' said Veronica.

'Can I give you a piece of advice? Leave him, he'll never change.'

She stood there for a few seconds looking at the two women then turned mumbling quietly that she needed to go. Both women stood in silence as they watched her fade away and around a corner. Angela bent down and picked up a lipstick from the kerb.

'I think you missed this?'

'Thank you. The woman needs help.'

'A consequence of living with an uncaring husband.' This time Angela heard the double meaning in her own words.

For the first time, Veronica turned and looked at Angela directly. Her head tilted slightly her eyes viewed Angela as if she was seeing her for the first time.

'Mmmm, it must have taken a lot to come and help me?'

'Well, yes there is that.' responded Angela. 'My son wanted to stay and watch you get duffed up.'

Veronica managed a smile, smudging her usual poker face.

'Where is he now?' Veronica said glancing around.

'He's with my daughter in that café over there. I need to get back to them.'

Veronica nodded and glanced at glanced at her watch. 'Well, I have a meeting this afternoon.'

'Really. Are you sure?'

'Yes. I have a change of clothes in my office.' replied Veronica as she smoothed down wild strands of hair.

'Well, I hope your afternoon turns out better than your morning. Turrah.' She turned to walk away.

'Angela.'

Angela stopped. 'Yes?'

'I would really appreciate it if the other women didn't get to hear of this for now.'

'I understand,' replied Angela.

Veronica nodded. 'Thank you.'

And for the first time since she'd met Veronica, Angela saw something different; A thread of respect, sewing some understanding between them.

13

Gethin

Gethin sat on a noisy rambling train, viewing the undulations of the Welsh landscape. The sounds felt familiar, the mountainous view consoling.

He was beginning to understand his reluctance to coming back to this luscious green land. In his desperate quest to abolish her existence, he'd sabotaged any prospect of regaining the connection he longed with the place he called home.

He'd awoken in the morning to find his feet dirtied; small pieces of gravel caught between his toes. Had he tried to get into the garage to retrieve the photos of her? It had shaken him. He'd left a message with his therapist's secretary. Some things he couldn't hide from anymore. He could have done something stupid… dangerous, even.

The breaks of the train screeched, the carriages rattled and slowed until it stopped with a jerk. A few people around him stood up. Gethin being closest to the door, pulled the latch with the force required and the echoes of several door clicking and clacking open mixed with several whistles and rubber soles hitting the platform were the sounds of his childhood.

He left the station and turned right up the main street with the small map in his hand of Trigoed, a small town surrounded by hills, mountains, and sheep- marking the landscape with black and white blotches. Clusters of small, wooded areas added a patchwork of greenery to a patchwork landscape that Gethin associated with Wales.

After twenty minutes of walking uphill towards Coed Derw, a minibus trundled past him. The driver honked its horn and smiled. The youngsters sat behind him were a motley crew. Some boys sat at the back of the bus with hair like rats' tails and gave him the "V" sign. He smiled and returned the gesture in jest. They screeched with laughter. An adolescent boy stuck his head out of a small window and shouted, 'Get a fucking life, you old man'.

Guess I'm not far away then.

On the back of the bus as it moseyed away down the hill, Gethin read "Coed-Derw Children's and Young Adults Residential Care Home". Underneath in smaller print were the words "We dare to care ... Do you?"

Gethin turned left onto a smaller road flanked by several sycamore trees with branches that arched across the road like grappling hands. Their patchy bark always reminded Gethin of burnt skin that scabbed and flaked.

Further down the road, Gethin saw a large car park hemmed in by a red brick wall and a set of wrought-iron gates which were open. Beyond it, he recognised the building that was once called Radcliffe. Despite the spring sunshine, it had a cheerless presence.

His eyes travelled upwards to the rows of pointed arched windows framed by darker brickwork like several sets of suspicious eyes glaring down at him. Dirtied net curtains hung like veils in some windows whilst other windows obliterated any hopes of sunlight with stacked boxes, bottles, stuffed toys, and other such items. Gethin absorbed the surrounding scene. He'd expected noise, lots of it. All he heard was the distant sound of a plane that flew overhead and the occasional warble of an unseen bird.

He passed the gates and crunched his way across the carpark towards what he believed to be the main entrance, a set of large studded wooden doors, one of which stood slightly ajar. Once inside the old stone portcullis, another smaller façade made up of large, reinforced glass panes reminded Gethin for reasons unknown to him of a mental institution.

Beyond this, Gethin could see a long white corridor with several doors coming off to the left. On the right were several low-slung benches running the length of the wall. They reminded him of the type he'd once used for gym lessons in his youth. More arched windows above looked out onto some kind of inner garden with a few small trees and bedding boxes.

Gethin pressed the large button on the intercom. He heard a loud buzzer echo down the corridor. The young boy who sat on a bench halfway down the corridor looked up at Gethin and scowled, then dropped his gaze back towards his scuffed boots.

A few seconds later, a woman appeared out of a side door dressed in a yellow twin piece and her lacquered to stone. Her heels clicked on the old grey tiles as she scurried towards him and pressed something. He heard the click of a lock before she pulled the door open.

'Hello, Mr James, come on in.' She stood and watched the door behind him click and lock then returned her attention to him with a closed lip smile.

'I've been expecting you. I'm Olivia. We spoke on the phone the other day.'

He reached out to shake hands.

She reciprocated with a curious expression.

'Hello Olivia, it's lovely to meet you. I hope I'm not disturbing you too much?' He couldn't help but glance at the boy sat a couple of metres away from them as he spoke.

'Oh no, not at all. Everybody is out today at a charity fun day.' She chuckled 'This is a rare and quiet day. Count yourself lucky!'

He smiled. 'Good to hear. I'll stay out of your way as much as possible. Just point me in the right direction.'

She leaned up close to him and whispered, 'Mr James, that is a splendid idea as I simply forgot you see, to put your visit in the diary before Mr Cleverley left with the children.'

Gethin tried to ignore the strong pungent smell of honeysuckle and showed concern for her little disclosure. 'Now don't you go worrying yourself Olivia, I'm no crazed psychopath, honest!' He widened his eyes for effect.

She chuckled. 'Oh, Mr James, you are funny. Now sit yourself here for a minute. I'm just popping back to the office to get the keys. Back in a jiffy.'

Olivia disappeared into one of the side offices again, leaving Gethin sat in the long corridor with the young boy. He started knocking his foot against a wooden leg of the bench. Tap... tap ... tap. The young boy seemed somewhere else as he stared at the floor. Gethin wondered why he hadn't gone with the other children.

'Hey, what's your name, buddy?' asked Gethin.

The boy stopped tapping. He didn't look up. Said nothing. Then started tapping again. This time faster. Tap ... Tap ... Tap ... Tap. Tap-tap.

'Here we go.' She smiled and jangled the keys near her face. 'The keys to our archive office. Not much there now, I must say. Follow me, Mr James'. With this, she turned on those tiny heels as if impervious to the repetitive sound of the boy's boot that echoed down the corridor.

Gethin stood and followed. As she approached the young, dishevelled boy, she coughed into her clenched hand in a contrived manner. The boy stopped. He didn't move a limb as they walked past in silence. The only sound heard the low monotone hum from the white strip lighting high above their heads.

At the end of the corridor, they turned left. Gethin followed her down another short corridor. The walls had an array of framed photos of children doing a variety of activities. Some larger photos showed larger group photos. They reminded Gethin of school class photos, but not as formal. He stopped for a moment to explore one of the larger photos.

'Oh no, I'm afraid there's no time for that. Come, giddy up, Mr James.' She smiled.

He forced a smile, then continued to follow her down a small and dimly lit stairway. At the bottom were two closed doors on either side of him. Olivia turned to face the more ornate wooden door on the right.

She pushed the archaic looking key into the keyhole then suddenly stopped before turning it to unlock the door. Gethin could hear the thump of his own heartbeat in the small, darkened space. Was she having doubts? Then she did something that shocked Gethin.

She coughed into her hand and with a quick flicker of her eyes, she shot Gethin a deliberate glance. He tilted his head to the side and frowned. Then reached into his pocket for his wallet. She brought her chubby little fingers with pearlescent painted nails to her face and tapped at her over rouged cheek. He was about to express his disapproval, then thought better of it. He needed to get into that room.

As he opened his wallet, she turned her head away in mock respectfulness. He pulled a crisp five pound note out and offered it to her.

'Hmmm,' she said with a curt nod. And folded the note once, twice and again and pushed it into her skirt pocket.

Gethin watched as she unlocked the door, flicked a light switch, and stepped back without a word- gesturing him into the cold cheerless room. There were several metal cabinets of different sizes, a variety of framed photos of different sized stacked against one wall, a wooden bookshelf with very little on it except a few boxes with what looked like children's toy things and a single table and chair. On the table were box files stacked high. Under the table was a small two bar heater. She tottered over to the window and pulled the roller blind down.

'How rude of me, Mr James. I haven't offered you a drink. Tea, coffee?'

Gethin shook his head dumbfounded. 'No thanks, Olivia. I think I have everything I need right here.'

She smiled, tight-lipped. 'Oh yes, I think you do. Some of these files go back to when this building was Radcliffe, mind you.' She did a little shiver of discomfort for effect, as if saying the word was like poison on her tongue. 'Well. Happy researching, Mr James.'

She went to leave, then stopped. 'Just one thing, I need you to leave by twelve-thirty.' She looked at her watch 'Wonderful, that gives you a full two hours.' Then she left, leaving the door open a sliver.

Gethin stood in the small room feeling uneasy. The arrangement disquieted him. He pushed these thoughts aside, took his jacket off and folded it over the back of the single chair in the room. Next to the table, he placed his satchel. The first thing he wanted to discover was if someone by the name of Penny had attended Radcliffe. He would check old records of children living at the homes since the seventies, then if time, he would look at staffing records at the home to shed some light on the woman Deborah called Nonnie.

He stared at the old metal cabinets; they had key holes but no keys. Holding his breath, he pulled at the top drawer of the largest cabinet. It opened with a scratching of metal on metal. He breathed out, relieved he wouldn't have to go back upstairs to speak with Olivia.

The first hour rushed by. Files littered the floor and the desk where he sat. His eyes ached a little in the dimly lit room. The age range of the children who entered the care system surprised and troubled him. He focused on not becoming emotionally drawn in by the sad and traumatic lives of these children. That wouldn't help them, or him. Finding the truth might. He set to work unhindered.

Each child's records also listed foster carers they'd lived with. He came across Mrs Solomons' name a few times and smiled. Yet, he still hadn't come across a file for someone by the name of Penny. As he pulled out the last drawer in the cabinet, he wondered if the woman on the phone had been mistaken. Perhaps there had never been a Penny at Radcliffe.

He flicked through files without removing them from the cabinet to save time. Only lifting those that might be of interest to him. As his fingers rolled over fans of paper, he saw something. He pulled the old brown file out. A young girl by the name of Trisha had been fostered and returned to the home after three months. The name of the foster carer was Jean Smith. Smith! He jotted the name and address in his notebook. Circled it and jotted Makos above it with a question mark?

He sat for a moment before tapping his fingers against the cabinet, aware that two hours was no time at all if things were to continue at this pace. He also needed the toilet. With time chasing him, he took the stairs two at a time and moved brusquely through the cold long corridor. He glanced right, hoping not to see her. To his surprise, the young boy from earlier remained slouched under the window. His feet were now tucked under the bench, his expression bored and resigned to his situation.

'Phhwwt, Kiddo, where's the toilets?'

The boy lifted his head and looked up at him through thick, dark lashes. He jerked his thumb behind him.

136

Gethin responded with a shrug.

The boy shifted his eyes towards Olivia's office, then leapt from the bench. Thankful, Gethin imagined, to have an excuse to move.

'Quick, follow me, it's down ere,' he said in lowered tones.

'Right-y-o', responded Gethin, trying to conceal his amusement. He took him along another shorter corridor, running alongside the other side of the central quad. An array of large and smaller photographs decorated plain magnolia walls. They flickered in his peripheral view like black and white film reel as the boy stomped ahead in haste.

Then Gethin stopped. Backtracked. He turned to stare at the large black framed photo, catching his own reflection for a moment. So many faces. So many children. He moved in closer. Not sure if he'd imagined it.

'Oi butt, thought you needed the bog.'

There she was. Penny sat on the grass holding another young girl's hand, smiling sweetly. The setting looked like the grounds outside. Oak trees and sycamore framed the large group of children. Although she looked younger, hair perhaps a different colour; hard to say with a black-and-white photo. She smiled at him from the past. He looked down. The framed picture had a date, *Sep 1975*.

He turned to the boy stood further down the corridor, with his hands pushed into his khaki bomber jacket. He eyed up Gethin with suspicion.

'Have a look at this photo for me.'

'Ahh man, don't be a dick, if old rattlesnake finds me gone.' He pulled his finger across his neck and made a cutting sound.

Good name for her, he thought. 'It'll be worth a pound note?'

The boy scowled at Gethin, then sauntered up to him.

'See that girl there? Do you know her?' He pointed to Penny in the photograph.

Still with his hands deep in his pockets, the boy shook his head.

'Nope.'

He pointed to the girl who sat next to Penny with long blonde hair. 'What about her?'

The boy stared at the photo for some time. 'What about her??'

Well, do you know her?

'Yeh, my older brother fancied the pants of her, Mun.'

Gethin turned and looked down at him waiting for him to disclose a name.

'No one talks about ur you knaw. Yu can't go round flapping yur gob about ur Buttie. Rumours as it, if you say ur name you'll be jinxed. I bet old rattlesnake didn't even realise when she put that picture up who she was.'

Gethin frowned and nodded. 'What if you whispered it?'

'What's it worth?'

Another pound note.

'Tidy.' The boy leaned over and whispered her name 'Penny Hughes!'

Gethin pulled back and stared at the boy, his eyes simmering with low level annoyance.

'Look again.' He pointed to the girl sat on the grass with Penny. 'I mean her.'

'Ah man, I'm telling yu that's ur name.' He prodded at her picture. And tutted.

'Where is Penny now?'

The boy looked at Gethin through slit, suspicious eyes. 'Yu fucking kidding me. Give us my cash. I need to get back for the snake starts fanging out.'

Gethin pulled two-pound notes out of his wallet.

'Jeez, Mickey Mouse wallet. Like t-ang out with the yung uns do yu?' The boy snatched the money and grunted something as he lurched away back down the corridor.

Gethin called after him. 'My girlfriend bought it for me!'

The boy lifted his middle finger at Gethin as he continued down the corridor and round the corner.

Gethin stood staring at the photo for a while. Was it possible the boy had made a mistake? Gethin unconsciously shook his head. He'd seemed pretty sure. If the other girl was Penny, who was the woman found dead at Dulwich Park who sat next to Penny in the photo? Gethin rubbed at his temple. The ring worn on the murdered girl's finger said Penny. H. He looked at his watch. There wasn't much time, and he needed the toilet. Now he moved quicker. He knew things had just become more complicated. Much more complicated.

He returned and started on the second filing cabinet. This time he was sharper, more focused. He pulled records out, scanning like a bird of prey. In the second drawer, he found old records of children who had lived at the institution. They were ordered alphabetically. Gethin wasn't sure how far back the files went. He fingered through the tags, searching for surnames beginning with 'H'. There was Hack, Harris, Harrow, no Hughes. Gethin wanted to roll a smoke but continued his search. He squeezed his eyes shut and then opened them to relieve the strain, a ring of dull ache around each eye.

Each file he retrieved contained a history of individual children going back to when they first entered the care system, including photographs. Yet, he still couldn't find any other evidence that proved someone called Penny had attended Radcliffe.

He went through several drawers and covered surnames from A-Z, suspecting they could have filed some under the incorrect letter. There was nothing. He sat back in his chair, exasperated. He was no wiser as to who *she* was. The girl found under the azaleas at Dulwich Park. She'd existed, and she'd been at Radcliffe and a club called Makos, and possibly been friends with another girl at Radcliffe, who went by the name Penny. His head ached. A coldness spun down his spine as he considered with more certainty that someone, somewhere, might have reason to conceal this young woman's identity.

Gethin rolled a smoke and sniffed along it before slipping it into the inside pocket of his jacket pocket for later. His eyes darted towards the other photo frames, gathering dust against the wall. He glanced at his watch before leaping from his chair. Perhaps there were other photos of the girls, further proving their presence at Radcliffe. With deft fingers, he flicked through the photo frames. He found nothing. For a moment he thought about how lost he was becoming in these strange loops of truth and untruth. The word "palters" came to mind. He slouched in the chair, knowing he didn't have much time left. Only then did he pay attention to the boxed files, stacked in front of him, in plain sight, yet so invisible.

He leaned forward to read the scribbles in pen on their spines. They appeared to be dated. Two yearly finance accounts. Gethin peered towards the door. Would he risk it? He had ten to fifteen minutes left. At least he'd hear her brusque quick steps down the old stone stairs. He moved like an arrow forced from its bow. He shut the door to the small room, grabbed one box, and opened it.

The paperwork, to his surprise, wasn't in any order. Bunched together over a two-year period. He flicked through receipts, invoices, charitable donations listed and logged on pieces of card, which were signed. The box he had picked up was from April 1976 to April 1977. the visible generosity of local businesses to the homes, who had contributed televisions, tape recorders, garden furniture and games for the children, surprised him.

He came across two sealed A4 brown envelopes with the word "private" scribbled across the front of them. The sound of him clearing his throat seemed like an intrusion in the silence. As if the room itself objected to him being there.

Could he peel back the glued flap of the envelope without ripping it? He tried until the sound of paper slowly tearing caused him to cave in and tear at it without care. Inside he found Radcliffe headed paper, listing many expenses and donations.

He scanned down the list of company names, then moved onto the next page. He went to flick onto the third page when he stopped. Towards the bottom of the page, in almost illegible handwriting, was the name of a company, *Black-tip Construction Ltd*. The company had made a large donation to Radcliffe: £150. Mr Wayne. H. Thomas had signed alongside the generous amount. Gethin sniffed. Rubbed his nose. Back then, Mr Thomas, the superintendent, managed and ran Radcliffe Children's Home. So why did it make him feel so damn uneasy?

Another sizeable sum of money, another charitable donation of £145. In the space of a few months, two substantial amounts of money had come into the home from the same company. Without looking further, he took the receipts pages from the pile of paperwork, folded them, and dropped them into the front pocket of his satchel. He closed the box file and placed it back amongst the others on the table. As he put his jacket on, Olivia wrapped the door twice and walked in. She looked around the room, then back at the door. She smiled sweetly, like gone-off meat, at Gethin.

'I see you're a good timekeeper, Mr James, bravo.'

She scanned the room again as if checking nothing looked out of the ordinary, then waited as Gethin buckled his satchel. He followed her out and stood waiting whilst she locked the door behind them.

'Did you find what you needed for your research?' asked Olivia as they climbed the stairs.

'Yes, I did. Thank you, this is such an interesting building too. Lots of lovely original features' He knew he was pushing close to the edge. 'And some of those older framed photos in the corridor. This place must hold a lot of memories for some. I'm quite taken by this place.'

Olivia stopped walking and turned. She perused his face as if inspecting a child up to no good. Then she smiled. A smile that only reached her small, snubby nose.

'That would be down to me. I found some old photos in that very room, stacked and covered up. Forgotten. I cleaned a few of those gilt frames up and found a place for them in the corridor. Someone needs to make this place look more respectable.' She smiled. This time with self-admiration then continued with her quick march along the corridor.

'Yes, I think I've seen one of them. Continued Gethin following her. You've done a fine job, I must say. I was wondering about something. Something you might be able to help with.'

'Mmm, really. Now. Please be quick. The riff raff will be back very soon.'

'Have you ever heard of a Penny? '

Olivia stopped; her body stiffened ahead of him. She pivoted on her small, neat heels and glared towards Gethin. Her mouth suddenly appearing unnatural, pulled across her face in a snake like smile. Any minute a forked tongue would slice through the air towards him.

'WHO ARE YOU Mr James, and WHY are you really here?'

'Researching the demographics of children who come into the care system.'

Her eyes, like round beads of blackness, seemed to suck in the light. Shroud him in further darkness. She didn't believe him anymore.

'You have no business coming here and asking such questions. I know your type. Trying to cause trouble for this wonderful establishment. Please leave right this minute.'

She marched down the main corridor, Gethin close behind. He couldn't bring himself to apologize to the acrid woman. He heard the familiar buzz sound and pushed the heavy door open. The door clicked shut behind him as he left the building. He didn't look back. Imagined her stood there like a gatekeeper. A warrior unknowingly protecting something dark and ominous.

Once outside, Gethin took a deep breath, inhaling the crisp fresh air. He heard gravel being kicked up, then showering back to the ground in a repetitive fashion. It was the boy from the corridor, his worn jacket zipped up, hood up as if the weather threatened something more dangerous. He smirked at Gethin.

'Off then, are you? Old rattlesnake got to you, eh?'

Gethin grinned. 'Nah, I've experienced worse.'

The boy grinned. His stained and crooked teeth more visible.

'Gotta fag I can ave?'

Gethin went to say "no" but didn't. He pulled out the one he'd rolled earlier and held it out. The boy sauntered up and took it off him. He took his lighter out of his pocket.

'She killed urself in his bloody study like.'

He leaned in to take a light off Gethin, then gestured towards the more modern annexe on the side of the old building.

'Hung herself...'

'Penny, you mean?'

'Yup! They tried telling everyone she had died cos of some heart mutter. But we knew that ain't the truth.'

Gethin frowned and stared at the young lad. 'Heart murmur you mean, son.'

He shrugged. 'Whatever it fucking is. She was dead as a rusty nail and they lied to everyone bout it.'

'I was only a dwytty when it happened. I remember my brother being well sad like. We were told if we went gossiping bout her ghost would aunt us.' He scanned the building as he spoke, as if even being an older teenager the thought of it still haunted him.

Do you remember the carer everyone called Nonnie?

'Yeh, I do. He chortled. she taught me a few Italian words when I was young like. She always had these sweets called ...'

143

'Sherbet pips?' Gethin replied.

The lad raised his eyebrows at Gethin. Either wondering how he knew or annoyed he'd interrupted his regaling of a fond memory.

'What's her real name, do you know?'

'You're cracking me up now, mate.'

'Nonnie is her real name. Wait a minute.' He pinned his lips together as if trying to remember a name. 'That's it. Bloody ell. I remembered cos I stole one of her lanyards. Had a little crush on er see. Nonnie Iriti.'

He sucked on the end of the cigarette and blew out hoops of grey smoke up into the air above his head.

'I remember ur saying it means Helen in Greek.' He grinned a wide, toothy smile. Pleased with himself.

Before Gethin could ask any questions, several minibuses drove up the drive behind one another. They slowed as they approached the gravelly carpark. The first driver waved at the boy. Smiled. The shrill sounds of children's voices breaking the silence that crept around the buildings and its grounds.

'Gotta go and help get them off the bus. See yu but. Thanks for the smoke.'

Gethin stood for a moment watching as buses parked up. Youngsters of varying ages sprawled out of them, smiling and laughing. Before anyone started asking questions as to who he was and why he was there, he turned, kept his head down, and walked straight out of the gates and down the driveway. Until the children's voices were nothing more than gentle echoes on the wind, and the building receded, diminished by the dark shapes of trees and foliage and shadows behind him.

He rolled another smoke, walking back into town and considered the revelations given by the strange boy at the home. Could he believe him? And if a girl by the name of Penny Hughes had killed herself on the grounds of Radcliffe, where were her files? And why had she killed herself? Had the ring with Penny scribed into it belonged to her?

Gethin looked at his watch as he arrived outside the station. He had ten minutes. He bought himself a baguette roll and climbed the steps to the platform. The train pulled into the station, rumbling and screeching. He stood from the bench and brushed the little breadcrumbs from his lap. They scattered across the floor, the slightest burst of wind catching them and displacing them further afield. Gethin scrunched the empty wrapper and shoved it into his pocket before stepping onto the train. He needed to find Nonnie Iriti, and fast.

14

Angela

Angela stood in her small hallway watching as the patterned glass of the door smeared and distorted the shape of someone stood outside. She could hear her own breathing funnel through her nostrils. It was seven o'clock, and dark grew outside. She tapped her hand against her thigh fearful of who it might be. What if it was...

Another knock. 'Hello Angela. Is that you? It's Veronica.'

Veronica. Shit? Angela glanced down at her old grey joggers and stained blue sweatshirt. She swept a few loose strands of her blonde hair behind her ears, thinking what a mess she looked.

She opened the door.

'Hello.' Angela tried to hide her surprise.

Veronica stood with a large plate covered in foil in one hand and a leather holdall slung over her shoulder. She wore exquisite cream joggers and a matching hoodie: fine merino wool, perhaps? The growing darkness outside framed Veronica's body.

'A thank you for the other day. My favourite. It's still warm. Hasn't

146

been out of the oven long.' She glanced towards the bag which rested on her hip, her face twitched a little.

'And a bottle of chianti and some cheese for us. I hope you like red?'

Angela nodded. She couldn't remember the last time someone had made such a gesture of appreciation towards her before. She fiddled with the door latch, wondering what to say until she realised Veronica was waiting to be invited inside.

'How bloody stupid of me! Come on in.'

Angela led Veronica into the kitchen, her shoulders tense. Only a few days ago, she vowed never to be within a metre of her again.

'Yew. Is this how they left it for you?'

'Pardon?' Angela turned around to see Veronica eyeing up the mustard walls and black gloss skirting boards of her kitchen.

'It's horrendous, isn't it?'

'So were the previous tenants. Gave Lisa a terrible time. Truly vulgar family.'

Angela sniffed. She wondered if they had judged her in the same way given her stress levels the day she'd moved in. *Perhaps the house attracted women like me?*

Angela forced a smile and took the covered plate from Veronica. She couldn't find words to respond to Veronica's historical account of life at number ten.

'How do you live in it?' Continued Veronica.

Angela felt agitation creep up her spine. 'I don't live in it. I live with it because it's better, much better than what I lived with before.'

Veronica raised an eyebrow 'I see.' She paused. 'Seems this street attracts women like us.'

Angela wanted to kick herself. She realised her comment had given away far more than she had intended.

'What's this?' Her eyes fell to the plate she'd taken from Veronica.

'Oh. Pizza with anchovies for the children?'

Angela tried to hide her bemusement. It was clear Veronica spent little time with children. It was unlikely that any child, any normal child, would like pizza with anchovies. Before she could say something, Joel strode into the kitchen, curiosity licking his features. He stopped. Looked up at Veronica who towered over him. Then he glanced towards his mum, his emerald eyes glistening.

'Wow. You're the one who fighted on the street weren't you? And my mum had to come and rescue you.'

Angela saw that brief twitch of discomfort again as Veronica opened her mouth to respond to Joel, then thought better of it.

'My mum doesn't like you?'

'I have pizza?' Veronica's voice crackled like shiny sweet wrappers trapped inside a tightened fist.

It was the first time Angela heard anything near nervousness in Veronica's voice.

Joel continued to tilt his head as he searched Veronica's features. He didn't seem much impressed. Angela wanted the ground to open and whip her away.

'Joel. Don't be so rude. You mustn't say things like that. Apologise right now.'

Angela watched as his large, confused eyes danced between herself and Veronica. Then he shimmied up to her and whispered.

'I don't know her name, Mum?'

'I'm Veronica, but you can call me Roni.'

He grinned. 'Thank you for the pizza, Roni. I love pizza.'

Angela doubted he would love pizza with anchovies.

Roni nodded her head. Then laughed. A laughter that shot up from deep inside, like a burst pipe. 'You're an honest boy aren't you, Joel?'

'Yeh. Not like my dad.'

Angela placed the plates down a little heavier than intended onto the kitchen side and spun round. It made her feel a little off balance.

'Joel, go to the room and ask your sister to help set the table please.'

Jason slouched away into the room. Angela peeled the foil off the top of the pizza and begun to cut it into slices. She could sense the troubled silence in her small kitchen as Veronica took the wine, cheese, biscuits and even a few serviettes from her bag. Somehow, the considered gesture made Angela feel worse. In that moment she wanted to drop kick her son out the window. She shook her head a little unconsciously.

'And that's why I don't want children.'

Angela turned her head towards Veronica, relieved to see the corners of her lips turned up with bemusement. It was like an amber light slowly changing green.

'Yeh. They know how to embarrass the hell out of you.'

For the next five minutes, except for needing to know where crockery and cutlery were, a silence fell between the women as they busied themselves preparing the food and drink. Angela washed and chopped a quick salad whilst Veronica poured wine into glasses and set the cheese on a board with crackers.

There was something about the situation, preparing food in her kitchen with another woman that felt foreign to Angela. Uncomfortable even. She tried to make less noise and be more careful, each move she made felt exposed and on show. She pulled at the cutlery drawer, despite its damaged runner, with little sound. Used a lighter hand to take cutlery from it. Placed used cutlery into the metal sink avoiding the crash of metal hitting metal. Was this normal?

Angela reminded herself that only a couple of days ago, before the weird incident in Cardiff, she vowed she wouldn't step within a metre or so of Veronica again. And here was Veronica once again well within that distance, and this time stood in her kitchen. Preparing food, she'd made to eat with them.

Fate seemed to play a bizarre part in bringing them together.

'There. Perfect. This Brie looks delicious don't you think?'

Angela nodded. She couldn't remember the last time she ate it. Colin detested the stuff.

Despite the sudden appearance and show of appreciation for her help the other day, Angela knew she still didn't trust Veronica. This sudden appearance at her door seemed premature—somewhat out of character for someone like Veronica. She felt a similar way to how she'd felt the day Gladys had turned up uninvited at her house. *Was this perhaps another example of how people behaved on an estate? Or was her mistrust of others getting the better of her again?*

Angela swallowed, reminded herself that it did her no good thinking this way. The gesture, after all seemed considered. Generous even.

Half an hour later, Catherine who had said little at the dinner table left saying she was going round a friend's house. Angela didn't ask her when she would be back. And didn't protest when she had Daisy Duke on her shoulder again, despite the restrained look of horror on Veronica's face.

Joel, on the other hand, chatted away a while longer and filled the silences with incessant talk of his new friends on the street. Then, he'd disappeared upstairs to change into his pjs and have some time playing with his Lego before bedtime.

Roni stood and gathered the plates.

'Really, there's no need to do that.'

Roni paused. 'I appreciate you not mentioning to the others about what happened the other day.'

'I said I wouldn't.' Angela wondered if she should tell Veronica that she'd purposely avoided all of them since the party. She decided against it. Was there any point? She would only start asking questions. And questioning wasn't something Angela appreciated right now.

'The thing is Sophie's not good at the moment. We're all worried about her. And something like this. It might well… make her worse.'

Angela found Veronica's words difficult to believe. Worry wasn't exactly how Angela would have described Veronica's behaviour the night of the party.

'If the truth be known, Sophie's husband died of cancer. He'd been the love of her life. Their son is all she has now. The pain of losing her husband has made her more vulnerable recently. It was the anniversary of his death a few days before Lisa's party. And Sophie she just isn't herself right now because it.'

Veronica's words drifted into the background as Angela's mind filled with snapshots of the strange events at Lisa's party. Sophie amid it. The large and frightening man at the window. How he had later stood at the door and asked for Sophie. He'd claimed she had invited him.

Maybe Veronica had been trying to protect Sophie. Keep her from harm. Angela considered the possibility that her opinion of Roni had allowed her to see and judge the events of the evening through a tinted lens. And not seen what was really going on.

'Poor Sophie. That's awful. She seems so lovely too.'

'Not all the time,' quipped Veronica as she carried plates into the kitchen and returned with the bottle of wine.

Roni topped up their glasses as she spoke. 'Obviously, I'd prefer it you didn't let on that you know about her husband.'

'My lips are sealed.'

Roni smiled.

'I noticed you have a chess board. Do you play?'

Angela frowned. Surprised by the sudden change in conversation.

'Yes, I do. Usually against myself.'

'Really. That can't be much fun. Let's play. I love the game.'

'Okay.'

'Used to belong to the chess club in university.'

'University. That's impressive.' Angela felt a pang of envy. Before she'd met Colin that had been her dream. To go to university and do

Fashion Design. Of course, all that changed soon after meeting Colin. Her proximity to him had eroded much of her confidence. The last years living with him she'd felt robotic and detached from herself. It had been so much easier for him when her father had died, leaving her feeling alone and trapped. Even the house she'd inherited from her deceased parents had gone. Colin had squandered the lot on fast cars and prostitutes.

'Angela, you, okay?' The sharpness of Roni's voice pulled Angela back into the present.

'Yes. Fine.'

'There were only two of us on the course. Females I mean. And then she dropped out half-way through. It was hell being the only female, but I came out with a first.'

'And I'm guessing after the other day, you now work in Cardiff?'

Roni nodded, 'Yes. PR manager. Had to work twice as hard as any male there too, to get to a managerial position. What about yourself?'

'No, not for me. My children need me home with them.' She couldn't be sure if Roni believed her. Roni was a very shrewd woman. And imagined not much would get past her.

To her surprise, Roni just nodded and smiled.

'Shall we play then? I warn you I'm good.'

'Absolutely.'

'I'm not so bad myself.'

With what remained of the bottle of chianti, the women sat at the coffee table. Angela sat on the edge of the sofa and poured into both their glasses. Roni sat on a cushion on the floor and arranged some of the chess pieces on the board.

After ten minutes, the women fell into bouts of quiet concentration as they moved and lost pieces across the board. Angela wanted to win the game. She doubted she would as Roni moved her pieces with confidence. She heard Joel's playful sound effects as they tumbled down the stairs and dissected the silent concentration around them. Angela glanced up to see Roni's loose sleeve threaten to knock her wine glass. 'Watch yourself?'

Veronica moved her arm quick enough to spare the spillage.

'Angela. I want to apologise?'

'For what?'

'Come on. You know. The way I've behaved towards you recently. I shouldn't judge a book by its cover.'

'Ouch,' responded Angela. 'What's that meant to mean?'

'No, not like that.'

Angela sighed and took a gulp of her wine. She knew how she came across these days, defensive and brittle. Her own lack of respect had affected how others saw her. Most of the time she found solace in avoiding people altogether. A habit that started a few months after meeting Colin.

Veronica sighed. 'Look, we all behave strangely when we're avoiding or hiding something.'

This time Angela's eyes peered straight at Roni as if she was examining in depth each fleeting expression of her face. *What the hell? Is she implying she's uncovered something about me or is she trying to tell me something about herself?*

For a while, both women played the game in silence.

'Do your parents live near?'

Angela bounced back as she took Roni's rook.

'I'm impressed.'

Veronica took her move with the knight.

'No. They don't. My father job took them to London.'

Angela nodded and moved another piece. 'Checkmate.' She sensed the reluctance in Roni's voice to talk about herself.

Veronica looked down and frowned. 'You're the first person to beat me in two years.'

'There's more to me than what's read on the cover,' retorted Angela.

'Ding dong.' Veronica raised her glass to Angela and finished what remained of her wine.

'It's funny. Gladys said to me the night of the party that in time I might grow to like you — that we're actually quite alike.'

Veronica rolled her head back and laughed out loud. 'She said that to me, too.'

The air around them settled into silence again before Angela coughed.

'Can I ask you something Veronica?'

Roni grinned. 'Depends on what it is?'

'I saw you outside on the kerbside late one-night last week. It's odd because it looked like you were wearing a wig.'

Veronica shifted in her seat, straightened her back. 'A wig?' She grinned and shook her head as if puzzled by the suggestion. 'That's odd. Not me. Never worn one except for fancy dress. Are you sure it was me?'

'Well. I'm pretty sure. Perhaps with the stress of moving and everything...' Angela flicked her hand as if to brush her own question away.

'I guess it doesn't matter.' She smiled.

As Angela placed the chess pieces back into the box, Roni looked at her watch, then stood up.

'Did Lisa tell you she saw someone snooping around your house the other day?'

'Yes.'

Roni nodded and Angela had that feeling again, as if Roni wanted to say more.

'Lisa rang me in work. She thought he was behaving a bit suspiciously. He hasn't tried coming back?'

'No, not that I know of. Why?'

'No, nothing.'

Were Roni's questions trying to determine if the man in question had anything to do with her? Did they suspect it might be an ex? She couldn't understand why Roni didn't just come right out and bloody ask the question. She tightened her jaw, trying to push the thoughts away.

'Well. Time to go. Big meeting to prepare for tomorrow. I'd like to play chess again so I can beat you next time.'

Angela felt the red wine loosening her usual hypervigilance. Or it could have been the couple of vodkas she'd drank earlier. Yet, through the haze she knew Roni was lying about the night she saw her stood under the streetlight. After Colin, Angela knew how to read a lie well. She'd had enough practise. Gladys had said they were alike. They both kept secrets.

15

Angela

It had been someone's birthday, Ted's wife. The film reel of Angela's mind was sketchy in places. She didn't go out that often, but Ted's wife had invited Angela to her birthday celebrations in front of Colin. She remembered feeling embarrassed. *Fucking embarrassed!* It had been difficult for Colin to decline the invitation as they stood in a *Ralph Lauren* clothes store, him with several items of clothing folded over his arm.

As she stood staring at her reflection in the mirror, memories rolled in on waves that could drown her. She twisted a small strand of blonde hair as she recalled the awful evening.

He had taken the offer graciously from Ted's wife … she frowned trying to remember her name … Rosie maybe. She had a rare social evening out with her husband, who'd always preferred her at home with the children. She had worn a dress, a little dated, but she had updated it with a few well-placed darts and a new hemline.

Before leaving the house, she recalled how she'd fretted about walking in stilettos. It had been so long! The shoes, she would later realize, were the least of her worries.

Angela looked away from the mirror as she recalled the rest of the story. She moved to her bed and flopped down wondering why she had taken Roni's invitation up after all.

It was a stupid idea.

Roni had called her the day after her unexpected visit with pizza and wine, inviting Angela out for an evening with all of them. She had VIP tickets for a new club in town. She'd hesitated. After five minutes of Roni's art of persuasion she'd relented. And for a moment, as she listened to Roni's evening plans over the phone dared to feel something akin to excitement.

That night, she'd sat with Colin excited to be out in a nightclub drinking and talking with other adults for a change. She'd been presented to others, generously welcomed into the group and socialised with natural ease. Until the moment Ted took her hand and gestured towards the colourful flashy dancefloor. She'd turned towards Colin, flickers of light from the disco ball had illuminated the darkness she had witnessed in his eyes. She'd hoped... looked for his approval. It had been an uncomfortable moment.

And in his usual casual manner when in company, Colin had smiled at Ted, then turned to Angela.

'Why you asking me, honey, if you want to dance with Ted, go ahead, it's just a dance, love!'

It was then she had felt the heavy heel of his cowboy boot, hidden under the table, grinding into her toes until they felt they might break. All the time gesturing for her to take his friend's offer. She declined Ted's offer and watched as he'd shrugged his shoulders and walked off in disappointment.

The rest of the evening she had sat in mute, nervous confusion, detached from the rest of the group. Colin, on the other hand, had joked with everyone and even swaggered onto the dancefloor with several of the other wives in the group. He'd appeared every bit the loving husband as he waved over at her and gestured if she needed another drink.

She'd appeared anti-social to others. But his actions had seeped fear into every limb, immobilizing her. Her toes felt almost broken, yet it was the hollowness and hurt that sat in the pit of her stomach she found difficult to manage. She had become damaged goods.

For weeks later, she'd pulled details of the evening apart. *Was I flirting, not behaving appropriately? Was I making a fool of myself and not realising? Am I unattractive?*

Angela shook her head, trying to dispel the terrible memories from her mind. Then, as if motivated by something very different, she shot off the bed, grabbed her stilettos and handbag, and marched out of her bedroom.

Ten minutes later, Angela stood outside Roni's front door. She rubbed the soft skin of her lips together and fiddled with the collar of her jacket. Roni's shadow appeared behind the door. Angela tried to calm her nerves with a sharp, deep inhale of cool air. It didn't help much.

The door opened.

Roni smiled. 'Hi, you're the first to turn up. Come on in.'

Angela offered a brief smile in return as she stepped across the threshold into Roni's large hallway, her heels clicked onto the gleaming large white tiles. She glanced around, trying not to look too surprised. It was like stepping into fantasy. Everything was white. The floor, the wall, the carpet on the staircase and the ornate console against the wall. Angela's face must have said it all.

'Yes. I always have the same reaction from mothers. You've probably worked out I don't do children. I've never seen myself wiping snotty noses and dirty backsides.' She pinched her lips and shook her head to further express the fact.

'Remind me never to turn up with Joel. You'd have a serious meltdown.'

Roni laughed. 'I do let Lisa's and Sophie's children come round. I love them enormously, but I must admit I always make them come round to the back door and into the kitchen. The others tell me I have OCD.'

Angela stood there and lifted her shoulders.

'Anyway. Follow me. There's champagne to drink for us ladies tonight.'

Roni's kitchen had a large oak table at one end. On top of a vase full of white lilies, their orange pollen powdered the smooth wood at the base of the vase. The fragrance strong and almost overbearing. She hung her black patent bag on the back of one of the dining chairs.

On the other side of the kitchen, Veronica opened a glass cabinet and began taking out several glass flutes and lined them up on the granite work top.

'I'm pleased you came, Angela. You sounded uncertain when I spoke to you on the phone. I guess it was quite short notice?'

'I don't know, perhaps it will be good for me. It's not like anything bad is going to happen.' Angela rubbed her nose as she spoke and wondered if it was the pollen.

Roni paused and turned towards Angela. Her forehead mapped with small hairline fractures.

'That sounds like you're not sure?' Roni turned her back on Angela and walked towards her fridge. 'You understand that what happened at Lisa's party was nothing, right?'

Angela's eyebrows furrowed down towards her eyelashes.

Why would Roni say this?

She had apprehensions. She didn't want to mention the fact that it scared her shitless that there might be a sliver of a chance she might bump into Colin.

'Not at all. I'd forgotten about it.'

Roni reached into the fridge as if she hadn't registered Angela's response. She retrieved two bottles of champagne and put them on the side as the sound of the doorbell chimed in the sudden blanket of silence between the women. Angela watched as Roni clicked across her tiled kitchen floor and out into the hallway. She heard the door open and close. A familiar voice drifted along the hallway.

A minute later, Gladys waddled into the kitchen as if she had the most important job to attend to. Angela couldn't help but smile.

'Well, hello, lovely.' She turned to Roni. 'You not tell me Angela go too?'

Roni rolled her eyes. 'I must have forgotten.'

'You bloody not forget a thing.' Gladys put the cake down on the table and smiled at Angela.

'Hi. My, that smells bloody gorgeous, Gladys. What cake is it?'

'I Bake a medovik cake, and one for children too! *They* love my medovik cake.' She extended the vowel for emphasis as she narrowed her eyes towards Roni.

'Gladys, I know it's your speciality, but really, I can't help it if I don't like honey.'

'Pah,' exclaimed Gladys as she flicked her head feigning offence. She took a small bottle of what looked like alcohol from one of the deep pockets of her long cardigan and dribbled it over the cake.

'Good grief. I hope you didn't do that with the children's cake?'

'No, they prefer vodka!'

'Gladys … you can't say that.'

'Tsssht, I say always what's in my mind, Bossy!'

Gladys sliced the cake, plated it, and offered it to the ladies. Her expression implied they would be rude not to eat it.

'I pour lemon liqueur on top. It make it taste even better.'

Angela didn't mind, she loved cake.

'Gladys, Angela is saying she's not sure about coming out with us tonight?'

'Well, I didn't quite say...' Before Angela could finish, Gladys interrupted.

'Angela, you be fine. Is something else worry you?' Her eyes flickered towards Roni.

'You stay for few drinks with us. Then see how you feels?'

Angela nodded. Bemused again my Gladys's verb confusion.

Gladys nodded in agreement. 'Come on dear, a glass of champagne?' She grinned. 'Or I can go and get my ...'

'Nooo' both women responded together. Starting the night with Gladys's vodka read like disaster.

'You decide my vodka not good enough now. Eh?'

'It's too good, Gladys.' Angela looked down at her painted nails. She'd already chipped some. Not a good omen. Before she looked back at Gladys with a smile.

'Your vodka should have a written warning with it.' Roni said, as she forced the cork from a champagne bottle. It shot across the kitchen like a bullet just skimming Gladys's head bun.

'Cyka,' Gladys wailed as she felt across the top of her head.

'What did you say?'

'That's bitch in Russian, Ang ... I'm used to it.'

Gladys scowled at Roni.

'Gladys, it was an accident.'

Five minutes later, Lisa let herself in through the kitchen patio doors, bringing with her a rising sense of excitement for the evening ahead. The ladies greeted each other warmly, forgetting the cork incident.

'Oh Gladys, the children have already tucked into your cake and have their pjs on,' said Lisa, smiling.

'Well, I best be gone now. I have a film for the children to watch this evening, *E.T.*; a pirate copy.' She lifted her eyebrows for effect. 'You have VHS, not that Betamax rubbish, eh?'

Lisa grinned, showing her perfect gleaming white teeth. 'Yes, Gladys, but really. Who do you know who does pirate copies?'

Gladys tapped her nose. 'Roni not the only one.'

Angela shifted in her chair and fiddled with the cuff of her batwing sleeve. Why was she having that feeling again? That these women had something to hide.

'I'm guessing Sophie hasn't dropped Jason off at yours yet then,' asked Roni with a hint of judgement in the tone.

'Not yet.'

'She's never on time. At least some things are consistent and reliable with her.'

Gladys sighed as she wrapped her woollen cardigan around her protruding stomach. 'Okay. I go before children eat all my cake. Have a good time, and Angela, you change your mind and go, yes?'

As the sound of the door closing drifted from the hallway, Lisa turned to Angela.

'You're not coming out?'

'I don't know I…'

Lisa took Angela by the hands. 'Please come, Angela. I think it'll be good for you.' Lisa peered towards Roni for a few seconds. 'I can always come back with you if you don't like it. Plenty of clients tomorrow, so it wouldn't be a problem.' She waved Angela's hand up and down as she spoke. 'Please.'

Angela couldn't refuse. 'Okay. Yes.'

Twenty minutes later Sophie burst through the patio doors in her usual late fashion. She howled with excitement when she saw all the ladies. Angela thought she looked stunning; her dark glossy hair tumbled over a fitted khaki jumpsuit. She wore large hoop earrings and several bangles on her wrist.

Roni looked over and managed a smile. 'Only thirty minutes late.'

'You look stunning,' quipped Lisa as she stepped towards Sophie and gave her a hug.

'Thankyou.'

Veronica glanced at the clock. 'Okay. Now we're all here, I can finally ring for a taxi.'

As she left the room, Sophie took a chair next to Angela at the table. She squeezed Angela's hand.

'How is she, then?'

Lisa pulled a face.

'Oh, was I really that bad then? Joss sticks'. Sophie's voice fell to a flat whisper. 'Like I said the other day, babe. I thought she'd be cool about it. He was a nice guy. Didn't know what we...'

Lisa coughed into her clenched fist. Shook her head.

Sophie smirked and turned towards the glasses filled with champagne, which Roni had placed in the middle of the table on a silver tray. She stooped across and picked up a glass. 'Is this for me?'

'Yes. Drink up.' Lisa glanced over her shoulder.

Had she just told Sophie to shut up?

'I don't get it.' Angela piped up. Then hesitated. *Should she ask what was playing on her mind?* 'Even if you'd wanted to invite someone to Lisa's party, why would Veronica object?'

Sophie went to say something as Veronica walked back into the kitchen with her jacket and small silk purse.

'Done, booked for eight-fifteen, ladies.' She stopped and looked at the women. 'Everything okay?'

Lisa cleared her throat. 'Yep, all good. I was just telling the ladies I bumped into Gethin on the street. Didn't look his usual self? Pacing back and forth on Dina's path as if he couldn't make up his mind where he was going.'

'I don't understand why he's here. Dina told me his parents live the other side of Cardiff in Penarth. Why doesn't he stay with them?'

'I don't know. Maybe he doesn't get on with them or something.'

Roni pulled her lips back tight against her teeth. 'I find it strange. Why here with Dina?'

Sophie knocked her champagne back in one. 'I'm sure Dina said they went to university together some years ago. Fuckinella. Who cares? He's hot.'

'Actually. The night of Lisa's party, I popped round to my house to check on the children and found Gethin carrying piles of things into Dina's garage. It looked like photo albums or files. Don't you think that's weird? It's not as if the house belongs to him.'

Lisa took a large gulp of her champagne and twisted the glass in her hand as if the thought had provoked anxiety within her.

'And the strangest thing is that afterwards he moved his car so close to the garage door his bumper must have been almost hitting the garage door. Of course, I couldn't be sure because it was dark, but it was like he was determined no one was going to get in there.'

Angela sensed her words had ruffled the ladies' feathers. She caught the flicker of eye contact between Lisa and Roni. The only one who appeared mildly concerned was Sophie who continued to fill her glass. Not that she needed it. Angela recognised she had already been drunk when she had arrived.

'Ok, ladies, let's not worry about strange neighbours for tonight. lipstick, money, perfume ... done!' Veronica clicked her clutch bag shut.

'I need the loo before we go', Lisa said. She darted toward the downstairs toilet.

'That's not a bad idea. My pelvic floor isn't what it used to be.' Angela's nerves were getting the better of her. She couldn't ease the growing tension that tangled her stomach.

164

'Come on, ladies, the taxi will be here soon. Angela, you can use the bathroom upstairs. It's the second door on the left.'

She nodded and made haste upstairs, wondering if her heels might mark the white carpet. 'Bloody ridiculous, Mun,' she muttered to herself as she hit the landing. For a moment she stood at the foot of the stairs, forgetting which door she'd been told was the bathroom. She screwed her eyes up and reached out towards the small glint of a metallic door handle in the darkness. Then fumbled across the wall to find a light switch.

The overhead lighting filled the room with a sudden brightness. Angela squinted for a moment before realising she was in Roni's bedroom. She almost screamed, had her brain not processed what she'd seen as quick as it did. An opened wardrobe door revealed a flesh-coloured mannequin. On its head a wig. The same wig Angela had seen Roni wear the night she stood outside her house with the others. Its copper strands glistened to the shoulders. Angela's fingers hit the switch, consuming the room with darkness again. The sound of her own heartbeat swooshed through her ears. She closed the door and returned downstairs, willing her heartbeat to slow and her bladder to hold out until they reached Cardiff.

The ladies were all stood waiting and ready in the lobby. Sophie touched up her lipstick in the mirror above the console table. She smiled at Angela's reflection as she descended the stairs.

Roni stood at the bottom of the stairs, holding Angela's jacket and bag. For a moment Angela thought Roni suspected something as she stood there watching Angela, her expression unreadable before passing her belongings. Heat rose to her cheeks as she slipped her narrow arm into the jacket.

'The taxi is here, ladies.'

And as if on cue, they heard the car horn, signalling it was time to leave.

Angela sighed with relief as they piled into the taxi and waited for Roni to hide her keys under the terracotta pot near the door.

Doors banged shut as the skies blotted dark ink blue. Angela pulled her jacket collar tight around her neck. A cat run out from the roadside; the taxi driver screeched its brake, thrusting them all forward. Everyone laughed except Angela. She shivered as the taxi moved off again, turned right and took them towards the night.

16

Angela

A slight drizzle dampened the air as the ladies clicked and chatted their way down St Mary's Street. Angela glanced behind her at the castle illuminated in the darkness giving it an eery still presence. Ahead of them, neon lights reflected shifting colour across the wet pavement, like tendrils creeping underfoot. Crowds of people stood in small raucous groups waiting to get into bars and clubs. The sound of music came in waves from every direction, like jumbled thoughts. With her arm looped into Lisa's, she felt each muscle in her body tighten against the bombardment to her senses.

They turned left halfway down St Mary's Street into a quieter side street. Roni walked a few steps ahead with a small card in her hand. A few metres away, two well-dressed bouncers stood outside a large glass doorway cordoned off with red ropes. An air of excited anticipation filled the air as the women approached the new stylish bar. Roni waved the VIP tickets towards the bouncer. He nodded. Unlatched a rope and let them through to the sound of disgruntled customers stood in the queue. They glided up the decadent glass panelled staircase towards the double doors above.

Sophie pushed the doors open with excited enthusiasm. A warmth gust of air hit their bodies in a quick sharp move, drawing them in like metal towards a magnet. The atmosphere was like nothing Angela could remember experiencing before.

Music danced above their heads as they pushed their way through the hot traffic of people towards the bar. Angela trailed behind and peered over heads, looking for a toilet sign.

The pungent smell of expensive perfume and aftershave hit the back of her throat. Opium, Dunhill, Anais Anais, and Poison. She recognised them all. For a moment, a light-headedness consumed her. She touched her neck as she swallowed.

The place was a kaleidoscope of moving colour and sound. Sheets of moving laser lights sliced through people's bodies, then shuddered with the beat of the music. On her far left the dancefloor, made up of illuminated white tiles, eagerly awaited company. For a moment, seeing it took her back to a memory she'd rather forget.

Yet, a subtle excitement trickled through her veins. She noted the sensation with caution as she approached the long rectangular bar towards the back of the club.

A few people waited like standing shadows for their doses of liquid to help forget something or other. She watched as they held their drinks above their head, scared to spill a drop.

Roni slithered sideways, like a pro, and reached the bar with little objection from the crowd. A barman approached her seconds later; she smiled and leaned towards him. It was impossible to hear what she had ordered. He raised his eyebrows towards her, then nodded and disappeared the other side of the bar. He reappeared a few minutes later, holding a bottle of Cristal. Angela gasped. These women squandered money.

The barman lined four flute glasses on the bar with such concentration it made Angela retrain a chuckle of bemusement.

Sophie leaned in towards Angela and Lisa.

'It's definitely different in here, eh?' her voice was a few decibels higher than usual. Lisa nodded. Angela smiled.

How would I know if it was different or not?

She looked up at Sophie. 'What do you mean?'

Sophie grinned. 'Look around you. So much confidence and I smell wealth. And they look so young. Look at him over there.'

She glanced towards the two young men talking animatedly near to where they stood. Both wore shirts with their sweaters loosely tied around their necks.

'It's like their dawns have broken with a promise of better things to come. Don't you feel it?'

Lisa gave Sophie a subtle nudge to the hip.

'I think you've just drank too much champagne.'

'Some of these men like something more than women... money, and that's perfectly fine by me.'

As Sophie spoke, she caught the attention of a young man with an expensive looking suit, also stood at the bar. She returned a smile showing of her perfect white teeth. *How does she ooze with confidence like that?*

Roni must have seen the exchange too and leaned in towards Sophie. Her expression had hardened. They exchanged words before Roni returned her attentions towards the barman.

Angela crossed her legs desperate for the toilet and a quieter space just for a moment.

She leaned in towards Lisa.

'Did you see a toilet on the way in?'

'Yes.' Lisa tiptoed and pointed to the far right of the dancefloor.

'Do you want me to come with you?'

Angela shook her head. 'No. I think I'll be fine.' She waded through the growing lines of people, around the edge of the dancefloor and into the toilets.

She sat on the toilet and wondered what Roni had said to Sophie at the bar? It's as if Roni always wanted to dampen her exuberance for life, belittle her in some way. Despite their newfound friendship, frustration rose like silver mercury, heating Angela's mood. She despised any form of control that one person had over another. And for one horrible moment, she wondered if Roni's invitation was driven by darker motives, which she didn't understand yet; something to do with what she'd seen and heard at Lisa's party.

Angela walked out of the toilets a few minutes later and scanned the club to get her bearings again when almost immediately she saw Roni, towering over most people, waving towards her.

'We've found our VIP seats the other side of the bar.'

'Okay.' Angela followed Roni to a booth, one of many that ran along the back wall of the club on a risen platform. Above the salt, thought Angela as she folded herself into the semi-circular seating with its deep red velvet upholstery.

Neon piping swirled on the wall above the booth and licked their skin, turning them into chameleons. It reminded Angela of the night she'd saw the women stand under the tangerine glow of streetlights masked in their own skin.

Sophie entertained them with funny stories about other students on her psychology course. Did her wildness make her a free soul? Someone who understood what it really meant to exist. Or was the course she'd embarked on a way of teaching herself? Angela pondered: compared to the other women, she appeared the most dangerous. The kind of dangerous that wasn't filled with unkindness or cruelty but full of loose and unpredictable actions and choices, all the same. They were all still laughing when a barman carried a silver tray topped with flutes and champagne approached the table.

'Did you order more champagne, Sophie?'

'Fuckinella Roni. Why do you always assume it's me?'

Roni pulled a face that showed Sophie's question was ridiculous.

Sophie grinned. Did she enjoy these games of discord that rankled between them? It seemed that way? Angela rubbed her head. This tendency to overthink would ruin her night if she wasn't careful.

'Ladies, compliments of Mr Parklane at the bar.'

Veronica scowled towards Sophie.

'Oh, stop it, Roni. Lisa and I were just joking about at the bar. I called him Mr Whitechapel. He said he rather considered himself a Mr Parklane.'

'And I have a feeling he might own this place, not sure why. Just occurred to me now, really.'

Everyone turned to look at Lisa. 'Seemed pleasant enough. Tell him we appreciate the kind gesture. Thank you.'

The bar man nodded at Lisa with a small smile and left them. Angela's eyes followed him towards the bar where he stopped and exchanged a few words with a good-looking man at the bar. Behind him stood another man, older, and slightly stooped. He leaned over and said something to Mr Parklane, sneered, then disappeared in a stooped, dishevelled sort of way that unsettled Angela.

'Angela, would you like the honour?' Roni passed the bottle to her.

'Me? Ok, if you insist.' As she poured, the atmosphere between the ladies seemed to crisp thin. A silence fell upon the ladies as they watched Angela fill each glass. She felt her hand tremble as she poured. The unshakable feeling that her muddied senses were preventing her from enjoying the evening. Was she reading too much into situations?

Then, without warning, he appeared next to the table. 'Evening ladies, mind if I join you?'

Before anyone had a chance to respond, Sophie patted the velvet seating next to her and invited him into their coven.

There was something about the way Sophie held herself, how she used her voice, when a good-looking man appeared nearby. Angela had witnessed it at Lisa's party. How close to jagged rocks would this man guide his mast, wondered Angela.

There was no doubt this man with his olive skin and almond-shaped eyes was handsome. However, as usual, Angela switched on to his every move, as was her habit. She watched as he stroked his glossed back hair with smooth manicured hands. His white teeth gleamed as he bore a smile into Sophie with a jaw line as sharp and clean as his suit. Angela saw through the whole goddam bullshit look of him and instinctively turned to watch Roni's response to his sudden appearance. Veronica raised an eyebrow. Apart from this, it was impossible to know what she thought.

He leaned in and said something to Sophie. She giggled as they both looked towards Veronica. *Jesus, she's mocking Roni right here, with him.*

Angela's foot rocked under the table. *Why oh why do I do things I know aren't good for me?*

Mr Park Lane raised his hand and glanced towards the barman who had served them earlier. He nodded and strode with an eager pace to their booth.

'Another bottle of Cristal for these beautiful ladies. Make sure the champagne is at nine degrees Celsius. Just a little warmer than the normal eight for these ladies.'

This time, Roni visibly rolled her eyes in disdain.

'There really is no need ...'

He considered Veronica for a moment then smiled.

'Yes, you're right. This has nothing to do with need. I *want* to. There's the difference?' He exposed his full set of whites with another smile.

Veronica shifted in her seat.

Something didn't feel right. His manner reminded her of Colin's. That smooth surface that hid so much below.

'Dom, isn't it? I haven't introduced you too my gorgeous friends.'

'This is Sharon,' Sophie gestured towards Roni. 'And this is Diane and Sarah.'

Angela opened her mouth to say something until she received a sharp kick in the ankle from Roni. She froze.

'My pleasure, ladies!'

'No, the pleasure's all mine,' responded Angela in a flat mocking tone that surprised even Roni.

She leaned in and whispered.

'Never ever kick me under the table like that again. Do you get me? And the last time I looked; my driving licence read Angela Webber not bloody Sarah.' She pulled away from Roni and smiled towards the others.

'Ladies.' The barman set yet another bottle of champagne onto the table and removed the empty bottle.

Dom went to take the bottle from the bucket.

'Please, Let me?'

Lisa stubbed her cigarette and picked up the bottle before Dom could respond. She placed her hand at its base and her other at the top of the bottle.

'I see my champagne is in expert hands?'

Lisa smiled and continued. She placed her thumb into the punt at the bottom of the bottle and spread her fingers around the edges.

It was difficult to determine how he felt about the gesture. His jaw tensed as he watched Lisa pour the expensive liquid into tilted glasses.

'Little frothing.' Lisa smiled.

'Server in your past life?' joked Dom.

'No, my husband loves champagne, as do I.'

Dom flinched; it was so subtle a response Angela might have missed it.

'Come on, ladies, let's toast. Before you lot completely devour me.'

'To wealth and success!' Dom raised his glass.

'I second that', responded Lisa.

They all raised their glasses, their thoughts transferring from one another like a charge of energy struggling through a faulty circuit.

'Do you own this club, Dom?' Asked Lisa, leaning slightly round Sophie to gain Dom's full attention.

He sipped his champagne slowly before responding.

'Yes, I do. Why do you ask?'

'No reason, other than—how does your business survive with this kind of generosity?'

He smiled wryly. 'Let's say I have a keen eye. I don't do this for many.'

Lisa nodded, slipped her Virginia slims into her small purse and clicked it shut. With a polite and sophisticated gesture, she slipped past Sophie and Dom to go to the toilet. They stood to let her pass; she brushed past Dom closer than necessary. Maybe it was just the alcohol.

A few minutes later Roni turned to say something to Angela. Her hand caught her drink, sending the glass sideways. Its contents spilled onto Angela's satin trousers. She yelped in surprise and shot to her feet, catching her thigh on the edge of the table.

'Oh no! Sorry.'

'Don't worry.' Angela looked down at the wet stains across the top of each trouser leg. It surprised her; She didn't put Roni down as someone that careless. She rubbed down her one thigh, knowing it really wasn't going to help much.

'They might have a hand dryer in the toilets. You could use that.'

'Yes, there are two.' Both women cast their eyes towards Dom as if he had no right to even comment.

He raised his hands and grinned at the women, as if he found their response amusing.

Angela slipped out from behind the table. Roni followed and picked up their handbags.

'I'll come with you.'

As they head towards the toilets, Angela wondered about Sophie left alone with Dom. She glanced back at them before entering the toilets. What she saw unsettled her—a lot.

Inside the toilets, Lisa was applying more lipstick, concentrating on her application. She didn't see them walk in.

'Now I remember who you remind me of?'

Hearing Angela's voice, Lisa snapped her head round. 'Toilet again?'

'I accidentally spilled my champagne on Angela.'

For a second, Lisa's eyes flickered before she spoke. 'Use the dryer. That will help. Might take a while to do each leg. Is it worth taking them off and drying them?'

Little sparks of panic shot from Angela's wide unblinking eyes. 'You for bloody real? Me. Stand here? In my knickers, drying my trousers?'

'She has a point, Ang. Be quicker to dry.'

'It's just a bloody drop of champagne, for Christ's sake. It's not going to harm me like.'

Lisa put her lipstick in her chain mail handbag and clicked it shut. 'Well, I'll leave you ladies to it. Sophie's out there by herself.'

Not quite, thought Angela.

As the door shut behind Lisa, Angela leaned in towards one of the wall dryers to dry her trousers.

'Sophie seems to have taken quite a liking to this Dom?'

'Most men make a bee-line for her.'

Angela knew this wasn't exactly the entire truth.

'Why did she lie about our names?'

'Sophie thinks it's a bit of fun, like the sort of thing you did as a

175

teenager!'

Angela's expression said it all.

'It's all right. We're all still learning to understand Sophie.'

After ten minutes, Angela's trousers were dry.

'Come on. Let's venture on that dance floor.'

There was something in the way she said it, tight like a cork in a bottleneck. Angela's eyes narrowed as she searched her face doubtful that Roni meant it.

Now busier than earlier, she followed Roni onto the dancefloor, the smoke machine churned out clouds of white that dried her throat and twisted and turned through throngs of moving bodies. Sheets of colour laser lights spliced through the smoky atmosphere. Everything looked abstract ... unreal.

Through the haze, Angela glimpsed something. She closed her eyes—opened them again. Was it trickery? Her own eyes playing a devilish game on her. Had she really seen Sophie and Lisa leaning together in front of Dom and French kissing? With her limbs immobilised by the spectacle, Angela squinted through spaces between bodies thinking, somehow, she'd made a mistake.

Roni grabbed at her wrist. 'Come on.'

Angela pulled at the neck of her sweater, waving it back and forth, to fan her chest with cool air. Small rivulets of sweat threaded down the small of her back to her knicker line. She grimaced, not liking the sensation.

Then a Kim Carnes track, "Bette Davies Eyes", came on and more people filled the dance floor. Swept by the music, a welcome distraction, Angela let herself go. Concealed by smoke and laser lights, she danced like she never had before. Within seconds, strands of her hair stuck to her hot cheeks. She closed her eyes and swayed her body as others danced around her. For the first time, she didn't mind the fleeting contact of skin on skin as her tensions ebbed away.

Then a hand grasped her wrist and forced her eyes open. She heard Roni's voice blow heat into her ear.

'We are leaving to go to another bar soon.'

Before she could respond, she felt a pull at her wrist as Roni pushed through the revellers. She found it hard to keep her balance as she stumbled to the edge of the dance floor. Heat and noise swamped her senses. She reached forward and held onto the back of a chair to steady herself. Only then did she glance across the heads of people seated at tables and towards the back of the club. She saw Sophie reach under the table for her handbag and grab her jacket to leave the booth. But, no Lisa.

As if time itself had slowed, Angela watched in horror as Dom grabbed Sophie's arm with such ferocity it almost knocked her off balance. Angela glanced around her in panic. *Why couldn't anyone see it?* Even people stood nearby failed to witness the unfolding situation. He yanked Sophie towards him until his lips almost touched the side of her face. What was he saying to her?

'We need to leave.'

'What the hell is going on?' Angela tugged her arm away from Roni's grip and glared at her.

'We need to get Lisa from the toilets now.'

Angela glared at Roni. She wanted answers but realised this wasn't the time to ask. She glanced towards the toilets and nodded. Whatever these women were doing could affect her own safety, too. Something she couldn't risk.

Roni pushed past people without apology, Angela followed. The music suddenly sounded less intrusive, further away, as if heard through a closed door. People's mouths moved, but she heard no spoken words. All she felt was a base that thumped in beat with her heart.

'Sophie,' Roni called as she waved her arm to get her attention.

Sophie clocked them and moved faster now; her eyes wide with fear.

'What's going on Sophie?'

'He knew what my name was, Roni. I swear he did. How could he?'

'So, he didn't...'

Sophie shook her head. 'I don't think so. He expected something in return for his champagne. We should get out of here.' Her words trembled and juddered to a whisper.

Roni sighed. 'Christ, Sophie. Why did you do it? I'll get Lisa. Take Angela. Hail a cab and wait for us.'

Sophie just stood there paralysed, as if not hearing what was being said.

'SOPHIE GO NOW.'

She gazed with a blank expression towards Roni. 'Sorry. Something is all wrong!'

Angela tugged at Sophie. 'Come on.' Her ears crackled as the surrounding reality returned. Screeching laughter behind her, a blinking neon light. And Dom in the distance, his eyes pinned on them like weapons ready for action. Angela saw a young woman fall backwards onto a table. Glass flew in several directions and shattered onto the floor. Dom didn't even stop to see the damage he'd caused. His eyes always on them. He wanted something.

Lisa sauntered out of the toilets, oblivious of the rising troubles. She stood a few metres from them and smiled. Whilst Dom, who had clocked her shifted his direction and fast approached her from behind. Roni acted quickly and shot towards Lisa.

Angela felt her heart gain speed with each step Dom took. She backed away with Sophie.

'Lisa,' she screamed. 'Behind you.' Then, with one hand, she grasped at Sophie and tugged her through the crowds. All she could think of now was removing herself from the scene with Sophie in tow. The beat of her heart hit hard against bone. The smell of sweat and hair lacquer stuck in her throat. She looked back through the crowd once more before reaching the exit.

She could see Dom's outreached hand as he tried to grab Lisa. Somehow, he missed and grabbed the strap of her shoulder bag instead. Lisa jolted back, kept her balance then spun around in shock. She must have read the situation well. She released the bag. With no resistance, Dom stumbled back a few steps. It all happened in seconds.

People were sensing something was happening. Heads were turning towards the commotion. Then she saw him stood there leaning against a column as he lit a cigarette. A coldness trickled down her spine that caused a paralysis in her legs. As a burst of light from his lighter lit the end of his cigarette, he turned his head. He looked straight at her with that familiar smirk. She squeezed her eyes tight, counted *1, 2, 3.* She opened them again. He was gone.

Was her mind playing tricks on her again?

Angela forced her legs to move. She heard Sophie say something. It was incomprehensible. She reached out and pushed open one of the heavy glass doors in front of her. The sudden movement of cold air bombarded her senses. Bit at her skin. Burnt her lungs. She didn't stop before descending the glass staircase. The sound of her own stilettos snapped against each step like cracking joints. Fear and her own reflection in the mirrored wall drove her downwards. Away from danger. Sophie tripped and almost knocked Angela off her feet. She heard Sophie yelp as her ankle buckled under her but kept going, Sophie limping behind her.

She darted left and fled towards St Mary's away from the club. Black cabs with lights lit like beacons lined the one side of the street. With one quick glance behind her to check for Sophie, she bolted towards the closest cab, opened the door, and mumbled something involuntarily to the driver. Sophie jumped in behind and slid the door shut with such ferocity the whole cab rocked.

The driver turned towards them. He frowned. Angela saw his face soften a little as he took in the scene at the back of his cab. He slid the glass partition between them across.

'Alright ladies. You be just fine in ere. Who we waiting for?'

As if on cue, Roni and Lisa flew down the side street towards the High Street.

'Them.' Sophie pointed towards the ladies.

The driver nodded, beeped his horn, and flung his arm out the window to gain their attention.

Roni saw them first, pointed, then both ladies hurried towards the cab. Seconds later, the driver, sensing their urgency, indicated, and pulled away from the kerbside.

The two women raced towards the cab and flung themselves inside and slammed the door. The cab driver, as if sensing their urgency pulled out and away from the kerbside.

Angela's eyes flitted from one woman to the other in the darkened cab. Moving light like meteorite trails skimmed the sides of the cab as it sped through the hollow-hearted city. Angela wondered why she hadn't learned her lesson yet. Trouble and treachery always tarnished the promising sparkle of an evening out in the city.

'What the hell just happened?' Angela's words broke through the uncomfortable, dark silence. For a few moments, no one spoke. Angela could see Lisa's hands tremble.

Roni turned to say something.

'No! Don't bother. It's better that I don't know.'

She slumped back into the car seat, letting the ball of anger in her stomach fend off the tears. The realisation that there wasn't a soul she could trust might break her more than Colin already had.

17

Gethin

This time Gethin remembered parts of the night before like broken parts of a dream. He continued to wash the mud from his feet as images of Angela slamming a car door shut the night before broke through his tiredness. He'd heard other voices, too. The spray of the shower washed away the muddiness and he pondered if it had indeed happened or been fragments of troubled dreams. Angela had crept into his mind frequently, like a slinky—slow and fast.

He turned off the shower, stepped out of the bath, and grabbed a towel. Coldness nipped at his skin as he wrapped the towel around his hips.

Condensation dribbled down the mirror above the sink, breaking up his features like some strange visual aura. He shook his head, trying to dismiss the questions rooted at the back of his mind. Somehow, the images of Hazel and Angela were becoming one. Hazel's hair and pale skin merged with Angela's intense green eyes.

He dropped his head and stared into the white porcelain basin.

Memories he'd kept hidden from sight were like shards of unexpected light. Scenes in India, ragged children running barefoot along dust baked streets lined with large Hibiscus with their trumpets calling to him. He squeezed his eyes as he watched himself from a distance stumble into a parched yellow building with brickwork stained and broken in places. The sky above bleached by heat and faded memories. His pulse quickened, as if warning him to stop, that he wasn't ready. He opened and blinked at his own reflection that trembled on the wet glass. And there he stood, asking himself a question he'd avoided for years. Where did I disappear when Hazel died? India had swallowed him up, buried his pain among its beauty and banality. He'd caused her death and missed her funeral, and he wasn't sure he could ever forgive himself.

As he dressed, Gethin knew decisions had to be made. He would try to ring his therapist in London again. Would he even consider taking him as a client again after what he'd done? He pulled the t-shirt over his head, pushed his arms into the short sleeves which exposed the tattoo on the top of his arm. It wasn't something he did often choosing to hide it where possible. He had no recollection of having it, who did it, or where in India. He didn't even know what the symbols meant, and until now he hadn't wanted to know. Yet, each time he glimpsed Angela outside her house in the garden or getting in or out of her car, her appearance drew him back to another time. And now he wanted to know what these strange symbols on his skin meant. As he pulled his jeans up over his hips, the phone trilled downstairs. He zipped up and flew down the staircase thinking it might be Dina.

'Hello.'

A faint crackling like static drifted into his ear. He tried again.

'Who is this?'

'Gethin, is it you?'

'Christ, Deborah, It's you. Are you okay?

'I'm safe, at least for now.'

'I thought something… What happened?'

'The day after meeting you, I was beat up by a client.' She paused for a few seconds. 'It was a client Jean organised. Not someone who has come to me before. I guessed they must have followed me the day I met you.'

Gethin felt a wave of familiar guilt. What was it about him and putting women in danger? He'd followed Deborah that day in Bute town and persuaded her to contact him.

He sighed down the phone.

'Don't blame yourself. I knew what I was doing. There's something else. That day I wasn't being completely honest, couldn't be sure if I could trust you.'

'I get it.' Gethin pulled a dining chair towards him and dropped onto it like dead weight.

'Until Eddie showed me some article he found. I know about your other investigations. I kinda guessed you really want to help people like me inall.'

Gethin nodded into the phone as he recalled the investigation that was the catalyst that brought him onto the landscape of more serious investigative journalism. He wasn't the best, but he was learning fast.

'Who's Eddie?'

A silence buzzed in his head before he heard whisperings in the background.

'He's a friend.'

'Can you trust him?' The words caught in Gethin's throat. Could a woman like Deborah trust any man?

'Can I trust him? Would you trust someone who removes you from a hospital bed, knowing it might put his own life at risk?'

Deborah sighed. 'Eddie's the one who told me to ring you. Tell you about the key.'

'A key?' What concerned Gethin was why this Eddie had taken an interest in Deborah now and encouraged her to contact him.

'I have a key that Penny gave me before she disappeared.'

As neurons fired like pistons in his head Gethin tried to keep up with what Deborah told him.

'By the way, that's not her real name.'

'I know.'

'You do?'

He heard the click of a lighter. The sound of Deborah inhaling. He glanced at his tobacco box on the dining table, suddenly needing one himself.

'Before Alison disappeared, she contacted me to say she had to leave Cardiff and return to London. She wouldn't say why, but I heard the fear in her voice. She was scared, really scared.'

'Do you have any idea what had scared her?'

'I'm getting to it.' He heard a low tut of annoyance. 'she said something strange. I didn't understand, but the way she said it spooked me. He's back from the dead?'

'Do you know who that might have been?'

'No, but Eddie thinks it has something to do with Dom?'

'Who the hell is Dom?'

'Well, that will be the monster who put me in hospital. The man Jean works for.'

Gethin's thoughts flicked back like a tape-recorder in reverse to the day he visited Makos.

'Deborah, I visited Makos after you told me about it. I think I've met Jean. Someone left a photo of us sat at the café that day. I'm beginning to wonder if this Dom might have something to do with the place, too?' Gethin rubbed his scalp in slow circular movements, the sound of his hair scratchy like sandpaper.

'Yeh, he does. Eddie told me Makos is one of several businesses

Dom owns. But he keeps his distance he does, to keep his reputation. Apparently, his father helps him out, but there's few he trusts with his businesses and even fewer who know the real Dom.'

Gethin wondered if one of these businesses involved offering young, vulnerable children from broken homes for sex.

'The thing is most people see him as some hot shot city business owner. Like I did. I had no idea he owned me. And those who do know his business ain't gonna be a loudmouth. They've seen where you might end up. Face down at the bottom of Cardiff docks.'

He heard her inhale and pictured her in a white space with only the grey smoke that folded and misted the air around her and that single beautiful mole on her cheek.

'Eddie thinks there's a few down the docks who remember him as a young boy before he moved away. Maybe he thinks everybody has forgotten who he was.'

The more Deborah told him the more convinced he became Alison had fled Dom.

'Deborah, do you have any idea what Alison might have been up to?'

'I really don't know apart from … Well, you know what girls like us do. I'll contact you again soon. Eddie will meet you and give you the key.'

Seconds later, the line went dead. A flat line that droned into his eardrum. He'd sensed her anxiety, a fear that inflated the longer they were on the phone. Was it possible that someone had murdered Alison because of what she knew rather than a circumstance of what she did? He placed the receiver down, grabbed his notebook and scribbled the names "Eddie" and "Dom" in capital letters.

He would wait for Deborah's call but remain careful. Doubts regarding Eddie's motives for helping Angela plagued his thinking. Could Eddie be trusted? He might work for Dom and be trying to find out more about Gethin's investigation. Deborah was vulnerable and Dom might use her differently this time.

He tapped his pen on the wire binding of his notebook. Yesterday, he'd discovered the name of the foreign carer, Nonnie Iriti. If he could find and contact her, he might learn more about Alison and Penny. And how they knew each other.

Gethin remembered something from his college days- trust, then verify. He needed to check what he'd been told against what others said. If he could speak to Nonnie, he could also check the information the boy had given him at the care home and Deborah.

Gethin jumped from his seat, grabbed the BT directory, hoping this time, he would have more success.

18

Angela

Angela rubbed her eyes and glanced at her bedside table. Eight o'clock. She sat bolt upright, then remembered it was Saturday. No school. Panic over. She grabbed at her dressing gown and wrapped it around her naked body. Her sweater and satin trousers and underwear trailed in a line across her bedroom. Memories like splinters, sharpened by her growing wakefulness, pierced her mind.

She remembered being the first out of the cab. Without saying goodnight to the ladies, she'd strode away from their hushed pleas to come to Lisa's house to talk—she had no interest. She'd given them plenty of chances. And they'd proved the one thing she had always believed. There were so few people she could trust in this world.

Then she remembered. She'd seen him in the corner of her eye, in the shadows, stood there in only his boxers and a t-shirt. A vacant look in his eyes. Blank. It had made the hair whisper up on her arm. His silence. His stillness. Death-like.

She bent back onto the toilet and peed for what seemed like ages as other fragments of the evening forced themselves into view—Colin. Had she really seen him there? She couldn't be sure. The anxiety had got to her made her see other things she feared. A trick of lighting and sensory overload. As she wiped herself, she worried *what if it was him? What if he'd witnessed the women and whatever they'd done? Would he use it against her?* She shuddered. She knew Colin would use anything to take her son, and even Catherine, given half the chance. He had made it look like she was the problem so many times. Even the police had believed him. She'd had no one to turn to. Still didn't.

She flushed the toilet, feeling a heaviness far worse than she had felt for some time. She'd tried, really tried, to make it work with her new neighbours. She had wanted to learn how to trust them. To build some kind of relationship with others. She thought of her father, her mother—both gone—and longed to have their arms around her once more.

She carried herself down the cold wood of the staircase barefoot. It felt good. The children were still asleep. They must have been up pretty late. She stopped, turned, and scampered back upstairs. She had to check they were still there, asleep, and safe in their beds.

A few minutes later she stood in her hallway contemplating doing scrambled eggs on toast for her children, and bringing it up to them in bed, when she noticed a narrow rectangular box just inside her front door. She bent down and picked it up, along with the several other letters, all addressed to her. The motion made her spin. Nausea rose from the pit of her stomach.

She carried them all into the kitchen and set them down on the side, curious as to where the box came from. Then she recalled a BT operator informing her of a delivery a few days earlier. They were going to send a telephone lead to replace the older existing one. She smiled and mocked herself.

She filled the kettle, placed it on its base and flicked the on switch:

a red light came on. Then she picked up the box, took a knife out of the drawer and run its sharp edge along the taped seam at the one end of the box. She stopped and frowned. For a moment she thought she heard something, an unfamiliar sound which was hard to define. The kettle clicked and crackled as it heated. It must have been the kettle, she assured herself as she continued to tear back some loose tape from the box. She brought the box to her nose to smell it. She wondered if she expected the parcel to smell of Colin's aftershave, not willing to believe her own presumptions of where it came from. No. Instead, the box had an unusual musty smell, like nothing she had smelled before. Little lines appeared around the edges of her eyes as she scrunched her nose up at the unpleasant smell. *Should she open it?*

With trepidation she continued, her small, busy fingers pulled back the small cardboard flap. Her heart raced a little. Had something moved inside? Of course not, she told herself.

Then, with sheer horror, she witnessed several dark brown insects scuttle out of the opened end. They moved so fast that several of them were skittering up her dressing gown sleeve. Their spiky legs pricking at the soft skin of her arms as they moved.

She froze, tried to cry out. She felt her chest tighten. Her arm jerked upwards and sent the box spinning in the air. Cockroaches cascaded down like a black rain fall. This time, she felt the air leave her lungs as she screamed. She swiped at her hair as cockroaches crawled through it, becoming entangled as they tried to bury down into her locks.

She tore her dressing gown, flayed, and swiped at her bare skin, sending cockroaches everywhere. Within seconds, she glimpsed her children stood dumbstruck near the stairs. Her nakedness exposed in all its glory.

'Mum. Mum. Calm down. What is it?'

'Fucking cockroaches. Get them off me.'

Catherine darted down the stairs towards her mum.

'There's nothing on you. Mum. Calm down. I think you imagined it. You're frightening Joel. Here.'

Angela wiped a tear out of sight, took the throw Catherine held out for her, and wrapped it round her tightly.

Her eyes burned with an embarrassment that didn't feel familiar. She tiptoed from the kitchen into the hallway, not taking her eyes off the floor. The cockroaches had disappeared. She glanced towards her children. Catherine stood there with that familiar, wide-eyed stare. She thought it was one of her mother's episodes again. Like the time she was convinced that gnats were crawling all over her. For a second, she questioned her own sanity. She turned and scanned the floor. The box lay just inside the kitchen doorway. But it was the smell that clung to the back of her throat that told her she hadn't imagined it.

She turned to Joel who still stood on the stairs, appearing totally bewildered by his mother's behaviour. She tried her hardest to offer a consoling smile.

'Mum. Why are you jumping up and down like that?' He pouted his lips. 'Are you really crazy like Dad said?'

But Angela wasn't listening. Something else had caught her eye. There were objects scattered across the floor; they looked like Polaroids.

'Cath, could you take take Joel upstairs to get dressed... please.'

Hesitantly, Angela tiptoed towards the kitchen. All signs of the cockroaches were gone. They must have scuttled into corners and under cupboards. Angela felt sick at the thought.

She picked up several of the Polaroids at their corners with fingers like pincers. She held her breath to avoid the pungent smell that hit the back of her throat. It must be the smell of those disgusting things.

What she witnessed next took the wind from her. Images of the previous evening flickered like an unreeling film.

He *had* been there. He had witnessed the unfolding chaos. He would now cause even more chaos for her. She'd be called an unfit mother, crazy and alcohol dependent. And for years, she'd believed his narrative over her own. Would this one ill-fated evening undo everything? Even weaken her resolve to keep going.

The bastard was there all the time.

She felt another tear slip and disappear as it traced down her cheek to nothing.

There she stood at the bar and sat in the booth. The third photo was of Lisa and Sophie with Dom. Colin had scratched the word "sluts" into the photo.

Angela breathed out in brief spurts, as if her lungs were backfiring. Then the phone rang.

'Angela. Please don't put the phone down.'

Angela couldn't respond. She stood there with the phone near her ear, suddenly aware of the sprigs of green erupting on the tree outside.

'Are you okay? I had the windows open and heard you scream.'

Angela shook her head. 'No.' saying it didn't feel half as bad as Angela would have imagined. Yet, the silence on the end of the line sounded terrifying.

'Angela? Angela, would you like me to pop round?'

She shook her head again.

If he was taking photos of the ladies too, then they we all in danger. She could feel the crow's feet gathering at the corners of her eyes, clawing at her mind. He had been stalking her and she knew his behaviour would darken... worsen. There was no telling what he would attempt to do.

Angela's head ached. She struggled to find words to put together.

'Angela. You still there?'

'I'd rather come round to you.'

'Of course, you can. When were you thinking?'

'In ten minutes?'

'No problem at all. I'll have a nice cup of tea waiting for you.'

'I'll have Cath and Joel with me and probably Catherine's pet rat. They can't stay here.'

Another short silence. 'Tell you what. I'm making breakfast here for my two. I'll put some more bacon under the grill for them too. A bacon buttie can work wonders, alright?'

The dull blanket of grey sky through the window offered little light or colour as Lisa and Angela sat curled over the oak table. Slow and unrelenting raindrops ticked a familiar theme against the windowpane. Sunshine had all but disappeared from sight except for the shadow of a hazy warmth.

'This is creepy, it is. Has he done anything like this before Ang?'

Angela nodded. Using her fingers, she wiped away ketchup from the corner of her mouth and finished the last of her bacon buttie.

'Yes, he has. He used to follow me. Take photos, then accuse me of having affairs with someone I might stand behind in a queue at a shop or sat next to on a bench in the park. The fact I had the children with me every time made no difference.'

Lisa continued to stare at the polaroid and squeezed her bottom lip between her fingers.

'Have you ever reported his behaviour to the police? Spoken to anyone?'

Angela chewed on her gum. How could she tell Lisa that he'd threatened to put her away? Have her locked up if she ever tried reporting him to the police.

'He's a senior manager in mental health.'

'Good grief. Colin. Really?'

Surprised by Lisa's response, Angela frowned. Lisa coughed into her clenched fist, stood, and with an unnecessary haste collected the plates from the table and carried them away into the kitchen.

Angela sniffed and picked at the polish on her nails, wondering about the sudden change in the atmosphere between them. before.

Perhaps she feels awkward about last night and doesn't know how to approach it?

'Another cuppa?' called Lisa. Her voice a few notes higher.

Angela didn't respond. Something had struck her and sucked the air from her lungs. She realised what had been niggling at her senses.

Lisa's head poked around the open doorway.

Angela sharpened her gaze at Lisa.

'How do you know my husband's name is Colin?'

Lisa's shoulders slumped, her head dropped for a second onto her chest before she slid back to the chair and dropped onto it with a deep and exasperated sigh.

'I'm so sorry. We should have told you sooner.'

Angela bit at her top lip. She didn't like the sound of this one bit. 'Told me what?'

'That day, I saw Colin snooping around your house. I thought he was looking for us.'

'Us?'

'Yes, we stole Colin's wallet one night about six months ago in a club. We thought he was on the street trying to find us.'

Angela's head rolled back, and she swore into the air above her head. 'Fuck. Fuck. Why do you ladies keep lying to me? Why?' Images of Dom and his salacious smile as he sat between Lisa and Sophie threaded into her thoughts.

'Roni was the one who suggested he might be looking for you, and not us, because when he saw me, he put his head down and left pretty sharpish.'

'So that's why you made a point of ringing me that day.' Angela's jaw tightened. She rubbed at her temple. The memory of the two women stood on the pavement as she took surfboards from the top of her car returned. They must have stood there deliberating what they should do.

'Well, yes, and no. I was worried about you, too. If he was…'

'Don't be fooled. Colin doesn't forget a face even if you wore a wig. All he proved by that is that you are not the focus of his attention.' She paused. 'Even when he's really drunk or high, his ability to stay in control is almost supernatural.'

Lisa drew back, her eyes wide and unblinking. 'Roni was right. It was you at the window that night.'

'Yup. And Roni knows it was me too because I asked her about it last week … And the evening we were going out I saw the wig in Roni's bedroom.'

Shades of confusion darkened Lisa's features. Angela didn't care that much anymore. She'd had enough of all the cloak and dagger drama. She wanted to know everything these ladies were doing and what risks it held for her and the children.

'You don't know Colin, he's not just possessive, he's extremely paranoid. He'll convince himself that I'm involved in all this. And that you're out to destroy him.' Angela picked up her cigarettes and offered one to Lisa who had taken to pacing the dining room, her face as pale as porcelain. She stopped and slid one from the box.

'I'm so sorry. We didn't know how to approach you about it. I mean, you're so private about your past, and I just sensed whatever you've been through hasn't been pleasant for any of you. It would have seemed like I was prying.'

Angela flicked the lighter. It fizzed and sparked to life. The small, hypnotizing flame danced, luring her in like the sweet music of sirens. She gazed, unblinking, at the flame before Lisa leaned in with a

194

cigarette to her mouth. Angela offered the flame towards Lisa.

'So, you ladies steal men's wallets, then?'

Lisa leaned in; her hand shook a little as she lit her cigarette. Angela had the strange feeling that somehow their roles had reversed a little.

'Lisa nodded. Hmmm. Roni was right. After last night, she knew you'd already worked out what we do.' Lisa brought the cigarette to her lips, inhaled and blew out slow folds of smoke. 'We were all a bit surprised when Roni said she might invite you out for the evening with us.'

Was it possible that Roni had only befriended her to find out why Colin had appeared outside her house? Angela heard herself laugh. A nervous sardonic laughter that made Lisa stop pacing and glance over.

'No. Please, Angela. It's not like that. I think Roni trusts you, and that's big. For Roni anyway.' She blew out grey twirls like smoke signals. 'We all have issues on this street. I can't say how many times I've looked at that photo of me and my husband over there.' She glanced towards a large wedding photo above her Ercol. 'He walked out when I was pregnant with Becky, but I still can't take it down.' Lisa shrugged. 'Is that normal? Doubt it.'

'So how did you two become friends?'

'A long story, but put it this way, I was a pushover until Roni taught me how to smile at someone whilst still saying no. And I'm still learning. When she lets you in, you won't ever have a better friend. Yes, she can be such hard work, but if it wasn't for her, I wouldn't have what I have today.'

'You mean your salon?'

'No. My sense of freedom. I sought approval from everyone, always asking what others think. I still get like it sometimes, but nowhere how I used to me.'

If these women's paths had crossed with Colin's, they would know the man he was. This was the real chance of building a friendship on something they had in common—knowing the real Colin. The Colin who has so little respect for women.

Lisa stopped pacing and faced Angela.

'He's stalking you. That's harassment.'

'Do you think?' Angela couldn't find any other words to respond.

Lisa sat back in the chair and picked up the photo of her, Sophie, and Dom. She brought it to her nose and grimaced.

'Good grief. they smell weird.'

'Yes. He kindly sent them in a box accompanied by cockroaches.'

Lisa gasped. 'You must be kidding.'

Angela's breathing became jagged again as the memories of earlier that morning bled out. 'I can't bear to go into my kitchen. Most of them scuttled under the cupboards and under the skirtings.' She didn't want to give them the finer details of the fiasco that unfolded.

'I can help you with the cockroaches. Boric acid. That'll get rid of them before they cause an infestation.'

'That's why he used cockroaches. Of course. He wants to infest my bloody home. To let me know he's not going away.'

Lisa reached out and squeezed Angela's hand. 'Do you want to hear a funny fact? When you drink freshly ground coffee, a roach or two are also ground down with the coffee beans. You've probably tasted one before now.'

'Oh God, Lisa, really?' Angela scrunched her face up and shook her head. Lisa grinned and for a moment they chuckled together.

'On a more serious note. If Colin is making threats, perhaps it would be worth contacting the children's schools to let them know about him. The last thing you want is him turning up at their school.'

Angela shuddered at the thought.

'Coming here was meant to be a new start. Telling the school will be like dragging him back into our life.'

Lisa's expression softened. 'But he already is Angela and it's time you did something.'

Angela sighed. 'I was bloody stupid like to believe he'd just leave us alone.'

'Not stupid Ang. Hopeful. Like any good parent.'

Air caught in Angela's windpipe as she tried to hold back her emotions. No one had called her a good parent since her mother and father had been alive.

'I remember when I had to tell Becca's nursery about my husband, as my circumstances were going to change. It was the hardest thing I had to do. I sobbed the whole time I spoke. It's not an easy thing to do'

Angela nodded. Thankful that Lisa understood.

The pervading feeling that disclosing a truth about her life would bring even more trouble her way had always troubled her. As if the words themselves were drawing something despicable out of the darkness. Now she had to wonder about how far he would go to destroy her and take the children from her-—and that really was the last thing she wanted to consider.

Her thoughts were interrupted by a loud wrap on the door, which made both women freeze. Lisa slid out from her chair and crept towards the hallway.

'Oh. It's Roni.'

Seconds later Roni panic driven voice, charged through the silence.

'Christ Lisa. I opened Dom's wallet this morning. We might have an even bigger problem on our hands.'

Roni stopped mid-stride when she saw Angela sat at Lisa's dining table. Roni's expression said it all.

Lisa followed behind.

'It's fine, Roni. I had to be honest, as things have gone too far. Angela knows what we do.'

To Angela's surprise, Roni didn't protest. Something bigger was on her mind right now. And Angela guessed it might have something to do with the black leather wallet embossed with Gucci in her hand.

'Would you like a cup of tea?'

She looks like she might need something stronger than a cup of tea, thought Angela.

'Not yet. I need you to come and look at this.' She opened the wallet and pulled its contents out onto the table.

'There's something very strange going on with this man.'

'What do you mean?'

'Look at his credit cards.'

Angela leaned over and looked. Nothing seemed that different at first. Then she noticed. Two of the cards had different names on them.

Lisa picked one up, glanced at it, then picked up another.

'Christ Roni there's three or four different names here?'

Angela picked up one of the cards. A Diner's Club card. It read "Dominique d'Petri". Another one she picked up read "Aed d'Petri", and another said "Mr Timothy Davies".

'The question is, are they stolen, or has he set up false identities for himself? Either way, it's damn creepy and dangerous having this wallet in our possession.'

'Really, this is all too weird …' Lisa turned the gold Visa card round and round in her hands like a magician. 'Have you used any of them?'

'Yes, the Diner's card. The Tiffany rings we discussed.'

'Tiffany rings! Christ, ladies. A decent washing machine would do.' Angela tried hard to control the subtle tremble of her hand as she inhaled a hit of nicotine.

'We sell on expensive items. You'll be surprised at what seemingly respectable people do with their money.'

'So, who is he?' Lisa's voice became almost a whisper.

'Well. He isn't the local bloody vicar, that's for sure.'

Roni sounded unusually troubled as she moved towards the window. The sudden harsh downpour outside distorted everything. Houses smudged into each other. Colours muddied into grey.

'This is worrying. Very worrying. We haven't just stolen his wallet. We've stolen the very things he's hiding. I'm not sure he's going to let this go?'

Roni continued to stare out of the window as she spoke.

'This is Sophie's fault. I've had enough.'

'Roni. If he's up to no good. Will he really risk furrowing out and recovering this? He'd be an idiot if you ask me. He'd do the same as the others and cancel them. And we'll still have a window of opportunity to use the cards before the stolen and lost credit cards list hit the stores.'

Roni didn't respond. She stood with her back to the women then spun round. Her eyes burning through them like smoking cold ice.

'Sophie should never have done this. We agreed.' Roni's eyes shifted towards Angela for a second, then back at Lisa. 'We all know she's good at what she does, but last night was a step too far. She jeopardised everyone's safety again.'

Lisa saw Angela frown.

'We target married men, older married men. Sophie had this notion that these men needed validation sometimes even more than sex. And she was right. We listen to them, make them feel special and worthwhile and most of them never consider we are trying to steal their wallet.'

Lisa interjected. 'They take days, sometimes longer to report their wallet is stolen, even then, we imagine, they report it lost, less explaining that way.'

It struck Angela then. Was it possible these women weren't stealing just for the financial gain? Were they targeting married men for other reasons too?

Roni leaned against the windowsill her body darkened and silhouetted against the wet glare outside. She rolled her eyes.

'This is one bloody mess I have to make go away.'

'Sophie seemed convinced he knew her real name, too?'

'She was drunk. Maybe she imagined it?'

Angela pushed her cigarette into the glass ashtray. Had she called Sophie by her real name in front of Dom? It was a possibility.

'And your bag, Lisa? Please tell me you had nothing in it which would lead this man to our door.'

'Good grief. No. Matter of habit now when I go out. Same as always. Money and lipstick. That's it.'

'Good ...' Roni leaned across and picked one of the Polaroids off the table.

Her expression was like watching a rainstorm pass into a thunderstorm. 'What the fuck is going on?'

That was the first time Angela had ever heard Roni swear.

Lisa raced to the rescue. 'I tell you what. How about that cup of tea?'

19

Gethin

He ran his fingers down a few wafer-thin pages before finding her name. He kicked himself for not considering before that Nonnie could be her real name.

It was already past midday. The seconds seemed to slip past, as his mind cascaded with a waterfall of thought and action. He stared at the number. He hadn't considered what he might say if he managed to contact her. What if she didn't want to say much more about Radcliffe for fear of reprisals? It seemed possible, but Gethin thought it was worth a try.

As soon as she picked up the phone and spoke, he knew it was her. The woman who had called him late that February night. He stalled, fearing she would put the phone down as soon as she heard his voice.

'Hello Nonnie.'

Silence… 'I wondered how long it might take you.'

'It was you then?'

Another silence. 'Yes, it was. But it's complicated … risky. Risks which my husband didn't agree with. He still doesn't.'

'I understand.' Gethin thought carefully. 'Would it make any difference if I told you I care about what might have happened at Radcliffe and to Penny and Alison? I believe there are people who need to be exposed for their wrongdoings.'

The long silence down the line played out like tumbleweed rolling across the parched earth of an empty film set.

'Okay. Be here this Thursday. My husband leaves for work at ten-thirty. He's very protective and nervous. And he understands that what I know about Radcliffe puts me in danger. He's ex-military. Eyes and mind like a hawk. Park your car if you're driving in the lane down from the cottage.'

Gethin jotted down the address she gave. Just outside of Tenby.

'Gethin. Be careful. There are darker things at work here.' Then she put the phone down.

Without hesitation Gethin sat down to work. He drew a list of questions he wanted to ask Nonnie. He would also take the sketch he'd made of the tattoo on Alison's shoulder. Perhaps Nonnie could confirm that the dead girl in the park was Alison and not Penny? Just like the young lad had told him.

His watch told him it was already ten-thirty. He jogged across the small country lane towards a cottage with a small picket fence. Hedges partially concealed the cottage.

Being caught behind a tractor down narrow country lanes didn't seem like a good start. He swept a damp curl back of his face and hoped his lateness wouldn't deter Nonnie- god forbid from trusting and talking with him. He knocked the door with the old brass knocker and waited.

A minute after polite introductions he found himself sat on the edge of an old armchair in a room with a low ceiling, exposed wooden beams and an old French dresser housing an array of China stood against one wall. An open hearth with a fireplace gave the room an overall warmth.

He leaned back onto floral printed cushions. On the wall opposite was a carved ornate cuckoo clock, the style of which he hadn't seen for years. Below it hung two carved wooden cones on the end of small chains. Gethin couldn't help but admire their intricacies.

Nonnie disappeared then reappeared carrying a tray with tea and biscuits and placed it onto the coffee table between them.

'Milk?' she asked whilst pouring tea into small delicate bone China cups on saucers.

He nodded. 'Yes please, just a drop... watching my weight,' he joked bringing his hand to his stomach and patting it.

'No sugar then?'

He shook his head.

She passed him his tea. 'I should have known you'd have eventually found me... In some strange way that's what I'd hoped.'

'Was it your husband who put a stop to the call?'

She nodded. 'Of course. He works in social care. And he knows how *these* people sometimes close ranks to protect themselves and their reputation. He's experienced it himself first hand when he tried to help me. Nearly lost his job and reputation.'

'And now?'

She looked up at him and stopped pouring. 'I'm guessing if you've found me you know a bit more about Radcliffe?'

'Yes. But it hasn't been easy most people don't like to talk about the place.'

She nodded.

'You would understand if I said "we" keep our heads down and live our best life. That's not to say we're not scared. I know things that might put me at risk.'

She continued to pour tea and scooped a teaspoon of sugar from the sugar bowl.

'It still haunts me you know. All those vulnerable children, too many of them for me to protect alone.'

'The night I rang you, I was feeling desperate. The sense of guilt was too much for me. I had to do something. Reach out to someone. The police weren't an option. They saw most of the children as drug-fuelled troublemakers and delinquents. And rarely believed anything they said.'

'So why me? Why did you ring me?'

'I'd listened to you on a radio talk. You had genuine compassion for the work you do?'

'But how did you know I was investigating Alison's murder?'

'I didn't. It was a wild guess. I saw you at Dulwich Park sat on a bench near the pond, the day I went to pay my respects. A few days before, by chance or holy intervention I'd picked up a newspaper left on a train. An article highlighting the dangers of investigative journalism mentioned you and several other journalists. Your photo with several others was in it.'

Gethin shook his head. 'Jeez, that was when I'd went from reporting to proper investigative work. Few of us left.'

Nonnie smiled. 'Yes, and I noticed you seemed particularly interested in the welfare of children and young adults. I took my chances, did my research, and rang you hoping I was right about your reasons for being at the park. I'm glad I did.'

She stopped and passed him his tea.

'It's been tough. My husband worried about me and what I know. Sometimes he thinks people are watching us. He doesn't want to see me hurt by a past that he thinks will never be proven. I promised him I wouldn't call you again.' She sipped her tea.

'You rang me, it's different now.'

Nonnie offered a small plate of biscuits to Gethin. He took one more out of politeness than appetite.

'I knew it wasn't Penny. She was the stepdaughter of Mr Thomas. Although most knew her as Penny Thomas. Her mother's maiden name was Hughes.'

Gethin's cup stopped halfway to his open mouth as he processed what he'd heard. His skin tingled as he set the cup back on the saucer.

'You're telling me the real Penny didn't attend Radcliffe she lived on site because her stepfather was Superintendent Thomas who run and managed Radcliffe?'

'You have it in one.'

'Was he married to Penny's mother?'

'Strangely no. They were like common-law husband and wife. Mr Thomas always referred to Penny as Penny Thomas but if anyone asked her, she insisted her name was Penny Hughes and would always be Penny Hughes. I don't think she was keen on her stepfather.'

'Any idea why Penny hung herself?'

Nonnie rubbed at her eyes and sighed as if memories of that times troubled her. 'I see you've done your research. No. Although, back then it was obvious her mum and Mr Thomas were having problems. Her mum liked the drink and took pills for anxiety I heard. Where possible Mary avoided being anywhere near Radcliffe. It was if she hated the place. Maybe because it took up so much of Mr Thomas's time.'

'Things became a lot worse after Penny hung herself. They lied about the cause of her death. Tried to hide it it. They said it was out of respect for Penny and her unwell mother. I think they didn't want to draw any unwanted attention to Radcliffe.'

'And you left about a year after this?'

Nonnie raised an eyebrow towards Gethin. 'Correct. I left in 1978.

But Alison she ran away not long after Penny's suicide. For a while I tried to find her.'

Gethin went to ask something, but Nonnie continued. 'I haven't set foot in or been near that building since. It's a place where innocence isn't guarded, and evil is allowed to persist Gethin. I can still hear the whimpers and cries in my dreams, I should have done more, said something. I tried.' Nonnie picked up her cup and saucer. The China clanked as her hand trembled a little. She brought the cup to her mouth then replaced it shakily onto its saucer.

'We had the highest rate of runaways in Wales at one time, questions weren't being asked... well, not the right questions anyway. Another?' Nonnie offered the plate of biscuits to Gethin again. A subtle distraction thought Gethin.

He smiled and shook his head. 'No, thank you.'

'Gethin, there were a few times men would turn up in black fancy cars escorting children God knows where. We were told they were being treated by special sponsors of the home, to things like the cinema and bowling. I never believed it. Some nights when I had to sleep on site some of these children wouldn't return to Radcliffe until the early hours of the morning.'

'Did you ask them where they'd been or what they'd done?'

'Well. Yes. I would try to talk to them on their return, but it would be like; how do you Brits say it? err getting blood...'

'Blood from a stone,' responded Gethin.

'Yes, that's it—blood from a stone. Until I started noticing other things. What we called red flags.'

Gethin frowned 'What do you mean?'

'I noticed how some children who had been out on these little social treats began to act out of character, just a little at first but then the behaviours became progressively worse with some of them. They began to withdraw from activities they'd always shown an interest and enthusiasm for; staying in their rooms more you know. Others started sneaking out to buy alcohol and cause trouble in the villages nearby. And I'm talking children we'd never really had a problem with before.'

Gethin shook his head.

'There were a few teenage girls... and boys who slept in a room together, not for that,' she emphasised to Gethin.

'They refused to turn the light off and became aggressive if I explained those were the house rules. They were too frightened or too ashamed to talk.'

'Ashamed?'

'You have to remember some of these children came from tough backgrounds and neighbourhoods. They wouldn't even tell each other what they had experienced. There were things they couldn't speak about. But they all knew.'

'What about other staff at the home, did they notice the changes in the children?'

Nonnie looked up her expression one of resignation. She brushed long wispy strands of chestnut hair back, away from her round open face. She shook her head.

'I guess some of them did, but it was so easy to think it was normal behaviour from children who experienced neglect and abuse before they came to Radcliffe.' Nonnie stopped and glanced up at the open window. 'What you don't understand is that even some members of staff weren't to be trusted either. I caught one laid under the quilt with a young boy. He said he was offering the boy comfort. Like Hell was he! I thought it totally inappropriate and reported the incident too Mr Thomas. He never followed it up.'

It was at this point Gethin knew he needed to record what Nonnie was saying. He couldn't be sure how she would respond to it. Most people became very nervous and refused to say anymore.

'Later, Mr Thomas pulled me into his office. Told me an overindulgent mind had completely taken the incident out of context... My mind he was referring too. Can you believe it?'

'Do you think Mr Thomas knew what was going on at the home?'

'I'm not sure Gethin. I often wonder about this. The thing is you must understand there were so many things changing there at the time...'

Gethin took the opportunity. He pulled a small audio recorder from his pocket. 'Do you mind? It's really important I remember everything. What you're telling me could really change many people's lives Nonnie.'

Nonnie threw him a startled stare and cast her eyes towards the handheld recorder as if it was a gun.

Gethin waited for Nonnie to look up again. He dropped the tone of his voice as he spoke.

'Nonnie what you're saying you've witnessed at Radcliffe is vital to the investigation. You are one of the few people I have met willing to report what really happened there. Like yourself I've had my fair share of closed doors and threats.' He hesitated. 'Nonnie. People deserve to know what terrible things have happened at Radcliffe and why Alison was found dead in a city over a hundred miles away from where she grew up.'

Nonnie's crossed leg rocked up and down. Her eyes flickered for a second on Gethin. He knew he needed to stay something to persuade her to talk before she completely closed up again — maybe forever.

'When I arrived, you said that you hoped I would find you. Here I am, Nonnie. You and I can help men and woman find some justice for what happened to them at Radcliffe. I want to tell their story... and Alison's. They shouldn't have to hide away in shame as if what happened to them is their fault.'

She pursed her lips in thought and nodded.

'There are vulgar individuals out there Nonnie, who desire the thin veil of reputation to conceal their vile actions. The cost of their acts Nonnie, I have no doubt, will have followed these innocent children into adulthood. He stopped again and creased his forehead to ease the ache. 'Alcohol, drugs, promiscuity, prostitution, violence. I've witnessed and written about it. Lots of them never adjust to a normal life.'

'Okay, okay. I hear you!' Nonnie almost snapped the words at Gethin, her shoulders tensed, and she sighed loudly.

Gethin placed the small recorder on the table in front of Nonnie. He asked her for a paracetamol for his head and jotted down in bullet point what she had said earlier. After a few minutes she returned with two cold glasses of water and two pills. She handed him the tablets and he swallowed them down with the ice-cold water. This time Gethin noticed she sat at the edge of the chair. Her body now leaning in more. He glanced at her, smiled, and clicked the record button.

'You said things were changing at Radcliffe, Nonnie?'

She cleared her throat and shifted at the edge of the chair. 'Yes, the council ran Radcliffe. When I started working, we were mostly women. Then things began to change. Thy kept employing men, always men. Some of us started realising these men had few or often no qualifications, suited for their role at the home.' Nonnie stopped and gulped from her glass of water. 'Now I know how that might sound, we weren't jealous!' She placed the glass back on the table looking at the recorder with continued nervousness. 'One time, out of curiosity I went hunting for old posts advertising the positions. Something didn't feel right, something was going on. Of course, I rang Mr Thomas to express my concern. He gave me some err... cock and bull. Is that how you say it?'

Gethin nodded.

'Mm mm some cock and bull story about a new equal opportunities department who could override management decisions regarding prospective staff. Some of these men getting jobs weren't even providing references from past employers. A few of us ladies, well we felt let down. No one listened to our concerns about the professionalism of some of these male staff.'

'Couldn't you go direct too personnel to complain?'

'I did, they told me what Mr Thomas said was sort of correct. Labour had introduced some equal opportunities policy. Somehow it ended up as bit of a mess because anyone could apply for a role whether or not they had the experience! It was as if normal checks and references weren't required anymore. We even had male staff recommending their male friends. It was crazy?'

'After that we didn't feel as if we could complain about some of the behaviours we were seeing. I approached the man I'd found in bed with a child, he continued to say he was just comforting him! I told him I was going to put in a formal complaint about his conduct. He laughed at me. Said the equal opportunities team would be involved if I tried to start any disciplinary procedure against him.'

She stopped and took another gulp of water.

'I think Mr Thomas was thankful of some of these men because they could handle the more aggressive children and young adults. Some of us women felt neglected. It's like we had no power to voice our concerns. Some of the older female staff were being mocked and accused of being bitter because they no longer held the reins in the place. It was very awful for a while.'

'What finally pushed you too leave? The children obviously meant a lot to you?'

Gethin watched as Nonnie's face crumbled. She seemed to fold into herself, her eyes went blank for a moment. 'Turn the tape off ... please ... turn it off.'

The faltering in her voice like a crack opening in the earth's crust made the hairs on his arms stand upright like a thousand pins. He knew. In the void between himself and her folded body. He knew.

'I don't want this on record. There were two of them. One an employee, the other I'd not seen before. Like I said there always seemed to be men milling around the place unsupervised. It was a night shift. About one-thirty in the early hours. I had gone down to put the rubbish out for the next morning. He was waiting for me. They pinned me against the wall. Done things to me. I couldn't scream. I froze. Just froze. My punishment for speaking out.'

Gethin continued to sit in silence. His limbs felt heavy, yet his heartbeat in anger and sorrow for this poor woman sat opposite him. He leaned over and placed his hand gently on her hers. 'That's truly awful and I will do my very best to expose those who did this.'

'No one will ever know what happened to me. Do you understand?'

She cast her eyes towards him. In that second, he saw the steely strength this woman must have once possessed at Radcliffe. 'I tell you all this for the children, for them.'

Gethin understood. And nodded.

They sat in silence for a moment before Gethin bent down the side of the armchair and unfolded the flap of his satchel. He took out the small newspaper copy of the opening of the annexe.

'Nonnie. There is something I need you to look at. It's a newspaper clipping of the opening of the new annexe back in the seventies before you left. You're in the photo. You're not looking happy. Yet, everyone around you is. It looks as if you're peering towards someone in the crowd. Will you take a look?'

She nodded. And took the clipping from Gethin. He placed his finger on the small handheld recorder and checked for her approval. She nodded. He clicked record.

At first, she smiled, a solemn smile as her eyes took in memories of her past. Then she pointed to the councillor stood next to Mr Thomas and the Mayor.

'That's who I'm glaring at. Right there. Him. I'd caught him snooping around the girl's dorm, sat on the edge of one girls bed stroking her arm. I told him to get out. He'd been wearing joggers and a sweater and a cap. I had no idea he was a councillor. I felt disgusted seeing him stood with all these other people looking like a respectable member of our community.'

'You're pointing to the Councillor, Dylan Edwards.'

'Yes. I am.' She glanced at the small tape recorder and swallowed.

'And what about him, there?' Gethin pointed to the man in the Ray-Bans.

'Can't remember his name. I didn't see him around much; might have been because of the different shifts I took. He seemed Ok. From what I can remember he was involved with a lot of charitable work. His company built the annexe I believe.'

'Black-tip construction.'

'Yes. That's it? Always smart. Good-looking man. busy type. Had this habit though. This way of licking his lips whilst he spoke to you. Bit weird but I think it was some kind of tic.'

He clicked the recorder off. And leaned back in the armchair.

'Well done, Nonnie. I know what you've shared with me today has been difficult for you. And I can see how much compassion and love you had for these children. But I promise you this, I'll keep peeling back the rotten layers of this place and find those involved with what happened there. They will have their comeuppance.'

'Maybe'. Her eyes lingered on the photo then she stood. 'One minute.'

Nonnie left Gethin sat in the lounge and disappeared. She returned a couple of minutes later with a letter in her hand. 'I received this about a year after I left Radcliffe. I'm not sure how Alison found me.

Guess she was always a resourceful young girl.' She passed the letter to Gethin.

He unfolded it. It was handwritten in blue ink. The handwriting was surprisingly elegant full of loops and curves. Gethin wondered what he had expected. `

'She'd obviously created a new life for herself using Penny's identity, but she'd signed this letter with her real name, Alison.'

Gethin nodded.

'There's just one thing I have to ask. How did you know it was Alison's body found in the park back then? The police didn't have a photo of her suitable for the media.'

'But they did do an artist's drawing. Don't forget some of these girls relied on me like a mum. I witnessed them grow into young women. I just knew it was her.'

Gethin nodded.

'Read the letter, especially the last paragraph.'

Gethin skimmed over the letter, which stated very little concrete information other than she had settled into a new home, was busy looking for a job and taking up new hobbies. When he'd finished, he looked up at Nonnie.

'What do you think she means when she says...' He looked down and read out the last paragraph.

'Don't worry Nonnie I'm dealing with stuff. Now I understand that to live your life it's important you acknowledge the wrongdoing of others and endeavour to banish the memories of it. A kind of restitution. I think my future will feel more harmonious you see. I hope yours will do too.'

'I've often wondered what she meant by that.'

'Do you think Alison was, also abused at the home?'

'Yes. I think so.'

Gethin opened file 10.81 that now rested on his lap. He took out the sketch he'd made of the tattoo he'd seen on Alison's shoulder and passed it too Nonnie. 'There's a photo of Alison in a bar in Cardiff. She had this tattoo on her shoulder. Do you recognise it at all?'

She nodded. 'Yes, it does look familiar but honestly, I couldn't say for sure.' She shrugged and placed the sketch on the table.

'Wait.'

For a second time Gethin watched as Nonnie moved from her chair and disappeared. This time he could hear things being moved, rustling, and scraping of wood on wood.

She returned with a small photo album. She flicked through several photos then stopped.

'There.' She passed the open album to Gethin. The old cuckoo clock on her wall chimed as photos of children in flared jeans and polar necks and pinafores stared up at him. The photos had faded and yellowed a little at the edges.

'It's the only one I have of Penny.'

She passed the photo to Gethin. He recognised the young girl in the photo from the group photo he'd seen along the corridor at Radcliffe. Penny had the same straight dark brown hair and the blunt long fringe almost filtering out the sadness in her eyes. The same smile. She stood against a wall, just to her right was a large old and ornate mirror.

'Can you see it?'

Penny's cardigan had slipped off her one shoulder. He turned towards Nonnie. 'Good God. They have the same tattoos.'

'You're lucky I have this. Mr Thomas didn't agree with Penny fraternising with others at the home. He preferred her to stay away.'

Gethin responded. 'I think the question now is did they both have this tattoo whilst at Radcliffe or did Alison have it done later, after she'd run away from the home?' He rubbed at his temple as he jotted a few additional things into his notepad.

'Do you think their relationship was more than just friends?'

'It's possible. That sort of thing did go on. Having the same tattoo might have been a way to express what they felt or shared. It's strange though as I didn't see them together much. If they did, they must have been very clever about it.'

Gethin stared at the photo as if something might physically change in the photo and give him some answers he desperately needed.

He lifted his satchel onto his lap and took out his smoke tin and rolling mat. 'Do you mind?' he asked.

'Not at all. My husband smokes. She stood up too open a window. 'Speaking of which, we really don't have much time he'll be home soon.'

'I really won't take much longer.' Gethin opened the tin and smelled the rich sweet fragrance of the tobacco before rolling one and lighting it.

Do you know where Mr Thomas is now?

Nonnie gaped at Gethin in surprise. 'Don't you know? A few months after he leave... left Radcliffe he was dead. He'd moved to Flint, out in the sticks somewhere and committed suicide.'

Gethin rollie rested on his bottom lip unlit and hung in the balance. Both Mr Dylan Edwards and Mr Hughes had committed suicide. And something connected both of them to Radcliffe. Was this a coincidence or were they collateral damage for something bigger? Possibly some kind of paedophile ring?

Gethin stuffed his things into his satchel as Nonnie cleared the teacups from the table.

'I wondered if you'd mind me having that photograph of Penny.'

'Well, it's the only one I have of Penny, if you understand. But if it helps you find Alison's murderer, then take it.'

'Thank you.' He slid the photo from its crispy clear sleeve and dropped it into file 10.81, buckled his satchel and stood to say farewell to Nonnie. Her need to shine some truth on what happened at

Radcliffe had guided him to her. He appreciated her courage, despite the subtle flare of fear that something bad might come of her actions.

As they walked to the door, she passed him his jacket. 'It's good to have finally met. You're a brave and courageous woman. What you've tried to do for those children. We need more like you.'

She smiled and brushed his compliment away. 'It's them who were brave.'

He buttoned up his jacket. 'Stay safe, Nonnie.'

She shook her head for the last time before he stepped over her threshold into the wet Spring air.

As he closed the gate behind him, he looked back at Nonnie. A woman who had never wanted to be exposed to all those bad things. The cross on her chest caught the low sunlight and flickered slithers of light until the sun moved behind a darkened cloud and everything seemed cold again.

He jogged across the lane towards his car suddenly feeling as if he had less time. Whatever happened at Radcliffe, Gethin believed was the reason that Alison was dead.

20

Angela

Angela stood behind the large iron gates of the school waiting for Joel and Jason, her chest heaving from the physical exertion of running down Lewis Drive. She'd forgotten the time. Shoals of children were already spilling out onto the school path and fields.

Wearing only a thin Polar sweater and leggings, Angela folded her arms across her chest to keep herself warm. Her shoulders hunched up around her neck as the first spattering of raindrops fell on the crown of her head. Angela scanned the flurry of excited children hoping to see the two boys, before the beginning of another spring downpour soaked them all.

Always the bloody last out of the gates, Mun.

She lifted her hand and pushed her blonde hair behind her ears hoping her son would get a move on.

'Alri… Ang.'

Angela swung around to see Sophie stood next to her.

'Hey, I thought we agreed I'd pick Jason up today.'

Sophie smiled. 'I managed to get away a little earlier than expected. It all went well though.'

'Where's Cath now? Was she okay?' Angela chewed at her gum as she wondered how her daughter would have taken the whole thing. A few times she'd been ready to call over to Sophie's. Tell her she didn't think it was a good idea, that maybe it was too soon.

'She's doing okay you know. I'm not going to mention the cutting yet. I've just explained that I need a teenager to analyse as part of my course. She seemed happy with that. She's an emotionally bright girl.'

Angela laughed. 'Too bloody right. She'll know what you're up to, even if she doesn't say.'

'At least she didn't bring Daisy Duke. Don't think I could have coped with that.'

Angela rubbed up and down her arms, looked at the old trainers on her feet.

'Lisa gave me some stuff to put down for the cockroaches. I think it's working. I've pulled everything out from the kitchen, hence the way I look.'

Sophie's eyes darted to the few parents left waiting at the gates, then leaned in towards Angela. 'I wouldn't worry about what this lot think. Appearances aren't everything. Look at me.'

Angela nodded and smiled. Sophie had a style of her own; loose flowing skirts, patchwork velvet coats and earrings that almost hit her shoulders.

'Do you think you can help, Catherine?'

'Yes. I think so.' Sophie put her hand on Angela's shoulder. 'Part of my course is also being totally confidential about what I'm told. But I will need to share it with one tutor.'

Angela forced a smile and nodded.

'She liked some of my books on alternative and complementary medicine.'

Angela grimaced and shook her head. 'She wasn't that impressed by all that yoga and meditation stuff.'

Sophie chuckled and squeezed Angela's shoulder and smiled again.

'She'll be fine.' Sophie glanced towards the school. 'Where are those boys? Slow coaches.'

Angela's eyes scanned the school field and entrance. Only a few children trundled out now. She saw Joel and waved. He raced towards her like a kamikaze pilot, his shirt untucked and flapped like a billowing kite behind him. He lurched towards her and thrust his arms around her waist.

'Wow, hello honey. Where's Jason?'

'I waited for him in the cloakroom like you said, but he didn't come.' As Joel spoke, he peered up at Sophie.

'I'm sure he'll be in there somewhere looking for his school kit or lunch box. I should have reminded you, he's a dawdler.' Sophie smiled.

Despite her words, Angela sensed a subtle nervousness in Sophie's voice as she spun around as if expecting Jason to be there. Like some game was about to be played out by the two boys. 'I did tell him he'd be walking back with you and Joel.'

An eerie stillness now surrounded them. In the distance, parents and children dotted the streets with colour as they drifted their way home.

Angela worried that she'd missed Jason leave school. She had been a few minutes late to the gate. She swallowed and peered along Lewis Drive in the other direction towards the petrol station; some children often stopped at the garage to buy a ten-pence mixture.

'Okay, why don't you pop into the school and speak to Mrs Williams? He's probably still inside. Boys, eh!' Angela heard the tenseness in her own voice despite every effort to remain calm. She rubbed her chapped hands together.

'I'll stay here just in case he comes out.'

Sophie moved without hesitation down the school path towards the school. Angela watched as she picked up pace and jogged the last few metres towards the main entrance and disappeared inside.

Angela held Joel's hand, her grip tightening with each minute that passed until she saw a worried looking Sophie reappear with Mrs Williams. They exchanged a few words, then Sophie scurried back down the path towards Angela as Jason's teacher darted back into the school.

'They've said he was one of the first out-of-class today.' Sophie's voice rasped as she spoke and cleared her throat in a continuous manner, as if restraining her growing fear. 'They said he might have headed home without me.'

Angela glanced up the street. 'I would have seen him though?' The sharp burn of bile rose in her throat. 'Is there anywhere else he likes to go after school?'

Sophie's eyes continued to sweep the area. Then she stopped and turned towards Angela.

'Oh my God. Angela. What if it's him?'

Angela placed her hands over Joel's ears.

'I don't think Colin would do something like this…'

'No, not Colin… him?'

'You mean Dom?' Angela shook her head. Don't be silly. He doesn't know where we live?'

'Maybe he found out.'

'Sophie. I think you're over-worrying. Come on. I'm sure they're right and he's made his way home. Or gone to the park with his friends. Joel's done that to me before.'

Sophie nodded. Her large brown eyes soaked with desperation. 'Okay.'

They hurried up Lewis Drive as droplets of rain greyed and

dampened the path they walked. Angela held onto Joel's hand until they reached her back gate. He'd not spoken but Angela had felt his hand tighten around hers.

Sophie crossed the road to her house without a word.

'I'll check he's not at the park,' Angela called behind her.

Within a few minutes, with Joel tucked indoors with Catherine, Angela run to the park. The park burst with the energy of children on swings, climbing bars and slides—but no Jason. As she returned up the back path and across the road towards Sophie's house, she glanced down at her trembling hands and crossed her fingers. *God. I hope he's safe at home with Sophie. I should have been at those school gates on time. I know this is my fault!*

She knocked on the door with a sharp quick rap and waited. Her eyes wandered towards the open outhouse. Coats hung on pegs, an umbrella poked out of a wicker basket, shoes littered the floor. And there, amongst them, Jason's scuffed school shoes. She sighed with relief as she heard Sophie's voice and footsteps. The door opened.

'He's here then. Thank goodness.' She glanced down at his school shoes.

But something was wrong. Sophie stood there her eyes like two hot coals in snow. Red-rimmed with heat and emotion. 'Come in. Yes, he's here, he is.' Her words rushed and jittery. She gestured for Angela to step inside and shut the door.

'I've sent him upstairs to change. He's acting a little weird. Saying weird stuff. I can't get much out of him.'

Sophie walked into her kitchen. 'Coffee or wine?'

'Coffee please.'

'Sugar?'

Angela shook her head. 'No.'

Each second that passed Angela thought that Sophie's calmness was hiding something bigger. It didn't feel right.

Angela followed Sophie into her lounge, the mug of coffee warming her chilly hands. Sophie's house was how Angela imagined it to be. Full of eclectic and bohemian furnishings.

'Have you called the school to let...'

Sophie nodded as she took a sip of her wine.

Throws covered sofas, two bean bags littered the wooden flooring, and one wall had an array of photos, paintings, and prints covering the wall. Yucca plants and spider plants filled corners and hung from the ceiling in woven baskets.

A dark wood piano on the other side of the room took up a large space next to the dining table. Jason's school bag was slung against its side.

'Didn't know you played.'

'Not very well. My husband played, and Jason plays sometimes.'

Angela tried to conceal her surprise. She rarely heard Sophie speak of her husband. As she flickered her eyes around the room, she noticed there were no photos of him either.

A noise above made her look up. Jason sat on the open staircase, peering between the slats at both of them. His eyes and cheeks were red with emotion and shame. He snuffled.

'Hello, beaut. You had us all worried, you know.'

'Sorry.'

Sophie's voice interjected, more tense than before.

'Jason don't sit on the stairs. I've asked you to go upstairs and change, please.'

Jason dragged himself up from the open staircase and trudged up the stairs.

A strange silence filled the air as Angela sipped at her coffee. Why wasn't Sophie explaining anything? Something wasn't right. 'What's going on, Soph?'

Sophie brought her finger to her full lips and shook her head a little.

Angela got the message loud and clear. Once they heard Jason disappear, Sophie spoke in a hoarse whisper.

'Jason said a man called Dom gave him a lift home from school.'

Angela gasped and thrust her hand over her mouth. 'You've got to be bloody kidding me.'

Sophie shook her head and moved in closer to say something. 'No. I wish I was. He told Jason I had asked him to pick him up.'

This time, Angela could hear her own words split and crack through her vocal cords.

'He... he didn't do anything to Jason?'

'No.' Sophie's head shook in sharp excessive motion. 'That's the first thing I asked. She hesitated. 'This is bad though, real bad, isn't it?' Sophie stared into space as if lost in her own troubled thoughts.

'Sophie. What are you going to do? Are you going to call the police?'

Sophie sighed deeply and shook her head. 'That's exactly it. How can I? They will start asking questions. We can't risk it. And I think he knows we won't.'

Angela chewed on the inside of her gum.

If only I had been a few minutes earlier.

'It's a warning to us.' She spoke just above a whisper.

'Sophie I'm so sorry. I should have got to the gate earlier. Been there sooner.'

Sophie gripped Angela's hand tightly and moved it up and down as she spoke. 'Don't you dare go blaming yourself like that? Women do that far too readily.'

Angela responded with a tepid smile, not convinced by Sophie's considerate words.

'Why don't you ring Roni and Lisa? Tell them what's happened.'

Sophie turned and peered out the window towards her garden and the fields.

'He knows where we live Ang. How the hell can that be? And what if he tries to do something like this again? We all have children. What kind of man is he to do this?'

Angela tried to steer the conversation, 'Okay. Did you ask Jason what car it was?'

'He thinks it was a BMW. Definitely black. Yes, black. He said the windows were dark. I think he means tinted. We don't see many cars like that around here.'

It sounded like Colin's car, too. For one brittle moment, Angela feared Colin might play some sick game on them. Perhaps he'd discovered Dom's name.

'There's something else, too.' Sophie picked up an ornate wooden box from her coffee table and opened it. She pulled out a small rectangular piece of pink paper from it and passed it to Angela.

'He gave this to Jason.'

'What? It's a Monopoly note.' Angela brought the note to her nose to sniff.

'It's Polo, Ralph Lauren,' said Sophie. 'I can't stand the smell of it. Too overpowering for me.'

Angela felt her forehead crease in confusion. 'I don't understand this, Mun.' For a moment they stood staring at the note until Angela used to bad scenarios stepped up with a line of action.

'Right. Jason? Has he had anything to eat or drink?'

'Not yet.'

'Okay. He'll need something. Something sweet. I'll make a hot chocolate and sandwich for him. You ring Roni and Lisa. Ask them to come to yours as soon as possible.'

Five minutes later Sophie walked into the kitchen. 'I've spoken to both of them. Lisa doesn't have any more clients this afternoon and Roni is already home. They'll be over in half an hour.'

'Did you tell them what it's about?'

'No. Just told them it was urgent, and we really needed to talk. Of course, Roni found it difficult to leave it at that. But it's not something I could say on the phone.'

'Of course.' Angela agreed. She turned to face Sophie. 'Why don't you take these up to Jason. You know better than any of us how confused he'll be feeling right now.

Angela gave the sandwich and hot chocolate to Sophie and watched as she moved quietly up the stairs. She knew what Sophie would be thinking and feeling. Protecting your children from harm was a mother's instinct. Sophie would be feeling guilty. Wondering if her own actions had inadvertently caused her son harm.

Angela settled onto a bean bag and waited. She could hear them talking upstairs. For a moment she thought she heard Jason giggle. Then, she remembered that Catherine didn't know what had happened. She called her and explained she was at Sophie's. That she wouldn't be too much longer and to tell Joel that Jason was safe and home. Catherine had the sense not to ask questions. Angela knew they would come later.

As she moved back towards the bean bag, she heard a rhythmic rat tat tat on Sophie's front door. She glanced at the clock on the shelving. Only twenty minutes had passed.

She called up the stairs. 'Don't worry. I'll get it.'

Angela opened the door to a terse looking Roni and a puzzled smile from Lisa.

'Hello ladies, come in. Sophies upstairs with Joel for a minute.'

She closed the door and followed them to the kitchen.

'What's this about?' Roni pulled a small bottle of gin and another of tonic from her large leather bag. She reached up for glasses from the shelf, sliced a lemon even before Angela could string together a response.

'I think Sophie should tell you,' Was all Angela could muster.

'It must be serious for Sophie to ring us.'

225

'Yes, it is. She didn't want to say much over the phone. I suggested she should call. I hope this was ok?' Angela grimaced.

'Of course, it is Angela.' Lisa placed her hand on Angela's shoulder and smiled.

Roni passed a drink to Lisa and Angela. 'I have a feeling we are going to need this.'

The women made their way to the lounge. Roni sat on one of the large ecru beanbags, which didn't seem to suit her long limbs at all. Lisa sat in the L shaped sofa with Angela. A silence swept through the women as they sat and waited for Sophie. Angela brushed along the leaves of a spider pant on the small table next to her wondering how the women would take the news.

Sophie glided down the staircase without making eye contact with the women. She sat the other side of Lisa and poured more wine into her glass from the bottle left on the table.

She gulped down a generous mouthful of her wine before speaking.

'Sophie.' Lisa stretched her arm out and placed it on Sophie's shoulder and smiled. 'Slow down or we might not get a word out of you.'

'My new party trick... To get drunk and talk.' Sophie mocked.

'Oh Sophie. What have you done this time?'

'Charming.' Sophie took the Monopoly note out of her pocket and handed it to Roni.

She frowned. Bemused. 'It's a Monopoly note. And?'

Roni turned the note over several times in her hand.

'What's this about?'

'I don't know?' responded Lisa.

'It's Dom.' Sophie exhaled the words so quickly they might have missed them.

'The bastard managed to convince my son to get into his car.' Her voice cracked as she spoke. 'He gave Jason that Monopoly note. He's warning us and used my son to do it.'

Roni's eyes widened exposing too much white that it appeared almost unnatural. 'You saying he knows where we live?'

'No, I'm saying he could have done fucking anything to my son!'

Silence like the decreasing space between a heavy rock falling and hitting the ground pervaded the room. Lisa was the first to react.

'Poor, poor Jason. Is he okay, Soph?'

'He wasn't physically hurt. If that's what you're asking? Dom told him he was a friend of the families to entice him into the car.'

'I'm terrified. He's going to do something else, much worse. I mean, the children. They live in that park. I know Gladys keeps an eye out for them. But how many of us can honestly say we know where they are all the time? We've never really needed to worry before now?'

'Are you sure it was him?' Lisa continued to stare at the note in Roni's hand as she spoke.

'If I'm to believe what my son said. He told Jason his name. Too much of a coincidence, don't you think?'

'Sorry. I don't mean it to sound that way.'

Sophie shook her head. 'It's okay Lisa. I guess it's all been a bit too much to take in.'

Lisa pinched her lips together. 'I think I know why he's given Jason a Monopoly note.'

The way Lisa's words stretched out in a flat, slow rhythm startled Angela.

'What do you mean?' Roni asked.

A look of guilt and alarm flooded Lisa's soft features.

'My daughter passed me a Monopoly note the night we went out to Cardiff. I put it in my clutch bag thinking nothing of It… the same bag Dom pulled from my shoulder.

'Lisa, that wouldn't tell Dom where we live?' Roni's words rang with impatience.

Recently, Steven and Becky were squabbling over Monopoly with some friends. Becky was spoiling the game because she was scribbling on the notes. I thought nothing of it.' Lisa looked around nervously at the others. This was the second round of disturbing news of the evening and flumes of disquiet now swirled around the ladies, making it difficult for them to get a perspective on the situation.

'What did Becky write on the notes, Lisa?' Roni continued to stare into her glass as she spoke.

'Our address.'

Angela gasped and thrust her hand to her mouth.

Lisa reached into her pocket for her cigarettes.

'She practises writing her name and address. I've always told her how important it is that she remembers her address and phone number.' Her hand shook as she lit her cigarette.

'There's nothing written on that note.'

'That's because the Monopoly note Becky gave me was green, not pink.'

'Fuck. This is all we need.' Angela heard the hint of judgement in Roni's voice and felt her cheeks burn with restrained agitation towards Roni's lack of empathy towards Lisa. People make mistakes.

'It could have been worse. Jason is upstairs safe.'

Everyone nodded and Angela realised in that passing moment something inside her was transforming. She was becoming bolder, in a way that felt more authentic and calmer.

Veronica pulled herself up from the bean bag and began pacing back and forth Sophie's lounge.

She stalled and looked at the women in turn. 'Why hasn't he just knocked on a door and demanded his wallet back?'

Lisa blew out a long plume of smoke. 'Well, he has no real proof we took it does he? Anyone that evening could have taken his wallet?'

Roni shook her head. 'You're missing my point. If he believes we took it, and still hasn't approached us, or the police, then what is driving him?' She answered her own question. 'I think the man is some kind of sociopath. He's playing with us and enjoying it. The sick bastard.'

'What if he's capable of worse?' Lisa asked as she rubbed up and down on her cheek.

'He might be. But you can't think that way. That's how he wants you to think...to feel. We can help ourselves more by taking some necessary precautions.' Everyone looked at Angela; she swallowed.

'How?'

'I'm used to men like him. You could start by having some security cameras fitted to your houses?'

'Yes. That could work.' Roni's eyes flickered. 'That would include your house too, Ang.'

'I can't afford it. I'm selling what I have just to make ends meet.'

'We'll pay for you.' Lisa glanced at Roni as she spoke.

Roni nodded. 'Yes, we need to protect each other now. We don't know who he might target next. And you were with us that evening Ang.'

Despite the awful circumstances, Roni's words had dripped like syrup into Angela's ear. Her friendship with these women, one which she had wanted to nullify only a couple of days ago, now imbued her with a sense of belonging that seemed almost alien given the dangerous situation their actions had placed her.

Lisa pushed her cigarette butt into the ashtray. 'Also, if Colin is snooping, he's also a threat to all of us now.'

Angela peered at each woman.

Do I owe it to them to trust them?

Despite her uncertainty, she turned to Roni.

'Okay. Yes. I will. But on one condition. As soon as I can afford it, I pay you back.'

'And the children?'

'We need to be more vigilant. Let Gladys know. And if they go to the park someone has to be there at all times, even if Gladys is there.'

Everyone agreed with Lisa. Then each one of them fell into a silence.

Sophie shifted on the sofa, breaking the quietness. 'Remember that film about the husbands whose wives were robots, and no one knew at first?'

'Yeh. *The Stepford Wives.* I lived among them for a while,' Angela responded.

'Well, us lot are the antithesis of that. We all have our reasons for sure.'

'Yes, I guess so. But that doesn't mean all men are,' said Lisa.

Sophie's and Roni's expressions said it all. Lisa rolled her eyes and despite everything, they laughed a little.

'It's getting late and Catherine's with the children.' Lisa and Angela stood to leave.

As Angela scampered across the road with Lisa, a blood orange sky burnt the horizon. She thought of her own fears, the ladies' fears and the cruel games men play to hide their own fears.

She stopped at her gate and considered her words. What if the less she feared, the more she could take action? What if she could control her fears and turn the lens back onto men like Colin, like Dom? What would she discover or learn about them?

She locked her gate and sauntered down her path realising that despite her fears and the new challenges she faced, perhaps moving onto Dafydd Drive had always been the right choice after all.

21

Gethin

Gethin stretched and yawned. He couldn't remember the last time he had woken late. The warmth of sunshine as it trickled through gaps in the closed curtain filled him with a renewed positivity, heightened by his visit to Nonnie and what he had learned.

As he pulled the curtains across to let in more daylight, he saw the van parked on the kerbside. He scrunched his eyes against the light, then opened them again. Across the side of the vehicle were the words: *We can help make your home a safe and secure environment.*

Gethin stopped. His heartbeat raced a little as he hesitated to look down at his feet. For one sweet moment, he'd forgotten his nightly excursions. With a count of three, he looked down. His feet were clean, not a bit of dirt or gravel. He sighed with relief and glanced up towards the ceiling, then shifted his gaze back out of the window towards the van outside.

He knew his behaviour would appear bizarre to the female neighbours on the street. And there were a lot of them. The van meant one thing; the strange neighbour Angela was installing home security. His Adam's apple bobbed up and down as he swallowed.

Is she having security on account of me? Like I'm that scary, for fuck's sake.

He wanted to crack a joke about it. Laugh it off. Yet something else niggled at him.

In the kitchen, he poured himself a bowl of cornflakes, heated some milk in a saucepan and poured it over the crisp flakes. He stopped and looked down at Belflo's bowl, his food untouched again.

'Crap,' he said. He hadn't seen the cat since leaving to visit Nonnie the day before. He sighed and stared at his cornflakes as they shrunk back softened by the warm milk. Without a second thought, he slipped on his trainers in the hallway and opened the door to go find the damn cat.

Stood on the driveway, he peered up and down the street. A light breeze cooled the warm air. An unusual silence filled the street. On a weekend, the drive would be filled with bikes, scooters, children playing hopscotch, chalk marks on the road. But not today. The only glimpse of life were a few children playing in a garden at the end of the Drive and two suited men stood in Angela's garden and seemed to be arguing about something. He moved closer to the hedge and peered over. He saw one of them drop to his knees to look at something near the Cherry tree.

'You'd better go and knock on her door and tell her.'

The younger of the two men responded, 'Nope. Over my dead body, am I gonna tell urghh,'

The other man stood up, shaking his head. 'For Christ's sake I'll go and tell her then, init. But find something in the van to put over it. Whoever done this is one sick bastard.'

Gethin heard the van door open, then slam shut again.

He decided to take a look himself. As he appeared round the hedge one of the men walked towards Angela's front door and knocked. The other now stood in silence staring at a sheet of plastic that covered something on the grass.

'What seems to be the problem?'

The two men looked at one another, Gethin sniffed then rubbed at his nose. Neither man spoke at first.

'What's that?'

'There's a dead cat under there. Not a pleasant sight, mate. Sick really what they've done to that poor thing.'

Gethin felt the muscles in his arms tighten as he clenched and unclenched his fists. His eyes fixated on the shape and size of the covered mound that lay near the trunk of the tree. Then he heard her voice.'

'What's going on?' she directed her question to the man stood on the pathway. He didn't respond. She followed his gaze whilst strolling along the path. Then she stopped a few yards from Gethin, refused to acknowledge him stood there and crossed her arms across her chest. He could smell her perfume.

'What's that?'

Gethin reacted the quickest. 'I think it might be Belflo.'

Startled by his response, she stepped back. 'What!'

'I found him there Ms...' His voice fell into silence. He looked at the clipboard in his hand.

'Angela. My name's bloody Angela.'

'Sorry, Angela. Whoever's done this to your cat needs executing, my love.'

'It's not my cat.'

Her eyes flashed towards Gethin. Inflated with suspicion and mistrust.

Gethin moved past her towards the rectangular piece grey plastic, bent down and lifted the edge of the plastic sheet. All eyes were on him as he tried to conceal his shock. Belflo lay there, his fur dry and matted and lifeless. His mouth was partially open, exposing his teeth. For a second, Gethin had to look away. Where his beautiful lit-up green eyes once were, were two empty black holes. Gethin whipped the plastic back down onto him before Angela could witness the horrible spectacle. He coughed involuntarily as his mind reeled. He tried to stay steady as he stood up.

'Look, we're pretty much finished up here.' Said the man who had knocked Angela's door. How about we contact Veronica with the quote by telephone. I think that might be best?'

Angela nodded.

'And sorry about your cat mate. That's the craziest thing I've seen in a while.'

Gethin watched as both men retreated into the van on the kerbside, did a quick turn in the drive and sped up the street.

'It's my cat. So, I'll move him now.'

He witnessed the confusion on Angela's face and realised what he'd said.

'Well, not exactly. He once belonged to my girlfriend.'

He shook his head as he realised, he was digging a hole for himself. A hole that was too deep for someone who didn't know him well enough to understand.

'Catherine was fond of that cat. She used to feed him.' Angela glanced towards her house. 'She loves animals. Always been the same.'

'Hazel loved this cat, too.'

Before he could say much more, he watched as Angela folded the cat into the plastic as if it was second nature, lifted the carcass from the grass, and laid it into Gethin's' arms.

'What's so crazy? What did they mean?'

Gethin sighed. 'Do you really want to know?'

'Yes. I do.'

'Someone has gouged his eyes out.'

Angela turned white. 'Nooo, that's awful!'

He watched a little startled, as she flung her hands to her head. He sensed something else in her reaction.

'Do you know who could have done this?'

Angela shook her head. But here was something in her manner that made him believe she was scared, not just shocked.

'Are you ok?' His experience as an investigative journalist kicked in. He knew she was keeping something from him.

'Of course not. I'm just thankful my children didn't find it out here.' Without another word she left his side, walked back to her house and shut the front door on him.

For a while Gethin stood there with a dead Belflo in his hands, wishing he could be anywhere else than where he stood right now. And Angela's behaviour, he just couldn't fathom it. All he could think is that somehow, she might now who had killed him. The way she had glanced around the street when he told her about Belflo's eyes.

He looked up at the cherry tree that branched out above his head with tiny blossoming flowers. In that moment he realised that he'd forbid himself so much since Hazel's death that even the passing of seasons often went unnoticed.

It took Gethin half an hour to dig a hole and bury "their" cat. He slumped into a chair and swigged warm lager from a can.

He wondered if the whole thing had been a huge mistake. Should he have stayed in London? Had it been the case that drew him back to Wales? Somewhere in his psyche he knew it had also been a need to cleanse himself of Hazel, whose bones lay trapped in a dark place deep within him since her death. He'd hidden her from sight yet carried her with him for too long.

A knock on the door startled him from his sombre mood.

He didn't want to move from the sofa at first and sneered towards the hallway. Burying Belflo had brought him to his knees. He'd discarded that cat like the memories of Hazel. In that moment, he despised himself. He gulped down some more warm beer, hoping whoever it was would go away. A second knock told him that wasn't going to happen. He cursed as he stood up to answer the door.

She stood there, her appearance meek and uncomfortable. He wanted to laugh on account of the alcohol and his mood. She smiled with closed lips and thrust a hand forward. She held a card.

'For you. My daughter's pretty upset and wanted me to give this to you. She thinks I'm being a bitch.'

'Maybe she's onto something.'

'Are you drunk?'

'Why do you want to know?'

'I think I should go.'

He watched as she turned to leave and felt a panic rise from his stomach.

'No, please. It's not been a good day. Don't go.'

He watched as she stood there peering at him through narrowed eyes, trying to fathom his intentions. He suddenly realised he really wanted her to come in. She folded her arms tight around herself.

'Please. I could do with the company.'

She eyed him up and down again, softer this time. 'I can't stay for long.'

He nodded and shut the door behind her. She stood in the hallway fiddling with strands of her hair, anxious at being in such close proximity to him. Yet he wanted to embrace her. He didn't.

A few minutes later, they sat in the lounge. Bob Dylan drawled in the background.

'There's something I need to tell you.' She looked at the card still unopened in his hand.

In his tipsy state, Gethin wanted to say something humorous and flippant, to elevate his mood. To appear more relaxed to her. Instead, he told her things about himself.

'Do you know what I do?'

Angela stopped, glanced over her shoulder at him, and shook her head in obvious confusion at his question.

He knew he'd lost all sense of purpose again around this woman.

'I'm an investigative journalist and right now I have good reason to believe there are others watching me. Even want to hurt me.' He let out a sigh, emptying his lungs of heavy air.

He watched as her head tilted and her eyebrows knitted together.

'Your cat?'

'Yes. Belflo.'

'Maybe we have some things in common after all?'

'Maybe?'

He watched as she peered at him through curious eyes again. He knew in that moment he would want to tell this woman more. She would understand.

22

Angela

Angela sucked on the end of the cigarette and wondered why she'd talked about Colin to Gethin. She hadn't planned to. It just seemed to go that way.

She yawned. It had been difficult to sleep the last couple of nights. With security fittings, dead cats, and fears that perhaps she'd told Gethin way too much for comfort. Colin had always used her words against her. Would Gethin do the same? Punish her with her own words and actions.

She shook her head involuntarily, as if disagreeing with her own thoughts. Surely not. He seemed so different to Colin. The way his eyes rested on her as she spoke, like he really understood what she was trying to say to him. This strange man who had once been an uninvited presence in her new home had, in the short time she sat with him, somehow made her feel safe. Not because of his strength, but the way in which she relaxed and became more of the person she once was in a past that had withered after meeting Colin.

She glanced at Sophie. Had she just called her name?

'Penny for your thoughts?'

'Nothing. Just a bit tired.'

Guilt frayed at her edges. Would the women find her behaviour disloyal? Find it strange how she'd confided in the stranger next door? A man she'd claimed to mistrust. She remembered his response to what she told him, his calmness. He'd crossed his legs and tapped his knee as he listened; like her own father had done when she was a child. At first, the realisation of this had shocked her. She swallowed, knowing that she'd enjoyed the way he'd given his full attention to her. Yet, she understood there was a kind of senselessness in her ping-pong behaviour.

With her hands still clasped together in her lap, Angela remembered his words. He'd claimed, like Lisa, that Colin's behaviour was stalking. And his threats of taking her children she should report to Social Services, or even the police. Angela stiffened at the thought of confronting Colin's behaviour in this way. Gethin warned her, ever so gently, that he knew people like Colin. Their behaviour would become worse. That she didn't deserve to live this way. She'd wanted to cry in that moment. But held it together. A skill gained living with Colin.

'What is going on with you?'

'This sunshine, isn't it just wonderful?'

Sophie grinned. Angela knew she didn't believe her.

Angela thought about Belflo. Gethin told her the cat had belonged to Hazel before her death. That she'd left the cat with Dina to travel out to India to join him. That she'd been in a car crash on the way to the airport. His voice had cracked in that moment, and he'd stopped. And when she had reached out and placed her hand over his, it felt natural. He hadn't pulled away.

She watched as Jason raced down Roni's lawn towards them with his Batman mask on.

'Hi, chick. You having a good time?'

'I can't find Joel, Mum. We were playing hide and seek. I think he's good at this game.'

'Good grief, I hope you're not messing up Roni's house.'

He shook his head, his dark eyes curious as he looked at Angela.

'Someone said he came out here to hide. Me and Catherine are looking for him.'

'Catherine and I,' Sophie corrected.

He turned his dark eyes and peered out from behind his mask. You could tell he'd scrunched his little face up at his mother's instruction.

Angela looked up at Roni's house. The outside appeared as white and pristine as the inside, with a patio furnished with white garden furniture- and a small stone water feature that trickled in the warm sunshine. A variety of pots were filled with carefully selected blooms of varying whites and blues. Sweet peas trailed up lattice fencing on the one side of the garden.

'I think he went back inside.' Angela smiled.

'Did he?' Jason pulled his mask off; his hairline was wet and clammy. He tilted his head, then without a word he spun around and darted back towards the house as his words jigged in the air. 'I'm gonna catch him.'

Sophie raised her eyebrows as Angela stood, which stopped the gentle rock of the sun lounger.

'I'll just check in, see if he's okay?'

'I'm sure he's fine.' Sophie's words trailed behind Angela, who was already halfway down the garden. As she passed the patio table, a sudden gust of wind blew the small potted plant off the top, sending it to the floor with a smash. She disappeared into Roni's without even looking back.

Angela called his name as she slipped her shoes off and wandered around Roni's house. She checked the lounge, dining area, toilet, and hallway.

She passed Roni in the kitchen deep in concentration as she made a puree for fresh fruit ice lollies. The sweet smell of strawberries and pineapple filled Angela's senses. Red strawberry juice bled over the sides of the mixing bowl.

Angela strode into the perfect white hallway and ascended the perfect white staircase as she both worried, then scorned her own pathetic anxiety. She heard Sophie downstairs also call his name. It gave her goose pimples, or maybe it was just the coolness of the shaded staircase. Then she heard the excited sound of children drift from Roni's spare bedroom.

The children stood at the window, peering out at the streets below. They all turned and stared at her; bemused expressions on their small features. Becky spoke first.

'Is that Joel's daddy?' Her wide eyes twinkled. She blinked, then glanced back towards the window.

Although legs buckling under her, nothing had ever felt quite like this before. Angela made it to the window. Her heart thumped against her rib cage as she caught sight of him outside.

Within seconds, she was taking the stairs two at the time, terrified her legs would give way completely from beneath her. She could feel the involuntary shaking as she pulled at the door latch and sped towards Colin's car on the top of Lewis Drive.

Catherine's high-pitched scream filled the air with a sense of urgency as she grappled at Joel, who sat in the passenger's seat. Colin was yelling at her to let go as the car inched forward. She wouldn't. The gravel picked up on her bare feet as she sprinted across the road flew up like shrapnel around her.

'No. Get out, Joel. Get out.' Angela's vocal cords screeched. She could see Catherine being pulled dangerously close towards the car as she tried to keep hold of Joel.

Angela saw Gethin on the edges of her own reality. His car pulled up the other side of the road. His car door opened. What she saw next was Gethin's crop of curly hair as he yanked the driver's door open and reached in. A fist shot out of the car towards him. Gethin rocked sideways and avoided the contact, then swung round again and reached into the car, the movement so quick you might have missed it. She heard a bellow of pain as Gethin caught his wrist and twisted it using an Aikido self-defence move.

Angela sped to the passenger's side. Joel sat wide-eyed, pale, and terrified. He stared through her as if she wasn't there. He wasn't there. She released the car strap and whipped him from the car seat. His light thin limbs wrapped around her tightly as she spun towards Catherine, who now stood frozen at the kerbside.

Angela tugged Catherine away from the unfolding chaos and ran towards the house, her features distorted by smeared kohl pencil and fear. Colin's anger-fuelled words pound a path towards her, but Angela refused to look back.

'He's my fucking son. He belongs to me, you whore.'

Angela flung her back door open, shut it behind her, and locked it, still with Joel wrapped around her like a bandage. His heart thumped against her chest, making her want to cry out in anguish.

Angela pulled Catherine's trembling limbs in towards her. They stood huddled together like this as Colin's voice howled outside.

'You've broken my fucking wrist-—my wrist.'

A car door slammed; rubber wheels screeched on tarmac as the sound of a car drove off in haste. Through the mottled glass of the back door, Angela could see moving shapes that blurred into one another. She felt faint and moved into the lounge.

The phone trilled. Angela turned her weary body to quickly and the room spun about her. She stepped back in a vain attempt to steady herself. Her mouth went dry. The heat of her son's tense body wrapped around her, making it hard to breathe. In that second, she knew, *fall backwards Angela, for the love of God, fall backwards.*

When Angela came round, she felt her body shake in that all-too-familiar way. She frowned. Crouched down near the sofa, Gethin smiled at her. She tried to lift her head, then thought better of it, resting it back down into the cushions.

She saw Catherine cuddled into Lisa; her eyes stained still with teary slips of black. She tried to force the emotion that tore at her throat. She swallowed, trying to restrain the tears that threatened to run like thin streams of shame and fear.

Was this how it would always be for us?

She felt an ache in her stomach that pulled so hard she felt she might pass out all over again. Then she sat up panicked.

'Joel. Where's Joel?'

'He's okay. Gethin carried him upstairs. He's had some sweet tea and biscuits. He's okay. Sleeping now.' Lisa smiled. 'Sophie and Jason are up there with him.'

Angela felt the panic subside as she rested her head back on to the pillow and saw the blanket that covered her body.

Gethin stood up and sat at the end of the sofa. He had a few scratches across his cheek. Angela felt a warmth, like a heavy blanket being wrapped around her each time he looked at her *that* way.

Does this man care about me? Is this what it is?

She wondered.

'Okay, I believe you're in very capable hands here. I'll take my leave.' Gethin smiled at Angela, lingered for a moment as if wanting to say something, then left, saying, 'You're all going to be okay.'

Angela knew she didn't want him to go.

'He's a fucking maniac,' Angela said. The words felt like bubbles of air escaping her mouth. Each syllable felt gratifying, full of the disgust she felt towards the man. No matter what he did, she realised her friends were always going to see her as Angela, their friend. Surely there was some strength taken from that.

A few hours later the house fell silent. The ladies had agreed to take in turns checking in on her, and Gladys had popped around with a cake which Angela no longer had an appetite for but still appreciated. She had friends now. Friends that really loved her.

Angela ached all over as the evening drew to a warmer close. She soaked in a warm bath, changed into a comfortable pair of pjs, tied her hair away from her face, and settled to read. A luxury, or at least for a long time, it had felt that way. As she pulled the paperback from her stack against the bedroom wall, she heard a knock on the door. She froze, feeling the tingling sensations of fear returning. Would Colin be so foolish as to return so soon, again? Her body stilled as she listened with senses heightened by the day's traumas. Another knock. Slow and precise. Something told her it wasn't Colin.

With some trepidation, she made her way downstairs, light on her feet, and edged into the hallway, screwing her eyes into small beads straining to see who it might be.

She recognised his shadow and felt her pulse quicken. Her stomach tumbled with anticipation. She opened the door. It was Gethin.

'How are they doing?'

She responded, 'They're alright. Sleeping.'

As she watched his eyes, she could sense his need for her. For a second, she felt the old fears return.

'Would you like to come in?'

He nodded and walked past her. She shut the door behind him. He stood in the hallway and raised his hand to touch the slight bruise on her cheek. She flinched, a natural response for her. He didn't move his hand, and instead cupped the side of her face. She felt his soft, warm fingers slide towards the back of her neck. She felt his warm breath on her face as he moved closer; could smell the subtle hint of his aftershave and the sound of her own breathing lifting, then falling. He stilled, reading her response. She felt her lips curl upwards into a small smile. He pulled gently at her tied back hair—it fell onto her shoulders, still damp from her bath. She watched as he leaned forward and touched his lips on hers. His mouth warm and soft. And her body wanting to move closer, to fold into him.

But what if he turns out to be like Colin?

She felt the sensation in her body change. An icy fear crept in; she stepped back. Tried to gain control of herself as she watched his face crumple with confusion. She shook her head more out of disappointment with herself. She'd wanted nothing more than to live in that moment more. Her memories had worked against it.

He smiled at her. No criticism or mockery came from his lips. He took her hand and squeezed it.

'I understand. It's ok.'

She smiled back, feeling his blue gaze fall and collect inside of her. She rubbed her thumb across the top of his hand.

'Fancy a coffee?'

He grinned. 'Yes. That sounds like a great idea.'

23

Gethin

Gethin woke up with a film of sweat covering his body. For a moment, he forgot where he was. His neck ached from the awkward position in which he'd slept.

He glanced down at himself lit by the early morning orange glow that bled in from outside—still dressed and wearing clean socks. A wave of relief washed over him. Angela lay asleep on the sofa in front of him. He gently eased himself from behind her and grabbed his trainers, pulling them on without undoing the shoelaces. The night before, he remembered how she'd leaned onto his shoulder and slipped into sleep like a teenager. As she slept, she'd wrapped one arm around him, and he'd welcomed it and marvelled at how natural it felt.

He shut Angela's door quietly behind him and scampered down the path and across Dina's lawn. The streets light flickered off as he turned the key and pushed the door open. There were glimpses of a new day dawning as the door shut behind him.

In the kitchen, he clicked the kettle on and took a cup from the cup stand on the side. Cats covered the mug. He put it back and took another instead. When would he contact Dina and tell her Belflo was gone? He knew how much the cat meant to Dina. He'd already decided he would omit the gory details. It would just be too awful for Dina to hear. Having Belflo was her way of feeling close to Hazel.

As he sauntered into the lounge, memories of the night before flooded back to him. He'd been shocked to hear Angela mention a man by the name of Dom. The women, after a night out in Cardiff, believed Dom might be stalking them. Their fear of him forced the decision to have cameras installed in their homes. Although Gethin wondered if the women were doing it to protect Angela too?

She guessed he hadn't taken favourably to one of the women refuting his advances. He'd asked Angela if she could remember the club they had gone to—she couldn't recall the name.

He hadn't pursued the conversation as Angela had appeared anxious and still nervous after what had happened earlier. He didn't want to cause her more discomfort. What was it about this woman? *Why do I feel so protective of her?*

He glanced at the clock on the wall—it was nearing seven. He hadn't practiced Aikido for days. This morning he would spend some time doing some simple exercise, a little meditation to calm and focus his mind, then he would begin writing up a rough first draft report.

It's where most of his journalistic experience came to the forefront. The preliminary work and his research were always a challenge, had been since he began Investigative journalism. This was his third largest investigation, and each time he wrote up the final report, it seemed a little easier. He stood to change into his joggers when the phone rang.

Gethin frowned, his eyes flickered again towards the clock. For a strange moment, he wondered if it was Angela. He picked the receiver up.

'Gethin.'

'Hi Mark. Everything okay?'

'Listen Fella. Does Dina still have her fax machine?'

'Yes. Why?'

'Need to send you something. Check it's on. If it is, wait for two faxes. Show nobody. Do you hear, Geth? Bloody nobody.'

'Got it.' The fine hairs on Gethin's neck twitched and rose like fine bristles. Mark rarely sounded so nervous.

He raced upstairs into the small bedroom Dina used as an office. He flicked the light on and moved toward her desk, relieved to discover all was good—her telephone fax was lit up, and on. He rubbed up and down his arms as he stood and stared and waited, not knowing what to expect.

An empty photo frame sat on the desk. Gethin had removed the photo of Dina and Hazel from it a couple of weeks before. Now it was safe in the garage with other similar photos. For a moment, his mind wandered as he considered how he would explain everything to Dina. The dreams he'd had, the flickers of memory and what they might mean. Fragments of his time in India were pushing up from a dark place to reveal themselves. A time when everything that he thought would be his future had fallen away after one unexpected phone call. Hazel should have been on a flight out to visit him. She never arrived.

The sound of the fax machine coming to life drew his attention back to the moment. Dina's fax machine was one of the older models. It still used the thermal paper that yellowed with age. He knew this type of paper wasn't accepted in archives or as evidence in courts of law.

The machine buzzed and clicked before a sliver of paper became exposed on one side. He tilted his head sideways to see what was being printed. The machine stopped for a few seconds, then started again.

Another image became visible. They looked like bad photo prints. Once he was sure the fax had finished, he tore the curled soft paper away at its edge and unfurled the paper both ends with his hands out onto the desk. He pulled the roller blind open to let more light into the room. At the foot of one image, there were a few handwritten notes. It was in Mark's hand.

They investigated detective Superintendent Turner in 1976 for affiliations with the paedophile group, PIE. The whole thing had been laughed out of court and kept very much below the radar. But look at the newspaper on his passenger seat. The photo was taken a few years ago, after 1976. Turner doesn't realise this photo exists- yet.

And the other photo. You tell me?

It was the same detective who had initially led the team investigating the suspected murder of Penny Hayes who was now Alison.

The first photo showed Turner sat inside an unmarked police car. Callum had penned a small red arrow, which pointed to a folded newspaper on the passenger seat of the car. The title read *Magpie*. They were a group of paedophiles who campaigned for the Government to abolish or lower the age of consent. Gethin could feel bile rise in the back of his throat. He remembered reading a while back that a journalist had infiltrated their group at the end of the 1970s and proved that many of them were just men wanting sex with children.

Gethin glanced down at the photo below. The same detective stood with Mr Hughes and a younger looking Penny in his arms. Her head rested on his chest as she turned to smile at the camera. A woman, Penny's mother he imagined, stood the other side of Mr Hughes. They stood in a room that looked to be a study. Behind them, in the distance beyond the patio doors, stood Radcliffe flanked by the oaks and cedars.

The nausea pulled at his stomach. He knew how so many faces in positions of authority and deemed to be respectful members of society wore a civilised mask that hid the horrors that lurked beneath. What was the Inspector doing there? And why hadn't he pursued the links between the murder and Radcliffe?

An hour later, Gethin sat on the stair with the phone in his hands. He tapped the receiver of the phone against his chin. As he'd presumed. The company Black-tip Construction no longer existed. Gethin wondered if the payments were to Mr Thomas for something far sinister; for allowing a large paedophile ring to abuse innocent and vulnerable children at the home? He sets the receiver on the cradle and placed the phone back down on the small table at the foot of the stairs. If there was one thing he needed now, it was the key that Alison had left with Deborah. He desperately needed Deborah to keep her promise and ring him soon.

24

Angela

Angela stood holding the front door feeling a little worried by the sudden appearance of Lisa and Roni.

'Ang, we know this is bad timing after what happened yesterday. You've been through a lot, but could we speak to you?' Lisa asked.

'Can we come in?' interjected Roni, her manner more purposeful and to the point.

'Yes, What's this about?'

The women walked straight into the lounge and sat down.

'Are the children in?'

'Catherine isn't, but then that's normal these days. Joel went out for a walk with Gladys. Why's that then?' Angela glanced toward the several pillows still on the sofa from the morning. For a tiny moment her mind wandered towards Gethin's phone call, which had woken her. The way he'd explained why he'd left early, and how he wanted to see her again.'

'Angela, are you sure you're ok?'

'Yes.'

She saw Lisa glance at the pillows as she unpeeled her jacket, placed it across her lap and stroked it down. She looked paler than usual.

'And the children. They, okay? How are they doing?'

'There doing well... For God's sake, women, what is it?'

Roni responded. 'We've been trying to find out who Dom is. We started with the name Dom d'Petri.'

'Did you find anything, then?'

'Yes, we did.'

'Can I make a coffee for everyone?'

Lisa stood up as Angela nodded a yes and made her way towards the kitchen. It was as if what was going to be said she didn't want to hear.

'For a start we discovered there are a lot of d'Petri down the docks.'

Angela frowned. 'Bloody hell. How did you find that out?'

'I have a friend who works at the registry in Cardiff for deaths, births, and certificates. To be exact, Lilly is an old friend of the families. She's in her fifties now but she helped us out no end.'

Roni continued. 'We came across several Dominique De Petri's at the registry. Dom could be a shortened version of Dominique.'

'Lilly told us that one Dom d'Petri was born in 1910 and died in 1960 of gastroenteritis and bowel perforations. Nasty stuff. Now, one Dom did interest us. He'd been recorded as presumed dead towards the end of 1978. Witnesses say they saw him going out of the dock in a fishing boat. He never returned. A few days later, pieces of the boat rolled in with the tide on Barry Island. Now, Lilly remembered the incident because one man on the boat was a descendent of the Duke of Bute, apparently. It was in the papers. Strange what you remember...'

'I'm not sure where you're going with this ladies? Are you saying someone could have stolen this man's identity?'

'Well, maybe. But this is where it gets more interesting. Lilly rang us this afternoon saying she'd found some paperwork that might be of interest.'

Lisa carried in the drinks on a large white plate. 'Couldn't find a tray.'

Angela shrugged. 'Sorry, I don't have one.'

When Dom died at sea, he left a wife and son. The wife, a Welsh woman, Elisabeth d' Petri died of a drug overdose a few years ago in some run-down house in the docks. Lilly thinks she might have been a prostitute. She also discovered an adoption certificate for their son.

'This Lilly's a resourceful woman,'

Lisa nodded. 'She does this sort of thing for people tracing their family tree. She loves it and knows all the right people.'

'Oh.'

'As I was saying social services removed him from his parents' home and put him into care. Then later he was adopted by the Reeds. They gave him their Sir name. But his Christian name was the same as his father's, Dominique; it's a Maltese thing calling your first son by the same name.'

'Wow. So, the Dom we stole the wallet from could be the son? Returned to Cardiff? Kind of makes sense, wanting to go back to the place you're from.'

'Well. That's if it is him, but it seems to fit together well, doesn't it?' Lisa pulled a pack of cigarettes from her jacket pocket and lit up. Her hand trembled a little as she gestured towards Angela if it was okay.

Angela smiled. 'Yes, please.'

'It would explain why he doesn't have a Welsh accent and seems well so turned out—I remember those manicured nails.'

Lisa's lighter zipped as she lit her cigarette, then leaned across to light Angela's.

'Shame about his manners then,' responded Roni sharply.

'Perhaps some things just can't be eradicated from one's true nature.'

Roni twitched at Angela's response.

'Ladies, we're forgetting one minor detail here. We stole his wallet in his own club.'

Angela noted in greater detail the dark circles that ballooned around Lisa's tired eyes and her obvious discomfort with the conversation.

Angela knew her own experiences of life in recent years had conditioned her for such bleak scenarios and discussions. She wasn't so sure if Lisa, despite proving herself to be the most level-headed and sensible of them all was coping with all the recent revelations.

'You okay, Lisa?'

She didn't respond at first as if deep in thought about something.

'I'm not sure. When we first started playing our Monopoly game, it all seemed strangely harmless given the fact that we are stealing from these men. None of us ever question why we really do it.'

Roni appeared agitated by Lisa's honesty. Her lips thinned into two crisp lines.

'It's a bit late to be asking that now. Don't you think?'

'Maybe not Roni… I've been thinking about it a lot lately. I can't seem to not think about it.'

'Shit, I always look back and wonder about the choices I made. Why I made them? But now. I'm learning there's nothing in the past you can change. It's pointless you know.'

Lisa sighed. 'I don't want to do this anymore. I've realised you know, on the rare occasions that a man refused our advances, we tried even harder to draw him in to our own reality. It satiated our own belief.'

'Where're you going with this, Lisa?' Roni glanced at her watch and stood up.

'Well. If a man didn't fall for our seduction— no matter how heavy we came on, what did we do in response? Can't you see? We treated them like some kind of bloody royalty and didn't take their wallet, even when the opportunity arose.'

'Were we rewarding them for their loyalty to their wives or just relieved to discover that our beliefs... opinion of men were wrong after all? That good men do exist?'

Angela cast her eyes nervously at Roni, waiting for her response. Prickles of resentment darted off her. Angela wondered if she should try to change the subject. Roni didn't seem to like men full stop; she'd had her own disappointments. Too late.

Roni's voice was slow and deliberate.

'Let's just get this right. My understanding was that you and Sophie wanted a better life for yourselves and your children. To give them the opportunities that your income alone couldn't give them. The extra tutors, the holiday, swimming lessons... and let's not forget the retraining and the salon. From where I'm stood, it had nothing to do with men.'

'I'm not sure that's entirely true anymore Roni. All of us have experienced nasty shit with men. Even you.'

Roni scowled.

'None of us ever doubted we could do this. Maybe because we were hell bent, each in our own ways, to prove our theory of men, right? Perhaps that was what really motivated us.'

'Come on, ladies. Let's stay bloody focused here, Mun! It's Dom we need to keep our attention on. If you start thinking that way, it'll screw with you. Look at me.'

They both ignored Angela's attempt at self-depreciating humour. Roni still bubbled beneath. Lisa looked as if she was about to throw up.

She watched Lisa rub across her neck. 'You're probably right, Angela. For now, we need to stay focused on Dom.'

'Yes. She is.' Roni's voice cut like crystal. 'We need to really understand who we're dealing with. What he's capable of.'

'So' Lisa shrugged. 'What next?'

'I have an idea. You might not like it, but I think it's our only option.' Roni said.

25

Gethin

Gethin sat on a wooden bench on the pathway running alongside the River Taff in Bute Park. He tried to look casual, despite the rising discomfort in his chest. What if he'd been wrong to agree to meet Eddie? He scanned with sharp and alert eyes and waited for someone that might register as the person he'd spoken to on the phone the night before.

The damp rollie stuck between his forefinger and middle finger before he dropped it between his legs to the floor and killed it with the sole of his shoe. He flicked his eyes down the long path as he heard the turning of quick bicycle wheels and pedalling. An older man on a bike whisked past.

Why had Eddie rung him last night and not Deborah?

Gethin doubted either of them trusted each other much. Eddie's voice had been deep but soft. He'd reassured Gethin that Deborah was perfectly safe with him. That she was in the safest hands she'd been in for a long time. And that he planned to take care of stuff for her.

Gethin listened carefully to his instructions before the line had left a buzzing in his ear and lots of other unanswered questions in his head. Gethin rolled his shoulders in small circular motions—he had to relax, feel a bit more in control of the situation.

His stomach rumbled as he continued to sit and flick his eyes around the park. He wondered if he looked suspicious sat there by himself. His wristwatch said it was already two o'clock. Eddie was late. Thoughts flew around his head as haphazardly as paper planes. Would Eddie actually turn up? Could this be a trap? What if he was protecting someone else? Someone who knew that Deborah and Alison had been friends. His mind flitted from a faceless Dom to Detective Superintendent Turner and Jean. He knew there was something missing. Something he couldn't see. Two people who had connections with the home had committed suicide. Both Alison and Penny were dead.

As he continued to sit and wait, he ran his mind through some familiar Aikido moves, just in case he would need to defend himself. Why was this Eddie so keen to protect Deborah? Perhaps Eddie had already discovered what the key had unlocked. Perhaps that had been his motive all along.

He lifted his sunglasses and rubbed at his red and dry eyes. He hadn't slept well. He squeezed his eyes shut a few times to release the ache. Too many things on his mind and he struggled to keep things compartmentalised. Today, he needed to. So much rested on him discovering what Alison was doing before her death. As he slipped his glasses back down onto his nose again, his eyes fixed on someone moving in the distance.

He wondered if this broad, tall man with tight-curled hair was Eddie, then watched as he turned left away from the river. Gethin glanced down at his hands and the fine lines that mapped his skin and sighed. As air passed his lips, he felt something. The hair on the nape of his neck prickled upwards. He stared ahead, knowing someone stood behind him. He controlled his breathing again with his Aikido practise of Mushi. Prepared his body for action.

He heard his name. Without turning around, he replied. 'Eddie?' The man he'd seen walking along the path slipped onto the bench next to him.

Gethin could smell Armani aftershave and leather. He also noticed that Eddie had a crooked nose, and suspected he'd been a boxer. For a few moments they sat in silence, perusing the view around them as if they were two old men enjoying a rare moment out.

Eddie removed the small black backpack from his shoulders and placed it on the bench between them. 'Take the bag.' Gethin felt his mouth go dry. He glanced up the path, then back at the bag.

'What's this? How do I know I can trust you?'

Eddie laughed. 'You can't. All I know is that Deborah trusts you. You've asked her lots of questions about Radcliffe. About Alison. She thinks this will… let's say, make things clearer.'

'So, where's the key?'

Gethin watched as a young girl cycled past next to her father. The wind caught her hair and lifted it away from her shoulders like wings.

'She asked me to go to the house. Find what was there first.'

'A house?' Gethin swallowed. Deborah hadn't said it was a key to a house. He shifted his eyes towards the rucksack again.

'Yup. A house with walls and windows and a door… in London, Ladbroke Grove. Hell of a place she had there.' Eddie paused. 'Someone else got there before me. It looked like Beirut. Turned the place upside down. I guess they were looking for this.'

His large, soft tanned hand tapped the rucksack.

Gethin's brow creased liked linen on a hot day.

'It's a child's shoebox. Deborah knew there were only so many places a person who'd spent time in care hid things. Clever doll was right. '

'But why … Why are you helping her?'

Eddie looked off across the river without a word and shrugged.

'I don't know. Pain recognises pain, I guess. No man should ever beat on a woman. You get me. And Deborah. Well, we understand each other. And I ain't aving anyone lay a finger on her now. I'm taking me and her away from all this crap. That's why I got a favour to ask you in return for this.'

Gethin could see Eddie's jaw tighten. A nervousness seemed to creep into his features. For a man of his size and nature, it surprised Gethin.

'Before all this shit gets out, give me enough time to get us out of here. When Dom finds out, it's me who took Deborah from his private clinic. He'll have others searching for us. He's been acting so weirdly lately, anyway. There's a chance he might already have worked it out.'

Gethin shifted in his seat and nodded. For the first time in a long time, he knew he was making decisions that would help another female live her life.

'Where will you go?'

Eddie turned and smiled at Gethin but said nothing.

Gethin understood. There were some things he didn't need to know. Eddie intended keeping Deborah safe and the less others knew, the safer that would be for both of them.

'This man called Dom. I heard he's into stalking women who visit his club too?'

Eddie squinted up towards the sun, crow's feet framing his rich chocolate eyes.

'Shit. You're onning about the Monopoly note women, aren't you?' Eddie didn't hide his surprise as he slipped his hand into the inside of his *Members Only* jacket, causing Gethin to tense in anticipation. The jacket itself seemed strangely inappropriate, given the warmer weather. Eddie retrieved a blackjack from the inside pocket, unwrapped its sticky paper, and popped it into his mouth. Gethin's shoulders remained tense as he spoke.

'Monopoly women. I don't understand?'

Gethin's nostrils filled with the sweet smell of liquorice as Eddie chewed and talked.

'They stole his wallet, didn't they? Got the better of him. Few do. They play his kind of games, and he liked the fucking challenge.'

Gethin grimaced as he tried to keep up. 'Games?'

'The night they fled the club with Dom's wallet, one of them dropped her handbag. Inside was a Monopoly note with a child's scribbles on it. He became obsessed with that bloody note. I nicknamed it "his little precious". Just from a few scribbles on that note, he compiled a list of addresses and sent me out looking for them.' Eddie glanced along the path. 'The thing is, Dom doesn't like losing, and those women exposed his weakness.'

Gethin dropped his head and stared into his lap. Angela hadn't told him the whole story. Why? Did she not trust him? Then it struck him. What if she was trying to protect the women? He believed Angela was far stronger than she gave herself credit for.

'He was determined to find them. I'd go as far as saying obsessed. You see, that evening he'd held onto his wallet instead of putting it in his safe. It was a mistake that sparked something in him.' Eddie shrugged and fell silent for a moment.

'Mind you, that his old man turned up a while back hasn't helped. Not seen Dom like it before. He keeps him on a pretty tight leash.'

'What's his father's name?'

'Fuck knows. Everyone calls him Missier. He looked at Gethin. 'Shit. Deborah's right. You ask a lot of questions.'

'Part of my job.'

'No shit, Sherlock. I would never have guessed.' Eddie fell silent for a moment as he picked bits of the sweet from his teeth. 'I swear he's trying to work the old pooty-tooter into an early grave which wouldn't take much cos his lungs already rattle like a burnt-out engine.'

Gethin watched as Eddie wove his fingers together, turned them out until his knuckles popped and cracked.

'I've heard a few rumours about the old geezer, but the circles I shore are full of people talking shit on someone. I make my own opinions and that old man—let's just say he ain't got much juice left in him. The way I see it, the old man's trying to make amends for any shit he might 'ave done to Dom. More than my shit of a father did.'

Gethin nodded and pulled the rucksack towards him as Eddie stood up—suddenly anxious that Eddie might actually have a change of heart.

'Time to shoot.'

'Just wondered, this Missier, does he ever work at Mako's?'

'Yup, Dom prefers him there, out of the way, out of his skin, and out of trouble.'

A toddler nearby laughed excitedly as pigeons swept down to peck at bird seed scattered on the path.

'I think Deborah wanted to find out for herself what happened to her friend. In the end, I persuaded her to stop looking through that bloody box. There's stuff in there that doesn't seem right for her to see. Do what you have to do with it.'

Gethin watched as Eddie stood there for a moment, as if wanting to say something else.

'Bit of advice. When Dom obsesses about something or someone, it rarely ends well.'

Gethin watched, unable to move a limb, as Eddie glided away

262

through throngs of people, then turned right and disappeared.

Gethin opened the rucksack, glanced around once, then lifted the lid off the tattered pink shoebox to peer inside. He could see paper, filled envelopes, floppy discs and something that looked like a miniature camera. He blew through his lips, placed the lid back down, pulled the drawstrings and threw the rucksack on to his back.

A cold crisp wind come up off the River Taff, as he stood. The sun sunk momentarily behind a cloud. Everything around him seemed to lose its colour a little. The Taff rushed by in a hurry, its crystal dappled surface gone grey. Gethin sighed. He needed to get back to Dina's so he could sift through the contents of the shoebox.

Gethin rattled on Angela's door. No answer. He cupped his hands and leaned into the small window trying to see inside. He stopped and peered towards Lisa's house next door; the shifting bright images of a television shone light into the growing darkness outside.

He wound round into Lisa's and knocked on her door. Waited in the dying light with his hands buried deeper into the pockets of his jacket. The stiff wind that swirled in the small patio area below the kitchen window pestered the shrubberies along Lisa's back wall.

Muffled footsteps, then the disfigured shape of Lisa behind the shifting patterned glass of the door appeared. He could hear metal scratching along metal as the key turned in the lock. The door opened. Lisa stood there with dark circles cupping tired eyes and a forced smile that told Gethin something wasn't at all well.

'Hi Gethin. This is a bit of a surprise. Everything alright?'

He nodded, knowing they both knew things were far from alright. 'Lisa, I've just been round to Angela's house. No one was in. I wondered if you knew where she was?'

She held the door tight to her body with fingers turned white as they gripped it. Gethin sensed at any moment she might slam the door shut on him. She studied him with narrow eyes, as if on the precipice of life and death.

Then confusion swept across her soft features like a mini tsunami—as if uncertainty of what she could or couldn't say—causing great unease and pain. Her fingers gripped even tighter around the door's edge as it slid slowly towards him.

He softened his voice.

'Please Lisa. Angela told me what's going on. Dom. He's dangerous. I think he might know where you all live.'

Lisa's face crumpled as she nodded.

'This man won't stop. It's not just about you stealing his wallet. He's involved in a lot of other nasty stuff and that wallet can prove it.'

He saw the flash of fear strike in Lisa's eyes.

'Please Lisa. I need to know where she is.' He felt the desperation in his voice and like a spark of fiery light created by solid matter striking solid matter, he realised that which he had denied himself. The foul mouthed; gutsy neighbour of Dina's had broken the walls that had kept him locked inside since Hazel.

'She's gone to Dom's club with Roni.'

He blinked in disbelief. 'Which one?'

Lisa blinked back. 'Lemon.'

For some strange reason, the word *Lemon* reminded him of a shark. He brushed the sweeping image away.

'It was Roni's idea. She didn't want us to be continually looking over our shoulder. Living in fear is no way to live. They have the wallet with them.' She stopped and bit at her lip again.

'I think Roni thinks by giving it back, Dom will stop threatening us.'

'When did they leave?'

'About forty-five minutes ago.'

He realised he must have arrived minutes after they'd left.

'That's good Lisa. Now listen. Dom is dangerous. Lock your doors and windows and wait.'

He'd heard the laughter of children coming from inside Lisa's house, including the voice of Catherine.

'Don't let anyone leave. Not even Catherine. I'll bring the others back here. Got it.'

Lisa shifted her body from one foot to the other as Gethin walked away.

'Will he try to hurt them?'

Gethin stopped halfway down the path and turned. 'Not if I get there first.'

26

Gethin

There were already smudges of people gearing up for a night out. Youngsters full of anticipation jostled for space along the paths of St Mary's Street. Gethin pushed his way through, shoulders punching shoulders as he headed towards the Lemon club. A splinter of day remained to the West of the city, obstructed by buildings that loomed like dark giants on a stark horizon.

Gethin turned left into a side street, hoping his own sense of direction wouldn't let him down. Ahead the neon sharp lights of the club told him he could keep his faith despite his breath fragmented by pace and uncertainty. Now he would need to muster all his senses of resilience. The word "tomiki" injected itself into his mind—to be fluid like water.

He approached the entrance of the club. The bouncer was over six-feet-tall, with an inhuman torso and arms that might stop a tank in its tracks, he looked Gethin up and down and smirked. He ignored him and focused on his intention. To find the women who might be inside and invite them to leave. He walked straight past the bouncer and up the stairs. His reflection bounced off several mirrors. He avoided the distraction and remained calm as he hit the top step. The sound of a walkie-talkie crackled behind him.

He glanced up at the small camera above the double doors in front of him. Nothing could deter him now. The door swung with ease as he pushed it open and stepped inside. The heat hit his skin as if he was stepping from a plane into a hot and unfamiliar climate.

Small prismatic crowds filled the area around the bar as coloured lights turned and moved with the beat of music. The low hum of people chatting, and occasional laughter carried in the thick air. A multitude of fragrances bit into his throat. He coughed. He had to stay focused. The sign for the men's toilet hung over a door to his far left. He edged round the still empty dancefloor. Twinkling lights scattered across the ceiling above him. He couldn't remember the last time he'd stepped inside a club; it wasn't really his thing. Hazel had persuaded him a few times, as she had loved to dance.

He spotted another bouncer tall and muscular eyeballing him on the other side of the dance floor nearer the bar. *Where were they?*

Gethin noticed there were several alcoves running along the back wall behind the large bar area. Using the bathroom would give him time to think about things and draw anyone who planned to harm him into a quieter area with fewer people around. The tactic had worked before, especially with those who misunderstood his strength and skills. Like the entrance, the heavy door swung open with ease and hit the wall behind with a loud thud.

The urinals were clean and, to his surprise, didn't smell as they so often did in such places. He idled towards them and unzipped, his body alert to sound and movement behind him as he traced the fine hair lines cracks in some of the white tiles in front of him. To the right, a mirror in tinted rectangular squares gave him a view of the door. He heard the door opened and flickered his eyes towards the mirror without turning his head.

A young man suited up, his tie loosened, his top button undone, swayed in and nodded at Gethin. Gethin nodded back curtly as he watched the man disappear into one of the cubicle toilets behind him.

Gethin closed his eyes and breathed and waited. As he zipped himself back in, he heard the door open again, but no thud followed. This time Gethin turned his head around to find the bouncer he'd saw earlier at the bar side stood there eyeballing him. With an air of confidence, Gethin turned his head away, zipped his jeans, then turned to wash his hands at the small sink.

The bouncer took a few steps into the bathroom and scanned the space before looking back at Gethin, who had a full view of him in the mirror. His pinprick eyes cast close together gave a mean look and his nose was a mess, a boxing nose, thought Gethin. The tattooed words, *My mother, my heart* twitched at the top of his right arm as he flexed his muscles. The snake tattoo on his neck slithered and pulsated. He continued to stare at Gethin as if his meat quota for the day had not yet been satiated.

'Lost or something?' said Gethin as he wiped his hand on a rolling towel and turned to face him.

The bouncer scowled. His fists tightened as his head thrust forward in a ridiculous show of aggression.

'Okay! Fight club it is then.'

The bouncer launched himself at Gethin, his right arm raised as if to cause a fistful of harm. Gethin stepped sideways, blocking the bouncer's flailing arm with his left hand. His right hand flew through the air and slapped the bouncer with immense force across the face. His fatty jowls quivered as his head ricocheted sideways by the powerful impact; dazed weasel eyes tried in vain to comprehend what had happened. He stood immobilized for a few seconds. With an instinctive speed, Gethin continued. He grabbed the bouncer's thick arm, rapidly rotated his hips, dropped to his knee, and took the bouncer off his feet. All two hundred pounds of him slammed into the floor. The thud of his head hitting hard tiles rendering him unconscious. Gethin, without hesitation pivoted on his knee and felt the man's fat plump wrist for a pulse. *Phew, He's still alive!* He'd forgotten how powerful the kokyu nage move was. He stepped behind the bouncer's body and rolled him into a recovery position.

As he stood up, he heard the flush of a toilet and a door open behind him.

'Poor man has passed out; he'll be okay in a minute.' He watched as the second man blinked. His eyes screwed up as he focused on the dark mass that lay across the grey, white tiles of the floor. Recognition flickered like a ray of light in confusion.

'Humph. Deserves it anyway. I swear that arsehole stole my wallet in here once.'

Gethin said nothing. Just thankful that the altercation had been short and quick.

The man scrunched his nose. 'Urrghh, fuck; that stinks.'

They both looked down at the bouncer. Gethin felt his stomach flip a little. Without saying another word, he stepped over the beat bouncer, washed his hands again and left. He needed to find the women.

A kaleidoscope of colour swirled from the lights near the DJ box as he walked with a briskness that stood out from the normal crowd, towards the quieter alcoves behind the bar.

It was then he glimpsed her white, Blondiesque hair. Roni sat next to her rigid and eyes fixed defiantly towards Dom, who sat across from them. He must have seen Angela's alarmed expression as she caught sight of Gethin. Dom twisted round, saw Gethin and shifted upright in his seat with a smirk that told Gethin he would need to be very cautious.

Gethin saw Roni's lips move as she spoke, her expression still fixed on Dom. If she was scared, she hid it well. As he continued to skim the furthest edge of the dance floor and make his way towards where they sat, he saw the bouncer stood at the bar watching him.

Another older familiar looking man who also had his eyes on Gethin turned, exited the bar, and made his way to another door on the other side of the club. All Gethin had to do was stay calm and get the women away. In the ten minutes he'd had to flick through the items in the shoebox before going to Lisa's earlier, Dom's name had cropped up several times.

At times like these, he knew his Aikido training might play its part in protecting him and others. He glanced back towards the women. Roni pushed something across the table towards Dom—his wallet. Gethin looked above. There were no cameras in this area of the club. Clever, thought Gethin.

As he passed tables surrounded with smiling and jovial faces, he focused his breathing below his navel in a further attempt to stay calm and keep his adrenal running through his veins under control.

He approached the table as Dom cast his eyes away from the women in an arrogant gesture of control. The smirky expression gone, he smiled. He sat even more upright and broadened his chest. These subtle suggestions of aggression didn't go unnoticed by Gethin. He saw Dom's eyes flicker towards the toilets.

'He might need seeing to if you're wondering. A "house clean" might be required.' Gethin pointed to his backside and pulled a face. He knew this kind of behaviour would confuse Dom. Agitate him and force him to make mistakes.

'We finally meet, Gethin.'

Dom stretched his hand out. Gethin ignored it and glanced towards the women.

'Well. Well. You have to be fucking kidding me.'

'That's not very polite,' responded Gethin.

Veronica slanted her eyes at Gethin, then at Angela. 'What have you done?'

Angela shrugged 'Nothing to do with me,'

Both women looked up at Gethin, their lips thin lines of confusion as to why he was there.

'Ladies, it's time to leave.'

Dom's jaw tightened as words seethed from between his lips. 'I think not. The ladies stay.'

He leaned back into his seat, his face like stone despite the smile he used to conceal his simmering temper. Gethin caught the subtle nod of his head, too.

He turned to see the bouncer that grabbed his upper arm as if it was heavy debris that needed clearing. Gethin stayed grounded and continued to control his heart rate.

'C'mon, out!'

'That's not going to happen unless these ladies leave with me. Please let go of my sleeve.' Gethin's eyes bore into the bouncer, unflinching. Calm.

Gethin scanned around him for other approaching dangers, then sized up the bouncer gripping his arm. He would be lighter than the beef he'd handled in the urinals. He took several deep breaths, preparing his body.

'Out.' The bouncer repeated as he once again attempted to shove Gethin towards the exit. Gethin could see sweat glisten on the bouncer's face as he realised, he'd miscalculated Gethin's strength.

In one fluid motion, Gethin moved to the side of the bouncer, took a firm hold of his meaty hand with his right hand from above. Simultaneously, he rotated his body clockwise and swung his left arm upwards to contact the bouncer's right elbow. As Gethin expected, the bouncer screeched with the sudden shock of pain, released Gethin's arm and staggered backwards.

Gethin brushed down his sleeve. 'Ladies.'

As the ladies stood, Gethin's hand whipped across the table like a Geckos tongue and swept up the wallet before Dom could react. He slipped it inside his jacket.

Dom threw an angry, side-on glance at the ego-bruised bouncer. The bouncer needed little persuasion to quell his humiliation. He lurched towards Gethin for the second time, trying to grab his wrist. Gethin deflected the intended grab and caught the bouncer's hand with both of his to employ Sankyo—a painful wrist lock that caused more harm the more you tried to resist. The bouncer cursed and screeched in pain as he fell to his knees. With a familiar agility, Gethin placed his foot between the bouncer's thighs- then with one quick move of his knee he'd knocked the bouncer out. His body quivered like jelly as he fell backwards and hit the carpeted floor.

From the corner of his eye, Gethin saw Dom lift a walkie-talkie from his pocket. Angela's arm spun outwards and sent it flying through the air. Had he witnessed a faint smile lift the corners of her lips? He didn't have time to consider it.

Dom had stood up as the women inched away from the table. He shot a look at Gethin.

'I'd watch yourself. Groping around in the fucking dark for little titbits can be a dangerous game for someone like you.'

'I'll take my chances,' responded Gethin.

'Ladies.'

Both women continued to back away, this time the fear in their face palpable and set like concrete.

It was the fluorescent red light that reflected on the metal of the cylinder that Gethin saw first before the gun levelled with his forehead.

He lifted his arms up. 'Woah! There's no need for that.'

Dom's eyes were dark swirls of hate that fixed onto Gethin and dripped with hostility. Gethin backed away slowly from the muzzle of the gun, hoping he would draw Dom to the darker area of the club and away from the women.

The women fled the scene unopposed. From the corner of his eye, he saw Angela look back in his direction, her features troubled before she disappeared through a set of doors.

Dom's lips curled. And for a moment, Gethin wondered why he hadn't attempted to stop them.

Using the hara, Gethin tried to control his heartbeat, which now beat a storm in his chest. He would have to be quick and acutely efficient to get out of this before more bouncers became alerted to what was going on.

'You knew where they lived. Why didn't you just call the police, Dom? I guess all those elocution lessons haven't taken the docks out of you after all.'

Gethin knew the fine line between agitation and craziness. He didn't believe Dom would shoot him. Distraction was Gethin's only weapon. To make Dom think of the past and remove him from the present. It would help to slow down his reactions to any moves he planned to make.

Dom smirked. 'You've been snooping into things that ain't your business.' His eyes narrowed as his face inched closer to Gethin's. 'And where the fuck is my girl, Deborah?'

'Somewhere safe, recovering from the beating she had.'

Gethin heard the tones of accusation in his own voice and kept going.

'I also heard you like picking up little boys from school... Is that part of your sick gameplay, too?'

His deep, momentary frown surprised Gethin. Maybe Dom didn't do it? Then, like the push of a light switch, he stopped and glared at Gethin with eyes like black coal hammered from the darkest of places.

'You know fuck all.'

With the gun still at his forehead and hands still raised high, he knew if he was quick enough, he could disarm Dom. Like a manual in his mind, he flicked through his knowledge of basic reaction time. If done quick enough,

Dom wouldn't register what had happened until it was too late, and Gethin had disarmed him.

Gethin looked sideways, as if seeing something. In that split second, Dom flicked his eyes in the same direction. Gethin's left hand flashed upwards, taking hold of the gun hand, twisting it as he moved to Dom's blind side. In seconds Gethin had drawn Dom's arm down, grasped the gun with both hands dragging Dom off balance.

Dom grunted. sweat glistened on his shiny waxy skin in the play of light and shadow. He staggered forward; his elbow joint forced straight at Gethin's left hip.

Without hesitation, Gethin thrust forward and rotated his hips anticlockwise. Dom stood no chance even as his other arm tried to reach for Gethin's legs, to relieve the pressure on his forearm, which was being forced to rotate with Gethin. With a resounding crack, his hinge joint snapped. Dom screamed in agony and dropped the gun. Gethin kicked it, sending it scuttling across the floor and under a table. He bent forward, his lips to Dom's ear.

'I know what you've been up to and soon everyone else will know, too.'

Dom scowled with dark amusement and his eyes glistened with something that Gethin couldn't grasp.

'You don't get it. Some people just can't be messed with.'

Gethin stood to leave. He felt a strange coldness trickle down his spine. Dom's tone thickened the air with a familiar threat. He glimpsed someone moving fast to his left through crowds of people. His black beetle eyes fixed on Gethin as he shoved others aside without apology.

As he moved closer, Dom shook his head. The bouncer stalled, then turned. His shoulders dropped as if disappointed he wouldn't get to disperse some of that pent up testosterone.

Dom shifted his weight, dragged himself up from the floor, and spoke through gritted teeth.

'I'll send my regards when you're six feet under.'

Gethin gave a curt sarcastic nod, pivoted to face the exit, scanned around the club once more then strode between the growing crowds towards the exit, all with an air of unhurried calm despite the trickling sensation that ran down the back of his neck.

Once through the double set of doors, he flew down the stairs, took a left, raced across St Marys Street and down towards Westgate Street, where he'd parked up. He jumped into the car, turned the keys, and pulled away, wondering if the women had been wise enough to head straight home to Lisa's.

27

Angela

Angela leapt out of the cab before it stopped and flew across the road towards Sophie.

'Sophie.'

Sophie's window wipers squealed back and forth, flickering movement in the darkness. She clicked the engine off and wound her window down.

'Hi. What's going on?'

Angela watched as Sophie glanced over her shoulder towards Roni, who stood the other side of the road in silence as their cab turned and disappeared down the street.

'Can you come over to Lisa's?'

'What now? No. It's late and I have to get Jason to bed. What's up with Roni? She looks. Well. Weird.'

Angela persisted as Sophie slipped out of the car and moved her seat forward to let Jason out of the back of the car.

'It's really important. We went to Lemon to return the wallet.'

Sophie's mouth fell open. 'What. Why didn't you... Why.' Sophie shook her head in disbelief.

'Roni thought it would stop him from chasing us like wild animals. We had to try.'

'I don't think that was such a good idea. And by your expression, I think for once I might be right.' She glanced towards Roni again. 'What happened?'

The faint, tinny sound of music drifted from Jason's headphones in the backseat's darkness. Then Jason scrambled out; his cassette recorder fixed to his hip. He smiled with a toothy grin towards Angela as his head nodded to whatever music absorbed him.

'Shitloads that I can't explain here,' whispered Angela as her eyes wandered towards Jason again.

Sophie blew out, a little exasperated, as she stepped out of her car and locked it.

'Ok. But give me fifteen minutes or so to shower and put Joel into his pjs.'

'I'll come in and wait with you.'

Sophie shrugged and grinned. 'If you insist. You'd better tell Roni. I really wish she'd let me do some Reiki on her, you know. Are you sure she's okay?'

Roni stood like a dummy; her body sliced by light in darkness from the lamppost behind her. Drizzle quivered and glistened before disappearing into the blackness.

'Could she get any weirder?' Sophie waved briefly, then turned and ushered her son up the path towards the front door.

'I'm staying here with Sophie. We'll be over in fifteen minutes,' called Angela.

Roni didn't respond at first, a bright beam of car light further down the road distracted her. Angela knew straight away it was Gethin's car. How could she forget? She felt a strange air of relief descend over her.

His window wipers moved back and forth like soldiers marching to combat before he slowed and parked up alongside Roni.

She heard the faint buzz of his electric windows as they disappeared into the shell of the door.

'You ladies okay?'

The rise and fall of his chest and the strained tone in his voice surprised Angela. The effect of his obvious concern for their safety made her feel sharper, as if the world about her had suddenly come more into focus.

She nodded. 'Fuck knows. Ask me later.'

Despite the growing fear that Dom might retaliate with something far worse, seeing Gethin had made a difference. How could she say that to him? She knew she'd responded in the safest way. And if she wasn't mistaken, she could have sworn she saw him grin a little before his expression flooded with familiar concern.

'Don't stay outside. I'll park up then meet you at Lisa's. It was Lisa who told me what you crazy ladies were up to.'

Angela could see Sophie nod at her side. Through a forced smile she whispered, 'Please will someone tell me what the shippy dick is going on here?'

'It's a long story, Sophie, it is. All you need to know for now is that he can be trusted.'

'Well, Yeh. I always had that impression of him, but no one cared to ask me.'

As a mute Roni disappeared into Lisa's house and Gethin continued onto Dafydd Drive, the women quickened their pace with an oblivious Jason close behind.

Sophie glanced up at her house and sighed. 'He's done it again, you know. Left his bedroom light on.' Angela glanced up and saw the red glow from the upstairs window and smiled. Her own son often did the same thing.

Sophie turned the key with some force to open the door. 'Damn lock needs replacing, it's getting worse.' With her shoulder, she pushed the door open and clicked the hall light on. A bright, bare bulb lit the hallway. The hallway was bright orange, with a bar of fuchsia pink running along the upper wall. Angela wondered why she hadn't noticed it properly before.

As Jason took his high-tops off in the hallway, Sophie pulled the headpiece away from his one ear.

'Upstairs, Jason, and straight in the shower. We're going over to Lisa's for hot chocolate before bed.'

Jason's eyes beamed with renewed excitement as he trundled upstairs.

'Don't forget your dressing gown, too.'

But he didn't hear her, his headphone fixed against his ears again.

Angela flicked off her shoes and made her way to the downstairs toilet next to the kitchen. Sophie kicked off her leather boots and peeled her long velvet patchwork coat from her body and hung it on the rail in the hallway.

Angela sat on the loo and heard the kettle as it filled in the kitchen as Sophie hummed to herself. Upstairs, Jason thumped about like an elephant. She heard Sophie call upstairs to Jason, asking him to settle down.

Taking a piece of tissue, she wiped herself. She noticed blood and groaned. Really. Of all the evenings, it had to be tonight. She shuffled forwards, holding her knickers and skirt, opened the door a little and called Sophie. Everything was still. There was no reply. She leaned out a little further as she grasped at her underwear and trousers. Then called out again. Could she hear music upstairs? Sophie must have gone upstairs to hasten Jason along.

She closed the toilet door, rolled off a load of tissue, stuffed it between her legs and pulled her knickers and trousers back up. It would have to do for now. A few seconds after flushing, Angela heard pipes rattle as she washed her hands. It sounded dead eerie in the silence. She bit at the inside of her gums, telling herself to stop being ridiculous and let Sophie know she could fix her cranky pipes.

A minute later, she stood in the hallway and glanced into the kitchen. Steam rose in swirls from the kettle. Coffee mugs stood on the side, still empty except for a teaspoon in one. She moved into the kitchen and poured the boiling water into the waiting mugs despite being eager for them all to head straight over to Lisa's.

It had gone quiet upstairs. Too quiet.

She turned and stared towards the staircase that dissected the lounge. Why did her heart thump so hard in her chest? She dismissed the feeling that pervaded her senses as she placed the teaspoon into the sink full of dishes. A pile of Sophie's yoga clothes hung in a heap above the tumble dryer spilling down the front.

She picked up the hot drinks and carried them into the unlit lounge. She stepped in something gritty and wet with a barefoot.

In the darkness, she put the drinks down next to Sophie's stereo system and flicked the lounge light on. It didn't work.

Christ sakes Sophie.

A nervousness crept up her body like cold spongy tentacles as her own fingers crawled across the wall, feeling for another light switch. Click. The dining room filled with diffused light. Her eyes scanned the floor and rug. Large dirty shoe prints trailed from the lounge window to the bottom of the stairs. The curtain rippled with a night breeze. Angela stood there frozen. Those icy tentacles had a vice like grip on her lungs. She couldn't breathe as the silence seemed to bellow with all her fears. She gasped out, then gulped in air. In a desperate attempt to calm herself, she breathed out slowly between pursed lips.

Her wide stare trailed the footmarks up the first few treads of the slatted staircase. Nausea invited itself and clenched in spasms at her empty stomach.

Who was it? Dom, Colin. Or an opportunist intruder trying their luck on a single mother.

Her hands trembled as she worked hard to think rationally. So many times, in the past, she'd experienced terror and survived it. She looked at her watch stunned by the fact they'd only been in the house seven minutes. Her fear had swallowed and immobilised time. She fought back. Sophie needed help, someone could be upstairs with her and Jason. She knew all so well, the time it took to alert the others, damage could be done.

For a moment she doubted herself, her sanity. Had the last few months sent her paranoia rocketing into the abyss?

Jason was upstairs vulnerable. Sophie hadn't been well for weeks the girls reminded her. If she stayed and helped, would she put herself in danger... and her children? She stood there, swallowed, and continued to take deep breaths to calm herself. But her hands ignored her efforts and continued to tremble.

Sophie was her friend. She'd never had friends like this before. She backed into the kitchen, pulled at a few drawers until she found a large, sharp-bladed knife. The cold metal reflected what light fell on it.

She wouldn't use it. Of course, she wouldn't. Like she hadn't the times Colin had threatened to harm her. It deterred them, didn't it?

With trembling hands grasped around the handle of the blade, she made her way towards the staircase again. She tried to take deep breaths; her throat tightened, making it difficult.

She moved light on her feet up the staircase with her shoulders hunched around her neck; her eyes glistened with fear in the darkness. The tick of the wall clock sounded loud and invasive. She stopped. What was that? She could hear muffled sounds. Whimpering.

Too fearful to call out, she stood there listening. She continued to edge up the stairs, her senses heightened to the tiniest of sounds. The radio no longer heard. She cursed Sophie for not changing light bulbs. As her foot lingered with trepidation above the next step, something flickered to her right above her. Too late. She felt someone grab her scalp, then a sharp painful strike to the side of her head. She blacked out instantly.

'Please Mummy wake up, Mummy please wake up I don't want you to die.'

His voice, tearful and desperate, penetrated her hazy reality. Angela lifted her hand towards the side of her head. It throbbed with a pain she'd become accustomed to.

She heard Sophie's voice floating towards Jason's desperate pleas. 'I'm here darling, see over here.'

Shadows appeared in her vision, blurred at first in the dim red light of Jason's bedroom. She saw Sophie crouched on the floor next to the radiator. Her face covered by tousled and matted looking hair.

She could hear Jason's whimper, but she couldn't find him. Then she saw the shadow of a person loom above her. Someone was in there with them.

She blacked out again.

The sudden sharp pain in her side as his foot struck her caused Angela to screech out in agony. A bolt of pain seared up the right side of her torso. Her stomach spasmed and she wretched as her eyes tried to focus.

'Please. No.'

Angela's throat felt dry. Her wrists hurt from the rope that tied them together-—so tight it hurt whenever she moved. Her side ached. Then she remembered someone had kicked her. She turned her head sideways, feeling the roughness of the carpet on her cheek.

A smell scorched her nostrils, bittersweet, like rotten eggs. She wretched again. Her throat scorched further with bile. She daren't move. Stood over Sophie was a man she thought she recognised.

'Wakey, wakey bitch… we've been having fun whilst you've been sleeping. Haven't we, Jason?' At the mention of her son's name Sophie lifted her head. Her black eye-make up smeared down her face, as torment tore at her restless eyes. And her hair, her beautiful hair on one side of her head, was now shrivelled and sparse.

'Please don't hurt my mummy anymore.'

Angela tilted her head back and strained to see where he was. She could see Jason hunched in the corner of his bed. His knees up near his chest. His arms clasping them tightly. The whites of his eyes like beacons of sheer terror.

Sophie must have seen him too. Angela heard a desperate and wretched sound pass her lips and the full horror of her situation became clear: He'd chained her to the radiator.

'Don't worry about your Mumma. She enjoys playing games.' He cackled, a haunting and hollow sound.

'See, Mumma I ask your son a question if I like the answer, he wins; if I don't like it, then we burn a bit more of this. We do.' He tugged at Sophie's head so hard you could hear the crunch of her neck bones. Her head flopped forward as he let go.

He struck a match. Its small flame igniting, filling the room with soft yellow light. He watched as it burned down to his fingers. Then the room faded back into a dark red. In those minutes, Angela knew it wasn't Dom or Colin knelt there. It was someone older, someone who resembled Dom, with those dark features and olive skin.

'Please. Let him go. I'll do anything you ask. Please.'

As she spoke, he leered towards her, quick as an imp.

'Do I look like him? Do you see a resemblance?' He laughed. A sharp merciless cackle as he leaned in towards Sophie, his nose almost touching hers with a grotesque glare in his eyes, he pretended to bite at Sophie's face. She reared back in terror, hitting her head on the back of the radiator. She cried out, more in anguish than pain.

Angela watched in horror as he stood and moved like a hungry, scuttling insect towards Jason. Unable to move, to help; she watched as he yanked Jason like a rag doll by his hair from his bed.

'Don't touch him.' Sophie screamed, as her son's slight frame flailed frantically in the air before dropping with a thud onto the floor. The smell of his urine added to the noxious odours in the air. In that second, she felt something different. Sheer anger, unlimited anger, infinite anger that swelled inside of her.

'Please, no more. Tell me what you want. I'll do anything. please just don't hurt him anymore' She wept. The sound of the metal chain clanked against the radiator as Sophie tried in vain to reach out and comfort her son.

'He's the dead spit of his dada.'

Sophie looked up and, with a coarse whisper, pleaded. 'If you're Dom's father. Why do this? He's your grandson.'

'That piece of shit stopped being my son after living with that family of God botherers.' He shook his head and sneered. In the red light of Joel's room his face appeared contorted, as if a hundred years of evil moved just below the skin.

'My son should ave listened to me all of them years ago. He thinking he was bigger n better cos that other family made im soft. I'm gonna show im different. Finking he could put is and my ard earned munny away for im there instead of me.'

Only then did something like a faint pulse register with Angela—a memory from a few days before. A man called Dom d'Petri, who had died out at sea. Was this him?

Returned from the dead.

'Dom don't know ow to treat you women proper. Needs me to put you in your place. In your box.' His hollow laugh could sink a thousand ships into blackness. 'Dom junior never does thing proper see.' He shook his head. 'Going to some stupid bloody counselling to stop his ways with the ladies. Needs me to sort his shit out.'

'You and your kid ere,' he slapped across Jason's head hard, he fell sideways and screwed himself into a small ball. 'Came along that night un spoilt everything.'

As he spoke, he kicked out at Sophie. Angela watched, willing herself to not speak as the anger inflated her. All the years of abuse she'd experienced, she knew one thing. Men like these were cowards.

'He changed after seeing this little rat here.' He gestured towards Jason.

'Told him to fucking leave it. Would he?'

He stood up and paced the bedroom floor, his eyes becoming more feral the more he spoke.

'He started forgetting is sponsibilities to his papa.'

Angela watched as he thrust his leg out again and kicked Sophie straight in the head. The blow sent her head reeling backwards onto the hot radiator again.

'He's not gonna sideline me, his papa, for some fucking skittish kid, and his mother.'

'You monster. You think after this you're going to disappear like before.'

Angela squeezed her eyes together, knowing what would come next, but at least his attentions would be on her and not Jason. As she saw his foot come towards her, she squeezed her eyes shut tight. Seconds later she felt the wetness between her legs as her bladder bled from the impact.

She didn't see Sophie's bloodied hand reach out towards her son's crumpled body as her world bled back into darkness.

28

Gethin

Gethin looked through Lisa's window and across the road towards Sophie's house. There was still no sign of them. He tore at a fingernail with his teeth. 'It's been over half an hour now. Is she usually late?'

'Always.' Roni inhaled, filling her lungs with nicotine. She coughed. 'We're used to it. Relax for God's sake.'

'I'm sure she's just sorting Jason out. It is late. He's usually in bed by now... as is these lot.' Lisa looked up at the ceiling, as the children giggled and chatted upstairs.

Gethin couldn't relax. He continued to look out as the rain ran down the window, smudging and distorting everything outside.

He doubted any of the women fully understood who Dom was... He remembered Eddie's warning; Dom didn't like to lose.

'I'm going over there to check everything's okay.'

Roni jumped up. 'That's really not necessary.'

Gethin sensed Roni still didn't trust him.

'Something isn't right.'

'I'll come too then.'

Only then did he realise it. She sensed it, too.

'Roni. I think it's best you stay here with the others. They need you.'

He saw her twitch. She felt challenged. 'No. She is our friend, I'll come...'

'Bloody hell, Roni. Why do you always have to be so... so bloody confrontational and controlling?' Her voice broke a little, as if her words were snapping in two.

'You were the one who said we should confront Dom. Look where that got us?'

Roni froze. Her eyes flickered left and right, then left again as if processing a thousand thoughts at once. She sat back down without saying a word.

'Don't you ever consider that you might not always be right, Roni?'

Stress lingered in Lisa's voice as she spoke. It was obvious to Gethin that this outburst by Lisa wasn't natural for her. As soon as she'd spoken, her features seemed riddled with guilt.

'Please Roni. I need you to stay here with me.'

'Does anyone have a key to Sophie's house?'

'I do.' Lisa jumped up, relieved she had something to do. 'I'll go and get it.' She went to the kitchen.

Gethin knew he had to tread carefully with Roni. She had kept these women safe. Disciplined and strong minded, she would not accept him coming into their world and trying to take charge.

'Roni. It's not my place to say. If it's important to...'

She put her hand in the air and shook her head from side to side in a slow, sombre manner.

'Lisa's right. If they all trust you, then so should I. I...' She went to say more but stopped. 'Please go now. Something doesn't feel right about all this.' Gethin nodded.

Lisa returned with a key and gave it to Gethin.

'If I'm not back in ten minutes, ring the police.'

They both nodded and glanced at one another.

He jogged across the street in and out of shadows, feeling the rain dampen his skin. He shivered.

He reached Sophie's door and lifted the letterbox to peer inside. The silence gnawed at his suspicious senses. There was no sign of the women or Jason—no chatting or movement. Silence slithered around in the darkness. He eased the key into the keyhole and turned it. Careful to make as little sound as possible. The door clicked open and sprung away from its frame, as if urging him inside. He stepped into the small hallway and glanced around him, scanning the detail.

The kitchen light was on, dishes, clothes, milk on the side. He moved into the kitchen and felt the kettle. It was still warm, not long boiled. He looked upwards, listening for sounds. Something told him not to call out. An instinct.

He saw a sweeping brush leaned against a wall cupboard, lifted it and pulled the bristle brush off its end without a sound. Then, held the wooden pole like a bokka, at an angle in front of his body as he moved towards the lounge.

He saw large dirty footprints across the rug. His eyes flickered towards the moving curtain. A coldness filled the air as he glanced upwards through the slatted staircase.

A child's blue light sabre was strewn across one step. The sight of it made his heart slip a little. It was too quiet—far too quiet. He edged towards the bottom of the staircase; a small pair of trainers sat neatly on the bottom stair.

Then the smell hit him; Nauseating and noxious. It clawed at his nostrils, lodged itself in his throat. He held his breath for a moment. It wasn't good! Something or someone was burning upstairs.

He felt his senses heightened. His eyes narrowed to slits as they locked into the darkness that loomed above. He placed a foot on the first step of the staircase, using his diaphragm to reduce the sound of his breathing and movement. Never had his Aikido training come to his aid like now.

He heard something. And felt his body wanting to react. Taming his senses, he felt he was prowling through fear itself, like a silent warrior—such was his intention.

He continued upwards. The wooden pole raised diagonally and close to his chest so as not to make contact with any surface and make his presence known. Then he heard it. The muffled whimpers of a child, a sound so haunting it could stay with you for life. Gethin continued. Made it halfway up the stairs without a sound. He could hear voices now. Desperate pleas. Sophie's voice sounded hollow and beaten into a jagged place.

'Please don't make him do it, let him go please, he has nothing to do with this!'

Gethin closed his eyes as the sound of his blood gushed through his temples like a tide forcing itself through narrow rocks. Then, from somewhere in the past, something drove him further. Here, at the precise moment, he needed to be. He could save her. His will now stronger than his fear.

'You stupid bitch, he has everything to do with it, init. You and your son need to disappear.'

The door, an inch or two from closed, sliced the darkness with a weak red light. He turned on the landing, sliding against the wall. He knew some form of horror lay beyond that door. The sour smell stronger here than downstairs.

He heard a child's cry, so desperate he fought the sinking of his own soul as he moved closer.

Where was Angela? What if something terrible has happened to her?

His foot hit something. Damn! He looked down. A child's small toy car rolled across the carpet, whirring and flashing.

He stood motionless, waiting. Let him come to me, use his aggression against him, he remembered from his training with Essani. The words spilled into the dark, silent space as he waited. The door moved. His instincts told him to wait. Patience in these situations had been part of his training.

The door opened. Gethin caught a glimpse of the silver edge of a knife in his left hand. He knew he would have to appear vulnerable, to encourage an attack in an open position. Gethin dropped the wooden pole away from his chest. Taking the cue like an ignorant puppet, Gethin saw the intruder lunge towards him. With maximum effect and purpose, Gethin shifted right of him and swung the wooden pole in an arc, striking Dom Senior's temple with a brutal crunch. He folded to his knees and dropped backwards, unconscious from the impact. His body lay across the open doorway and in that second, in the shadowy light Gethin recognised him—the man on the stairs from the day he'd entered Makos. An old man stooped and unkept. His path had crossed with Dom Senior's before. He swallowed, then moved his attention to inside the room.

The sight that met his eyes burned into his retinas. Sophie's son had only his boxer shorts to protect him, and his body looked fragile, his face exhausted. His dilated pupils seemed to pulsate with fear. He could see the child's ribcage inflate and deflate at speed.

Across from Jason, her knees folded under her body awkwardly, hung Sophie. The one side of her head was charred and burnt, her beautiful long dark hair gone, just an exposed scalp with only small strands of burnt and shrivelled hair. The smell was pungent. Gethin willed himself not to vomit.

He scanned the room for Angela. He couldn't see her. His stomach plummeted as he tried to stay focused.

He picked Jason up first, grabbed a blanket off his bed and wrapped it around him tightly. He held him close for a few seconds. His body shivered despite the sticky red heat in the room; Gethin knew the boy was going into shock and had to act quickly. He eased him back and looked into his dark chocolate eyes.

'I need you to be brave now, son, for your mum. She needs help, but I can't leave her. Go, as fast as you can to Lisa's house and tell her to call the police straight away. Do you think you can do that for me?'

His head shook up and down in quick jerks. 'There's a brave boy.' Gethin squeezed his arms and smiled. He lifted him across Dom senior's body and led him quickly to the top of the stairs. They had a few minutes before he would come round again. He watched Jason descend the stairs thinking he would find something to tie Dom's hands together behind him.

Tap.

Tap.

Tap.

Gethin, startled by the sound whipped around to where Dom Senior still lay unconscious on the floor and Sophie slumped onto the radiator, not moving. He heard it again. The noise came from the wardrobe the other side of the window.

'Angela?' He raced across the room and flung the wardrobe door open to find Angela folded up inside, tied and gagged. She peered up at him dazed, he could see the swelling and bruising on her face. A silent fury rolled inside him, but he knew he needed to stay focused. Reaching in, he helped Angela out of the wardrobe and removed the gag from her swollen face.

'Angela, listen to me. You must get out of here, get help. Jason is on his way to Lisa's. I'm worried he might not make it. He's disorientated and might go into shock.'

He untied her hands, pulled her in towards him, and hugged her tightly for a moment.

'Go now before he comes round.'

She looked down at Dom's father. 'Angela. Go now.'

She stepped over him and disappeared down the stairs.

Without a second thought, Gethin bent down and searched Dom Senior's pockets. He pulled out a small silver key and unlocked the hand cuffs that chained Sophie to the radiator. She was semi-conscious as he lifted her.

'Come on, Sophie. Put your arm around me.' His eyes darted toward him still lying there as he whispered his instructions to Sophie. He knew they were running out of time.

Making an extra effort to be gentle he lifted her upright and swung his arm around her back. He felt her arm move around him, a weak grip on his side. With all his body strength, he held her tight against his hip to support her weight. She whimpered with pain.

'My son.'

'He's safe, Sophie we need to leave now. I need you to try and walk, okay?'

Gethin led Sophie out of the room. He felt her body stiffen as he helped her over his unconscious body slumped across the doorway.

Sophie clung to Gethin as they shuffled down the stairs. Each step caused her to whimper in pain and clutch her ribcage.

Then, without warning, Gethin felt a forceful impact from behind that knocked him forward off his feet. He couldn't breathe, winded by the ferocity of the impact. He felt a sharp sting across his jaw. Seconds later, the three of them tumbled down the open staircase like fallen puppets. Limbs flew in different directions. The world tumbled in and out of focus. He heard Sophie cry out and the sound of body parts as they scrunched against one another and wooden surfaces in a tangled mess. As his own body hit the bottom he heard a crack, followed by an intense sharp pain. Then the world went dark.

Gethin's head throbbed. He opened his eyes and squinted in the low light of the room. He struggled to focus properly. As he tried to move his shoulder, he grimaced in agony from the pain that shot up his right arm. He peered down. His arm was stuck under Sophie's back. From its distorted angle he knew it was broken.

Pain swirled around him, dizzying his senses. He lifted his head to see around him. He had landed on the small square platform separating the larger staircase from the smaller one below. Sophie's body dangled like an abandoned old rag doll over the edge of the landing platform. The smell from her burnt scalp close to his chest a reminder of the depravity she had endured.

Where is he!?

He turned his head. Something moved. Dom was limping across the floor in short, small bursts, the blade still in his hand. His eyes cold and concentrated. Only then did he see Jason's silhouette crouched under the staircase, in darkness, against the back of the sofa. His eyes wide and unblinking, his knees tucked tight into his chest frozen by terror.

Despite the pain, Gethin raised his head using his neck and chest muscles. He swung his left arm across his chest to push Sophie off his hand. The searing pain made his eyes blur for a second and his stomach spasmed, vomit splashing across his shoulder. He pulled his hand free. Twisting his legs round he planted his feet over the remaining three steps and onto the floor below.

Using the wall for support, he forced himself up onto his feet. He held his arm tight to his side as he strode towards Dom Senior trying to blank out the intense pain that shot up his arm that made his vision blur.

Without warning he saw a blade slash the air near his face.

'Couldn't keep your nose out of my son's business could you.'

His face smeared with a salacious grimace of hunger.

'You got that stupid girl Deborah beat up cos of your questions. I made sure of it.'

Gethin sensed every muscle in his stomach tighten. The urge to believe this man's words, a force he had to reckon with. He cleared his mind of it. Stayed focused.

As he continued to inch forward with the blade this Gethin inhaled deeply, readied himself. In one swift move he pivoted on his right leg and leaned back to avoid the knife flashing towards his face. Then like a kamikaze, he swung his left foot in a cutting arc towards his knee swiping Dom Senior's right leg from underneath him. He crumpled to the floor, with a howl of agony. The knife fell from his hands and skittered across the floor towards Jason who remained frozen and unblinking in a dark unreachable place.

Gethin gasped for air and felt his body fall to the floor, exhausted by the exertion. He watched as Dom Senior's contemptuous eyes glued themselves to the knife. *This man doesn't know when it's done.* Dom Senior pulled himself up and moved despite the grotesque shape of his foot dragging behind him, crooked and flaccid. He inched closer and closer towards Jason, a determined smear dirtying his features. Desperate, Gethin reached his arm out in one last attempt to stop him. His fingers grasped at the hem of his trousers and pulled with what strength he had.

Jason's hand, like the tongue of a hungry lizard swiped the knife up and drew it in towards his chest in seconds. The long blade protruding upwards from in between his knees.

Off-balance, Dom Senior lurched forward. The blade sunk into his chest without a sound. His weight forcing the knife deeper until Jason, terrified, collapsed under his dead weight.

Gethin could feel the world swirl around him and wondered why as his eyes surrendered to the fierce pain swamping his body, he saw Angela floating into his mind's eye lifting Jason away from the dead weight of a killer.

29

Gethin

The street lit by flashing blue and white lights looked like something straight out of a movie, not some small town in Wales. Paramedics moved in a morbid dance with police officers and a special squad. Crowds gathered on either side of the street, in coats and dressing gowns. Several small orange lights bounced about in people's hands as they sucked on cigarettes in the dark. Others hung out of windows watching the drama below in silence.

Gethin sat inside the ambulance having his arm tended to by a young attractive paramedic. The brightness of the ambulance hurt his eyes as she continued to talk in a calm manner informing him that the saline drip with painkiller would soon ease the pain.

He looked around and frowned.

'Where are Sophie and Jason? Are they okay?'

'They're already on the way to the hospital. Sophie has a lot of injuries that need immediate attention, and Jason is in shock. Once I've secured your arm, we'll be on our way too.'

Gethin nodded. 'And Angela. The other lady?'

'Yes,' She nodded her head towards another ambulance. 'She's over there speaking to those officers.'

Gethin squinted and saw her with two officers near another ambulance. One officer scribbled in a notepad.

'They tried asking that poor little boy questions. We warned him not to.' She tutted with disapproval.

'One police officer even requested that he travel in the ambulance with you to the hospital. Can you believe it?' With this she tutted again to show just how much she disapproved.

'Thank you.'

'I also told them you would be available to talk once you had received pain control and this arm of yours is in a cast. They'll probably follow us to the hospital.'

'Yes. They often want to take statements as soon as they can. Not always possible though.'

'I agree.'

Gethin nodded as he kept his eyes fixed on Angela. She looked different. Something in her manner had changed. She must have sensed something and turned to wave at him. He saw her wince as she raised her arm. He waved back as a warmth enveloped his chest. A feeling he'd almost forgotten since Hazel.

'And… and the…' He didn't have to say anymore.

'Not so lucky. The knife wound was fatal. I've heard the blade went straight between his ribs and into his heart.'

Gethin sighed feeling a strange wave of relief. His mind drifted to the terror that had scorched Jason's features and wondered how a young boy would overcome this.

'Hello Superhero.' Angela stood outside the ambulance, the one side of her face still swollen. The way she looked at him made him want to reach out and hold her tight.

'How you doing? You ass-kicking ninja.' He also winced. He should have known! Despite her words of humour, he could detect the strain in her face, the palpable tears that she continued to restrain.

'Ask me when the painkillers start kicking in.'

She smiled and lifted herself into the ambulance and watched as the paramedic wrote notes onto paper on a clipboard. She wanted to say something else. He could feel it.

'I'm sorry. I didn't realise Jason hadn't even left the house.'

He reached out with his left arm and clasped her hand. He watched as her eyes glistened through a tepid smile. She wiped a stray tear away before anyone could witness it.

'I didn't imagine it then.'

She shook her head. 'I had to come back to get Jason. I guessed then he hadn't left. He wouldn't have wanted to leave his mum.' Her body trembled as she folded her fingers tightly around his hand. He squeezed to comfort her.

'I'm hard work you know—a brave mess?'

'Aren't we all,' said the paramedic offering a fleeting smile towards them before returning her attention on her clipboard.

'I'm not so tidy myself,' he quipped with a broad smile.

They continued to hold hands in comfortable silence for a few minutes before Angela pulled away.

'I'm not really supposed to be speaking to you right now. I thought you might want to know I heard those two police officers over there. He'd staged his disappearance years ago when they were investigating him for all sorts of thing fraud, abuse, GBH. They think he hid in Malta for a few years. Didn't even know he was back in Cardiff.'

He nodded. It was becoming difficult. His eyelids were becoming heavier as the drip took effect. 'Angela you've been hurt too. You need to see a medic.'

'Not tonight. I've refused. Roni is back at the house with all the children and Catherine. Good God, she's not keen on children at the best of times. We're all going to sleep at Lisa's tonight. Lisa's driving to the hospital to stay with Jason.

Angela's voice became distant. Gethin wanted to lie down, to fall away into the silky darkness.

He heard her words. 'I'll get going now sleepy.

He heard her step down from the ambulance and wanted to stop her.

He turned his head towards the paramedic with all the strength he could muster. 'Guess it would be too much to ask you to roll a cigarette?'

She grinned. 'You guessed right' she said with a kind but firm voice as she lifted his other hand and checked his pulse. Then he faded into a deep welcoming sleep.

30

Gethin

He heard the clicking of her heels across the white flooring of the hospital ward. Seconds later her head haloed with light auburn hair appeared around the doorway of his small hospital room.

'Well, you don't waste time, do you?'

'No, I don't.'

Roni smirked and walked over to his bed.

Gethin saw her eyes flicker towards the direction of the escalators. He judged she would have walked right past Deborah.

'A secret lady-friend?'

Gethin grinned. And glanced down towards her hands. 'See how much you care about me? Not a chocolate or bunch of flowers in sight.'

Deborah's visit had been unexpected even for him. She'd wanted to come in and thank him in person. She'd also discovered through Eddie that it was Dom's father who had arranged for her to be beaten up. He'd made Dom believe it had been a punter. That punter has ended up in a worse state than Deborah. Eddie had also learnt from some friends down the docks that Dom Senior and Jean went back a long way.

'Are you listening, Gethin, or is it the drugs they've given you?'

'She had a distinctive mole below her right eye.'

'Did she?' The corners of his mouth turned up.

'I can't tell you her name right now. That would be too foolish. I'd have to kill you.'

'You bet? I happen to think a lot about Angela, like the other women.'

He shook his head. 'It's not like that. Let's just say she has a personal history with Dom... and his father.'

'She's risking it coming here then. There's a journalistic fest beginning to gather outside.'

'She's a resourceful cookie. Bit like you.' He raised an eyebrow and grinned.

'You thought I'd moved onto the street to investigate what you and the ladies were up to didn't you?'

Roni moved to the other side of his bed, put her leather handbag on the small armchair and looked out the window across Cardiff.

'Yes.'

'And now? He scrutinized her. There's another reason you've come here before the others to see me. Isn't there?'

She folded her arms. 'Well now we're linked to all this because of Dom and his father. I want to know if you're going to write about us in your report. I'm guessing that is what you do being an investigative journalist?'

He laughed. 'I see, you've been doing your homework.'

She turned to face him; her arms still folded tightly across her chest. 'I can't let that happen. These women did what I said because they trusted me. I have a responsibility...'

Gethin tried to pull himself upright on the bed. He winced with discomfort.

'Roni, I admire the way you want to protect your friends.'

He tapped the bed beckoning her to sit. She moved from the window and sat on the plastic covered chair next to his bed instead, a small smile drove her lips upwards.

'Who or what have you been investigating?'

'The murder of a young girl connected to a children's home near Cardiff.'

'I see. And Dom, his father. What do they have to do with that?'

He viewed Roni with a sense of bemusement. 'Don't hold back on account of me lying here in pain.' He saw a sprinkling of unfettered fear in her eyes. 'All you need to know is that your little game of Monopoly is safe with me. Although I would strongly suggest finding another

way to punish men.'

She spoke with a tightened jaw. 'So why did you pick the wallet up and pocket it at the club?'

'Let's just say I was doing you ladies a favour. The wallet needs to disappear.'

He watched as the tautness in Roni's face dissipated a little. Her head moved up and down, yet he understood there were other questions that sat on the edge of her thinking waiting to be dropped into their conversation.

For a few minutes a wide silence settled between them. She looked towards his arm as if she'd suddenly remembered he lay in a hospital bed with a severe injury.

'What did they do?'

'Gave me general anaesthetic so they could re-align the bones. It's called a displaced fracture.'

She pursed her lips a little. The only sign that Gethin's words affected her. Another silence.

'It's a big coincidence though? You have to admit?'

Gethin frowned for a second before realising she was talking about the street again.

'I guess. Maybe our paths crossed for many reasons?'

Roni tilted her head. 'Yes. I'd be blind if I didn't see what's going on there.'

Gethin detected the protective tone in her voice.

'Yes. She's quite something?'

He didn't want to say any more. Gethin glanced down at the white sheet that covered and restricted his body, edges tightly folded underneath. He knew something had shifted and relented inside him since that day he'd set eyes on Angela stood at the window.

'Have you heard anything about Sophie and Jason?'

'Yes, I've just come from their ward. The doctors allowed them to stay together. She's still sedated.'

She stopped for a moment and Gethin watched as a shadow of pain filtered across her inscrutable features.

'They covered her scalp up, so it's really hard to see what's going on underneath. Jason's awake though. I took him some sunflowers.'

Gethin frowned. 'Sunflowers. Christ Roni. The kid will be wanting toys and chocolates and hugs.'

Roni shrugged. 'Well. Sunflowers will help to make him feel positive. Happier.'

'So, there is a heart in there somewhere?'

'Maybe.'

Roni tapped at her knee again. Gethin glanced down at her long fine fingers knowing another question was brewing.

'What I don't understand, is why Sophie? Our Sophie?'

'I think the night you ladies turned up at Dom's club it all changed for Dom.'

Roni shook her head. 'It still makes little sense. To hurt Sophie that way because of a stolen wallet?'

Gethin realised Angela had said nothing to the others. He imagined it would be out of respect for Sophie.

'I don't think it was just about the wallet Roni.'

Her eyes shot towards him. 'What am I missing?'

'Only Sophie can answer that!' He felt bad for withholding it from Roni. She cared deeply for the women, but he knew it was the right thing to do. If Sophie wanted the women to know fragments of her past that was her decision, alone, to make.

Roni's blank expression didn't hide the confusion that danced in her eyes.

'Okay. I understand.' She unfolded the soft leather flap of her handbag and took out a pack of low-tar cigarettes. She offered the pack to Gethin who took one out with his free hand. They both sat in silence inhaling and exhaling swirling clouds of grey-white smoke.

Roni leaned back in the chair, small frown lines appearing on her pristine forehead. 'They are the only family I have you know. I would do anything that helps them in this man's world.'

Gethin glanced at his cigarette in the aluminium ashtray, the hot orange tip cooled, burned out.

'Why don't you tell them Roni?'

Roni turned visibly perplexed by his words. 'What do you mean?'

His eyes traced the slight bumps on the white plaster cast encasing his broken arm before he took a breath.

'Come on Roni. It's obvious.'

'What is?'

'You prefer women?'

'Fuck you, Gethin.'

'I don't think you'd really want to do that. I'm the wrong sex?' Gethin's humour failed to soften the rising defensiveness spilling outwards as she stood and grabbed at her bag to leave.

'Roni. Okay sorry. It's not my business. Don't go. Please.'

He watched as Roni stopped near the doorway, her back and shoulders rose and fell.

'What if they find the thought of me repulsive?'

He could hear the desperation in her hushed tones. The need to sound steady and resilient.

'Don't you think that's a chance worth taking?'

She turned and faced Gethin. 'I might be all out of chances.' She turned and walked to the end of his bed. 'I was married once you know?'

'Now, that does surprise me.'

'Does it? Well. I guess it was more a marriage of convenience looking back. What you'd call a union of cerebral posturing.' She stopped for a moment as if deep in thought.

'It's strange you know, I read Austen, Bronte, Mitchell. Could never quite understand my pleasure in reading them when the feelings experienced by these women eluded me in real life. I guess marrying David was my attempt at imitating fiction.'

'What happened?'

'When we separated, he started seeing a woman he'd once claimed to despise. Fifteen years his senior with a penchant for S&M. Last I heard they were throwing parties… that kind.'

'Oh. I see.' Gethin grinned then let a chuckle escape.

'I'm guessing you've never had an invite.'

'No thanks!' Roni's eyes sparked a little.

Within seconds, they were both laughing out loud, great hoots of laughter that tumbled out of Gethin's small single bed ward and into the long corridor. He was glad to see Roni laugh a little. She wiped loose tears from her reddened cheeks.

'Bloody hell, what you two laughing at?'

Angela walked in with a newspaper, a cactus, and a bruised eye. Joel stood grinning at her side as she placed the cactus on the cabinet next to the bed.

Gethin flashed his eyes at Roni, she shook her head. A plea to say nothing.

Angela continued.

'They didn't need to amputate it then?'

'Guess not. The fact I suggested they preserve my arm so I could take it home as a keepsake changed their minds.' Angela chuckled and laid the folded newspaper next to Gethin.

'Thank you. And the um, cactus?'

Angela rolled her eyes. 'Yeh. I know. Catherine's idea. Apparently, flowers are no good, they just die. She said cacti are tough and can survive most things like rats! That girl. She intrigues me more every day.'

'Mm. Actually. She does have a point.'

'Not as many as your cactus does.'

She looked towards Roni. 'Good news. Sophie's awake. Still very drowsy. Lisa's down there now with her two, Catherine and Gladys. The wounds to her head are only second-degree burns which means it's highly possible her scalp will recover, and her hair should grow back.'

'How have you found all that out?' Roni asked.

'I cornered the doctor just before I came up here. He went on about cell regeneration, skin grafts and blood supply. Think I might have switched off at that point.'

'And Jason?' Responded Gethin.

'Jasons sat up chatting away to Becky as if nothing ever happened. Gladys is clucking and warned under no circumstances should she bring a bottle of vodka into the ward. And the children have already tucked away half the box of chocolates I bought.'

'The officer. Has he left yet?'

Angela shook her head as she looked towards Roni.

'No. He's still there trying to ask questions. Is that even right you know? I wanted to tell him to bugger off. I have to say I'm impressed with Jason. He told the police officer he didn't want to talk until his mummy was awake to sit with him.'

'Clever kid. That's exactly the right thing to do.'

'Did they want to talk to you again?'

'Yes. I've already been to the station this morning to give a witness statement.'

Gethin sensed tension rising from Roni again. There were things she didn't grasp yet, and she knew it.

'I'm sure Sophie will tell us what this is all about in her own good time.' Roni's words settled in the air waiting and untouched.

31

Angela

The smell of a hospital always bothered Angela. That disinfected clinical smell, trying to conceal all that pain and tragedy. She glanced over at Roni as the elevator door clanked and clunked together. She hadn't spoken since leaving Gethin's ward.

As the darkened lift rattled downwards, Roni remained silent. She wasn't leading, telling Angela the quickest way to get to Sophie's ward, who the most reliable nurse would be or what they must do to help Sophie. Something was wrong and Angela sensed it.

The doors opened, the doctor stood in the elevator with them, marched out in front, clipboard to his chest and disappeared through another set of double doors on the left.

A few minutes later, they were in Sophie's ward. Lisa sat in the chair next to her, rummaging through her bag for something. She looked up.

'Hi. Gethin doing okay?'

Angela nodded 'Yes, he'll live.' She walked around Jason's smaller bed, which lay on the floor alongside Sophie's. With the extra chairs provided by the nurses, the space now seemed tighter... smaller and confined.

Where's the others?

'Catherine's taken them to the canteen for something to eat. She's so wonderful with them, you know. And Gladys had to go back for her 'little sunshine,' it seems his condition is worsening.'

Sophie, her encased leg suspended in the air opened her drowsy purple bruised eyes.

'Poor Gladys she's so busy with him at the moment she missed everything recently.'

'Maybe that's a good thing.' Chirped Angela.

'Anyway, you should see the doctor who checked in on me this morning?'

The women smiled and shook their heads. Except for Roni.

Angela stood next to Lisa. Roni stood at the end of the bed, her back against the wall. Quiet.

Sophie's bruising was taking hold, spreading like a virus across her smooth skin. In some areas it looked dark purple, almost black. Angela admired Sophie. Despite everything, she was keeping a brave face, wearing it to cover what lay beneath.

'Ladies, this stuff they've given me for the pain is terrific. Who needs meditation when you have drugs?'

The women laughed, except for Roni. Her expression unreadable yet creating an invisible divide between herself and everyone else. Angela was sure the other ladies felt it, too. She had caught Lisa's eyes flicker out towards Roni momentarily, then turn back towards her bag. She pulled out her cigarette holder and took out one of her slims.

'Anyone?' She glanced towards the nurse's desk outside. 'We can, can't we?'

'There's no law that says we can't. What do you think will happen?

We'll get arrested or something?'

Lisa's face turned blank as a white sheet for a moment. 'Hilarious, Ang. I'm sure in years to come they'll tell us how bad smoking is for you too!'

Roni still said nothing.

Sophie coughed. 'You okay, Ron?'

Roni flicked her hand, as if attempting to push the question away. 'Yes.'

They all turned to look at Roni, knowing she wasn't telling the truth.

Sophie continued. 'Well. I guess there are things you ladies want to know.' She glanced at Angela.

'Good God no. I said nothing. Not my story to tell.'

Sophie nodded.

'And really. You don't have to say a thing. You've been through enough and...'

Sophie looked at Roni as she spoke. 'Please Lisa. I need to. As strange as it sounds, I'm only discovering myself what this is about. It's as if my mind had become fragmented—detaching facts to protect me. I've read about such things on my course.'

Sophie spoke, an endless piece of music with arpeggios and broken notes, she expressed a dark past that most of the women could relate to. And all the time she spoke, her eyes flickered between all three women. But mostly fell on Roni, as if wanting to draw her into their circle, as if sensing like the others that Roni was standing on the peripheral, as if she was ostracising herself from the group of women who loved her. As if the finely tuned strings between them had been plucked on too vigorously, as if at any moment they would snap under the pressure.

'I've shut it out for so long.' She lowered her voice to a whisper. 'I so desperately wanted Jason to be Brian's that when I moved onto the estate, I told everyone he was. Less complicated that way.' She went quiet for a few second and searched Angela's eyes.

'A fresh start. That's all I wanted. After a while, I convinced myself he *was* Brian's. Isn't that so strange? How we can conceal the truth even from ourselves.'

'Not so strange, really. It sounds like some kind of trauma.'

'I see it now. Like a picture book inside my head. Pages that were missing suddenly appeared with shape and form like those children's colouring pages. You know the ones you add water to, and something appears that you didn't-couldn't see before.' She jerked her head from side to side, short jolting movements as if still not quite comprehending her own words.

'It was in some crusty bar at the back of some hotel in Roath. It was open after-hours, somewhere to go if you didn't want the night to end.' She paused. 'Or you just wanted to forget who you were.'

'I remember the bartender now. His smile. The way he seemed to look after all those lost souls in the place sat hunched over drinks, chain-smoking, some of them in dark corners and their minds in even darker places. I was so bloody naïve and stupid and lost.'

Lisa stood up and pulled a tissue out of the flowered box, put it into Sophie's hand as tears tracked down her swollen bruised cheeks, to her jawline and precariously hung there for a few moments then fell away, creating a tiny wet darkened patch on the white sheet. The tissue remained in her unmoving hand.

'He wore a cap so low over his head I could hardly see him. I never saw those eyes. But I remember his smell.' She sneered as if repulsed by the memory. 'Whenever I smell that after-shave it makes me feel so ill.'

'My sister convinced me he'd put something in my cocktail. She told me later; the barman had come into the toilets as Dom Junior had zipped himself back up. I had passed out. The way my sister put it, hanging over a small basin like a rag doll. To this day, I don't remember how he got me into those toilets.'

'That's truly awful, Sophie.' Lisa reached out and cupped her hand over Sophie's. 'To lose your husband—and then, then that.'

'The thing is, after Brian died. After I'd nursed him to his death, someone from his office gave me another briefcase he'd kept at his office. I'd thrown it into the shed. Not thought anything of it. I didn't want something else in the house reminding me he was gone.' She sighed, a broken whistling sound. 'About six months later, I decided to clear out the shed and came across the case again. I'd forgotten about it, to be honest. But then it struck me why would my husband need another briefcase?'

Angela shuffled as she continued to listen. She leaned back into her chair, feeling the skin on her face tingle.

'I became determined to find out what was inside. I didn't have the combination to the lock. So I ended up prizing it open with a few long nails and a hammer. Wish I hadn't. Inside were letters and cards and photos.'

Lisa gasped.

'All that time I'd been grieving for a man I didn't really know. A man whose heart I never understood. Fuck, after reading some of those letters I realised his heart had never even been with me.'

Angela looked down at her legs. She bit into the soft tissue of her cheek. Moments like these challenged everything she was. She knew how to keep secrets. She believed, honestly believed, that no one kept secrets like the ones she'd kept. Now she was beginning to see this was untrue. she witnessed that each one of her new friends had secrets intrinsically linked to who and what they had become.

'Come on now. You've gone so pale and you're upsetting yourself with all this.' Lisa's words although meaning to be kind now sounded restrictive, as if she wanted Sophie to put her past into a pretty pink box and tuck it away on a shelf out of sight. Angela understood Lisa didn't mean it to sound this way.

Roni coughed into her clenched hand.

'I went off the rails. God, I was awful, Screwing any man in sight. But Dom, I didn't even know that was his name until last night. He unnerved me, I remember that. Even in all my messed-up craziness I knew he was kinda dangerous.'

'Isn't he just.'

'Back then, I don't think I cared about myself anymore- until my beautiful son changed all that for me.'

'I'm so ashamed now. That woman doesn't seem like me anymore. I'm so sorry. everything we've been through is because of me and my, my stupid jealousy.'

'It isn't. It's because of Dom and his father.' Lisa's words spliced the air with a sharpness not usually associated with Lisa, our Lisa.

Sophie smiled weakly. 'The strange thing is that night at Lemon as we sat there drinking champagne. He seemed familiar. It's like somewhere inside I knew who he was, but it wasn't surfacing; showing me, if that makes sense?'.

Angela found herself nodding. She understood more than she wished to.

'God, I love that boy. It scares me how much Jason looks like them. What if he...' Her voice drifted into another silence. We all knew what she was considering.

'Jason is a wonderful young boy. Kind and considerate—just like his mum.' Angela looked towards Sophie wide-eyed wondering how such words had stumbled from her own lips. She'd never felt safe in the company of other women to voice such opinions of others. Shuffling from one foot to another, she watched, with a strange, unfamiliar apprehension lodged in her throat.

Sophie smiled; a warm appreciation glimmered in her eyes. Angela felt a warmth blot her insides.

'It's the truth lady, don't bloody forget it.'

Lisa laughed. 'I can't help thinking about the day you first moved onto the street Ang. Now listen to you?'

'I'm getting there!'

Roni stood motionless, an unreadable expression still blanketing her face. She licked her dry lips. She went to say something but coughed instead, as if her words might wedge in her windpipe. Angela wondered if Roni was finding it all too much. Roni who scrutinised the miniscule. Roni, who was always in control. Roni, who always knew what to do, now stood staring into the space between herself and the rest of them.

Angela wondered if this was Roni's weak spot. Hearing and seeing the real physical damage men could afflict on women.

Then, without warning, Roni spoke. Her words were clean and sharp and matter of fact. 'Ladies. I think you should know... I prefer women.'

Angela noticed Roni's back straighten a little as she spilled the words out. As if she refused to crumble under the weight of her words.

'Of course, you do,' Angela moved to the bedside cabinet and poured a glass of water from the jug and took it to Roni.

'You'd better drink this. You've gone white as a dewdrop in spring, you have. I'm afraid they don't serve champagne in hospital.'

Roni's eyes anchored in on Angela. 'You knew?'

Angela pulled a face and shrugged 'Nope! Not exactly. But now you've said it.' She paused. 'It makes total sense!'

Roni's eyes flickered between each woman as if she was trying to read their response to her words.

'I know this is the wrong time and I'm...'

'Actually. It makes sense,' continued Sophie. 'All that self-control. I could tell somewhere underneath all that perfection you constantly worried about what we thought about you. Yet, would we have believed in ourselves as much as we do now if it hadn't been for you Roni? I certainly wouldn't have thought I was good enough to go back to college- to study at my age.'

Angela piped up. 'And that's coming from Sophie, your soul mate.' Everyone laughed.

Lisa walked around the bed and held Roni's arm. 'Do you think we would let your sexual preferences effect how we feel about you?'

She sighed. 'I can only begin to imagine how awful it must have been keeping that locked away for so long. To me, that would feel like never allowing a part of who you are to flourish.'

The others nodded in agreement. 'I'll second that,' Angela responded.

'It's fine. I'll work it out.'

'Oh, come here.' Lisa wrapped her arms tight around Roni.

Angela noticed Roni's body stiffen in response. Then, in a manner so unfamiliar for Roni, she hugged Lisa back.

'Can I ask you something, Ron?' Sophie's voice had a surprising hint of playfulness considering what she'd been through. 'Is that the reason you've always hated wearing dresses and skirts?'

'And don't forget the Drakmaar aftershave you wear. The first time I realised it was aftershave, I thought you had a secret male friend,' piped up Lisa as she smiled warmly towards Roni.

Roni rolled her eyes, appearing bemused by the sudden honest outbursts of their observations.

'I wonder if keeping secrets, holding truths in the dark is self-abuse?' Sophie twisted the tissue she still held in her hand. 'Can it be as harmful as any other form of abuse?'

'Yes, it can hurt to keep secrets. Veronica said. 'And it can destroy parts of who you are—eats away at everything- even friendships.'

'And it's exhausting. Trying not to slip up, constantly having to be vigilant,' responded Angela.

'Isn't it an interesting thought,' quipped Lisa? 'Many of these secrets are like uninvited guests.'

The delicate skin around Angela's eyes crinkled. 'I don't get you?'

'Well. From where I'm sitting, I think a lot of these secrets might be a symptom of abuse, or even neglect?'

It went quiet again. Each woman thrust into their own past, reflecting on their own failed relationships. Did any of them truly have what they'd hoped for in marriage? Did all of them allow their world to revolve around their men in the hope that they would receive kindness and love and respect in return? And what about the secrets they keep? Had they all believed that to survive after marriage, these secrets would keep them safe from judgement, harm and shame? It seemed less of an accident to Angela—the fact she'd moved onto a street with women who had all suffered because of failed relationships with men. They were now opening up to each before all those secrets destroyed the good in all of them.

She remembered the evening Roni had come round to her house with pizza and wine. Had she not hinted that her marriage had been loveless? She'd neglected her own needs. And her husband, on reflection, had used her to climb the corporate ladder. And Lisa, her husband had abandoned her, left her pregnant with a young child. And what about poor Sophie? Would she overcome all this? Angela hoped like the other women she would. They wouldn't, she imagined, let it be any other way. They would do what it took and being part of that thinking felt like one of the best feelings in the world. Angela had found her tribe. All of them flawed, but all of them trying to do their best.

For a moment, Angela's mind drifted off to the games the women had played out, the nights they hunted, like wolves for their unsuspecting prey. Now, she saw them differently. Had each one of them unconsciously acted out their resentment towards men in the only way they knew how? She thought of Colin. There was one more hurdle to jump to be free of his abuse. A warmth flooded her insides, as she glanced around her newfound friends. This time she had the support needed to do it.

32

Gethin

As soon as he left hospital Gethin set to work. Without a moment to lose, he pulled everything from the shoe box once more—a boiling cauldron of unknown information for Gethin. It had become apparent that individual wrong doings were becoming part of a larger scale paedophile ring. Opening Alison's little shoebox now felt like he'd taken the lid off Pandora's box.

He'd already moulded a starting point for the report highlighting that his investigations had unearthed a series of failures by the police force, local government, institutions, and members of social services to protect the rights and wellbeing of the children at Radcliffe, including Penny and Alison.

He'd decided from there he would outline facts regarding how liberalism, and the weight given to equal opportunities in the work-place when employing new staff in the seventies, had affected the case. How Labour Party policies on equal opportunities had given potential paedophiles an unprecedented supply line; an infrastructure of opportunities to access vulnerable children. He would also mention how men in positions of authority like Detective Superintendent Turner were members of PIE, a paedophile rights campaign that even now, the beginning of the eighties, has affiliations with the National Council of Civil Liberties.

He would write about the cover-ups by people in positions of authority, including the cover-up of Penny's suicide and the reasons for it. And finally, he would conclude by describing the impact of abuse on people like Alison, Deborah, and other children into adulthood. The public had a right to know what was happening in these institutions and the long reaching effects of these men's horrific actions.

For hours he pored over Alison's diaries. There were several from 1975 up to 1979. They had dates, times, and terrible descriptions of some of the sexual abuse handed out by men, including Detective Superintendent Turner and Dylan Edwards at the home.

He cross-referenced some of her diary inserts with what Nonnie and Deborah had told him- Even the young lad he'd met at Radcliffe.

After them, Gethin combed through the floppy discs, letters and small film reels taken with the tiny Minox camera of which he'd never seen before.

He only stopped for a cigarette or coffee break or a bite to eat with Angela. These were pleasant reprieves from the dark world and often unpalatable read of Alison's diaries.

She listed additional names, with numbers, of those also abused at the home with phone numbers. Some of them he'd contacted. Encouraged them to talk. How exposing those who had done terrible things would help others to come forward. He made sure that he was clear about his intentions—even as adults they sounded fearful of repercussion, if they spoke out.

Gethin glanced at the floppy discs and small Minox camera with film cases that littered the table. It seemed Alison might have lost her life acquiring the information he was now delving into. Forced into a brutal metal mask in death because she dared to tread paths that uncovered the things that others wanted kept in darkness. She hadn't worn an iron cage for being a gossip but because of her attempts to navigate a dark world and expose it to others. The final year of her life, she had collated discs and reels of evidence. This woman had planned her own exposure but understood that hard evidence only would prove in a court of law what she already knew.

He realised much of what Nonnie had told him matched with what he'd read in Alison's diaries. The only thing Nonnie hadn't realised was the developing relationship between Penny and Alison all those years ago. They had as teenagers planned to run away. It was sadly apparent that Penny had suffered emotional and psychological abuse at the hand of her stepfather. Alison had recorded an incident Penny had told her about.

A knock on the door interrupted his thoughts. He opened the door, distracted by what he'd read.

Angela stood there. 'Going well then?'

'It's not an easy read, Ang.'

'I didn't think it would be.'

'Willing to listen if you need it?'

He shut the door behind her and went into the kitchen to pour them both a coffee.

'There's evidence to suggest Penny's stepfather, Mr Thomas abused her.'

Angela bit at her top lip.

'Alison wrote about an incident Penny had told her. Her stepfather had returned from Radcliffe one evening in a rage, it seems. He'd dragged Penny and her mum from their rooms to his study.'

He poured coffee from the percolator into the two cups.

319

'The heathen forced them to strip and chucked them into the garden. Made them stand out there until her mother collapsed in the cold. It was two weeks before Christmas.'

'Nothing shocks me much, Gethin.'

Gethin stopped and turned towards her. 'Not all men.'

Angela smiled. 'You need a break from all this. I mean, your doing this with one hand! And have you spoken to your parents yet?'

Gethin nodded and without warning, he bent across and kissed her gently on the lips.

'What was that for?'

'You're my sanity in all this craziness. And in answer to your question. Yes.'

'Did it go okay?'

'Difficult. I've hurt them very much.'

'You've done the right thing.'

He passed a mug of coffee to Angela, picked his tobacco tin from the side, and offered one to Angela. She shook her head.

'I'm trying to give up.'

He took one from his tin and lit up. 'Did I tell you I spoke to Dina yesterday too? I asked her about India. What happened to me? She wouldn't at first. Wanted to wait until she saw me in person.'

'I'm guessing you pushed her to tell you in your persuasive, gentle manner.'

'It's instinct.'

Angela tilted her head and smiled. 'So?'

'After hearing about Hazel's death, I disappeared. No one could find me. Dina came out to look for me. Found me working on a farm in Goa. I was a mess and taking drugs.'

He saw the surprise on Angela's face and suddenly felt deeply ashamed. She sipped at her coffee and glanced out of the kitchen window.

'We all do things we don't understand when under extreme stress or pressure. Don't be too hard on yourself.'

By late afternoon, Angela had left leaving Gethin to continue his report. He'd discovered the truth about Alison. In her later years, after she'd escaped from Radcliffe, Alison had pursued retribution on the men who had abused her and others at Radcliffe. She had walked back into the very places where the darker nature of men years earlier had stolen her youth. Her aim had been obvious. To seek out those who hid behind a mask of respectability in society and the power held in their hands.

There were Polaroid snaps and photos taken with the small Minox camera, the photos, although thumbnail size, proved much of what she'd recorded in diaries and notebooks. This woman had been sharp and clever in her activities. She'd moved around in their circle, gaining their trust. Pretending that she herself was a member of PIE and some kind of predator. She'd taken tremendous risks. Risks that exposed how many people were involved in these sordid affairs.

Three names. Each one with contact details written alongside. Two of them had red lines struck through them. One name was Dylan Edwards. Gethin knew he was dead. Killed himself with car exhaust fumes. The next name was Wayne. H. Thomas. He'd killed himself with an insulin overdose.

The third name was Dom d'Petri. It had a question mark next to it. Had Alison known he hadn't died out on a boat? That he had feigned his own death? He remembered the letter read out to him at Nonnie's. He believed Alison had hunted down each man and killed them for the awful things they did and let happen, at Radcliffe.

As late afternoon drifted into the evening, Gethin still struggled to discern what had happened to Alison. He flicked through her diaries again and again, who had killed her? Gethin sifted through what remained in the shoe box. At the bottom was a train ticket receipt dated Wednesday 20th October to London Paddington from Newport Station. After ten minutes, he found an address amongst some other papers for a property in Ladbroke Grove. The one Eddie had told him about. He vaguely knew the area after visiting Portobello Market a few times.

By two o'clock in the morning, Gethin flopped into Dina's sofa. His back ached and his eyes itched from tiredness. He'd finished the first draft of his report. It had, been difficult to write. The women danced in his peripheral view, their image reminding him that once they'd been alive. Although not religious, he hoped his actions had given them some peace, wherever they now were.

He'd completed several long paragraphs stating it was impossible to ignore the possibility that the investigation had been purposely mishandled to conceal facts that, if exposed, would shine a light on the leading investigator, Chief Superintendent Turner and his close affiliations with paedophile groups and Radcliffe.

Alison had written the extent of the abuse at the children's home in a raw and exposed factual style. Translating this for readers had required a sympathetic touch. And at the end of it, he wanted no accolades for his exposition. No rewards. Only for justice to be done. For some of those who walked the corridors that few walked in his country to be brought down, to descend into Dante's Inferno. To Gethin, being a great journalist was far more than finding a great story.

In a few days, when the report was ready, he'd need to return to London. He knew many broadsheet papers would be hungry for his articles. Headlines reporting other inadequate ways in which Scotland Yard runs its departments, his article couldn't have appeared at a better time.

He tilted his head back, relieved that he'd achieved so much in the few days he had spent planning, collating, and writing the report. Yet, as he slipped into a deep sleep, he saw Alison's face caged. And the question that had started his entire journey still whispered from her lips.

33

Angela

She stood with the telephone in her hand, watching Catherine point to her watch and mouth, 'I'm going next door. I'll take Joel with me.'

Angela gave her a thumbs up and watched them cut across the garden towards Lisa's house as she listened to Gethin over the phone.

He'd returned to London and since then the publication of his damning report, things had gotten a little crazy.

'So, after they questioned Chief Superintendent Turner, they searched his house. One of the officers discovered paedophilia materials in a small room he'd built and hidden in the attic. It's berserk right now. Every newspaper, including the tabloids, is gunning for him.'

Angela, although pleased that things were turning out well for Gethin, had mixed feelings. With all the attention he was gaining right now, she didn't think she would see him again. And she'd surprised herself by just how much she missed his company since his return to London.

Dina and her husband were back next door and although she found them good neighbours, it was nothing compared to having Gethin around. But, telling him how she felt might be a step too far. She didn't want to pull him away from something that he obviously loved to do.

'But the most important thing they've discovered is a large sum of money that came out of his account two days before Alison was murdered. Mark is chasing a lead who says he saw him with Dom Senior in a pub in Finchley later the same day. He had it on CCTV. It looks promising.'

Angela had tried to keep up with the news, buying a newspaper daily. She knew that Scotland Yard, under the pressure of criticism, were stomping down hard on any misdemeanours of their staff. They had some internal cleaning up to do, one paper said.

'Angela. You okay. You've gone quiet?'

'Yes, still here.'

The small sequins in her jersey top caught the light from outside, causing shifting circles of light to dance across the wall opposite as she moved. Her finger twisted through her blonde hair as she considered the decisions she'd made, decisions she wanted to share with Gethin.

Actually, share, like it mattered to him too.

'I've decided to do it.'

There was a moments silence on the line. 'You know we'll all be behind you.'

'The diaries, I never realised that one day they would help me too.' Angela had written in her own diaries. When living with Colin, she'd found them a distraction from her reality, even if the stuff she wrote sometimes described his awful behaviour towards her and the children.

'And you have witnesses. Me for a start.'

'Thank you. I also spoke with Roni. She has a cousin who is a very good solicitor. And she's offered to put me in contact with her. I'm no fool though. He's a very clever man. He'll use what he can to fight me.'

Her voice took on a more vulnerable tone. 'It took moving on to this street to make me realise I could do this. I just had to find the right time to do it.'

'Sometimes the right time chooses us.'

'Fuck, Geth. That's profound.' She heard him chuckle. The sound made her tingle with a desire she had never thought she would feel again.

'Right. I'm on my way round to Lisa's for Becky's birthday gathering. See you in a few weeks.'

As Angela placed the phone back on the receiver, she knew for sure that Gethin, like her friends, understood the unusual wells of courage she had attempted to drink from in recent weeks.

A few minutes later Angela stood in her garden, absorbing the sunlight and fresh air. Things felt so different now. She remembered the steel grey skies of the morning she'd arrived on the street, chain-smoking her way through a pack of Bensons, high on anxiety and nicotine.

She glanced down the street. All was quiet. Most of the children, she imagined, would be inside Lisa's house for the party.

She looked up at the cherry tree, its thick green foliage dotted with ripening fruit in beautiful reds and oranges. It made her smile. Only now had she finally noticed the fruit that grew and ripened in her own garden.

About the Author

Graduating from a fashion and marketing degree, I worked as an assistant fashion buyer in London before returning to Wales to embark on an Art and Design PGCE. Within two years, I began working with SEN children and loved the way my artistic background supported the sensory curriculum needed for this post. During this time, I produced several short stories for pupils, bringing them to life with story sacks. With some encouragement from friends I signed up for several writing and craft courses. Now, I try to bring my love of design into my work as a writer. My short story, A Special Hero, is published in Anansi's Spring Anthology 2023. The Secrets They Keep is my debut novel. I now live in Monmouthshire, with my partner, sons and Cookie- the much loved and excitable boxer dog.

You can connect with me on:
- https://www.worsleyrites.com
- https://www.instagram.com/claire.worsley9
- https://www.tiktok.com/@worsleyrites?lang=en

Printed in Great Britain
by Amazon

24541734R00191